Scandalous

He traced the line of her collar with one finger, and she felt the air rush out of her lungs. "Always so starched," he said. "So neat and *correct*."

"Yes, sir. I do my best."

"Perhaps you try too hard, my dear." Slowly he slid the pins from her hair, and she felt it tumble down around her ears. He ran his fingers gently through the mass of curls, sending tingles down the length of her spine.

"I . . . I think . . ."

"You think too much," he said softly. "Sometimes a woman ought to just feel."

He curled one hand around the small of her back, bringing their bodies close, his face inches from hers. The touch of his mouth to hers was like nothing she had ever dreamed of . . .

Scandalous

SONIA SIMONE

AVON BOOKS ◆ NEW YORK

SCANDALOUS is an original publication of Avon Books. This work has never before appeared in book form. This work is a novel. Any similarity to actual persons or events is purely coincidental.

AVON BOOKS
A division of
The Hearst Corporation
1350 Avenue of the Americas
New York, New York 10019

Copyright © 1994 by Sonia Simone-Rossney
Inside cover author photograph by Terry Lorant
Published by arrangement with the author
Library of Congress Catalog Card Number: 93-91641
ISBN: 0-380-77496-8

First Avon Books Printing: January 1994

AVON TRADEMARK REG. U.S. PAT. OFF. AND IN OTHER COUNTRIES, MARCA REGISTRADA, HECHO EN U.S.A.

Printed in the U.S.A.

RA   10   9   8   7   6   5   4   3   2   1

BOOK ONE

Chapter 1

Boston, June 1850

At two in the morning, half-numb from the cold, what Zeke Malloy wanted more than anything was a very long, very hot bath. He thrust his hands beneath his shirt to warm them, flinching at his own ice-cold touch against the bare skin of his belly. He'd been crouching for over an hour behind a low barricade of rotted crates and barrels, and the muscles in his thighs ached. The smell—a mix of guano, old fish, and rancid whale oil—would linger in his coat long after the cold had left his bones.

Still, he had little to complain about; he'd assembled this pile of wreckage himself, choosing the most fetid debris he could find on the littered dock. His enemies had gotten wilier, but he hoped they weren't so suspicious that they'd stoop to picking their way through a pile of malodorous garbage. He looked over at his partner, Jim, who was absently carving a pattern into a broken barrel stave. Some nights, waiting for something to happen tried them as sorely as the danger and the cold did.

Zeke crawled over to Jim, moving as slowly and silently as a stalking cat. "You going to be ready for Blodgett when he makes his move?" Zeke kept his voice lower than the sound of the oily waves lapping the pier.

Jim's grin was hidden by the woolen muffler

3

around his mouth and nose, but Zeke could see his eyes crinkle. "You ever knowed me to be anything but ready for trouble, boss?"

"Just making sure, you old mountain goat. Most of Blodgett's boys have already gone to drown themselves in ale and barmaids at the Sea Cow. Blodgett and Sid are the only ones left."

"Guess that means they're fixin' to bring prisoners in."

Zeke nodded soberly. "Jim, are you sure you're all right about this? It's just the two of us tonight. Nate's taken enough risks as it is. I don't even like having him drive, but we've got no choice."

Jim drew his beetled eyebrows together, offended. "In the Rockies, I could take on a grizzly with nothin' more'n a dull pocketknife and a mean hangover. I reckon I can handle that fancy-pants city boy."

They watched, crouching motionless in their hiding places, as Sid wheeled the last loads of cargo up the gangplank and onto the jaunty white clipper *Chérie*. Provisions for the trip, crates of whiskey, dry goods. Nothing special. Not yet, anyway. Zeke felt a cough building in the back of his throat. It brought tears to his eyes, but he made no sound. He'd been at this game far too long to give himself away so easily.

Jack Blodgett, a tall, clean-shaven man, appeared at the top of the long gangplank, his thumbs tucked into a silver waistcoat that shone like a beacon in the moonlight.

Zeke nudged Jim with his elbow. "There he is! They'll be loading the captives any minute now."

Jim scowled. "You don't have to poke me. I told you, I'm ready for him."

Sid scurried back down the gangplank, his round spectacles glinting in the dim light. Zeke held his breath as the little man trotted down the dock, passing only a few feet from their hiding place. Sid put thumb and forefinger between his teeth and gave a long whistle. A large gray cart covered with a dark tarp rolled out from behind a warehouse.

"That's got to be them," Jim whispered.

The cart eased to a stop a few feet from the gangplank, and the driver, a hulking fellow Zeke knew only as Ox, jumped down. Sid and Ox unlatched the back and jumped into the wagon. A moment later they reappeared, dragging an old man, a young woman, and a boy of about twelve.

The captives' faces were dark as coal dust in the moonlight, except for the woman, whose skin glowed a soft copper. Their hands and feet were bound with iron shackles. All three made enough noise to wake the dead, the woman pouring forth a volley of insults, the young boy and old man joining her with shouts and cries for help. Sid and Ox ignored the racket, unconcerned about interference. On these docks, you could slit a man gut to gullet without a soul bothering to ask why.

Sid plucked a baby from the covered cart, and the infant let loose a stream of urgent, frightened shrieks. The woman squirmed violently, trying to twist free of the driver. "You gives me my chile, you damn bastards! Gives me my chile, or I'll send yo' ugly selfs to Hell!"

Zeke forgot his aching legs and numb fingers as he fought to clear his mind of emotion. If he let his anger take over now, he risked making a blunder that might jeopardize the three captives' lives. Four captives, he corrected himself. Blodgett would sell the baby into slavery as well, probably to a different master than the mother's. Blodgett wouldn't let a little thing like human feeling stop him from turning a quick profit. Especially when he already violated the slavers' own code; the people Blodgett captured and sold were nearly always freeborn.

Zeke knelt as still as any predator, waiting for the

perfect instant to make his move. Soon Sid's attention would be diverted with securing the chain and lock that would bind the captives together until they reached the auction block.

Zeke touched Jim's forearm, silently cautioning him not to move until the time was right, and eased a revolver from his belt. He rested his thumb lightly on the cold hammer.

Sid began linking the three prisoners together in a coffle, threading a chain between their shackled wrists. Not knowing what to do with the baby, whose screams had reached a fever pitch, he tucked it awkwardly at his waist, pinning it with one elbow. The woman lunged at him, stumbling as she fought the shackles. Sid growled at her, pushed his spectacles up on his nose, and fumbled at his waist for the key to the heavy lock. The baby wriggled, and Sid struggled to keep hold of both the child and the lock. Ox stood placidly by, watching Sid's trials with a sleepy blink.

Zeke released his grip on Jim's arm, cocked his revolver, and pointed it at the sky. He squeezed off three shots in rapid succession, the sound explosive above the captives' cries.

The horses pulling the cart screamed and reared, their breath white in the frigid air. Sid, still clutching the wailing baby, let loose an oath as he dropped his keys. They glinted in the moonlight, the ring wedged between the coarse planks of the dock, dangling precariously over the water below. The chain began to slither to the ground, slipping through the prisoners' shackles.

Another team of horses thundered down the dock, pulling a black carriage, its driver cloaked from head to foot.

"Oh, Christ, not again!" Sid moaned, sparing the black carriage a wild glance as he grasped at the loosening chain.

"What is it, Sid? What's goin' on?" Ox wrung his

big fists, looking helplessly to his smaller, shrewder friend.

The carriage's driver lifted a long-barreled gun and peppered the dock with shot, sending the gray cart's horses into a renewed frenzy. They veered and broke into a gallop, desperate to escape the noise and the stink of gunpowder. Finally prodded to action, Ox lunged to catch the horses, missing the reins by inches. He tore off after the frightened pair.

Sid cursed again. "Damn your worthless hide, Ox, it's a trick! Get on back here!" Trying to balance the wailing baby on one hip, he squatted and frantically tried to pry the key ring from between the planks, his fingers shaking.

"Mother of Christ, Sid, what the hell are you up to down there?" Blodgett shouted from the top of the gangplank.

On his knees now, Sid set the baby on the ground. "Boss, you gotta get down here right away!" His voice shook with frustration. "It's Malloy's god-damned—"

Sid broke off with a grunt as the woman prisoner shook her wrists with a well-aimed flick, sending the heavy chain crashing against Sid's pointed nose. His spectacles flew into the air, landing a few yards away in a pool of something black and oily.

"Good girl," Zeke whispered. He and Jim abruptly emerged from behind the barrels with a chorus of war whoops. Zeke fired his revolver directly over Sid's head. Sid clawed frantically for his spectacles, cradling his bleeding nose with his other hand. The gunpowder made him cough, and his eyes were streaming. When he spotted Zeke and Jim, he grasped at the knife in his belt. Zeke kicked the blade out of his hands, sending it clattering along the dock and into the water with a splash.

Sid scrambled to his feet, squinting without his spectacles, fumbling behind him for some sort of weapon. His hands found a narrow plank among the debris, and he held it in front of him like a club.

Jim rushed forward, and Sid waved his plank wildly. It connected solidly with Jim's sleeve, but the wood was soft and rotten. Jim laughed and stepped up to the smaller man, lifting him by his vest until the man's face was even with his own.

"What do you want me to do with the little rat, Zeke?"

Zeke smiled coldly. "Give him a bath."

Jim grunted his assent and tossed a kicking and cursing Sid into the black water.

Zeke shot a glance at the *Chérie*. Blodgett was taking the gangplank in long strides, waving a gleaming six-shooter. "Jim," Zeke hissed, "get them into the carriage."

Jim worked to pull the chain free of the prisoners' irons. "You keep yo' hands off me!" the woman screamed, thumping Jim with her shackled hands. "Ef you don't lets me go, I swears I'll cut off yo' balls and feeds 'em to you raw!"

Jim winced as the metal restraints glanced off his cheek. "Damn it, woman, we're trying to help. Ouch! . . . Jesus, we're not . . . ouch! Damn you, now stop that!"

"What's the problem, Jim?" Zeke asked, his jaw tense, his eyes fixed on Blodgett.

"They won't . . . ouch! I don't think she trusts us, boss."

"We don't have time for her to trust us, Jim. Get her into that carriage if you have to drag her. I'll keep Blodgett occupied."

Blodgett had reached the foot of the gangplank. He lifted the gun, squinting to take aim in the dark.

"Don't try it, Jack," Zeke called out.

Blodgett's face contorted with hatred. "Damn you sons a bitches to Hell and back again!" he screamed into the darkness. He waved the six-shooter wildly. "Our deal doesn't cover you stealing my property, Malloy! I should kill you tonight and get it over with."

Zeke gave a grim smile, holding his revolver casually leveled at Blodgett's belly. "We both know you won't do that, Jack. My boys know too much, and I'm the only one holding them back. What did you do with your prisoners' free papers, by the way? It would make my life easier if I could get them back now."

Jack's eyes gleamed in the pale light. They were a strange color, a clear golden yellow, like a snake's. "I don't need to stay in Boston, you know. You're making it worth my while to take my trade elsewhere, Malloy, and when I do, I'll cut your guts up for dog food."

The dark horses stamped behind him. Zeke felt the cold night air on the back of his neck, and heard Sid splashing in the water, struggling to get back onto the dock. "You know what you have to do to get rid of me. Release my sister."

Blodgett gave an ugly laugh. "She belongs to me now, Malloy. You sure are taken with that half-breed filly. If I didn't know how noble you were, I might think there was something more than brotherly interest between the two of you."

Zeke cocked his pistol again. "Annabelle was never meant to be a slave."

"Somebody should have told your daddy that, Malloy. He sold her off like he would any other prize filly."

Zeke battled the rage that pierced his heart like a shard of ice. "She was his daughter."

"By his nigger whore," Blodgett sneered, his mouth curling.

Zeke fought to keep his trigger finger still. Annabelle's safety rested in this son of a bitch's hands, and in the hands of his band of thugs. Zeke wouldn't be the one to sign her death warrant. But Jesus, it would be pure pleasure to put one neat bullet in this bastard's heart.

Jim had yanked the chain free, scooped up the wailing baby, and was trying in vain to push the three prisoners toward the dark carriage. "You've got to get in now. You're just gonna have to trust me, ma'am. Ouch! Damn it, ma'am, please don't do that again. If you just get into the damned carriage, we'll take you someplace safe."

"Get yo' hands off my chile!" the woman screamed, hysterical. "Gives me my baby, fo' I tears yo' heart out!"

Jim's voice broke with frustration. "You can't even hold him with those things on yer wrists. If you just get in, you can do whatever—"

He gave a muffled groan as she took another swing at him. "I'll kills you!" the woman screamed.

The carriage driver jumped down from his seat.

"Nate, get back up on that bench," Jim growled.

The driver lifted the hood obscuring his face, showing himself to the three prisoners. The woman stopped short, taking in the driver's dark face and gentle eyes. "It's all right, ma'am," Nate said gently.

"We have nothing left to say to one another," Zeke told Blodgett coldly as he edged his way backward to the carriage, never lowering his revolver. It was well past time to get the hell out of there.

"Don't we?" Blodgett's face lit with a weird smile as he lifted the Colt, cocked it, and fired into the darkness.

The bullet screamed past Zeke, grazing the carriage's black paint. The woman prisoner leapt into the carriage, and the others followed, Jim cradling the wailing baby.

Zeke found himself crashing into Jim as he jumped into the carriage. He almost twisted the handle off the door as he slammed it shut. The carriage lurched and veered sharply, and Jim plopped the baby on the distraught woman's lap, only to stumble over the tangle of shackled arms and legs. Zeke sank against the seat and shut his eyes.

The woman screamed as another bullet lodged itself in the wood above their heads, competing with the deafening sound of hooves on the wooden dock.

Zeke barely looked up. They'd done it. Somehow they'd managed to free all the captives, and nobody had gotten killed. He slid the safety on his revolver and checked the chamber: one bullet left.

"Jesus, boss," Jim muttered, gingerly touching a cut on his lip. "Some nights, workin' for you is one hell of a ride."

Chapter 2

〜〜∞〜〜

Zeke glanced up from his whiskey glass at the two men sitting in front of him. They looked as sheepish as boys caught filching melons from a summer garden. "Damn it, do you two have any idea at all what you risked tonight?"

Nate spoke first. "Jim had nothing to do with it, Zeke. I acted on my own."

"You acted like a goddamned fool. This is a dangerous enough game, Nate, but for you it's a fatal one. You know what will happen if you get caught." Zeke kept his voice icy, hiding his own concern and love for his friend. "You showed your face, the single worst thing you could do."

Nate set his mouth into a grim line. "I'm sick and tired of my color keeping me from helping you properly."

"Your color will get you lynched if Blodgett finds out who you are. Don't make me live with that."

"And what am I supposed to live with?" Nate exploded. "Those are my people, Zeke. Was I supposed to sit there and watch that woman get dragged back into slavery—and my two best friends get killed to boot?"

Zeke glowered into his glass. He should never have let Nate help him in the first place. Nate stood to lose everything—his successful business, the beautiful wife who adored him, even his life—in the service of a cause most people despised.

Zeke had agreed to the dangerous game for his own reasons, accepting the risk to his own life. But to gamble with the lives of his friends . . . that was something else again.

He turned on Jim next. "And don't think you're off the hook, mountain man. What the hell was that all about out there?"

Jim grimaced. "Aw, boss, what was I supposed to do?"

"You were supposed to get the captives into the carriage without taking all night."

"You try and tell that woman—that Indigo—what to do if she don't want to. She kept clippin' me with them irons until I wanted to deck her one myself. And I was gonna give her the baby as soon as she—"

"No excuses, Jim. Indigo was angry and frightened, as anyone in her place would have been. You weren't supposed to reason with her, you were supposed to get her body into that carriage. Why didn't you just pick her up and dump her in?"

"You only had fancy-pants and his pearl-handled six-shooter to deal with. I had to handle a faceful of iron and spittin' woman. Crikes, I hope we never get a gal and a baby again."

Zeke sat back wearily, sick of venting his frustrations on his friends. "So do I. Listen, you two, I don't know how much longer we can run these rescues. Blodgett wants to break the stalemate—the shots he fired at us tonight are just the beginning."

"He won't do squat, boss," Jim said confidently. "If he gives you so much as a black eye, me and the boys'll blab to everybody from the mayor on down. Even the slavery boys don't like what he's doin', grabbin' free folks off the street and sellin' 'em into chains."

"He made some noise about giving up his operation in Boston," Zeke said thoughtfully. "I gather we've made his business considerably less profitable." He allowed himself a tight smile.

Nate spoke up. "And if his southern clients found out where he gets his goods? No master likes to think of his slaves mixing with freeborn men."

Zeke ran his fingers through his hair. "I don't know if we can count much on Blodgett's clientele. He supplies his customers pretty cheaply, and his specialty can be hard to come by. The kind of man who buys an eleven-year-old for a whore probably doesn't care much where she came from."

Nate thought about this a moment. "Zeke, are you sure Blodgett really does have Annabelle?"

"All I've got is his word," Zeke said grimly.

"Even if he does have her," Nate ventured, "can we trust him to tell us the truth about her conditions in captivity? He's hardly the sort of man to keep his word, Zeke, especially to you."

Zeke looked up at Nate in frustration. "You think I don't know that? But how can I risk it? If I turn Blodgett in, he says he'll give Anna to his men. *All* of his men. Then he'll kill her. As long as there's some tiny possibility that he hasn't already done both, I have no choice. We can keep hounding him, hope to wear him down, but we can't bring him to ground."

"She's one woman, Zeke. And there are so many."

Zeke's expression was bleak. "She's my sister."

Nate nodded, conceding the point. He reached for the whiskey bottle, and Zeke raised an eyebrow. Nate didn't drink often—his wife didn't like it. But then, Nate's wife would like very little of what the three of them had done tonight.

Jim's pale Adam's apple bobbed, and he laid one bony hand on Zeke's arm. "It's been rough before, boss, and we always come through it. Fancy-britches's got a bee up his butt, and we're gonna have to lay low for a while, that's all."

"I hope so," Zeke said, appreciating his friend's attempt to comfort him. He poured another drink and raised it with a wan smile. "To tell the truth," he said, "bad as Blodgett looked tonight, I'm dreading tomorrow more."

Nate grinned. "Interviewing *another* secretary, Zeke?"

Zeke scowled. "They keep quitting on me."

"I can't imagine why," Nate said. "You bark at them morning 'til night, demand they keep your own peculiar hours, and refuse to tell them the slightest detail about what you're really up to in the middle of the night. And you treat them as if all females were brainless."

"Would you prefer I give them the name and address of every Underground Railroad station from here to Canada?" Zeke asked coldly.

"Missus Biggins is a female, and she ain't brainless," Jim muttered in defense of the woman who ran Zeke's household with good-natured efficiency.

Zeke laughed and took another sip of the whiskey, glad for the warmth it offered him. "Agreed. Nonetheless, the crop of females I'll be interviewing tomorrow will no doubt be not only brainless, but probably sexless, dried-up Boston hypocrites as well."

Nate looked at Zeke with something like wonder. "I forget you're not a northern man. The southern part of you seems so far away these days. Even your accent's gone."

Zeke scowled. "The southern part of me's the only thing that's worth a damn. If the bastards didn't keep slaves, I'd head for home in a Yankee minute."

The men were quiet as Zeke downed his whiskey, thrust his arms into his coat, and headed off to check on the rescued captives. The fugitives were hidden in the snug underground shelter behind

Zeke's house, where they would be safe and warm and well fed.

Zeke cursed as the night air filled his lungs. Even the whiskey couldn't keep the cold away. It wasn't doing much to dull his worries, either. He thought again of Jack Blodgett, and his cold yellow eyes. He had to be stopped. But if Zeke got himself killed in the process, Annabelle would have no one on earth to save her from that snake. Not, he thought with disgust, that he was doing such a great job himself.

A hot bath, he thought again, and another couple of drinks as soon as he'd checked the fugitives. It would be light soon, but maybe he'd manage to get in a few hours of sleep.

At just past five in the morning, Liberty Brooks sat upright in her narrow bed. Mr. O'Donnell had begun his morning singing practice in the next room, running through the entire latest music-hall repertoire. He had spoken with her about it in the dining room, assuring her that he would secure a place on the stage any day now. Liberty knew from experience that his practice would last a full hour, until he dressed and shaved for his real job as a bank clerk. She also knew that no amount of burrowing beneath her pillows would drown out his unmelodious honk.

Boardinghouse life, she thought, was always rather chancy. If you found a place that was clean, the rooms might be dank and windowless, or the meals inedible. If you could eat the meals, the place was overrun by mice, or you walked into your room one day to find the landlord rummaging through your dainties.

She remembered her parents' small house in Ohio, yellow marigolds growing in trim rows along the front steps. The streets in town met at perfect right angles, and even the fields were laid out in a neat checkerboard. Everything was bright and tidy. Twin Oaks hummed along like a spinning wheel.

Not Boston, where the streets met crazily, without any apparent rhyme or reason. Where people didn't know one another, and didn't care to. And the noise! Hooves clattered in the street from dawn until midnight, whistles and brass bells called people to work, stevedores swore and grunted on the docks as ships steamed in and out of the harbor. After Twin Oaks, where even in town it was no trick to hear the buzzing of a single bee on your front porch, Boston was deafening.

Liberty smiled. She wouldn't have traded the city's chaos for all the peace and quiet in Ohio. Cultivated, respectable Boston had captured her imagination since she'd been a skinny tomboy with a carefully guarded dream. She'd come here with nothing—nothing but a fierce desire to erect a barrier between herself and the pitying smirks she'd known all her life. Here she could live a life of honor and principle. Here she could give her heart and soul to the fight against slavery.

Mr. O'Donnell hit a quavering high note, and Liberty grinned. There were a few things here she hadn't expected, but the dream had remained. She was going to be the most respectable, most refined, most *honorable* damned crusader this city had ever seen.

It was time to propel herself out of bed and into the new day. The morning air made her shiver as she splashed cold water on her face and propped a small round mirror on her trunk. She unbraided her unruly chestnut-colored hair and brushed it vigorously, trying to unsnarl the stubborn kinks. If she pulled it straight back from the temples and rolled it into a hard, tight bun, it might look reasonably professional until noon. She shrugged out of her nightgown, pulled a clean chemise over her head, and stepped into a pair of drawers that had been mended too many times. The linsey-woolsey gown was looking rather threadbare, she thought ruefully as she worked the twin rows of buttons up the front.

The sounds and smells of breakfast were beginning to float up from the downstairs dining room. Liberty pinned her bonnet to her hair and thrust her stockinged feet into a pair of worn boots. She scowled at her reflection. The green straw poke bonnet had come with her from Ohio, and its decoration of blue calico flowers had wilted the first time she'd tried to sponge it clean. It was eminently respectable, and perfectly hideous. Next month, she promised herself, come hell or high water, she'd buy a new bonnet.

She took a deep breath. Today would be different. Today was the day she began her search for a new job, a new life.

Right after breakfast.

The marketplace overflowed with movement and color. A wizened old woman in a red kerchief handed a freshly killed chicken to a plump housewife, the rest of the feathered inventory clucking around her feet in small wire cages. A ripe, auburn-haired wench, all of fifteen, hawked plums and cherries. Her cheeks pinkened at the attentions of the dapper young men who leaned against her stall, drawling compliments and filching fruit.

Liberty would never get over her wonder at the variety and vitality of the big city, for all its ills. She rarely came to the North End and had never seen this bustling market before. Her modest breakfast had been no match for the long walk, and her stomach growled at the smell of grilling meat. Deciding the purchase of a new pair of stockings could go one more week if her stitches were very fine and close, she gave way to temptation and bought a savory sausage. The spicy mustard made her eyes mist over. With her newspaper clutched in one hand, the sausage in the other, she wandered the square looking for her street, finally finding it nearly where she had started from. The buyers and sellers in the busy market jostled her and one another as she wiped the mustard from her fingers with a handkerchief and stepped from the noisy square into the cooler, darker street.

Picking her way through the lane, she began to have misgivings. A rat as big as a housecat trotted along a windowless wall. A pair of seamen, clinging drunkenly to each other, swaggered down the lane, singing snatches of rude songs. The taller of the two touched his dark blue knitted cap as he passed, murmuring, "Begyrpardn, ma'am," and leering amiably. The shorter gave a loud belch, which she scrupulously ignored.

Perhaps she should simply abandon this particular venture. As she looked back to see how far through the slum she'd have to travel to return to the bright marketplace, she heard a high-pitched feminine voice.

"Hey there, sugar, ya lookin' for work?"

Liberty looked up to a nearby balcony to see a trio of young women no older than she who, on first glance, seemed quite glamorous. The woman called out again. "Whattsa matter, sweetie, cat gotcher tongue?"

Now Liberty noticed that the woman's low-cut dark purple dress was stained in the armpits and starting to fray at the hem and neck, and her face was coated with a thick layer of white powder. Liberty straightened her shoulders and offered a polite good-day.

The woman licked artificially red lips and arched a black eyebrow. "Oooh, she's very nice. Hey, girls, get a load of the lovely manners. Manners is real

important here, honey. You could be a real professional, first class." The other two women propped
themselves listlessly against the railing.

Liberty had not the slightest idea how to deal
with such persons. As she was trying to formulate
a reply, her heart leapt into her throat as a hand
grasped her elbow. Starting violently, she found
herself looking up into a pair of eyes as hard and
yellow as topaz stones. The man was tall and blond
with pleasing, regular features and a strong jaw. He
was expensively—if somewhat gaudily—dressed in
a royal purple waistcoat, acid green silk cravat, and
a luridly pink rose in his buttonhole. His eyes bored
into Liberty, making her sway a little dizzily.

"Is this young woman disturbing you?" he asked,
referring to the harlot on the balcony. His voice was
silky and mesmerizing, but somehow icy as well.

"Captain Blodgett," Liberty replied, regaining
her composure, "what a pleasant surprise to
see you here." Liberty's cousin Millie was practically engaged to the man. Having met the
captain several times, Liberty did not see the
attraction.

"You have the most peculiar interests for such a
pretty girl," he said, his yellow eyes glittering as
he glanced up at the prostitutes.

"Not at all," Liberty said, acutely aware of his
hand on her elbow. "My . . . acquaintances and I
were merely discussing the tragic lack of respectable
work for females. Perhaps if we attained the vote,
the streets of Boston would be a more honorable
place."

She wondered at herself. Captain Blodgett had
just plucked her from a decidedly unseemly situation, yet she felt no relief to see him.

"Nonetheless, I feel compelled to ensure that my
lovely and rather naïve young friend not come
to any harm," he said, his voice all butter. "If
these . . . ladies were to, say, have one of their

brutes clout you over the head and spirit you away, what would your poor parents do then?" He smiled so smugly, she thought he would lick his paws.

Liberty forced herself not to grimace. Blodgett invariably treated her like a stupid child. His reasoning—the reasoning, in fact, of her entire family—was that her attempt to live independently in Boston was a foolish experiment destined to end in disaster any day now.

"My parents," she lied, "would trust my judgment. I am perfectly capable of looking after my own affairs, Captain."

"I don't know that I can agree, my dear. I'm afraid this neighborhood is quite dangerous for a respectable girl walking by herself. What on earth were you thinking?"

Liberty bit her lip, annoyed. She hated to admit to Blodgett that she was looking for a new position again. She had changed jobs nearly five times in two years. "I read an advertisement for a position with lodgings. I was simply looking for the address."

"I rather doubt the North End is an appropriate environment for such a sweet young thing," Blodgett pointed out, his breath smelling very faintly of rum. "I was about to get a cab to the Common. Would you care to join me?"

"Well . . ." She hesitated. An internal voice told her not to go with this man, but even the mile's walk to the Common seemed long, and her feet were already throbbing. Her spirits began to sink. She had spent half the morning getting here, and all for nothing. Blodgett was right; she couldn't possibly take a position in this neighborhood. "That would be extremely convenient," she finally sighed.

The pair walked down the dark alley to a broad cross street, where Blodgett flagged a hack. As they entered the dark hansom, Liberty asked absently, "Captain, what brings *you* here? As you've said, it's an awfully unsavory neighborhood."

His brow clouded and his yellow eyes flashed fiercely for a moment, but he regained control almost instantly. "I keep an office here. For . . . shipping. Complicated matters, rather boring for charming young ladies, I assure you." His tone invited no further questioning.

Liberty started to retort, but there was something stormy and a little frightening in his eyes, and she decided that perhaps, just for today, she could allow such a remark to go unchallenged.

. Four hours later, Liberty's feet felt as if they were on fire. Another position filled. It was hopeless. Every place she tried had found another girl.

She had moved to Boston two years ago thrilled by the prospect of being independent, of enjoying the freedom of city life, and of teaching eager, gifted pupils. But she had slowly come to realize that some of her dreams had been the foolish woolgathering of a green girl, and that an easy and amusing life was the lot of a very tiny minority in this world. She'd accustomed herself to the pittance the schools called a salary, to the stockings mended too many times, to out-of-fashion bonnets. She even derived some degree of pleasure from her thrift, every week working out the knotty puzzle of how to make ends meet.

And living in Boston was a privilege, she reminded herself, well worth such minor hardships. Why, at the Antislavery Society meetings alone, she had met some of the most renowned abolitionists in Boston. Respectable, honorable men and women. More than anything else, she longed to be like them.

She rubbed her sore feet painfully and grimaced to see that her boot soles were wearing through—

again. She wasn't sure the cobbler could fix them this time.

It was time to face the cruel fact that, as a woman alone without family to help her, she could not make a living at her chosen profession. Lady teachers in Boston made less than a third of what their male counterparts were paid. On her tiny salary and long hours, she found that she had virtually no time to devote to her cause.

She straightened her back and adjusted her bonnet. Liberty Brooks was not the kind of woman to give up the modest gains she had made just for the sake of a little material comfort. It was simply a matter of finding the right position—one that would allow her to pursue her passion. She unfolded her newspaper and peered again at the tiny print, looking through those advertisements she had not circled, wondering if she might have missed something. Her eye lit on one she had not yet considered.

POSITION AVAILABLE

Boston speaker seeks amanuensis for routine corresp., kp. affairs in order, &c. Requires exclnt. spllng., must write clearly & in good hand. Good pay, comfortable lodgings. Only hardworking, respectable indiv's of reliable character need apply.

An amanuensis? Liberty had only the vaguest notion of what the title might mean, but it sounded like clean, respectable work, if nothing else. She promptly wrote a carefully worded letter to the address outside of town listed in the advertisement.

The reply came the next day, a short note from a Mrs. Biggins asking that Liberty appear for an interview. The note made no mention of the details, or just who her employer would be. But the very uncertainty gave the job an air of infinite possibility.

The day was warm and clear, and Liberty decided to walk to her interview rather than take the coach. A stroll through the woods would let her clear her mind and compose herself. Inhaling the clean scent of the pines, she covered the soft forest floor with a long, purposeful stride. The sun lazily dappled the trees, painting hundred-colored shadows, and the air was cool and still.

The rhythms of the forest swallowed all sense of time, so she was pleasantly surprised to emerge from the wood to find a neatly painted blue and white sign pointing to her destination: HAVEN HOUSE, ONE MILE.

The open road was dusty and hot but soon revealed a house surrounded by trees. Thank goodness for some shade, she thought, wiping her damp brow with her handkerchief. The blue-gray slate roof was massive above the elms and chestnuts surrounding the house.

Flanking Haven House was a deep, wooded gorge, very dark and cool. A stream trickled lightly through its heart, and wet purple violets grew along the bank. A modest bridge crossed the stream and led to the back door. Liberty followed the stone wall surrounding the house until she found a large green gate, then crossed the bridge and peered through a window into the kitchen. A small, plump woman, her white hair tucked into a simple linen cap, poked at a black stove. Liberty knocked timidly at the door, suddenly feeling a little unsure of herself.

The woman answered the door with a sweet smile. "Yes, dear?"

"I'm here to answer the advertisement, for the position," Liberty began. "For the amanuensis? I've had a letter—I'm Liberty Brooks," she added at the woman's puzzled look.

"Oh dear, I am becoming a silly old thing. Of course, the secretary. Well, come in, my dear, come in."

"Haven't you had many replies, then?" Liberty asked as she stepped into the kitchen.

"No, no, I expect it's too far out of the city for most young ladies nowadays. Seems they're all so busy catching husbands. Which you won't get far with in this household," the woman added, chuckling to herself. "Well, for goodness' sake, I suppose I'd better run and fetch him. Would you like to freshen up, dearie?"

"Oh, yes, very much," Liberty gushed, relieved at being able to rinse her flushed face and smooth her unruly hair.

The housekeeper showed her to a small, neat room with a mirror, basin, and large bath. Liberty splashed her face liberally with cool water, dried off with a large linen towel that smelled lightly of lavender, and emerged feeling and looking very much fresher.

As she returned to the kitchen, she nearly collided with a tall, imposing man. Her heart skipped a beat in a way she distinctly disapproved of. So this was the "speaker"—none other than Ezekiel Malloy, one of the foremost political lecturers in Boston. She felt an odd rushing in her ears. Foolishness, she chided herself. Frivolous, weak foolishness. She took a deep breath, held her body very straight, and looked at him again.

He was tall and powerfully built, with broad shoulders and a slim waist. His black hair fell around his ears in soft, thick feathers like raven's wings, giving him a savage, untamed look that was not strictly fashionable. His eyes were clear, cold green, seeming to reach into her very soul, demanding answers to questions still unasked. They had an almost cruel directness, but behind that steel gaze she thought she could see gentleness and pain held carefully in check. His face was haughty and fine-boned, his tanned skin and powerful hands belying his overall appearance of elegance and mannered leisure. Her heart hammered wildly as he surveyed her with a patronizing smirk, one eyebrow lifted.

"This, I take it, is what presumes to be my new secretary?"

Liberty's eyes narrowed. She'd been to hear his lectures, had been entranced by his passion and his fire. But if her high-handed idol thought he could dismiss her so readily, he had another thing coming. She needed this job, and she was determined to get it. She lifted her chin, meeting his piercing gaze.

"Now, Mr. Malloy," clucked the plump house-keeper, "with us needing a new girl so badly, I don't know what you can be thinking."

"That's enough, Mrs. Biggins," Malloy said, his voice a wall of ice.

"How a body can be so smart and still so uncivilized is beyond me, it truly is," Mrs. Biggins huffed, before quieting herself nonetheless. Mr. Malloy's tone did not allow room for argument.

Zeke Malloy slid his eyes up and down Liberty's faintly shabby figure, walking around her slowly as if to take in every detail. She felt acutely aware of her worn dress, her curls slipping precariously from beneath the green bonnet, and the shocking state of her poor boots. Her face grew hot under his appraisal. "Perhaps you'd like to check my teeth?" she snapped finally, unable to bear the strain of his gaze.

"I beg your pardon?" He seemed shocked at the impertinence of her speaking at all.

"I can hardly see how you are going to determine my qualifications for this position by looking me over like some prize pony," she said crisply, sounding a good deal more sure of herself than she felt.

His eyes narrowed. "Miss, Miss . . . ?"

"Brooks. Liberty Brooks," she said, annoyed that he could not remember even than much from her letter.

"God help us, a poetic name," he said. "Miss Brooks, then. I am an excellent judge of character, and I will appraise yours in any way I see fit. Is that clear?"

"Perfectly," she said coolly, cursing herself for the hot rush of blood that flooded her cheeks.

"Have you held this type of position before?" he asked abruptly.

She thought of the boardinghouse, and her pitiful stockings. "I write in an excellent hand, and my spelling is impeccable. In addition, should you have need, I consider my compositional skills to be beyond reproach," she said quickly.

"But have you experience *per se* as a secretary?"

"I am also reliable, scrupulously discreet, and more than willing to work long hours. I am well accustomed to hard work, I assure you."

"But have you worked as a secretary before?" he insisted, the green eyes pinning her like a butterfly on a collector's board.

I need this job, she told herself, willing her knees to refrain from knocking under his pitiless gaze. "Why, of course. I believe I mentioned my experience in my letter," she bluffed brazenly. "Of course, it has been several years. I hope you will not fault me if a few of my skills seem a bit rusty."

Somehow, lightning did not strike her dead on the spot.

"I see," he said.

His scrutiny was becoming unbearable, and Liberty fought the urge to bolt from the room. Her knees felt as if they were made of rubber, and her stomach churned wildly.

"There is," he said, "one additional matter, one of extreme importance. My politics are, frankly, a touch radical. I am an abolitionist. That does not offend you?"

She nearly breathed a sigh of relief. He believed her. She was going to get this job after all. "Not at all. I share your philosophy wholeheartedly." Her voice was almost a chirp.

"*That* will not be necessary. I simply don't care to waste time arguing incessantly with my employees."

"Of course." She would have liked to strangle him, but she set her face in a prim mask, although her heart beat against her breast as if it would burst.

"Well," he said shortly, "you don't appear to be painfully stupid, and I suppose Mrs. Biggins will grow to be rather fond of you. You shall live here. I must have my assistant at close hand at all times. The position is yours, providing we do not encounter any unsavory elements when we check your references."

She stiffened slightly, "Sir, my character is beyond—"

He waved her protests away impatiently. "Yes, yes, of course. Excuse me, I have more important matters to attend to than the hiring of staff. Good day." He turned on his heel and walked out of the room.

Her head swam after the peculiar meeting. Somehow, despite his thoroughly disagreeable demeanor, she felt the room oddly lacking now that he had left. "Well, he certainly has a . . . distinctive personality, doesn't he?" she said brightly.

"He can be a right nasty so-and-so, and no mistaking it," the older woman replied. "But you handled him just fine, dearie. He's a good man at heart, you know, and I'd do anything for him. And he's a great talker—the speeches, I mean."

"Yes, I've heard Mr. Malloy speak," Liberty said softly. Ezekiel Malloy was one of the best-known abolitionists in Boston, and his passionate, deep-timbred voice had haunted her dreams for months after she'd heard him speak.

But for all that passion, his restraint was legendary. Not content to nibble away at slavery from around the edges, he held some of the more hot-headed, emotional wings of the movement in public contempt. She shivered, remembering his cry ringing through the lecture hall—*Pull slavery out by the roots!* He seemed to consider groups like the Underground Railroad to be doing little more than pruning a few troublesome branches.

"I declare, it must be a fine thing to understand politics," said Mrs. Biggins amiably. "I don't expect I ever will myself. I'll tell you, dearie, it tickles him just pink knowing you take to the movement like that, and don't you pay one bit of attention to his sassing you about it."

"It's sweet of you to say so, Mrs. Biggins, but I don't know that Mr. Malloy and I are likely to spend much time in friendly political discussions," Liberty said, gazing dubiously after him. She turned brightly back to the older woman. "So . . . you are the Mrs. Biggins who wrote to me?"

"I am, dearie. Mr. Malloy's a mite prone to losing track of himself when he's between secretaries, so I just take a few things off his desk as I see the need. I did give him that nice letter you wrote, but I'm sure he never read it. But I noticed right off that your handwriting was real pretty, and the words sounded fine, too."

"Does he go through many secretaries, then?" Liberty asked nervously, somehow knowing the answer in advance.

"Oh, my word, yes. That's why he started accepting ladies as applicants. Mr. Malloy has his peculiar ways, to be sure." At Liberty's dismayed look, Mrs. Biggins quickly added, "Oh, but, dearie, you'll get on fine, just fine. You've got a good spirit, and that's the important thing."

"I'm glad to hear that, Mrs. Biggins," Liberty said, sounding unconvincing even to her own ears.

"Would you like to see the rest of the house?" Mrs. Biggins asked, obviously pleased with her new companion.

"Yes, please, very much."

The house was pleasantly large without feeling impersonal. Rich red and blue Persian rugs adorned inlaid parquet floors. Interesting little nooks revealed plant stands and Chinese porcelains and doors to mysterious rooms. Haven House, although some distance from the city, was thoroughly modern and efficient, and Mrs. Biggins proudly pointed to the water closet attached to the first floor.

While they toured the rooms, Liberty's mind returned again and again to the imperious Zeke Malloy. He had not told her the demands and duties of the position, or tried to find out if they would be to her liking, and she still didn't know what she was being paid. He had asked no pertinent questions that could have determined her intelligence or aptitude. He was arrogant, self-important, and rude. Perhaps she should make her apologies to the kindly Mrs. Biggins, and continue looking for another position.

But something would not let her leave. It was not only her need for a new place to work, or her weariness at sore feet and mended stockings. This man was one of the most important speakers and thinkers in Boston. His influence was enormous. He dined with poets and senators. His ideas about the role of females within the movement required, in Liberty's opinion, considerable adjustment. But who better than she to show Mr. Malloy that a woman could be as devoted to abolition as he was?

And her first reaction to him? The disturbing pounding in her heart, the peculiar shortness of breath as he stood near her? Did these perhaps play some role in her decision?

Instantly she struck the thought from her mind. It was certainly not for any such weak, foolish emotion that she chose to work for Ezekiel Malloy. Wasn't she, in fact, overcoming her powerful dislike for the man? No, rather she was taking a step further down the path of honor she had chosen for herself.

Mrs. Biggins chatted merrily on about the efficiency and comfort of the house, while Liberty followed her, firmly telling herself she was doing the right thing.

Chapter 3

A rrangements were made to move Liberty's trunk from the boardinghouse to her new quarters, and she was soon comfortably installed. Her room was small but bright and scrupulously clean. She was pleased to see potted plants in the deep windowsill: ferns, aspidistra, trailing ivy, and a luxuriant, brilliant red geranium. Certainly Mrs. Biggins's hand, she thought. It was so like the gentle older woman to soften a room with green, living things. The bed was trim and cozy, covered with a snowy wickwork coverlet.

She arrived in Mr. Malloy's study promptly at seven-thirty on Monday morning, crisply starched and ready to begin work. She had been awake since before dawn, struggling with her hair and agonizing over which gown was most suitably austere. She would not give Zeke Malloy the satisfaction of finding her frivolous, weak, or in any way simperingly *female*. But already she could feel the traitorous curls slipping from the severe prison she had devised for them not thirty minutes before.

As she waited for him to look up from his writing, Liberty's mind began to race nervously. It was bad enough to be starting a new position, with the inevitable self-consciousness and insecurity that implied. Now, in the light of a new day, the lie that had gained her employment loomed menacingly. The abolitionist movement was the purest thing she knew, run by paragons of virtue. The was no room for liars, no place for self-serving charlatans. She almost wished Malloy had demanded the names of her former employers, so that she would have been spared certain humiliation today when he realized she was a barefaced fraud.

But Mr. Malloy was so busy that he scarcely seemed to notice her at all as he irritably ran his long fingers through his mane of jet black hair. He was in grave need of a haircut, she decided—he looked quite savage. He rifled through a tall stack of papers and files, searching in vain for some misplaced item.

Abruptly he shifted his gaze from his desk, fixing her with steady green eyes as he said coolly, "Why, Miss Brooks, you've decided to begin work. How delightful." He drew his watch from his pocket and eyed it meaningfully.

She forced her hands to remain calmly at her sides rather than clenching them into fists. "I trust I am not tardy, sir. By the clock in my room, I am several minutes early." She refused to give him the satisfaction of a display of womanish timidity.

"Of course," he said, the iced green eyes masking any true emotion. "I begin at six, often earlier. In point of fact, you are perfectly punctual, my dear." His cool smile did not reach his eyes.

My dear? She wondered irritably how he would react if she called him her blasted *dear*.

Ignoring her annoyance, he continued, "I shall be blunt—the situation here is disastrous. I've been without a secretary for nearly a month, and you can see for yourself the bedlam that has resulted." He gestured with disgust at the piles of pamphlets and letters scattered across his desk. "Mrs. Biggins is not much for this kind of work, and I'm quite particular about the way I like things done."

Liberty remembered Mrs. Biggins's discreet management of Malloy's affairs, but didn't think it an appropriate time to point the matter out. She pasted on a faint professional smile and said, "Well, that's behind you now. Let's get to arranging these papers, shall we?"

He frowned and pushed a sheaf of letters into her hand. "These are invitations to speak. Write that I'm pleased by the offer but must regrettably decline—you know the sort of thing. Avoid the usual obsequious language, and I hope you can work silently. Can you manage that?"

"Of course I can manage that," she said, barely keeping herself from snapping as she took the file from him. He pointed her toward a small cherry-wood desk equipped with a stack of smooth, heavy paper, a bottle of green-black ink, and several fine-pointed pens.

As she sat down at the desk, her throat tightened in panic. Maybe she didn't write as well as she thought she did. What if she spilled the ink? Maybe she would take too long. She jumped as he growled from behind her, "What are you waiting for, girl?"

"Composing my thoughts, Mr. Malloy," she said with considerable restraint.

"You don't get paid to compose your thoughts, you get paid to compose my correspondence," he replied. "Kindly begin at once."

She felt him glaring at her. Anger cleared her head, and she picked up a pen, looked over the first letter, and addressed a reply. He seemed satisfied that she knew at least how to make the letters of the English alphabet, and returned to rattling through his bookshelves and muttering to himself. When she had finished the stack of replies, twelve sheets of creamy paper were neatly filled with her impeccable handwriting.

He looked them over. "Hmm. Adequate. Here's a draft of a flyer for my next lecture. Please take it to my printer to set and print up. Tell him two hundred copies. The driver will know where to take you." He turned away, dismissing her.

She took the flyer and headed briskly outside, slamming the door and counting silently to ten. Angrily she brushed her wayward curls from her forehead and set about her errand.

She found the driver, a rather rough-looking fellow named Jim Sweetwater, in the kitchen garden. His plain, unshaven face creased with laughter as he chatted with Mrs. Biggins, who looked very fetching among the lavender and savory herbs, her white lawn cap sweetly framing her round face.

"Excuse me, sir," Liberty broke in, embarrassed, "Mr. Malloy would like me to take this to his printer."

"Right away, miss. But it's *Jim*, if you please. Good day to ye, Audrey," he said to Mrs. Biggins, tipping his hat and smiling shyly.

The driver might look a little rough around the edges, Liberty mused as Jim drove her into town, but he handled the horses with a careless, almost elegant ease. The day carriage was simply but richly equipped, upholstered in a fine fawn broadcloth and drawn by a pair of perfectly matched bays. The leather harnesses were polished to a subtle, lustrous gleam, but there was no trace of frippery about the rig; the horses sported no ribbons, the upholstery no purple Turkish tufts. They drove through a small section of modest businesses at the bottom of Beacon Hill until they reached a rather large brick building with a painted sign: FREEDOM PRINTING COMPANY.

"I'll just let ye off here, miss. I'm off to run an errand or two for Missus Bigg'ns. That woman keeps me busier'n a bear in a beehive. I'll be back to fetch ye in a couple of hours—it don't usually take no longer than that." And he started off as soon as her feet hit the street, leaving her blinking and a bit confused about what exactly she was to do.

The printshop was vast and thunderously noisy. The smell of grease and mysterious chemicals filled the air, and a series of loud, rhythmic, gunshot-like bangs resounded amid the rumble of the other machines. She shouted at one of the men that she had some work to be printed, and he wordlessly pointed her to a door with a neatly lettered sign: OFFICE. She knocked on the door without result, so she turned the knob and went in.

Standing behind the desk was a handsome black man dressed in a linen shirt, silk waistcoat, and dark wool trousers. Smiling and raising one eyebrow, he was leaning over a lovely light-skinned girl of about eighteen. When she saw Liberty, the girl ran from the room blushing, leaving the man to call out after her, "Please have those invoices ready by noon, Miss Davis. May I help you?" he asked Liberty. His voice was smooth and gentle and caressed the ear with the faintest trace of a silky Virginia accent. He looked directly into her wide startled eyes.

Liberty found herself unconsciously lifting one hand to her errant curls, trying to smooth them back into place. She would definitely buy a new bonnet the instant she got paid. "Oh, I'm . . . I'm Liberty Brooks," she stammered, "Ezekiel Malloy's new amanuensis."

"Excellent!" the man replied with a delighted smile. "I'm glad Zeke has finally seen the light and hired a beautiful woman to work for him. You should have seen the battle-ax he had before. Perfectly terrifying."

She smiled nervously. "Mr. Malloy said to bring you this," she explained, handing him the flyer, "and to tell you that he wants two hundred copies."

"And I suppose he wants them in two hours, as usual," muttered the man. "Oh, very well, Zeke knows he can get what he wants from me. I'm Nate Jackson, by the way."

"I'm pleased to meet you. I'm Liberty Brooks."

"Yes, so you've said," he observed with a smile.

"Did I? Yes, I suppose I did," she said, laughing nervously. "Silly of me." She felt the color rise in her cheeks.

Nate's smile widened to a dazzling grin, and she grinned back, beginning to relax. "Sorry," she said, "I'm not usually so goose-headed. Today's my first day with Mr. Malloy, and I suppose I might be a trifle nervous."

"Well, congratulations. Zeke's a fine man to work with, once you get to know him. Mind you, he never really stops being a bastard, but that stops bothering you after a while."

Liberty laughed. "You seem to know him rather well."

Nate's handsome brow furrowed slightly. "Zeke Malloy gave me a start in this town when no white man would consider helping a black man start a business," he said soberly. "He went to the bank for me to get a loan, helped me rent this building, even got a friend of his from New York to give me a good price on the equipment. I owe him everything, really. He's a good friend."

"I had no idea he could be like that," Liberty said.

"Most people don't. That's the way he likes it, I guess. I never could understand why he's such a bear most of the time. Maybe he's just tired of being civil to people who detest him. It's a tough world for individuals who insist on talking about what they believe in."

"I'm afraid I know that condition all too well, Mr. Jackson," Liberty said with a wry smile. She thought bitterly of the countless times she had fished her father out of drunken arguments. Her father, the only abolition man within a hundred miles of their Ohio farm, was impressive and intelligent when sober. But he became bitter and irascible after a few shots of rye whiskey. His caustic tongue and radical beliefs had landed him in vicious brawls more times than Liberty cared to remember.

Nate interrupted the painful memory with a laugh as musical and soothing as his speaking voice. "My dear, I was going to take lunch with Miss Davis in there, but I think I'd rather spend it with someone who's not quite so frightened of me. Would you do me the honor?"

"Well, I don't know," she said, still a bit anxious with this elegant man and his debonair smile. How could she be certain he was the respectable person he seemed to be?

"*You're* not frightened of me, are you?" he challenged lightly.

She couldn't resist a challenge, especially such a charming one. "No, of course not," she laughed, meeting his gaze. "Very well, I'd be pleased to have lunch with you."

The two of them feasted on a fine meal Mrs. Jackson had prepared for her husband, and Nate regaled Liberty with amusing stories. The flyers were ready ahead of schedule, but Nate and Liberty became so absorbed in their conversation that she gave a little jump when she noticed the clock behind him. "Good Lord, is that the time? Mr. Malloy will be furious, and Jim—"

"Don't let Jim give you any trouble," Nate said with a chuckle. "Just tell him the presses were busy and the flyers took longer than expected. It was a pleasure meeting you, Miss Liberty Brooks." He extended his hand.

"Likewise, Mr. Nate Jackson," said Liberty lightly as she shook his hand. They came out of the building laughing, with one of the shop men carrying the heavy bundle of flyers, to see Jim leaning sullenly against the coach.

"Oh, golly, Jim, I'm so sorry, they . . . took longer than expected." Liberty stumbled on the lie.

"Ye don't have to hornswoggle me, miss. Nate and Zeke's just the same—could talk the ear off a snake when they're of a mind," Jim complained without much vehemence. Nate and Liberty suppressed their giggles and apologized gravely to Jim, who waved them off with an air of amiable exasperation.

Mr. Malloy gave the flyers a perfunctory glance when Liberty returned. "Nate does good work," he muttered. "Did he give you any trouble about doing it so quickly?"

"No, not really. He seems to be a fine man," she piped bravely.

Zeke glanced up at her with a smile that reached his eyes. "So Nate's charmed you, has he?"

Liberty, embarrassed, said stiffly, "Mr. Jackson is an intelligent and informed conversationalist. We had an enlightening discussion of Lysander Spooner's excellent article and Bowditch's rebuttal." Which was true, partly. Nate had also told her she had skin like Turkish gold and eyes that beckoned like the seven seas, but there really wasn't any reason to tell Mr. Malloy that.

Zeke fixed his eyes on her appraisingly. Mrs. Crump, his last secretary, had loathed Nate Jackson. She could never bring herself to accept a black man who was witty, charming, and more well read than she. Of course, Nate had flirted with Liberty—Nate flirted with all of Zeke's secretaries, even the hated Mrs. Crump—but that was unimportant. What was important was that Liberty felt comfortable with Nate, that she could see him as a human being. Nate's color didn't seem to matter to Liberty at all. Zeke hadn't counted on that from this prim little miss.

"Excellent job, Miss Brooks. I'm very pleased," he said with genuine warmth.

Liberty was astonished. She'd spent all morning

laboriously writing his correspondence, horrified lest she make the slightest error, and he complimented her on her ability to run a simple errand! She knew that geniuses often had odd quirks, but had never realized they could be so irritating. "Thank you, Mr. Malloy. It was a trifle, I assure you," she said coolly. "What shall I do next?"

Zeke scowled. Liberty Brooks was the best assistant he had found in years. She was efficient, knowledgeable, and, beneath that god-awful bonnet, he thought she just might be beautiful. She got along well with Nate and was unfailingly correct. Mrs. Biggins adored her already.

So why did he find her so profoundly irritating?

"You're just bristling with enthusiasm, aren't you?" he muttered.

"I beg your pardon?" she asked, feeling somehow insulted.

"I believe I spoke clearly enough. Very well, there's a project I've been meaning to get to for months. Do you see that carton?" he asked, pointing to a large box stuffed to overflowing with newspapers and pamphlets.

"Yes," she said slowly, somehow knowing she wasn't going to like this.

"Each of those papers has at least one article pertinent to the cause. I want you to cut out those articles that are relevant or interesting, and organize and index them."

Liberty's heart sank. This was the moment of truth. He would throw her out onto the street, after she had gotten so attached to her charming little room and the kindly Mrs. Biggins. How would she know which articles were supposed to be "relevant" or "interesting"? What did he mean exactly by "organize and index"?

"You can do that, can't you?" he asked impatiently. "Do you have some question?"

"No," she squeaked. "No questions."

* * *

Jack Blodgett looked contentedly into the mirror, pleased with the new waistcoat he had bought. Scarlet and deep pink embroidered roses curled cleverly around the lattice pattern woven into the cornflower blue silk. He pulled on a golden frock coat that set off his thick sandy hair and brows and echoed the color of his amber eyes. Women were mesmerized by those eyes. Like birds by a snake, he chuckled to himself. He broke off a length of sewing silk and used it to remove an invisible particle from between his perfectly even teeth. He turned his head slightly to one side, admiring his heavy, masculine jaw. Impeccable, he decided.

He trotted confidently down the stairs, taking a heavy watch from his pocket. Four-fifteen. Well, he had kept his attorney waiting for a bit, but he always felt he was sharper in his business dealings when his appearance was flawless.

The attorney, Josiah Sprigg, was a pinch-faced, bespectacled man whose fingers struck Jack as unpleasantly long. "I trust you had some excellent reason for keeping me waiting?" he squeaked in a papery voice.

Blodgett barely controlled a shudder. "I did, and it's none of your business," he said coldly. He loathed this desiccated man, but a discreet attorney was not to be cast aside lightly, especially in Jack Blodgett's line of work.

"I'll come directly to the point," Sprigg said in a shriveled voice. "As you know, I have been reviewing your uncle's will, trying to find some fault or loophole."

"Well? Anything?"

"Nothing," the gray man squeaked sadly. "I'm afraid the conditions still stand. You will have to marry in order to receive the inheritance, and you're running out of time. Should you remain unmarried by the first of the year, the money will go to his sister."

"That meddling old bitch," Blodgett muttered. "It would be pissed away in no time with all those brats of hers. The softheaded old cow is always bailing one of them out of some trouble. She'll be dead soon anyway, and leave it to those shiftless little monsters when she finally does pop off. What the hell good will that pile of money do then, split up among eight fools?"

"Then you must marry. Is the idea so distasteful?" Sprigg asked, one beetled eyebrow raised significantly.

Blodgett swore under his breath. Damn his uncle anyway for sticking him with this. He knew the old bastard was cackling with glee, if you could cackle in Hell. "I'd think that was obvious," he snapped. "How can I keep the operation running with a meddling female snooping around?"

"So you plan to continue the . . . operation? It carries certain risks, and with the money your uncle—"

Blodgett interrupted the man. "I make a very tidy profit from the operation, and it provides me some excitement. I get little enough pleasure from this life. You're not going squeamish on me, are you?"

"No, of course not," Sprigg said, rubbing his long, papery hands together thoughtfully.

"What I need is a simpering little china doll who doesn't ask questions," Blodgett mused.

"And the delightful Miss Goodall? I was given to understand that she was the perfect, er . . . woman of your dreams."

"She wasn't as pliant as I thought. As soon as I proposed, the minx was full of very pointed questions about how I make my money. Even wanted to see the books! . . . God, I hate scheming women. No, that's definitely out."

Sprigg wrinkled his high forehead and set his

fingers lightly to his lips. "Perhaps," he squeaked unctuously, "you have been, if you will pardon the expression, barking up the wrong tree."

"What do you mean?" Jack asked warily.

"I mean, perhaps you need a young woman with *more* schemes."

"What the Devil are you talking about?" Jack snapped, impatient to be rid of the unpleasant man and the entire business.

"You might consider one of these newfangled females—one of Elizabeth Cady Stanton's disciples, perhaps—with an endless collection of causes. Preferably one who has a notion to do a great deal of charity work after you're married. If she sat on enough committees and church boards, in addition to keeping house for you, she'd never have the time to look too closely at anything you might do."

Jack Blodgett sat back in his chair, a broad grin splitting his face. "I've always thought she was a nice little piece. Who'd have thought she'd be useful, too?"

"I'm sorry, Captain Blodgett, I don't quite follow you."

"I have just the candidate in mind. An earnest little mouse who'd never in a million years manage to get a real husband. A cousin of Millie's. She talked my damn ear off in the taxi with some nonsense about giving females the vote. What thinking man would put up with that? She'll jump at the offer. Just let Handsome Jack put the moves on her, and she'll melt like hot butter."

"Er, perhaps you should approach her with a little more . . . discretion. You do have some time to woo the young lady. No sense in scaring her off, now, is there?" Sprigg chuckled mirthlessly.

"Mr. Sprigg, I have more women in a month than you've had in a lifetime," Blodgett said with a twisted smile. "You just look after my legal affairs and leave the seductions to me."

"Of course, you do have a way with the ladies," Sprigg piped, the thin lips curling into something that passed for a flattering smile.

Jack Blodgett lit a fat cigar as soon as he had shown Sprigg to the door. He laughed out loud as he chewed and puffed.

Who would've thought it? Liberty Brooks was so pert and fresh, even in those old-maid clothes she wore. She was a little tall for his taste, but he bet she'd be a hellcat in bed. And she was ever so faintly dusky, exactly the way he liked 'em. If he squinted his eyes just right, she could pass for a pale, pale nigger. His mouth watered as he thought of her tender small breasts, imagining his big hands marking the lush flesh. The respectable misses were always the most fun in bed, even if you had to force 'em a little. They loved it really, even more than most women, when a man acted like a real man. That was the secret. No matter how much they cried, really they were loving it.

He shifted uncomfortably in his chair at the thought of his fist entangled in Liberty's soft, chestnut curls. Where was that bitch Emily? Two years as his maid and he still had to chase her down every time. He'd have to get rid of her soon; she was getting too quiet, boring. She didn't have any fight left in her at all.

He would give it to her, all right. He would give it to her good.

Chapter 4

As the days passed, Liberty's job began to make more sense to her. She was astonished to find that there was very little her new employer asked of her that she couldn't puzzle out, and since he seemed to assume that she, like most women, was blindingly stupid, her mistakes did not strike him as evidence of overt fraud on her part. His mood was often foul and his instructions cryptic, but he had unexpected moments of kindness that helped soothe her hurt feelings. He was a sharp and demanding employer, but after a few days she came to be able to interpret his vague directions and determine what he really wanted.

On her third evening in his house, Liberty sat in the study proofreading a long article he'd written.

"So this is how a lovely young woman spends her evenings."

Liberty jumped. She hadn't heard him approaching, but Mr. Malloy's long, lean form now filled the doorframe. *Lovely?* Something about the way he said the word make her feel strangely awkward. "Your step is very light, sir," she said. "You startled me."

"Oh, dear, how dreadful. We can't have you being startled, can we?"

Liberty started to glare at him but saw that his eyes had warmed to a leaf green, and his smile was not unkind.

"The best remedy for that, you know, is not to shut yourself up in a dusty old study after hours," he continued. "You'll be seeing ghosts before you know it."

"Oh, but I just have these few more pages to proofread, and then I can—"

"The article can wait until the morning," he interrupted. "Were you this dedicated when you taught school?"

"I was worse," she said with a rueful smile. "I was up at five and in bed after eleven every day except Sunday."

"Good God, I thought *my* schedule was crazy. What could have possessed you to work that way?"

"I'm used to it," she said lightly. "I grew up in Twin Oaks, a little farm town downriver from Cincinnati. By five in the morning, I'd be ankle-deep in dairy muck, breaking up the ice in the cows' water trough."

Zeke looked with new eyes at this proper, upright girl. Cows' trough? Dairy muck? Ohio was still pretty remote, and twenty years ago even Cincinnati had been not much more than a cow town. "So you're a country girl?" he asked.

"I suppose I am in some ways. I miss the feeling of being alone out there in the fields, with only the birds to keep you company. But I came to Boston when I was nearly twenty, and I don't think I'd ever want to go back. I have . . . odd ideas for a girl in Ohio. I'm much happier here," she finished abruptly, looking down at her hands, uncomfortable at having revealed so much.

If she wasn't careful, she'd be telling Mr. Malloy about her father's drunken arguments with those proslavery philistines, or about her gentle, half-Indian midwife mother. Most people assumed Liberty was a full-blooded white woman, and she did not care to be seen as a noble savage, or an "immoral Injun woman," or any of the other two-dimensional characters people imagined when they heard the word *Indian*. She would be Liberty Brooks, a respectable, honorable woman. Nothing more, nothing less.

"I see," Zeke mused. He was looking at her as if she were a mysterious package just waiting to be unwrapped. The thought made her a little dizzy. "Miss Brooks, would you join me in the parlor for a glass of sherry?"

"Well, I don't know if I . . . I mean, I've never had . . ." she stammered. Was it, after all, strictly proper for an unmarried woman to drink spirits alone with a man?

Zeke laughed. "That's all the answer I need. Come along now."

Unable to resist his rare good humor, she followed him downstairs. The parlor was large and comfortably masculine, its walls painted creamy white. Haven House was luxurious, but lacked any trace of pretension. Its owner now poured the sherry into two small glasses and handed one to Liberty.

Liberty sat gingerly in one of the heavy upholstered chairs, eyeing her glass with suspicion. Her mother had never touched spirits and had warned her that they were poison for native people.

She took a cautious sniff at the golden liquid. Well, it certainly *smelled* inviting. She shut her eyes and gulped it down, her eyes widening as the sherry slid down her throat like liquid fire. Trying to stifle her coughing and sputtering, she murmured, "Delicious . . ."

Zeke smiled. He had not expected the girl to be accustomed to spirits, but her blushing attempts to cover her distress were a joy to watch. She was delightfully transparent. "I'm pleased to see you enjoying your sherry, my dear. Allow me to pour you another."

"No!" she said quickly. "I mean, no, thank you."

She added, embarrassed, "I prefer to be temperate in all things." She folded her hands in her lap and studied the parlor floor as if she had never before seen its dark Turkish rugs.

Zeke leaned lazily against the stone fireplace's carved mantel, cupping his glass in one hand. He looked at her through half-shut lids, the suggestion of a smile on his lips. "You are a prim little thing, aren't you?"

"Prim?" Surprised, she looked up at him. "No, sir, I do not think I am prim, but I am respectable and careful. I believe these to be virtues."

"You've been misinformed," he said flatly, toying with the stem of his crystal glass. "Respectability is a lie, and caution a damned trap. Trust someone who's seen a little more of the world than you have."

"A *man* who's seen a little more of the world than I have," she corrected ruefully. "All manner of dissipation and debauchery is condoned when practiced by men, but women are required to be modest and seemly at all times. I prefer to save scandalous behavior for important occasions."

He lifted one black eyebrow. "My dear, you intrigue me. Tell me, pray, what occasions might those be? I would hate to miss any scandalous behavior on your part."

Liberty had thought he was being friendly, but something in his face changed her mind. His smile was almost predatory. "I was speaking metaphorically, of course, Mr. Malloy. I hope that doesn't disappoint you." The edge in her voice belied the sweetness of her expression.

He smiled wickedly. "Of course not, Miss Brooks. I am relieved to hear it."

Liar, she thought, studying him as he sipped his sherry. There was something restless about him tonight, a tension in his graceful frame. He lifted his eyes from his glass to meet hers, and suddenly she longed to smooth the unruly forelock of black hair that fell over his forehead. Her gaze dropped back to her lap, her mind racing for a suitable topic of conversation.

"May I ask, Mr. Malloy, what your position is on the constitutionality of slavery? Do you believe it requires a formal amendment to abolish?"

He paced the room like a cat, crossing to a shelf laden with books. He thumbed through a heavy volume bound in dark red leather. "No, you may not ask. I dislike discussing politics outside of working hours, and I especially dislike discussing politics with women."

Liberty gripped the arms of her chair, willing herself not to begin a tirade. Rome was not built in a day, and Ezekiel Malloy would not be reformed in a single evening. She would bring him around to a more reasonable view in time. They sat a few more moments in silence, when Liberty ventured, "This is certainly a fine house. Has it been in your family a very long time?"

"Miss Brooks, I loathe small talk," he replied icily, not looking up from the book he held in his hand.

She clenched her fists to keep from drumming her fingers in annoyance. Why on earth had he invited her here if he was going to refuse to talk to her? He honestly was the most irritating person she had ever known.

"You've never married?" she found herself asking bluntly. She regretted it instantly. What could have possessed her to ask such a personal question, and so clumsily? Her cousin Millie was right; she would never be anything but an awkward half-breed country girl.

Clearly startled, he set the book, forgotten, back on the shelf. Liberty ardently wished that the floor would do her the favor of opening up and swallowing her forever, so that she would never have the chance to disgrace herself again.

"No," he said, his voice curiously cool. "Never. And I never will. Marriage is an unnatural institution, wholly unsuited to the instincts of man."

"Why, Mr. Malloy, I find myself agreeing with you," said Liberty, looking up at him in surprise. "Although I would sooner say that it is unsuited to the needs of woman."

He raised a scornful eyebrow. "Marriage was *invented* by women. All a woman wants is to trap a man into supporting her, her brats, and a team of dressmakers from the sweat of his honest labor. And what does the man gain from this arrangement? Nothing he couldn't pay for in any bawdy house in Boston."

Odd, she thought. She wondered how a man could be so enlightened about slavery and remain so blindly pigheaded on the subject of women. "You can't be serious, surely, Mr. Malloy," she said, warming to the subject. "A wife is laundress, housekeeper, teacher of those 'brats' you mentioned—on whom a mother expends a great deal more energy than a father ever does, I assure you. She is up at first light preparing breakfast for her lord and master, who arises an hour after her to eat his meal at leisure, and she works by candlelight long after he has gone to bed—provided she is allowed to escape the brute's embrace for the night. As for the team of dressmakers, I daresay men lose a great deal more money on drink and gaming than any wifely wardrobe would require. What need has a slave of fine clothes?"

He crossed the room to stand directly behind her chair, placing his hands on the upholstery above her shoulders. She felt suddenly like a very small mouse at the mercy of a very large cat.

"It's husbands who are the slaves, my dear. You'll forgive me if I don't elaborate—there are mysteries of marriage a gentleman doesn't discuss with pretty young virgins."

Liberty flushed from the roots of her hair to the tips of her toes. "Honestly—why is it a man can never go ten minutes without thinking of—" She broke off, not knowing how to finish her sentence. She suddenly longed for another glass of the sherry—anything to keep her from wringing her hands and blushing like a fool.

His laugh made her shiver a little. She took a deep breath and wrenched the conversation back to safer waters. "Surely you don't find every woman so ignoble, Mr. Malloy." She willed her voice to a cool, low pitch. "After all, there are many wonderful female workers for our cause."

Zeke released his grip on her chair. "I'm sorry to have to tell you this, my dear, but most of the ninnies who call themselves abolitionists are among the worst hypocrites this city of liars has to offer. Men as well as women."

Liberty felt a knot of anger tighten in her chest. She turned in her chair to face him. "Hypocritical! How can you say that—and about people who risk so much?"

Zeke's eyes went cold. "Risk? What do those self-important fools know about risk? Let me tell you something, my dear. There's more to freeing the slaves than sitting in a Boston parlor gossiping and stitching quilts. If you knew a tenth of what—of what some men risk every day, you'd run back home to your cozy little farm in Ohio." He broke away from her gaze and crossed the room to pour himself another drink.

Liberty's mouth felt dry. Mr. Malloy's manner had changed as quickly as the sky in a summer storm. His voice was that of a man who had lost all faith in his fellow human beings. "People do heroic things every day," she managed, swallowing hard to keep her voice from cracking. "Men and women both. You, for one."

Zeke tilted his head back and drained his glass

in a single motion. He shut his eyes for a moment, as if to collect himself. "Your heart will break if you go about believing in heroes, sweetheart."

A hard lump burned in Liberty's throat, but she stood her ground. "Think of all those people working for the Underground Railroad, sacrificing their safety to help slaves escape to freedom. Surely that must mean something, even to you."

Zeke wheeled on her and flung his empty glass against the fireplace, where it splintered into a thousand glittering jewels. Liberty started up and out of her chair. The perfume of the sherry rose in her nostrils as she stared, shocked, at the wet shards on the hearth. She looked back at him, finding for the first time something in his eyes that truly frightened her.

He crossed the room toward her in an instant, grasping her roughly before she could protest. His fingers bit into her shoulders as if her stiff wool dress were gossamer. "You know *nothing*, do you understand me? What will it take to get you to leave off your stupid prattling?"

Liberty felt the hot sting of tears behind her eyes. What had she said to make him so angry? She tried again. "The people who run the Underground Railroad *are* heroes. I've known that since I was old enough to stand." Her voice sounded small to her own ears, a child's whimper against the roar of a hurricane. His eyes whipped her like sleet, and she looked away.

"What you heard were fairy tales." He took her chin in one hand and forced her to look up at him—at his hard jaw and angry mouth, at those terrifyingly cold green eyes. "The truth about the Railroad is that it's full of fools and cowards who lack the guts to face their enemies head-on. A thousand men and women rot in slavery for every lucky idiot the do-gooders manage to save. Scarcely a one of them has even the empty-headed idealism you do."

"Do you really believe that?" Liberty whispered.

"I don't believe it, sweetheart, I know it."

He let her go, and she felt a pang of disappointment. For a moment, she had felt as if his soul had brushed hers when he'd looked into her eyes. And suddenly she was sure that if he'd only open himself to her again, she could bring some light to the darkness within him. She knew it not in her mind, but in the deep, certain core of her heart.

"I don't know how you can endure it," she said, surprised that she'd spoken the words aloud.

His eyes shuttered and he was gone, as closed to her as he'd been from the beginning. "I endure because I have no choice," he said, his voice a harsh, enigmatic whisper. He turned his back to her. "It's time you were in bed, Liberty Brooks."

She stared at the broad form of his shoulders and the line of his back, searching for some chink in his armor. She found none.

"Very well, Mr. Malloy," she said, gathering her skirts and her dignity to rustle past him. "Good evening."

The night was clear and cold, and Zeke was glad of the pot of fragrant squash soup warming his hands. He walked briskly through the orchard, trying to clear his head. The girl had taken him by surprise, with her wide, mesmerizing eyes. He only hoped he hadn't let those eyes see too much.

Once, he had let himself be like her—naïve and full of hope. Maybe that was why it enraged him to hear her express those same sentiments so prettily. Because his own ideals had long ago hardened into a deep, gnawing anger at the hopelessness of it all. The years had passed, and nothing had changed. For every soul he helped to freedom, he could hear the cries of a thousand more echo through his mind, reminding him that all his efforts were not enough. Not enough to end the suffering. Not enough to shield his sister.

He stopped when he came to a rough, split-timber cabin. There were cracks between the boards big enough for a small bird to fly through, but the walls didn't need to keep the drafts out. Zeke swung the door open and stepped into the bare, cold room. He heard a high-pitched noise as a bat skittered past, its black wings almost touching his face. Moonlight poured through the window as he knelt on the floor, set the pot by his side, and felt along the floorboards for the expert, nearly invisible seam that marked the trapdoor.

In moments Zeke was lowering himself into a small, dark room with two doors as invisible as the trapdoor above had been. If the trapdoor were ever discovered, one would find only this small, homely cellar, with a few cabbages and potatoes moldering on shelves and some broken tools hanging on rusted hooks. But behind a second hidden door were two wide underground halls, tightly built to keep out the damp. Each was massive, much larger than the cabin, and had taken months to build. Narrow but comfortable beds lined the halls, and the shelves were filled with preserves and a fresh loaf of bread Jim had brought out earlier.

Zeke tapped on the hidden door—twice quickly, then twice again. The young boy appeared, smiling broadly. "Evening, suh."

Zeke smiled at the boy, who wouldn't be a child much longer. "Evening, Tom. Care to help me with this pot of soup?"

Tom grinned and nodded rapidly.

"You a good man," Indigo said to Zeke as she saw Tom bringing the steaming pot into the hall. "I don't know who you be, or how we goin' to thank you."

Zeke rummaged among the cupboards and found a few heavy bowls. "No need for any thanks. You've had plenty taken from you already; it's about time somebody took responsibility for giving a little of it back."

Indigo ladled the warm, steaming soup into bowls, and the three fell happily on the broth, laden with sweet squash, chestnuts, and smoked sausage.

Zeke leaned against the smooth plaster wall as he watched the group. How many fugitives had he seen by now? It was hard to tell. Sometimes they came in a flood, dozens of grim, silent souls pouring into the halls, forced to sleep on the floor because the beds were all taken. Other months it was a mere trickle, and the underground rooms grew dusty and cold from lack of use.

The group ate with obvious pleasure, all but old Jake, who sipped quietly, his face lined with pain. His feet were covered with bandages.

Zeke had been wrong about this particular band. These were runaway slaves, not the free blacks Blodgett generally kidnapped. They had managed their escape unusually well, but Jake had walked through forests and swamps without shoes, and his feet had been cut to pieces. Zeke had already had Dr. Stone in once to see the old man, but perhaps it was time to do so again. Stone was almost as good a friend as he was a doctor. He'd listened well in the backwoods of South Carolina, learning from the Cherokee medicine men who'd told him which plants reduced infection and swelling and how to help a woman muster her strength for childbirth.

"I'll go into town in the morning and get the doctor to attend to your feet," Zeke said, longing tonight to spend a few more moments in idle talk instead of making his way back to a cold, empty bed where he would get no sleep.

Indigo turned to Zeke. "You be a southern man," she said softly.

Zeke looked at her with surprise. He took her simple statement as half compliment, half accusation. "Most people can't hear my accent at all anymore," he said. "I've been living in Boston for years."

"I be listening for the voice of a southern white man 'most all my life," she said without a trace of self-pity. "It always be the voice of somethin' bad or shameful till now."

Zeke noticed that her baby was as pale as butter toffee and had blue eyes. "I'm sorry," he said. Indigo was beautiful, and beauty was dangerous for a slave woman.

"I be grateful to you for showin' me that anything can be holy, even that voice," she said. "It goin' be the voice of freedom to me from now on."

"It's late," he said brusquely, suddenly wishing himself a hundred miles away. He would get Dr. Stone tonight. Jake seemed to be in pain; his feet shouldn't wait until morning. Zeke would ride into town and wake Stone up. Maybe the cold night air on his face would exorcise his demons—at least for a few hours.

Giving them the usual reminder about the secret knock and keeping quiet during the day, he left. They should be safe here. This was Massachusetts, not Georgia, and the slave catchers were far away. Even Blodgett wouldn't be able to ferret out the well-hidden halls. The cabin was on private property. They would not be found.

And he could not bear for another instant the forgiving, gentle look on Indigo's face.

The ride was as cold and punishing as Zeke had hoped. Still, Indigo's face floated in front of him like a ghost's, taunting him, tormenting him. Shame welled in his throat. He remembered his own nights, too many of them, in the slave quarters. He had been only a boy, but that was no excuse. The girl had succumbed to his caresses, which had been clumsy at first, then more expert. She had even sighed, closing her eyes as he explored, finding out how to make her shudder and cry out in pleasure. He thought it was just possible that she had liked him, at least a little. He had never forced her, never knowingly hurt any woman, but he realized much, much later that his very position as the "marster's boy" had left his lover with little choice.

Shame sliced him like a knife every time a beautiful young fugitive lowered herself into those wide, plastered halls with their soft beds and full cupboards. Their eyes seemed to look at him and *know*.

But suddenly it was no longer Indigo's face that floated before him, piercing his heart like a dagger. It was someone else. Someone with eyes as cool and dangerous as the sea.

The horse beneath him nickered nervously, sensing the rider's restlessness. Zeke drew his breath in sharply as he realized whose face pulled at his soul. What did Liberty Brooks have to do with any of this? She wasn't involved, didn't know a thing about the whole tangled mess of Blodgett, Annabelle, and the fugitives who made their way in and out of Zeke's underground shelter. That tangle had begun to feel like a noose, squeezing the life out of him. On nights like tonight, he could scarcely breathe beneath the grip of the deadly words: *honor*, *enemy*, *slave*.

Sister.

Zeke felt his throat tighten. He spurred the bay beneath him, pushing the beast to run harder. Better to break his neck than to suffer this unending stranglehold.

The horse suddenly bucked sharply. Zeke gripped the bay with his thighs, fighting to calm the terrified beast. He struggled to keep his seat as the world pitched at crazy angles around him. It took every shred of physical strength as the bay shuddered and stamped, but finally it ceased its deadly twisting, allowing itself to be soothed. Something had startled the poor brute—the movement of some small animal, perhaps. Zeke stroked the massive, sleek neck and murmured quietly, willing his own heart to slow its racing.

He almost laughed out loud at his own will to survive. What, after all, did he have to live for? The fugitives? Nate and Jim would fight to keep his work alive long after he was gone. And Annabelle . . . Annabelle could be dead by now, or else a broken shell in a waterfront whorehouse, the light and life driven from her eyes. Annabelle had green, laughing eyes the precise color of Zeke's. And of their father, damn his black and twisted soul.

And yet, though it seemed Zeke would never be free of this curse his father had laid on him, he was suddenly almost happy tonight. He clucked the bay back to a trot, feeling the horse's strength beneath him. He was still alive, and there was something to be said for the business of breathing and eating and sleeping.

And loving? It was a fantasy Zeke rarely indulged. He thought again of Liberty Brooks. *She was respectable and careful*, she'd informed him in her crispest tone. It was the kind of thing his older sister would have said. Everyone had found Constance Malloy an admirable female—everyone but Zeke, who knew the cost of that brittle shell.

Pain flicked at his heart like the curl of a snake's tongue, but he repressed it. He clenched the reins in his fists. Not tonight. He would not think of Constance's betrayal tonight.

Chasing thoughts of Liberty away was far more difficult. There was something healing in her eyes, a glimpse at redemption. When she turned her steady, trusting gaze on him, it was easy to think that he had given up his dreams too easily. But what was she hiding behind that unwaveringly respectable facade? There was something wild in her, something that belied her primness and the dark wool costumes she hid in. He couldn't let himself believe in her promise of redemption until he answered that riddle.

The bay's trot jarred him back into the moment, and he spurred the horse to a gallop. He hadn't trusted anyone in a long time, yet he was almost tempted to trust Liberty. But not blindly. First he would shake her up a little, nudge her a bit off center and see what she revealed.

Zeke's *admirable* sister had caught all her flies with honey, not vinegar. He smiled at the cold wind on his face, thinking that maybe, just maybe, a little honey would make an effective bait for the paradoxical, intriguing Liberty Brooks.

Chapter 5

L iberty faced her first morning off with dread. Working for Ezekiel Malloy, she had the unimaginable luxury of two full days off, Thursdays and Sundays. Of the half dozen things she longed to do—read, take a good long walk, work on her new shawl—she had one social obligation to discharge first: a visit to her cousin Millicent Goodall.

The two girls had spent nearly every waking moment together until Liberty was eight, when five-year-old Millie was packed back to Boston by a mother who refused to further suffer the indignities of frontier life. When she was thirteen, Liberty had visited her cousin in Boston, returning to Ohio consumed with envy for the Goodalls' enormous, lavish house, bustling servants, and Millie's seemingly inexhaustible collection of gowns.

The older Liberty got, however, the less entranced she was with Millie's luxuriant life. Since Liberty had moved to Boston, she dutifully saw her cousin's family once a month, smiling glassily through interminable dinners, dodging questions about when she was going to get married.

She liked her uncle Harry well enough, a stout, red-faced man with a deep, infectious chuckle. It was Aunt Lucinda who tried Liberty's patience. Lucinda perched stiffly in the parlor, stabbing mercilessly at her embroideries, lecturing Liberty in a piercing voice on the correct comportment of young ladies. Lucinda managed a disapproving look or remark every time she caught sight of too tall, too outspoken, too *Indian* Cousin Liberty. And, indeed, something about her aunt always made Liberty feel not so distantly savage.

Millie, luckily, had more of her father's jollity than her mother's brittle nervousness. Still, she chiefly occupied herself with the awesome task of snaring a husband. She was devastatingly pretty— small, pleasingly voluptuous at nineteen, and bright and quick as a songbird. Her warm green eyes and apricot complexion were surrounded by a delightful mass of honey-colored ringlets that shook when she danced, laughed, or stamped an angry little foot.

The Goodalls' home was nothing like Haven House. Lucinda's domain shrieked her every passing fancy, whims dictated by various ladies' magazines. Its many rooms were stuffed with curiosa. One year owls had been all the rage; a bedroom had promptly been papered in an owl print, and no fewer than thirty stuffed owls glowered from mantels and bookshelves throughout the house. Another year Lucinda had been caught by the mania for things Japanese, and silk fans, delicate porcelains, and rice-paper screens littered nearly every room. An allegedly Veronese purple divan squatted atop an orange and blue woolen rug from the Indies. The resulting jumble threatened to shatter Liberty's nerves every time she entered the house.

Millie poured tea from a blue and gilt Russian teapot as she and Liberty sat straight-backed on the divan. Liberty had been grateful to find another guest in Millie's parlor—Jane Redburne, the graceful, red-haired wife of Uncle Harry's business partner. Mercifully, Aunt Lucinda was upstairs under cool compresses, suffering from a headache, so they had the morning to themselves.

"Your Mr. Malloy sounds perfectly disagreeable," said Millie, dropping two lumps of sugar into her tea to punctuate her statement. She looked quite fetching in her apple green silk morning gown, pert green bows restraining her blond curls.

Liberty, uncomfortably aware of her own stodgy dark dress, sipped her tea thoughtfully. She shivered a little, remembering his eyes when he'd been so mysteriously angry the night before. "He's quite brilliant, of course."

"He has an excellent reputation as an antislavery speaker," Jane agreed, her voice as cool as her hair was fiery. "Although he is, of course, rather unenlightened on the question of females." Jane Redburne was the picture of Bostonian sophistication, swathed in a matte silk gown the color of eggplant that managed to look opulent yet thoroughly respectable.

"Ooh," Millie gushed, "I do like men who are brilliant. At least I like men who are clever, and it's nearly the same, isn't it?"

"Well, I don't know about that," Liberty murmured.

"Men who're handsome are the best, though," Millie pronounced as she greedily bit into a tea cake, littering the zebra-skin rug with sticky crumbs. "Is he handsome?"

"He is," Liberty confessed. "Quite tall and lean, with dark hair and green eyes and a fine jaw."

"He sounds quite the Spaniard. Is he swarthy?"

"No, not at all. I believe he's Black Irish."

"Ooh!" Millie gasped, eyes wide. "An Irishman! Mummy'd skin me alive if I so much as winked at an Irishman."

"He has the look of Protestant Irish, at least," Jane added, looking coolly down at her gloved hands.

"Lots of 'em are awfully handsome," Millie added, as if this settled the question. "Dark with green eyes! Oh, darling, we'll get to work on him at once—we positively must! The first thing to do is to eliminate any competition. Does he have a young woman he fancies?"

"Millie, I really don't think it would be appropriate to—"

"You must make quite certain of that," Millie chirped. "He's probably got a mistress hidden away somewhere, or at least a charming young lady whose father wants her married off. And you must be ruthless, darling, perfectly ruthless in ferreting out these women and disposing of them. I am so awfully glad you finally took my formula for removing freckles. You're actually rather presentable these days. You're still a trifle . . . well, but I shouldn't think you'd ever have any trouble, you know, *passing*. For one of us, I mean."

Liberty's face flamed. She trusted that Jane would have the good manners to ignore the remark, but that didn't make it any less humiliating. Millie and her family considered Liberty's half-Indian mother a terrible social handicap. Liberty watched the cuckoo clock tick unrelentingly on the mantel, impatient for the ugly little creature to emerge and tell her it was finally time to go home.

"Really, Millicent, the man's . . . associations, or lack thereof, are hardly an appropriate subject of conversation for ladies, especially young unmarried ones," Jane reproved.

Millie rushed on, unmindful. In many ways, she was the same girl who had left Ohio at five years old, headstrong with the confidence that came from thinking she was the center of the world. "Don't you think you might want to get some more feminine dresses? And perhaps we could do something with your hair. . . ." She looked at Liberty with an appraising squint as she launched into another cake.

"No, I don't think so," replied Liberty with a sigh. "Honestly, Millie, he's terribly disagreeable and not in the least interesting, I wouldn't dream of trying to snare him. Don't *you* have any suitors these days?"

"Oh, darling, of course I do," said Millie with a toss of the famous curls. "None who are very suitable. The ones Mummy likes bore me to death, and Daddy disapproves terribly of all the ones I like. Well, except Jack," she said with a mischievous little smile.

"What? And you let me sit here, going on about dull old Ezekiel Malloy? What's the captain up to these days?" urged Liberty. She actually liked hearing Millie's accounts of her young men. Not nearly as simple minded as she sometimes seemed, Millie often parodied her suitors with wicked precision.

"Well," Millie began, "I don't think Jane knows him. He's terribly attractive, of course, Jane. His name is Blodgett, Captain Jack Blodgett. He's very tall, with great broad shoulders and blond hair. His eyes are awfully queer. Yellow and dangerous-looking, like a wolf's."

Liberty, who was quite certain Millie had never seen a wolf, sat back with her cup in her lap, pleased to have successfully changed the subject.

"And he's frightfully funny, and he says all manner of lovely things, but I rather get the impression he's a bit . . . common beneath it all."

"Common? What do you mean?" Jane asked.

Liberty, remembering the captain's overdressed vulgarity, knew very well what Millie meant.

"He quite grasps at things. His eyes were as big as goose eggs when he saw the emerald necklace Daddy bought for me in Paris."

Liberty knew the necklace; she herself had been awestruck by it. She could have lived in a good hotel for the rest of her days on what Uncle Harry must have paid for it.

"And he's impertinent, always wanting kisses and things," Millie continued, fussing prettily with her ruffles.

"Oh, that does sound terrible," Liberty mocked.

Millie giggled. "I think he's perfectly savage, really, beneath it all. It's why I like him so much. I do hope I can keep it from Daddy and Mum."

"He's rich?" asked Liberty, already guessing the answer.

"Terribly. He owns four clippers and simply dozens of riverboats. And mills and things, I think. I don't know, exactly. He's awfully closed-mouthed about it. Anyway, he wears the most smashing clothes. I'm trying to find out more in case I decide to marry him."

"Has he asked you?" Liberty asked, a bit shocked. Captain Blodgett had not exactly behaved like a betrothed man when she'd run into him in the city.

"Of course he has! Practically the first time he met me," Millie said, smiling like a plump, smug cat.

"Really, Millicent," Jane reproved. "You must let your parents guide your judgment on this gentleman. A riverboat captain . . . Well, seagoing men sometimes have certain . . . peculiarities. I know your father is very concerned that you marry a decent, respectable gentleman."

"Perhaps Jane shall meet him sometime," Liberty said.

"Oh, I am so very glad you mention that," said Millie with a gleam in her eye.

Liberty's heart sank. Millie's gleams nearly always meant trouble. "Why is that, cousin?" she asked with growing dread.

"Well, we must all get better acquainted, of course. There just happens to be a bit of a soirée here for the Fourth of July, and I thought it'd be awfully fun if you came."

Expensive, fashionable clothes. Endless rounds of shallow chitchat. Worst of all, there might be waltzing. "I don't know, Millie," Liberty said cautiously. "That really doesn't sound like—"

"Oh, I do hope you'll come," Jane said quickly. She leaned forward with one gloved hand on Liberty's sleeve to press the point.

"Yes, you must." Millie pouted attractively. "We've given a dozen parties since you came to Boston, and you've never so much as dropped in to say hello."

"I've so much to do," Liberty said. "And it isn't really my cup of tea, now, is it? What on earth would I find to talk about with all those people?"

"You could talk about your causes. Jane here is frightfully antislavery, and we've invited some of those people around."

Liberty raised her eyebrows in surprise.

"The more dignified ones, of course," Millie rushed to explain. "None of the fanatics. There are some deliciously exclusive sewing circles on the Hill these days."

Liberty tried to envision discussing abolition with jewel-encrusted society matrons. "I don't think—"

"Oh, but, darling, it'll be terribly serious—you'll enjoy it. Even your Mr. Malloy is coming, I believe."

"Mr. Malloy will be there?"

"Yes, Daddy says Malloy's getting awfully big in Boston, and one simply has to invite him. But you needn't worry about it—there will be so many lovely people there, you wouldn't have to speak to him at all, I'm sure."

"Well, I suppose I might be able to do some good . . . for the cause," Liberty said. Her heart fell. "Oh, but I don't have one single thing to wear that would fit in with a crowd like that."

"I had an idea you might say that," Millie purred.

Liberty eyed her cousin warily. "What have you got up your sleeve, Millie?"

"Daddy bought me a marvelous dress when he was in New York last month, but it's not really my color. A touch too cool, or too warm, or too . . .

something. On the other hand, it would be *sublime* on you."

"It's set, then," Jane said, leaning back.

Liberty sighed. "Don't be ridiculous, Millie, how would I ever fit into a dress of yours? It would hang across my bosom like a potato sack, and my legs would poke out the bottom by at least a foot."

"My dressmaker's a veritable miracle worker," Millie said airily. "And it has a lovely swooshy flounce simply perfect for taking down."

"Oh, I don't know at all. I really don't think—" Liberty stammered.

"Well, I've already taken it to Madame Cécie for the alterations. She took measurements from that dark thing you left here last winter, so the least you could do is try it on."

Liberty winced. The "dark thing" she had stored at Millie's was her best winter challis, and she hoped the dressmaker would return it in one piece. "You really are impossible, do you know that?"

Millie nodded happily, eyes shining.

"This does not mean I'm agreeing to go to your party—I'm just trying the dress on. To satisfy your relentless curiosity, you little cat."

"Of course, darling. Just to please me." Millie was fairly licking her paws over her success.

At long last, the afternoon was over, and Liberty gathered her shawl and reticule. The beads were worn off at the bottom, but she thought the little handbag had a certain gentility. She had missed the last stagecoach, but the walk would take only a little over an hour.

"My dear, shall I give you a lift?" Jane asked, touching Liberty's elbow lightly.

"Oh, no, it's not the least on your way," Liberty said.

"Nonsense. I'm more than happy to take you," Jane insisted, pressing Liberty's elbow more intently. "I have some matters I should like to discuss with you. About antislavery," she said in a lower voice.

Liberty was a bit startled. "Why, in that case, of course. That would be very convenient."

Jane's coach was finished in a smooth plum broadcloth trimmed with smart black tassels. The coachman wore a black uniform with a silk hat. Liberty tried to picture Jim in a silk hat, and found she could not imagine such a thing.

"I was very surprised to see that Millicent had such a sensible cousin," Jane said once the carriage door was safely closed.

"I suppose she might seem a trifle high-spirited, but—" Liberty began, rising to Millie's defense.

"Quite," said Jane dryly. Her pursed lips left little doubt about what she thought of Millicent Goodall. "However, that is her parents' concern, not mine. I gather you value the antislavery cause."

"My father raised me to see slavery as debauchery and vice. I think it's why he named me as he did," Liberty said. As a child, she had privately longed to be a Maria or a Susan, something ordinary.

"It was fated, then," Jane said with delight. "My dear, I am a most vehement supporter of the cause, although my husband thinks it grievous foolishness. I may embroider antislavery designs on quilts and handkerchiefs if I like, but he denies me anything resembling real action."

Liberty clucked her tongue. Someone as elegant and well-bred as Jane Redburne could surely be of great help to the movement. "How frustrating for you," she said sympathetically.

"It's maddening to be required to choose between moral rectitude and my marriage," she said. "But I do what I can, including inspiring others to take action where I cannot."

"Do you mean Millie?" Liberty asked. "You can try if you like, but I don't really think she's fertile ground for moral reform. She's a bit too—"

"No, no, my dear, not Millicent. *You*." Jane's voice vibrated with the thrill of conspiracy.

Liberty's eyes widened. "But I'm already working for the cause. I help Mr. Malloy prepare his lectures and tracts."

"What use are talks and pamphlets if no one will act?" Jane asked. "I'm talking about getting to the heart of the matter—helping the fugitive slaves themselves."

Liberty was quiet for a moment. Sheltering runaways was among the boldest ways to strike out against slavery, but it was difficult and dangerous. The Fugitive Slave Law mandated sharp penalties. And after last night's outburst, her employer's views on the subject were perfectly clear. Mr. Malloy would never sanction such emotional, foolhardy measures. Liberty felt a chill along the back of her neck as she thought of the broken glass littering the hearth in the parlor.

"I don't see how I can help you," she said sadly.

"But you can, Liberty. You're still unmarried. You can act as a free woman. And I'm given to understand that Haven House has a surfeit of space. Surely you could find a place in the barn or the stable for a young man in danger."

Liberty felt the chill again. "Mr. Malloy is violently opposed to sheltering runaways. It would ruin him and make his work impossible. He's trying to get the Fugitive Slave Law repealed, as we all are, but he won't go against the law. He's quite set on the matter. Please trust me, Jane, he won't budge on this."

"Then you can keep it a secret from him. I've seen it before—it can be done. You must help this poor young fugitive. The family he's with will need to move him soon, to keep him from being discovered. If he's caught and returned to the South, he'll die. Can you let that happen?"

Liberty wrung her hands. "Please, Jane, don't ask me to do this."

"It will be much easier to keep a secret from your employer than it would be for a married woman to keep the secret from her husband."

"You don't know Mr. Malloy. He'd see it in my face in an instant. I don't think I can manage it."

"You can. To save the life of this young man, you will find the strength. You're a sensible young woman. And you will do this." Jane's voice was urgent, commanding.

To save a life. The notion struck Liberty at the heart.

"For a few nights, perhaps. *If* you absolutely cannot find another place," she said, trying to ignore the sinking feeling in her chest.

Jane sat back in the seat, clearly pleased. "Of course. Only for a very short while. And perhaps I will find another place for him. It will all work out perfectly well, you'll see."

But as the carriage pulled up the long drive to Haven House, Liberty feared it would not work out perfectly at all.

Chapter 6

It was only three in the afternoon when Liberty arrived, and she was pleased to have a few hours before dinner to work on the shawl she was knitting. She had left her wool in the parlor, and when she went in to fetch it, Mr. Malloy stood by the fire with a brandy in his hand, his shoulders tensed as if poised for action.

She hoped he wasn't still angry about last night. The thought made Liberty's heart race disconcertingly. How on earth would she ever manage to hide a fugitive in this man's house? She'd be lucky if losing her job was the worst that happened.

She collected her knitting gingerly and hoped to slip out of the room without incident.

"Don't you own anything that isn't gray?" Malloy asked abruptly.

"Of course I do, Mr. Malloy," she replied, stung. "I wore my black bombazine only yesterday."

"Of course," he said wryly. "How stupid of me. Look here, I need to speak with you."

"Yes?" she said, trying to control the mixture of hurt and anger she felt. How dare he be so uncivil about her appearance? She rejected all the ribbons and flounces such a man would be likely to detest. In fact, she could see little difference between the way she dressed and the way he did.

His face took on a forcedly pleasant expression. "I have some . . . ideas for my next lecture that I'd like to go over with you. Would you be willing to discuss them with me over dinner this evening?"

She frowned. "I thought you didn't like to discuss politics outside working hours." *Or with women*, she thought.

His eyes chilled to green ice. "I should have thought you would welcome an opportunity to work on a more complex project, Miss Brooks. Perhaps you would prefer to review the details of a new filing system, instead."

Liberty bit her lip in confusion. Normally she ate with Mrs. Biggins or by herself in her room.

"Of course, Mr. Malloy. If you require my presence at dinner, that is your privilege," she said coolly, despite her nerves. "You dine at eight, I believe?"

Zeke did not fail to note the flicker of distaste that crossed her face. Damn the baggage! Was his company so abhorrent?

He composed himself and bade her a pleasant good-afternoon. *Honey*, he reminded himself, *not vinegar*. He'd have to control his annoyance at her correct little pose if he was ever going to find out what she was hiding behind that wall of steel.

They met stiffly at dinner, the length of polished table putting a good eight feet between them. Sculpted points of lead crystal in the chandelier caught the glow of the candles and scattered warm shards of rainbow across the table. The linens were pure, glowing white, stiffly starched and pressed. The silver was heavy and old, the wineglasses voluptuous crystal globes.

"You've had an enjoyable day, I trust, Mr. Malloy?" Liberty asked, her voice carefully neutral.

"No, Miss Brooks, I have not. I have had an unutterably wretched day," he replied, instantly quelling any attempt at pleasantness.

Liberty sighed inwardly and resigned herself to a long, awkward meal. Mrs. Biggins and Daisy, the cook's helper, wordlessly brought in dish after dish: roast loin of pork with wild mushrooms; slender, bright green spears of asparagus bathed in pale yellow hollandaise; tiny red potatoes with butter and herbs; tender rounds of baby carrots sautéed in butter with a thin drizzle of maple; hot soft rolls begging to be split and spread with butter.

The smell of those rolls baking had been torturing Liberty for the last half hour. She hadn't had a bite since the cakes at Millie's, and she was famished. Before she could launch into the feast, Mr. Malloy pulled himself erect in his chair with an ominous expression.

"I will say grace," he intoned. He went on for what seemed like hours. She bent her head over her plate and struggled to keep her mind on his carefully chosen words, but the aromas kept teasing her attention away. It was almost as if he were intentionally tormenting her. His voice rang on and on in rich, measured tones, and she could nearly taste the tender white flesh of the pork loin, the tangy creaminess of the hollandaise. Zeke's mouth twitched upward suspiciously when, to her horror, her stomach let out a loud, angry growl.

Finally he was finished, and she fell to her meal like a starved woman. She heaped everything on her plate in a jumble, her carrots sliding dangerously close to the hollandaise. Eagerly she took bite after bite, her eyes half-shut with rapture, not looking up until Zeke's resonant voice interrupted the exquisite fulfillment.

"You are enjoying your meal, my dear?" he asked, his amusement apparent.

Her cheeks flamed. She swallowed hastily and murmured, "Quite."

"But you've left out the most delightful part."

"What?" she asked.

"Why, the wine, of course. Won't you have some?"

"Oh, I never as a rule . . ." She forced herself to put her fork down for a moment, touching her napkin demurely to her lips.

"Come, come, my dear," he said suavely, "eating this meal without wine is positively criminal. Just a drop, to complement the roast."

"Well, I suppose just a drop wouldn't hurt. . . ."

He poured her glass nearly to the top. She watched him carefully as he lifted his own glass, swirled the liquid gently to better release its bouquet, and brought it to his lips. She copied him with studied nonchalance. "Oh, my!" she whispered after with her first mouthful. She took another sip. Somehow she tasted a hundred things in that crystal glass. Chocolate, oranges, Moroccan spice, and Venetian perfume, the smoky tang of incense and the ripe freshness of pears, all wrapped in a sharpness like . . . walnuts? It was unlike anything she had ever tasted.

"Now have a bite of the roast," he coaxed.

"Oh, my," she said again. She took another sip of the wine, shutting her eyes in delight.

Zeke raised a sardonic eyebrow. "Haven't you ever had wine before?"

"No," she confessed. "My parents always drank ale or cider." She neglected to mention her father had also drunk whiskey, telling herself it wasn't really important. "Isn't wine supposed to intoxicate one awfully quickly?" she asked, peering ruefully into the glass.

Zeke laughed indulgently. "Absolutely not. It's simply an accompaniment to food, like a sauce or a seasoning. Why, look, you've finished your glass already. Here, have another," he offered generously. The stream glowed bloodred in the warm light of the candles.

He refilled her glass again and again, switching to

Sauternes when the poached peaches were served, and still later he filled small glasses with sweet, smoky port.

Fighting a losing battle with her mutinous hair, which had been suffering severe constraint for hours longer than usual, Liberty attempted to secure her last valiant hairpins. But she managed only to dislodge them, freeing a tumble of curls. "F'rgive me," she said gravely, "but I do hope I may be informal with you, Mis'r Malloy."

"Of course," he said indulgently. "In point of fact, I wish you would call me Zeke. So much less formal, don't you think?"

"Absolutely. And you must call me Lib'rty. Lib'ry." She giggled. "My, this room is awfully hot," she said tugging at the buttons at the throat of her dress.

Zeke laughed. "Do you think so?"

"Do you know how to dance?" she asked suddenly.

"Dance? Well, yes, I suppose I do."

"The waltz? Have you ever danced the waltz?"

"Yes," he said.

"Is it very wonderful?"

"It's a perfectly charming dance," he replied.

"I've never . . . Would you be willing . . . to teach me?" she asked, looking very young and fragile.

"There's no music," he said, smiling.

"I'll make the music. You just worry about the dancing."

"Very well," he said, genuinely charmed. He was certain he had never heard that twang in her voice before. It seemed to soften her ruthlessly efficient edge. In fact, with her hair down and her dress unbuttoned to expose her throat, she was very different. Neither brusquely correct nor cloyingly coquettish, she was like a meadow rabbit, free and soft and very, very vulnerable. He took her gently in his arms, and she began to hum a pretty Chopin waltz, only slightly off-key.

He was acutely aware of his hand on her small waist. She was having an uncomfortable effect on him, which, thank God, she wasn't aware of. The curls that twisted free of every hairstyle she was able to devise looked exactly right spilled down across her shoulders. Her face was open and happy, and he noticed for the first time the clear golden radiance of her skin. He was surprised to find himself longing to touch that skin, to see if those fresh pink roses in her cheeks could possibly be natural, to feel if her skin was as warm and smooth and soft as it looked.

She chased all thoughts from his mind as she looked up at him from beneath a sweep of dark lashes, half singing the waltz. Her eyes were a smoky blue-green, the color of a restless sea. He pressed her to him, and his hips and legs spoke to her, showing her how to move, where to follow him. He surrounded her, and they whirled like twin stars circling each other as he lost himself in the blue-green mist of her eyes.

Dancing in each other's arms, they were quite alone. Mrs. Biggins had long since gone to bed; Daisy had walked back to her little cottage behind the meadow. Zeke drew Liberty closer and felt a surprising current down the length of his belly as her breasts pressed gently against him. The notes of the waltz died in the air. He stroked her soft curls with one hand, the other still cradling her waist. He was blind to everything except her mouth, tempting him like a moist plum.

As he bent to taste those ripe, moist lips, she grew strangely heavy in his arms. He drew back questioningly, then laughed out loud. Her eyes were shut, and her face was as calm as that of a sleeping child. She began to snore softly.

Well, it was his own blasted fault. He smiled,

picked her up, and, kissing her forehead once, brought her upstairs to bed.

He'd assumed she would wake up again immediately, but she was out for the night. He set her gently on her bed. There. She would sleep now.

He looked with regret at the stiff gown. How women could endure the tortures of the corset, he would never know. She'd wake up as stiff as a pine board if she had to sleep in that contraption. He'd just loosen her stays a bit, so she'd be comfortable in the morning.

He fumbled impatiently with the gown's long row of buttons, trying not to look down at what he was doing. Why the Devil did the baggage need so many buttons? He managed somehow to loosen the long row from neckline to waist.

Now he'd have to touch her. He lifted her to a sitting position, propping her against him. Her hair smelled wonderful, like rainwater. He tried to release her arms from the full sleeves, but they were too tight at the wrist. More buttons. He set her back down against the pillow.

To hell with it. What on earth could he have been thinking? His forehead was damp. Maybe he'd had a little too much of the wine himself. She was spread out motionless on the bed, her dress unbuttoned. My God, it looked for all the world as if he'd tried to molest her, when he was truly just trying to help.

Steady, Malloy. Not like you to let a woman throw you this way. He worked at the buttons of her sleeves, trying to ignore her small, high breasts pushed up by her stays. When he had loosened both sleeves, he propped her up again. The mantle of chestnut hair fell over his shoulder. He reached one arm around her waist to steady her, and she murmured faintly.

Oh, Good God, he thought with panic, don't wake up now. Her eyelids fluttered, and she shifted com-

fortably against him, her arm flopping dangerously
into his lap. She mumbled something incoherent
and sank heavily against his thighs.

He squeezed his eyes shut. How in blazes had
he gotten himself into this mess? He delicately
removed her hand from his trousers, which had
gotten uncomfortably tight. He slipped the gray
wool from her shoulders, keeping her upright with
the gentle pressure of his hand on her waist. Her
face was close to his neck, and he could feel the
soft rhythm of her breathing.

He looked guiltily at the clock on the bedside
table. The group of fugitives hadn't eaten yet.
While he had been trying to undress his beautiful
secretary, four hungry mouths had gone unfed.

He somehow managed to extricate her from the
dress and pulled gently at the gray wool until it
came completely free. He looked blankly at the
treacherous gray mass in his hand and flung it
onto the chair. Now the stays. Then he would get
the hell out of here.

They fastened in front with flat, white laces. Taking a deep gulp of air, he fumbled with the knot,
trying desperately to ignore the delicious distraction of her breasts. The wench had tied them in
a double knot, the way a mother ties a child's
shoestring. He thought for one wild moment that
he'd have to cut the thing in half to loosen it.

Finally he managed the knot and gently pulled
the lacing loose. She breathed a small sigh of relief,
and a bloom of color came to her cheeks. Her breasts
rose and fell with her breathing, their natural silhouette beneath her thin chemise somehow far more
entrancing than the display of cleavage pushed
together by whalebone stays.

Downstairs, he had been ready to kiss her. He
considered it again now. Her mouth was no less
inviting than it had been when she was waltzing
in his arms. Her arms were bare, her skin golden

and warm in her white cotton underthings. He bent over her. One chaste kiss only, and then he would pull the coverlet over her and go.

He paused an inch above her. He could feel her breath on his lips, steady and slow. This was something only a blackguard would do. An unprincipled swine.

The touch of her lips lit him on fire. Oh, Jesus, she was so soft. So beautiful and creamy and soft. He gingerly buried his face in her hair, inhaling the fresh smell.

He stood up suddenly. He was drunk. He had to be. This was obscene. The poor girl, alone in the city without any family to take care of her. He threw the coverlet across her and nearly ran from the room, shutting the door quickly behind him. What kind of amoral monster was he, to do such a thing?

He felt an inexplicable rush of anger, with himself and with the golden fairy child sleeping off her first drunk. She was a distraction, and that made her dangerous. He had too much work to do to spend his evenings chasing a girl who was a heady mix of wilderness and prim civility.

The cold night air had penetrated his coat by the time he had crossed the meadow. The sharpness of the wind felt sobering and real, nearly banishing the comforts he had left in the house behind him. He let himself in the cabin door and down into the underground hall, stopping only to knock briefly on the second hidden door.

"How's Jacob?" he asked Indigo.

"That doc fix him up just fine. That mess he give us to put on Jake's feet stink like an old dog, but he be walkin' around most of the day, just feelin' what it like not to hurt so bad."

"Good," Zeke replied, avoiding her eyes. "Is there anything else you need down here? I brought some of the roast from dinner, and a few vegetables, and a bottle of wine."

He was greeted by a round of jubilant hoots. "A bottle of wine?" said the young boy. "We ain't seen that in a dear long time."

The old man looked put out. "Ain't too Christian to be celebratin' our freedom by drinkin' the Devil's wine. We oughta be prayin' instead of gettin' our fool selves drunk."

Zeke felt abashed, but Indigo answered, "Jake, there don't be no harm in a nice sip of somethin'. The Lord drunk wine, it say so in the Bible. And if it be good enough for the Lord Jesus, I guess it be good enough for us. The gentleman be doin' us a kindness, and now you done made him feel bad."

Zeke shook his head. "No, no, if you don't want it, I'd be happy to bring something else. I'm sorry, I wasn't thinking—"

The woman took the bottle gently from his hand. "We be thankful for your hospitality," she said politely. "Thank you." She gave him a warm smile, the small gap between her front teeth making her seem very young, despite the baby balanced on one hip. "And we be mighty proud if you'd joins our party."

He smiled back at her. "No, I don't think I'd better. I have to confess that I've had more of a party than I can handle back in the house."

The group hooted anew, this time heartily joined by Jacob. "You and your missus having a celebration tonight?" the old man asked jovially.

"In a matter of speaking," Zeke said, smiling. "I mean, she's not my . . . That is to say . . . there isn't any *Mrs*. She's . . . an employee." He was thinking of Liberty dancing in his arms, her fragrant curls spilling across his chest, her languid, sea-colored eyes turned toward him. And thinking of her was making him stupid.

Indigo smiled and gave his shoulder a sisterly

pat. "There don't be nothin' so fine as courtin'. You takes my advice and you marrys that gal. It be a shame, a handsome man like you all alone. Anybody could see you's crazy about her."

"Oh," Zeke said, embarrassed, "we're not . . . It hasn't really . . . progressed to that point."

"He means he ain't kissed her yet," the boy burst out. The group laughed uproariously.

"No," Zeke said, joining the laughter. "Well, yes, technically. I mean, not exactly."

"You'll takes good care of that gal," Indigo said, her eyes sparkling. "You a good man, even if you don't knows it."

"I'll leave you in peace," Zeke said abruptly, collecting himself and making for the door. Really, how could he talk such nonsense to these people? He never would have told such stories to anyone in town, anyone he might see again. Strange that the only people he could trust with such pleasantries were the fugitives who passed through his life, keeping his secrets, not knowing even his name. With them he could be a man like any other. Even a man with a soft spot in his heart for a pretty girl.

As he walked back across the meadow to the house, feeling the grass wet the cuffs of his trousers, he reminded himself that he could not afford to give in to distractions. Other men might indulge themselves in wine and laughter and the smile of a beautiful girl. Other men had the luxury of giving in to tender feelings. But Zeke Malloy was not other men, and he was already embroiled in far too dangerous a game.

Chapter 7

"Distracted? That's the third time you've tried to read that article." Zeke's eyes glittered like the Devil's diamonds, cold and brilliant. He folded his arms smugly across his waistcoat.

Liberty's stomach knotted. She'd woken up feeling as if wild beasts had made their den in her head. And she had been *undressed*. Struggling to remember what exactly had taken place the night before—and considering all of the more obvious explanations—had greatly disturbed her. It had been some time before she could work up the courage to go down to breakfast.

Zeke had been insufferably smug all day, and there was no sign of his letting up. There was something in his eyes, something she did not understand. It was all so murky. Some time after the Sauternes, she had lost track of the evening, and she had yet to regain it.

"Distracted?" she said, trying for a crisp tone as she set the article aside and stood to collect a thick stack of papers from her small desk. "Distraction is another word for laziness, and I give it no quarter, I assure you, sir. If you've a moment, I have the letters you asked for this morning." She handed him the stack of correspondence and sorted through the remainder of the pile. "And here are the article summaries, and here is the list of speaking engage-

ments for the month. I should have a fresh copy of
that new lecture for you by this afternoon." She
bent her head over the papers, refusing to meet
his gaze.

What if he wanted to dismiss her? Oh, blast him
anyway for having poured all that wine down her
throat! Now he thought she was a drunkard, and
probably a slattern, too. This morning she'd found
her hairpins scattered beneath the dining room
table. A sudden, painful image of her father flashed
before her. John Brooks used to call her his "little
accomplice"; as a small child, she'd been as much
his friend as his daughter. But as much as she loved
her father, she had not followed him in this. Not
until now.

Alcohol doubtless affected Liberty more strongly
than it did other people, she thought with fierce
shame, mortified to have shown herself such a
weakling. All she could do now was to face the
consequences of her misstep—and vow she would
never be so careless again.

Zeke glanced over the stack carelessly. "You've
misspelled *Brownleigh* on this one. And this is the
wrong address for the Haverfords—they haven't
lived on Chestnut Street for over a year." He handed
her the pages with a smirk.

Liberty took back the offending letters. "I'm quite
sure I wrote them as they appeared in your book,
sir," she said quietly. "If the information there is
incorrect, I'll remedy it."

"The book is in order, my dear. You simply copied
it incorrectly."

She gritted her teeth. "Perhaps you're right, sir.
I'll try to be more careful in the future."

"What a little paragon of virtue you are," he said.
"Industrious, serious, and perfectly *correct*."

"Thank you, sir," she whispered, furious. The
praise sounded like insults in his mouth. But
she couldn't lose her temper, not now. After her
indiscretion—whatever it might have been—she

couldn't afford to let him think she was anything less than sternly professional. "Is there something else you wish of me?" She had to get away from him or she would certainly lose control and thump him square in the midriff.

"What an intriguing question," he said with a strange smile. "Oh, yes, I know. You can refile my articles alphabetically by author."

"But you just had them refiled by date last week," she protested. She had spent three long days crouched on the floor, sorting papers and going out of her mind with boredom.

"Yes, but I think I preferred the old system. See if you can have it finished by the start of the week, will you?" His eyes flashed, daring her to protest his capriciousness.

"I'm sure I can, sir," she answered. Her nails dug painful crescents into her palm.

"Very good," he answered. "Very good indeed."

The days crawled miserably until her next Thursday off. Millie had sent her a note that the dressmaker had nearly finished the alterations, and apparently one's actual presence was required to finish the job. So now Liberty had to go all the way to town to visit the Southacks Court shop and let some tyrannical seamstress pinch and pluck at her.

At least she'd be out from under Mr. Malloy's peculiarly penetrating gaze, she decided ruefully. He had not been ill tempered, but this new, confusing "friendliness" was almost harder to take.

And now that she thought of it, there were one or two pleasant errands she could run while she was in town. One consolation to this nerve-wracking job was that she was making more money than she ever had before, and her room and board were free. There was that little book of poems in Ticknor's that she could finally afford, with money left over for two pairs of good stockings. She might even try something besides black. She lay still for a moment in her narrow bed, letting the pink morning light fall across her face, thinking of bright chartreuse stockings.

After two warm scones with gooseberry jam and a large mug of Mrs. Biggins's strong coffee, Liberty set off with freshly polished boots and a full reticule. Zeke had taken the brougham, and Jim had the smaller cart, so Liberty took the crowded public coach into the city. After a ride that threatened to shake every tooth out of her head, she walked the last quarter mile to the shop, relishing the chance to stretch her legs.

The shop was elegantly decorated in white and gold, with MADAME CÉCIE'S painted on the window in gold letters. A very thin, very blond young woman stood behind a case of ribbons and silk roses, her fair hair pulled into a complicated structure of plaits and ringlets. She wore a slim, elegant dress of butter-colored taffeta trimmed with pale green braid. A chic cap perched on the blond curls.

"Can I help you, dear?" she asked with the merest note of derision at the sight of Liberty's unfashionable green bonnet and faintly shabby dress. "I'm not at all sure our merchandise is what you're looking for." She pursed her cupid's-bow mouth as if she had tasted something tart.

Liberty squared her shoulders and lifted her chin a fraction of an inch. "My name is Liberty Brooks," she said, her voice cool. "I'm here for a fitting."

"Oh!" the woman cried, embarrassed, as her disdain gave way to dismay. "But of course, you're Miss Goodall's cousin. I am sorry . . . I thought . . . Anyway, you're a little early," she stammered.

"Early?" Liberty asked, disheartened. She recoiled at the thought of sitting here for any length of time while this impossibly tiny, fashionable person fussed at her.

"It's only that Madame doesn't usually get here before nine," the woman apologized. "May I offer you a cup of tea while you wait? We have some lovely oolong." Her voice had taken on an almost unctuous quality, and Liberty mused that Millie must spend a fortune in here.

"I suppose I'll take a cup of tea," Liberty said in as grand a tone as she could muster. Since she was coasting on Cousin Millie's extravagant spending habits, she might as well enjoy it. Not that it brought her much pleasure to see this brittle shopgirl stumble over herself in an attempt to cover her earlier gaffe. The salesgirl was still entirely too dainty, too fashionable, and too blond. Next to her, Liberty felt ten feet tall and as untamed as Tecumseh.

As Liberty sipped her tea and tried not to fidget, a woman dressed in deep garnet breezed into the shop, her arms stuffed with taffeta, silks, and brocades. Impossibly, she was even tinier and more chic than the shopgirl, but she had coal-black hair and features too sharp to be pretty. She let loose a stream of French at the girl, and Liberty guessed that this was Madame Cécie.

Madame's French was too fast for Liberty, but the shopgirl's wasn't, and Liberty nearly choked, looking out the window to hide her laughter. The girl had confessed her mistake, and Madame Cécie was showering her with a torrent of abuse.

Abruptly Madame turned to Liberty and said, "*Ma chère*, I hope I have not kept you waiting too long. The girl, she is impossibly *stupide*. I hope you will forgive."

Liberty smiled. She liked this woman better already. As elegant and imperious as she was, she gave the impression of being a real person and not a china doll.

"Not at all, madame," she said.

"But your *cousine*—she has not told me the truth

about you, mademoiselle," Madame Cécie mused as she peered at Liberty. "*Oui*, you are too tall to be of the fashion, but it is the right way to be tall— like the statue. And the color of the skin—it is very good. Like summertime, eh? Or like the pears of Provence, gold and rose. It will be very pretty with this dress. Yes, I like very much."

Liberty was mortified at the unaccustomed praise. "Thank you," she said softly, wishing the floor would open up and swallow her.

"It is not the compliment—it is the truth," Madame Cécie said tartly. "I pay the compliment to the paying customer. You, mademoiselle, you are the model only, yes? I do not flatter the *mannequins*."

Liberty grinned. "I hope you won't be so frank about my flaws," she said.

"I will be ruthless, *chèrie*," the woman said with a sly smile. "It is good for the soul of the beautiful woman to hear that she is not perfect."

"I have no illusions on that score," Liberty said.

"Ah, she is a modest girl—very charming. *Bien*, we must begin. *Viens ici*, mademoiselle. Come with me to the fitting room."

The fitting was interminable. The gown was achingly soft, in a rose batiste so pale as to be nearly white. Liberty loved the way it felt against her skin, but the pins pricked at her mercilessly. True to her word, Madame Cécie kept up a ceaseless stream of comments, both flattering and unflattering. The fitting room had no mirror, so Liberty had no idea how the gown fit, or how the color looked against her skin. Her initial nervousness gave way to boredom as she made movements of a fraction of an inch, tolerated Madame's proddings, and sucked in her breath when she was told to.

"And what will mademoiselle be wearing underneath?"

Liberty was embarrassed. "These, I suppose," she said, gesturing to her sensible cotton underwear.

Madame Cécie was appalled. "This gown is not the straw bonnet for the cart horse," she said imperiously. "It is for the charming young lady, and it must be worn with the elegant underthings."

"But I haven't got—" Liberty began.

"The *cousine* will pay for the little extras, mademoiselle. *Eh bien*, we must have the very fine cambric chemisette and drawers, and the new stays, and some stockings."

Liberty's eyes gleamed. "Stockings?"

"*Mais oui, ma chère*. You must wear the stockings, eh? I will not have my gown worn over those atrocities you are wearing now. *Alors*, Suzanne!" she called to the shopgirl. "Bring me some stockings for mademoiselle."

The blonde brought several pairs of filmy lisle stockings in an array of colors.

Madame held the stockings against the dress with a practiced eye. "The rose—they are too light. The gray? *Non, c'est impossible*. Black? *Non*." She rifled through the sheer stockings. "*Ah, oui*—the teal. They are perfect. Eh, Suzanne?" She held up a pair of deep blue-green stockings, beautifully clocked.

Liberty reached out and felt the lisle. It was gloriously smooth, sheer, and soft. "They're lovely."

"Shall I make up some combs in teal and rose?" the shopgirl asked.

"*Non*," Madame said crisply. "A net of gold, and a hairpiece of roses. For mademoiselle, too much ribbons—it is not good. This dress, it is all innocence, very pure, very fresh. We must have baby roses, precisely the color of the dress. Not too dark, you understand?"

"Yes, madame," the girl murmured as she swept out of the room.

"That girl, she is grossly *stupide*, completely without refinement," Madame said. "And to finish, we have the gloves, the shoes, *et voilà*, mademoiselle is the most charming young lady in Boston," Madame pronounced with satisfaction. "The jewels, you will borrow them from *la cousine*, yes? Pearls would be best."

"Oh, yes, I suppose," Liberty said, wondering if Millie had really known what she was getting into. If it always took this much work to prepare for a party, Liberty could understand why Millie claimed she never had the time to read books or practice the piano.

After a seemingly endless morning, Madame Cécie finally released Liberty. The day had warmed, and the streets bustled with life. There was plenty of time to get to Ticknor's. Maybe she could even get a new bonnet—one of the new, smaller ones in blond straw, trimmed with a smart black ribbon. She had seen a very pretty one in the marketplace she had discovered. It would take no more than twenty minutes to walk there.

She quickened her step, smiling at the warmth of the sun on her face. Today might not be a perfect waste, after all.

Lost in thought as she walked, Liberty nearly collided with a broad, imposing figure in a sky blue frock coat.

"Why, Captain Blodgett, how delightful to see you again," she said graciously, masking her discomfort.

"Miss Brooks, it is a great pleasure," Blodgett said smoothly, his eyes gleaming as he took her hand to kiss.

"Isn't it odd that we keep running across one another this way? Do you know, I've quite forgotten exactly what it is that brings you to this part of town so often," Liberty said.

He blinked. "Exports, mostly," he replied, seeming faintly uneasy. "I have business on the docks, and there are plenty of men here to ... work in that business. Miss Brooks, I must say that I'm very pleased to have found you today. May I show you to my office? We can have a cup of tea there and discuss something that has been weighing heavily on my mind." His voice was urgent, and he took her elbow and began to walk before she had agreed to his invitation.

She felt a strange uneasiness, which she struggled to dismiss. Blodgett was, after all, practically engaged to Millie. And he seemed a perfectly respectable gentleman. Still, she felt a flicker of panic as she said, "Why, certainly, Captain, although my visit really must be brief."

His office was above the street and, although in a run-down building, was comfortable and well appointed. The furnishings were a bit ornate for Liberty's taste; his desk was intricately carved mahogany, the wallpaper a Byzantine green floral. But everything was of excellent quality, and she was certain the intricately carved sword on the wall behind the desk was some priceless treasure from the ancient Orient.

"Have you found employment, then?" he asked, his back to her as he started a kettle.

"Yes, thank you, I have. I'm working for Ezekiel Malloy."

The teakettle clattered onto the stove. "Malloy, eh? . . . Think I know him," he said nonchalantly into the stovepipe. "Hell of a fellow. Goddamned addlebrained fanatic, if I remember correctly." As he spoke, he stroked the lapels of his embroidered mauve satin waistcoat nervously, his big hands glittering with heavy rings.

"He's a . . . unique individual," she said, trying for tact. Zeke Malloy annoyed her no end, but for some reason she disliked hearing Blodgett speak ill of him. She was trying to determine how she could gently end her visit and be off when Blodgett suddenly whirled and dropped to his knees at her feet.

"Oh, Liberty, Liberty!" he cried, clutching her ankles, his face pressed against the newly shined leather of her boots.

"Really, Captain Blodgett, whatever can be agitating you so?" she said, mortified, trying discreetly to pull her ankles away from him. What on earth could have gotten into the man?

His voice was muffled as he said to the boots, "I haven't slept in days, eaten in a week! I can hardly think or even breathe. My limbs tremble, and my whole being aches terribly."

"My goodness, that certainly does sound disagreeable," Liberty said, pulling her legs free with a swift jerk, her usual sympathy deserting her completely. "You must by all means seek out a good physician. I *am* sorry, but I really must be going." She stood and made for the door.

"No, no, it's not a physical ailment that tortures me," he cried, impassioned, "but a wound to the heart. Cupid, alas, hath drawn his wicked bow, and I am struck! Struck!" He raised his face to her, and her heart fell to see a wide streak of boot polish on his cheek. She hated to see him make an idiot of himself.

"Please, Captain," she pleaded, "I really must insist you stop this at once." Listening to his problems with her impudent cousin was the last thing Liberty wanted to do. She felt sorry for the brute, of course—Millie could be as capriciously cruel as a cat with a bird—but there were limits to what comforts Liberty could respectably provide. If he hadn't been crouched there so miserably on the floor, she would have left immediately, but it seemed somehow too callous. And that streak of polish made him look like one of the ruffian children who lived in the alleys.

"But it is you, Liberty, you I desire!"

"Me?" she squeaked. How had she managed to get herself into this mess? "Now, Captain Blodgett, we both know that can't be true. You're nearly engaged to Millicent. She speaks terribly highly of you."

There, she thought. Now this insane man will get off the floor, and I'll be able to leave.

Blodgett cursed inwardly. "Ah, poor Millicent," he said, pulling himself to his knees, shaking his head sadly. "I was fond of her, it's true, but since I set eyes on you, she's ceased to exist for me."

"You want to throw Millie over for me?" she asked skeptically. "I'm sorry to say this, Captain Blodgett, but that seems rather unlikely."

"Oh, my dearest love, my life," Blodgett protested, struggling to his feet, "Millicent is but a flighty girl. You are a beautiful woman. She has no drama, no finesse."

"She's blond, adorable, and has a father who's richer than Midas," Liberty said matter-of-factly.

"Fishwife! She's a common fishwife compared to you! Whereas you, O mistress of my soul, you have the grace and pride of Diana," he gushed, clutching her hand to kiss.

"And you are to be my Actaeon?" she muttered, yanking her hand away and trying to keep her voice light. "Shall I have your own hounds tear you to pieces for your impertinence?" Honestly, she thought, what would it take to get this poor fool to stop this nonsense?

"Alas, you are cruel, blessed lady, to mock your poor slave so."

"I believe in the emancipation of slaves, Captain Blodgett," she said, more irritably than she had intended. He inevitably made her rather rude. She noticed that he was sweating heavily, making rivulets through the streak of polish.

"Liberty, beauteous, gentle Liberty," he cried, throwing himself at her feet again, this time clasping her knees. "Will you marry me?"

His embrace made her start suddenly and upset

his balance, toppling him backward onto the floor.

"I am so sorry, Captain," she stammered. This farce had gone much, much too far. "I'm afraid that . . . that your question requires a great deal of thought. I really must beg leave of your company now." She eyed the door, escape uppermost in her mind.

"My answer! What is to be my answer?" he bleated pitifully.

"I . . . I will give it to you in a few days," she replied, forcing an unfelt calm, unable to bring herself to look at him. "You certainly cannot expect me to make such a decision without time to think. Good day, sir." She turned briskly and crossed the room in a few steps, too shocked to regret leaving him in such a ridiculous position.

She had barely closed the door and run down the stairs when she was overcome by an almost hysterical desire to laugh out loud. She, married to Jack Blodgett! It was really too much. She had never heard such hogwash in all her life. If he hadn't been so pathetic, sprawled out on the floor that way, she would certainly have declined him then and there. Poor, silly man.

Blodgett pulled himself to his feet and lit a cigar. Well, that wasn't going to work. From the look on her face, she obviously didn't have much interest in getting married to a wealthy trader.

What the Devil was wrong with her, anyway? He stroked his cravat and puffed at the cigar. He was rich, good-looking, and charming as hell. Unnatural bitch.

She worked for Malloy. Was something going on between the two of them? Malloy was a cold fish, not a charmer like Jack, but women were odd when it came to these things. And she had that funny little catch in her voice when she said his name. Like some of her starch might have wilted a little.

He scowled in distaste. Maybe so. He could check it out the next time he saw Malloy. Which was due to be tonight, at sundown.

He frowned and took another puff of the cigar. Goddamned bitch had made him hard, even with her prissy ways. He absently unbuttoned himself and began to stroke his member, sinking back in his chair and closing his eyes.

He held her hands behind her back, and he was going to plow into her from behind. She was screaming. She was naked. No, she had her dress hiked up, and it was torn. No, she was naked, in shackles. He was moving closer to her, and she was screaming. He had a whip, and he was bringing it down on her back again and again. Screaming, screaming. He watched the black braid bite into her soft flesh, watched the blood well up like round red pearls, running down her back in rivulets, the braid cutting deeper and deeper.

Yesssssss. That did it. He threw his head back. She was a seductive little bitch, he'd give her that. He wiped himself clean with a handkerchief, buttoned himself, and took another puff of his cigar.

Time to get ready to meet Malloy.

Chapter 8

❧

Liberty walked toward home, feeling as if something had an iron grip on her chest, squeezing the breath from her lungs. She had been careful to avoid mentioning her lack of transport to Captain Blodgett, afraid he would insist on driving her. There was no question of waiting in the city for the coach; she would not risk running into him again.

The afternoon was clear and mild, and the meadows on either side of the road exploded with the brilliant green of new life. Stalks of wild tansy grew at the side of the road, the yellow buttons nodding cheerily beneath regal feathers of Queen Anne's lace.

Once she had overcome her original revulsion, she found herself turning Blodgett's offer over in her mind. For all her distaste, she could not deny that the attentions of such a successful man were flattering. He had asked her to marry him. She had not really thought anyone would. Her severity and unconventional notions had driven away most potential suitors.

She tried to think of Blodgett objectively. He was wealthy, handsome, and, aside from today, tolerably well mannered. She reasoned that he must be industrious and of good character to be so financially successful. He might not be overly bright, but perhaps that was not a terrible handicap.

What good, after all, was an intelligent husband?

One look at Zeke Malloy, brilliant and utterly insufferable, answered that question.

Just what did Blodgett do to make all his money, anyway? She knew he owned a number of ships, that he was an active trader, and that he did almost all his business with the South. Natural enough, she supposed, for a southerner by birth. Millie had mentioned to Liberty that Blodgett's family had never owned slaves, and that that had been a great hardship for them. How noble, Liberty thought, to endure privation rather than participate in an immoral institution. Surely that was a sign of good family character.

Still, he *was* a southerner. He spoke of states' rights and the protection of property, by which he meant Negroes. He spoke with pride of the slaveholding Founding Fathers. He used the word *nigger* as a matter of course. But in these he was not so different from many northerners she knew. To her chagrin, she realized even Uncle Harry had done all of these things at one time or another.

Her boots pinched her toes slightly, and she sighed. It seemed her feet had ached without cease since she'd come to Boston. What might it be like to have her own carriage and horses? To be mistress of a grand place like Haven House? To wear lovely things and eat marvelous food every day? She thought with a pang of those achingly soft lisle stockings.

If Blodgett was a little rough around the edges, was that so terribly important? An upright, moral woman could do wonders to civilize even an uncouth brute. Marrying Jack Blodgett would probably be the most sensible thing she could do. She allowed herself to picture, just for a moment, a life free of uncertainty, with time and money enough to truly make a difference to the abolitionist cause. And she could teach her passion for freedom and justice to her children.

A breeze came up across the meadow, making her shiver a little. *Children*. They did not, after all, materialize from thin air. The thought sent a shudder down her spine. Despite his dandified ways, Jack Blodgett reminded her of the dangerous, brawny bulls back home. His hands were weighed down with heavy rings, his fingers coarse and callused. Could she tolerate his touch? Both times she had seen him, his breath had smelled of stale rum and cigars. Could she bear his kiss? Were women even meant to enjoy such things?

He was gentleman enough, probably, to do his marital duty without unduly harassing her. In time, she might even come to feel some small pleasure. Was that truly the best she could hope for? Some small corner of her heart longed for more—precisely what, she wasn't sure. But she knew she could evince no real feeling for the man, apart from pity and faint dislike. She did not love him; she knew she never could. She was not even sure she could like him very much.

As she began to consider the matter more realistically, she realized that any plan to civilize the man was sheer fantasy. He clearly did not want an honorable crusader for a wife; he wanted a tractable, docile female. Even the headstrong Millie would make Blodgett a better bride than Liberty would. How could Liberty permit her work to be restricted to quilting a few coverlets for an Antislavery Society sale?

She could not marry, Liberty knew with renewed certainty; she could not marry anyone. She was cursed with a defect in feminine character; she was constitutionally incapable of bending her will to another person's. This stubbornness was unnatural in a woman, maybe, but she possessed it and would never overcome it. Better to continue the way she lived, fulfilling herself through her work. As for luxuries, they themselves would become a prison if she were not allowed to think and speak and act as a free woman, bound only by her own code of honor.

It was for his sake as well, she told herself, although the feeling of relief was overwhelming. She could not saddle any man with such a willful and unnatural wife. The late spring air filled her suddenly with a rushing joy as she felt her legs stretch with her fast stride. She was free, and her freedom beat in her breast like a bird, its wings strong and fierce. Her bonnet hung down her back. She laughed out loud and reached up to loosen the pins from her hair, letting it spill onto her shoulders. The warm afternoon breeze, ripe with the scent of pollen and grass and small wildflowers, tossed her hair around her face in chestnut waves.

She rounded the last curve and crossed the bridge to the back door of Haven House. The air in the gorge was cool and sweet, and frogs peeped happily in the stream below. She slipped into the house, shutting the door quietly and humming softly to herself, before nearly colliding with Zeke, who stood scowling in the doorway between the kitchen and the main hallway.

"You're late," he snapped. "Last week you were back a good two hours earlier than this."

Damn the wench, what in God's name could she have been doing all this time? He noted with disquiet the unruly mane of curls spilling down around her shoulders, and the deep pink flush in her cheeks.

"I walked home from town," protested Liberty. "Both the carriages were being used, and the coach runs so infrequently. I did mention my trip to town this morning," she said, flustered.

She was faintly annoyed that he had deflated her mood, but she was far more disturbed by her own behavior. How could she have permitted herself to return to Haven House in such a state? She lifted a nervous hand to her hair. Goodness, she must look like the wild woman of Borneo.

He noted her quickly concealed grimace, and his jaw tightened. "I expect you to arrange your personal life so that you can return to this house at a consistent hour. My time is valuable. I can't waste it worrying about whether you've gotten home safely."

"Oh, but, Mr. Malloy, I couldn't leave town early today," Liberty said evasively. She hadn't mentioned to him that she'd be at the Fourth of July party, and she felt foolish telling him she had spent her morning on something so frivolous as a party dress. "I had some . . . business to attend to, and then I went to buy a book. And I ran into a gentleman I know, Captain Blodgett, who had some . . . urgent affairs to discuss with me." She found herself rushing through her explanations, all the while annoyed at having to answer to him in the first place. It was, after all, her day off.

Zeke kept his face an unreadable mask, inwardly seething. How the Devil had Blodgett managed to find out about Liberty? Did the bastard intend to use her as some kind of weapon? Zeke would have to keep his glimmers of tender feeling to himself; Blodgett would strike at the girl with the speed of a rattlesnake if he thought it would undermine Zeke's opposition to him.

Zeke kept his voice hard and unyielding. "I hardly find that an acceptable excuse, Miss Brooks. I am, unfortunately, rather well acquainted with the captain, and I am certain his news could have kept."

He looked at her, her hair down, a rich bloom on her cheeks. Her loveliness startled him, the way a purple crocus peeping through the snow did.

"Well, he—he didn't seem to think so," she stammered, feeling her face color. "Really, Mr. Malloy, it is my day off, it's well before dark, and I am perfectly capable of managing my own affairs."

"What did he want from you?" Zeke pressed, taking hold of her arm. He was being unfair and he knew it, but at the moment he had more important considerations than fairness. The last thing he could afford was to let Liberty Brooks become the chink in his armor. "That man's a scoundrel and a liar. He couldn't possibly have anything to say to a respectable young woman."

Liberty felt her cheeks warm in an angry blush. How dare he imply that she was anything but respectable! She might look a trifle heathenish now, but she would show him just who he was dealing with.

"I beg your pardon, sir," she said crisply. "My conversations with *my* acquaintances on *my* day off are not your concern."

It really was too much, hearing herself justify a few moments spent with Jack Blodgett. Anyone listening would think she was actually *friendly* with the man. But she'd eat her green bonnet before she let Zeke Malloy dictate her associations to her.

Zeke fought to maintain a cool expression. Had she been flirting, if not worse, with Blodgett? She looked as lusciously rumpled as a dairymaid fresh from a tumble in the haystacks. All her seemliness and upright propriety wiped away by Jack Blodgett's cheap, oily brand of charm. Zeke wondered coldly if the bastard had bedded her. All it took was one look at her today to see she was not the ice maiden Zeke had hired, but a wilder, freer creature, a voluptuous temptress with a tangle of chestnut curls and the untamed grace of a tigress.

And she was lovely. Much too lovely.

"Excuse me, my dear," he said, releasing her arm, his voice chill. "I had simply mistaken you for an entirely different sort of female."

Liberty's throat constricted as she turned her back on her employer to head up the stairway. Since he was going to be unreasonable and infuriating, she intended to spend the rest of the afternoon in her room working on her knitting. "I'm afraid I don't have the slightest idea what you're talking about," she said coldly.

"I've known Blodgett for years," Zeke said nastily. "I wouldn't have thought such a proper little miss would interest him much. Evidently I was mistaken."

She turned back to face him, her jaw tightening. "Just what the Devil are you suggesting?"

"Watch your language, my dear," he said, his voice low and dangerous. "Any female who stays in my house will conduct herself like a lady."

She blanched at the thinly veiled threat. So he'd toss her out if she didn't scrape and curtsy, would he? Well, she'd see about that.

"Language be damned!" she growled, walking slowly back down the steps to meet him face-to-face. "Who are you to lecture me? I intend to keep whatever company I choose, during whatever free hours I choose. And I will not tolerate being treated like a child."

"Like it or not, while you are employed by me, I am responsible for your welfare," he pronounced, clenching his fists at his sides. He was torn between rage and desire. She was more beautiful than he had ever seen her, her blue-green eyes blazing with the fire of opals. She swore without blushing, and her voice held that hint of farm-girl twang he had heard the week before. Of all men to sully this exquisite, enigmatic, infuriating creature, how could it be Blodgett?

"No, Mr. Malloy," she said softly, enunciating with painful precision. "I'm afraid you're wrong. You are responsible for paying me a decent wage for my work. Your responsibility ends exactly there. You are neither my father nor my husband nor my guardian."

"I see," Zeke said coldly. He turned away from her for a moment, his temples throbbing, his fists still clenched painfully. "Then you intend to continue your *friendship* with this cretin?"

"He doesn't buff his nails or read Latin—that makes him a cretin to you, doesn't it?" she challenged.

"You're behaving like a fool," he spat. "Blodgett is involved in some very ugly business. You couldn't possibly understand—"

"How convenient." She curled her lip in an angry sneer. "I couldn't understand. Due to the well-known mental weakness of my sex, I assume. Don't think I don't know quite well what your problem with Jack Blodgett is."

Zeke gave her a dangerous look. What had Blodgett told her?

"You're jealous!" she crowed.

He turned his back to her angrily. "That, Miss Brooks, is without a doubt the most idiotic thing I have ever heard you say."

"You're jealous because Jack is charming and good-humored, and you're nothing but an arrogant, ill-tempered snob!"

He wheeled and grasped her shoulders with fingers like talons, his eyes hard and unyielding. "Maybe you two deserve each other," he said nastily. "When he's filled you with contempt and disgust, you think about the stuffy old *snob* who tried to warn you."

He released his painful grip and stormed from the room, slamming the door so hard that every windowpane in the house rattled.

Liberty rubbed her arm where he had held her. There would be a bruise there in the morning. Why did he have to be so horrible? She hadn't meant to say those awful things, and she hadn't meant to let him think she was friends with Blodgett. And she certainly hadn't meant to lose her temper and start shouting like some alewife. She fished in her reticule for her hairpins, and began hurriedly assembling her hair into its usual austere, professional style.

Good heavens, Mr. Malloy might assume she and the captain were . . . courting. She laughed nervously, and shuddered at the thought of the smirk Zeke would wear when he learned that she cared as little for the gaudy vulgarian as he did.

But more disturbing thoughts troubled her. When Zeke had grasped her so brutishly, she had not been frightened or even angry. Certainly she had felt none of the distress that had accompanied Blodgett's unseemly clutching at her ankles. She had barely even felt the pain of Zeke's punishing grip.

Instead, she had been seized by an inexplicable desire to touch that finely chiseled face, to see if it felt the way it looked—as strong and unyielding as granite. She had even, God help her, wondered if she could have ended the argument by reaching out just the smallest bit to . . . meet his lips with hers. She could have put her hand to his heart and felt its proud, heavy beat. The thought made her uncomfortable and confused.

She reminded herself that Zeke Malloy was brilliant, and an important voice in the movement. That was why working for him was such a privilege. He needed some education on the proper role of women. That was why she endured his difficult moods and his sarcasm. That was why she tolerated his heavy-handed, paternalistic attitude.

Wasn't it?

Of course it was, she chided herself. It couldn't possibly be anything else. Liberty Brooks had no patience with any kind of romantic, foolish twaddle.

She walked distractedly to the pump in the kitchen and worked the gleaming green handle, letting its squeak and gush drown out her thoughts. The water helped to cool her temper as she splashed her face.

Still preoccupied, she walked out the back door, painfully stubbing her toe on the doorstep. Her anger flared anew, and she howled and hobbled away, cursing roundly. She picked up a fair-sized stone and hurled it as far as she could.

To hell with Zeke Malloy and his imperious god-damned attitude.

"Why don't you tell me what the game is, Blodgett," Zeke said, his voice razor-sharp in the low light. The note had said to meet Blodgett here at Murphy's, alone. Blodgett couldn't possibly have thought Zeke was that stupid. Jim was flattened against the wall's rotted timbers, revolver drawn, and there were three more men outside. Zeke kept himself in the shadows, where he knew Blodgett had to strain to make out any form at all.

"Malloy, Malloy," Blodgett replied, his voice mock-indulgent. "Isn't it all getting a little boring? I go about my business, and every couple of weeks you hold a gun on me, or my boys hold a knife to you. Something's got to break the stalemate. Maybe one of us should just kill the other and be done with it." He laughed joylessly.

"It's a nice thought, but we've both got insurance policies," Zeke replied coolly. "You're as vulnerable as I am, Blodgett. There are too many of my men who know your operation, and I'm the only one holding them back from exposing and destroying you. When I'm gone, so is your protection. You can't kill them all, Jack, and you know it."

"Maybe not," Blodgett replied, his voice good-natured. "But I'm aiming to break up this tea party. It's been getting on my nerves. And with a little luck, your girlie will show me how."

Zeke froze in the shadows. He focused on the

hot red dot of Blodgett's cigar as the man paced the dirty floor. "Someone's been pulling your leg, Jack," Zeke said, his voice carefully neutral. "Of my many weaknesses, women aren't one."

"Well, prior to this point, I would have given you that." Blodgett chewed his cigar noisily. "I never figured you to be man enough to chase a little tail. But I've seen the filly you've got in your stable now, and she's a fine piece of work. You have my congratulations on acquiring the services of Miss Liberty Brooks."

"You've got it all wrong, Blodgett."

"You don't have to kid me, friend. This is your old pal Jack you're talking to." The cigar's red dot disappeared for a moment in a cloud of acrid smoke. "She's fine to look at, no question, but she's even better in the sack."

The room spun crazily around Zeke, and for one sickening moment he felt as if the sawdust-covered floor might rush up to meet him.

"Really?" he drawled. "I'm afraid I haven't taken the time to find out. Now that you have, I expect I'll pass." It took every ounce of self-control to keep the emotion from his voice.

"Oh, Zeke, my boy, terrible mistake," Blodgett said, jocular. "She's a wildcat, friend. She screamed so loud, I thought the boys would break the door down. I'm thinkin' of letting 'em take a crack at her next time, just so I can watch the little bitch buck."

Blodgett was lying. He had to be. At times Liberty might be a little wilder than Zeke had thought, but she was no whore. He knew better than to believe the crude bastard, better than to let Blodgett get the best of him.

"I don't care what the girl does, Blodgett," Zeke said. "She just works for me. It's none of my business if she wants to spend her day off rolling in the mud with a pig like you."

"Aw, but, Zeke, you're my pal. I want to be sure you get a little piece of this action. She's too good to miss. I wouldn't want my good friend Zeke Malloy to go without a taste of the sassiest bitch in Boston. And she does it for nothing, Zeke, just for the fun of it."

"Did you have anything you wanted to say to me, Blodgett, or are you going to talk about your perverted fancies all night?" Zeke asked, his voice clipped.

"Stay clear of me, Malloy," Blodgett replied, chewing the cigar angrily. "That's what I've got to say. One day soon you're going to regret interfering with my operation. I might just cut your bitch up for shark bait and drop what's left of her on that fancy front lawn of yours. Watch your back, Malloy, and your girlfriend's, too."

"I'll give that some thought, Jack. See you around," Zeke said, melting back into the growing darkness of the city.

The carriage rumbled beneath Zeke as he sprawled across the seat, his long frame nearly filling the passenger compartment. Jim was in the driver's seat, and the other men had been safely dropped off in the city. Zeke needed some space and time alone to think.

Liberty and Blodgett.

It wasn't possible. And yet . . . he had given the pernicious female ample opportunity to renounce Blodgett, and she'd chosen not to. That had to mean something. Didn't it?

He pressed his hands to his throbbing temples as he tried to think. The cold logic he prided himself on was evaporating by the minute. Squabbling with Liberty had been bad enough, but he was no match for the two of them coming at him from both sides, from hatred and . . .

And what?

Misplaced affection, he decided. Not love. Certainly nothing like love.

He glanced out the window at the shadowy world that flew past the carriage. He couldn't afford this. He had succumbed to some fanciful notion about the girl, but his notion of undermining her surface respectability had thrown him as off balance as it had her.

And look what he had discovered beneath those layers of starch. Was she Blodgett's lover? He remembered the roses in her cheeks, the fire in her eyes that her usual correct deportment couldn't hide. She had just come from that snake's lair. She'd admitted as much.

Zeke slammed his fist into the compartment wall, and Jim slowed the carriage. Scowling, Zeke tapped a signal for Jim to continue. She couldn't be permitted to erode his self-control this way. He couldn't allow *them* to get the best of him.

He pulled himself erect in the seat. He would simply have to regain the upper hand, that was all. If he'd given her a nudge before, this time it would be a full-fledged push. He was no schoolboy; he would master himself, and in so doing, he would master her. She would reveal herself to him. She would have no choice.

A thought teased at the back of his mind. *And what if she's innocent?*

He thrust it away. There were so many innocents at stake—so many fugitives like Indigo and her baby. And there was Annabelle, always Annabelle. Those still trapped in slavery had to be his first priority.

And if Liberty Brooks was simply another blameless player in this tragic game, she would have to prove it to him in the very near future. Because Zeke could no longer give her the benefit of the doubt.

*   *   *

Liberty looked up at the darkening cobalt sky. She had been out here in the woods for an hour now, and her temper was finally beginning to cool. She would have to go back soon. Mrs. Biggins would worry, and Zeke would say nasty things if she was out after dark. A few stars appeared on the horizon, bright pricks of white against a soft blue ground.

What did he want from her? What did he want her to do, to say? She had humiliated herself arguing with him and had infuriated them both in the bargain. Something about him invariably made her lose track of her carefully cultivated self-control.

Her reverie was broken by the sight of a small, dusty figure sprawled in the road ahead. Peering into the twilight murk, she hurried to get a better look, and she found a thin, dark-skinned boy, perhaps eleven or twelve, lying at the side of the road. His eyes were bright with tears, and his leg was bent back at an unnatural angle. One fat silver tear rolled down his cheek as he pleaded with her, "Please, miz, please help me. Nobody'll stop to help me. That bad man, he run me down wif his hosses, an' he don't even stop to see ef I's hurt. This leg be hurtin' me powerful bad, miz, please don't leaves me here."

Horrified, Liberty knelt to examine the boy's apparently broken leg. What sort of monster could run down a child and drive off? As she bent over him, she recoiled to see the flash of a knife blade. She drew a sharp breath as he neatly sliced the strings that held her purse to her wrist and dashed into the orchard, as fast and sure as a squirrel.

She leapt to chase him. The brat had picked the wrong victim—Liberty had always been the fiercest tomboy in God's creation. Back home she could run faster and spit farther than any boy for seven counties.

Must be getting old, though, she thought, her

lungs beginning to burn as she ran. Every stone pushed rudely up through her boots; every root seemed to reach out to twist around her ankles in the darkness. The boy ran through the woods, veering constantly to throw her off course. But she was close enough behind that she could, barely, keep him in sight. Just as she thought she could not possibly run another step, the boy burst into a clearing and darted into a tiny shack.

Liberty gulped painfully for air as she staggered after him, her hair disheveled, boots dusty, skirt torn where she had caught it in a patch of wild blackberry. As she stumbled into the cabin, an old man with grizzled white hair, poised to light a small lamp, gaped first at the boy and then at this mysterious white woman. "Boy, what the *hell* have you been doin'?" he thundered.

"I'm afraid he has something of mine. I'll just take it and be going," Liberty gasped, casting a look at the boy and holding out one hand. The child scowled, but he gave her back the purse.

The man looked furious. "Somebody had best tell me what's goin' on here."

"I was just playin', Jake. I swear, just playin'," the boy said pleadingly.

"There's no harm done," Liberty said quickly. She was angry about the child's dangerous "playing," but this man—his grandfather?—was clearly incensed, and looked ready to do the boy bodily harm.

The man gave Liberty a suspicious look. "Reckon you caught this boy stealin'. I'd say there was plenty harm in it. But don't you worry none about it, ma'am. I'll give him a good whuppin', and he won't bother you no more."

"A whipping? Oh, no, you can't. I mean, he was only playing. I'm sure he's not a bad boy."

"No, ma'am, he ain't a bad boy. Ef the Divvil gots hold of him, I reckon I can beats it out again. I hopes you can forgives the boy for stealin' from you, but it won't happen again. Good evenin' to you, ma'am." It was clear from the man's tone that he did not care to discuss the subject—any subject—with her further.

"I'm sorry to disturb you. I'll be off then." Her heart sank as she saw the young boy begin to shake with real sobs, not the crocodile tears she had seen by the road.

The old man turned his back on Liberty and busied himself with his lamp. His feet were wrapped in bandages, and bony elbows poked through the holes in his sleeves. Liberty stood a moment watching the stiff, proud back in the flickering lamplight, then left the cabin without a word. She returned to the warm brightness of Haven House, her pace slowed by a sadness that seeped down to her very bones.

Zeke did not return until the small hours of the morning. Liberty heard him stumble around downstairs, swearing angrily as Mrs. Biggins fussed and scolded. Liberty could not make out his words, but the tone was unmistakable; he was in a blind rage. She turned uneasily and buried her face in her pillow as she had done as a child when her courage failed her at night, hoping to hide from the demons of the darkness.

The next morning was hellish. Zeke had an odd new look in his eye—the hungry ruthlessness of a predator. He said nothing, but she caught him gazing at her as if he would devour her, bones and all. She flushed, her hand fluttering nervously to her collar, and looked away.

He set a pile of papers down on her desk, leaning closely over her shoulder. She felt an odd quivering in her stomach.

"Since you're so terribly efficient, you won't mind sorting through these for me." His voice purred with a strange new tension. "You know what to do by now—answer the letters, file the articles."

Liberty drew her eyebrows together. His words were perfectly innocent, but he seemed to be sending off a current of energy she was finding uncomfortably distracting. "Of course I can manage, Mr. Malloy. But I . . . I'd like to ask you a favor."

"Women are all alike," he murmured, his lips frighteningly close to her ear. "Forever asking favors."

"Perhaps we are forever asking favors because we have no rights," she pointed out. She shifted away, wringing her pen between her hands. "Really, Mr. Malloy, I can't think what's gotten into you this morning. Of course, if you don't care to listen to my request, I shan't force it on you."

He laughed softly, triggering a shiver up and down her spine. Perhaps she was coming down with something.

"Of course I will listen, my dear. How on earth could I resist you . . . or your unerring feminine logic?"

She forced herself to stop twisting her pen and shot him a nervous look. "Mr. Malloy, is there something you wished to say to me?"

He smiled, smug as a housecat. "Don't be silly, Miss Brooks, of course not. Please, go on."

"Well, I'd like . . ." She didn't know how to go on. He was behaving so strangely, and after having been so angry the day before. Of his many difficult moods, she found this predatory friendliness by far the most disturbing.

He lifted one black eyebrow and leaned back against her desk. "I'm waiting, my dear."

She profoundly wished he would stop calling her *my dear*. "If I could just . . . take this afternoon, to run a small errand—I don't think it would take very long."

His lazy smile froze into something far less pleasant. "What sort of errand?"

Liberty found herself speaking too quickly. "The very smallest of errands, I assure you, practically no errand at all. I merely wanted to see a friend for a short while. But if that isn't convenient—"

She broke off, dismayed by the turn in his expression. All she wanted to do was to see if she could find that little boy and the old man again, to try to help them. The sight of the man's bandaged feet had haunted her dreams all night, and this morning she'd realized that she'd have to do something to help.

Malloy's stare could have frozen seawater. "I imagined you were keen on honest, hard work, Miss Brooks. I hope I was not mistaken."

"No, no, of course I'll take care of anything that needs attending to. It's only . . . I had planned on making this one very small excursion."

Her heart sank as she took in the mountain of papers he'd placed on her desk. It was almost as if he wanted to keep her tied to her work all day—and half the night as well.

His jaw tightened almost imperceptibly. "I should think you had plenty of time for excursions on your days off, Miss Brooks."

Liberty longed to simply give the matter up, but she couldn't help thinking about that old man's poor feet. "Normally I have ample time, sir," she began, her voice a small squeak. "But there's someone . . . That is to say, I have a friend who requires my assistance."

"Your relationships with . . . *friends* will take place on your own time. Is that perfectly clear?"

Liberty tried again. "But in a way, it's for the cause. I mean, it's our work to help people, isn't it? And if I could help one individual, then wouldn't it really be like—"

Mr. Malloy cut her off. "I trust I was clear, Miss

Brooks. Quite frankly, I find myself uninterested in the needs of your one individual. Your energies to the cause are best served by doing as you are told."

It was no use. Liberty swallowed her anger and glanced again at the mountain of papers on her desk. "I see, sir. Of course, I'll get to work on these right away."

Chapter 9

Liberty spent her morning on the herculean task of dispatching the endless mass of papers. Mr. Malloy had ridden off like a madman, and Mrs. Biggins was busy experimenting with making puff pastry. Liberty had peeked into the kitchen after lunch to find the woman covered head to foot in flour, glowering at a lump of pale yellow dough on the kitchen counter.

By afternoon, the stack of letters and articles had reduced itself by a little more than half. If Liberty worked late tonight, she could return to the cabin and still finish the pile of assignments by morning. And with Mr. Malloy gone and Mrs. Biggins distracted, there could be no better time.

She put her shopping basket on her bed and put in a primer, a slate, a few stubs of yellow chalk, and a large handful of plums, covering the lot with a clean handkerchief. She only hoped she'd be able to slip outside without Mrs. Biggins noticing. Liberty did not care to attract their employer's attention with what he would doubtless find an ill-advised, useless project. He was always going on about how what really mattered were principles, not specifics. If he heard she'd spent her time—time he paid her for, after all—taking plums and books to a single wayward child, he'd be furious.

Liberty tucked the handkerchief into the basket

with a determined movement. One child *did* matter,
and she wasn't going to let Zeke Malloy's thoughts
on the subject dissuade her. It wasn't as if she
weren't going to finish the work he'd set out for
her, after all. She hoisted the basket onto one arm
and slipped downstairs and outside.

The day was warm, and she shut her eyes for a
moment to let the sun beat down on her upturned
face. The more time she spent in Boston, the more
she felt parts of her true self slip away from her.
When she felt like screaming, she found herself nodding politely instead. When she caught a glimpse
of herself in the mirror, she was shocked to see an
upright, rigid figure in somber bombazine instead
of a frizzy-haired tomboy with dirt on her nose. If
she'd met Zeke Malloy in Ohio, and not here in
Boston, she'd have picked a good fistfight with
him long ago. Liberty wondered if she could even
wrestle anymore.

But she'd kept her ideals and her sense of honor,
and for that she was grateful. A little modesty and
respectable self-control were surely a fair price to
pay for the privilege of working in the movement.

She headed purposefully for the orchard, inhaling the clean scent of grass and earth. It had been
nearly dark when she'd chased the child through
the trees, but she thought she remembered the gen-
eral direction.

Another thought nagged at the back of her mind.
What if Jane Redburne truly couldn't find anyone else to care for the runaway slave she'd mentioned? Liberty would have to find someplace to
hide the man—someplace Mr. Malloy would not
think to look. She groaned aloud. Jane had promised she'd try to find another place. But what if she
couldn't?

She pushed the premature worries firmly from
her mind. Even if worst came to worst, there was no
room for cowardice. She would not be responsible

for some poor young man's being forced back into slavery.

Liberty wandered for over half an hour before finally stumbling on the little shack. It saddened her that anyone would have to live in such a ramshackle place. And they wouldn't own the shack—or likely even rent it. It was on Mr. Malloy's land, and he had never mentioned any tenants, nor had she ever seen so much as a rental ledger. She suspected the boy and his grandfather had simply found this place and were quietly living here, hoping they would not be discovered.

Her first task, she realized, would be to make them understand that she wouldn't say a thing to Mr. Malloy. Once she'd gained their trust, she would be free to do what she could for the child and his grandfather.

Liberty knocked on the door, noting with distaste that the place could do with a good cleaning. Well, men were like that. Perhaps she could give the cabin a thorough sweeping out and get rid of the cobwebs that clung to the doorframe.

No one answered her knocks, and she frowned with frustration. She didn't want to invade their privacy, but as soon as she saw the two, she'd make them understand that she meant well. "Hello?" she called. What were their names? The old man's name was . . . Jake, she thought, and he'd definitely called the young boy Tom. "Hello, Tom? Are you here? Hello, is anyone at home?"

There was no answer. Liberty timidly turned the door handle. The cabin was even less appealing on the inside—a single room with unfinished walls and tattered oilcloth over the windows. A thick layer of dust coated the broken table and chair in the middle of the room, and a potato had rolled into one corner, sprouting white eyes that reached for the dim light from the window.

Liberty bit her lip. She hadn't thought of what

she might do if she couldn't find the little family. Well, since she was here, she might as well do what she could to spruce up the place. She looked in vain for a broom before stepping back into the orchard to make one from a branch.

Really, she thought, her lips tightening. Just because people were poor was no reason to let things go this way. She instantly dismissed the uncharitable thought. That poor old man could hardly walk with his feet bandaged that way, and it didn't seem they had a woman around to show them how to keep things nice. All Liberty had to do was to clean it for them once, and they'd see how much pleasanter it was to live in a tidy home, however modest.

Liberty gave one more call before she stepped back into the cabin. "Tom? Are you here? I'd like to help you! Hello, Tom? Where are you?"

No answer. She began to sweep the floor briskly with the makeshift broom, coughing as the dust flew up into her face. They didn't even seem to have any water; there was no pump in sight. She'd have to content herself with dusting and sweeping and throwing out that horrid potato.

Well, she thought, wiping the grit from her eyes, every project had to start somewhere.

In her underground hiding place, Indigo rocked her baby gently, her mouth set in a grim line. "Thass right, Sam. You sleeps nice and quiet like a good little man." A noise came from overhead—the scraping of a chair. Indigo could hear her own heart pounding.

Jake was sitting in the corner, his feet propped on a stool. "Damn it, boy," he muttered. "Ef we gets caught, we all know who to blame."

Tom's face was stricken with guilt. "Mebbe it ain't her."

Jake scowled. "Course it be her. You couldn't

keep yo' hands off her purse, could you, boy?"

Indigo shot them both a glare. "Hush, both of you. Jake, you as bad as the boy be. Keeps your voice down. She ain't goin' to find us if we keeps our mouths shut."

Jake's face twisted into a deeper grimace, but he kept his silence. Tom's eyes shimmered with tears, and Indigo felt a moment of pity for him. Boys his age were supposed to be a little wild; it was only natural. He'd thought the buckra woman's money would be a help to them. It wasn't his fault that this latest piece of foolishness might get them all shipped back into slavery.

So long as little Sam didn't start to cry, they would be safe. Indigo whispered a prayer beneath her breath. *Let us come through this, Lord. We come so far already, don't let us get caught now.*

They heard the voice again, and Indigo felt her blood run cold.

"Tom? Don't be frightened! Where are you?" The woman sounded far away, but she was a mere few feet from discovering their hiding place.

Keeps her away, Lord. Keeps her away, so I doesn't have to sin. As terrible as their escape to the North had been, Indigo had never had to kill anyone. She hoped with all her soul that this strange woman didn't find the two doors that led to the underground rooms. Indigo didn't want to stain her hand with blood, even with the blood of a nosy white woman who was trying her best to lure them out of this safe place.

Indigo shifted Sam gently on her lap, watching the baby's chest rise and fall with his even breaths. She didn't want to kill, but she wouldn't let her baby live in slavery. She remembered the night on the dock, and she shivered. They'd come so close to losing everything, before the gentleman had rescued them. He still hadn't told them his name, but Indigo respected his silence. He'd risked his own life for them, and she would be damned if she'd throw it all away now. She'd do whatever she had to do to protect her freedom and the freedom of her child.

"For God's sake, woman, will you leave off your wincing? You act as if I were going to eat you alive," Zeke growled.

Liberty had slipped in only an instant before Mr. Malloy arrived at home. Her pulse was still pounding in her ears, even now that she was safely settled in his office writing out his letters. She breathed deeply, willing her mind to slow its wild careening.

"I'm sorry if I've annoyed you," she murmured. "It won't happen again."

He stood behind her and leaned over her shoulder, closing his hand over hers. "There's no need to be frightened of me," he whispered in a voice that made her shiver.

She swallowed hard. "No, sir, I'm not frightened of you."

He laughed and released her hand, standing behind her so she couldn't see him. She longed to see his face, to try to read his eyes, but she did not want to show him her own flaming cheeks.

"Not afraid of me? Your eyes are as big as saucers."

Liberty was silent. What was there to say?

"Turn and face me, Liberty." His voice did not allow for the possibility of disobedience.

Liberty turned slightly in her chair, keeping her gaze pinned to the desk.

"All the way around, if you please," he insisted. "And look me in the eye for a change."

She turned her face up toward his. Her breath caught in her throat.

He held his hand out to her, motioning for her to stand. She stood before him in her dark wool dress, wrapped in layers of starched and pressed fabric, but she felt stark naked.

"I suppose I might have been a trifle short with you these past few weeks. It's time we had a little talk, wouldn't you say?"

Panic rose in Liberty's throat. "A talk? But we have highly interesting conversations every day, sir. Not that I would object to speaking with you now, of course. What I mean to say is—"

Zeke put a finger to her lips to shush her. She became wildly dizzy and realized she wasn't breathing.

"Hush, now, girl. By *talk* I don't mean that foolish prattle you've been force-feeding me to hide what you're really up to."

Liberty blinked up at him, confused.

"You're very good at keeping secrets, aren't you?" Zeke's voice was silky.

"I'm not the least bit good at it," she blurted. "In fact, I'm terrible."

He laughed again. "Perhaps you've even managed to fool yourself, then."

She eyed him warily. "I don't think I catch your meaning, Mr. Malloy."

He reached out to stroke her cheek with his thumb, and she had to fight to keep from flinching. He studied her face until her cheeks burned beneath his scrutiny.

"Have you been seeing much of your *friend*?" His voice was very low.

Liberty fought to make sense of this confusion. Which friend? Had he found out about her attempts to find the boy and the old man? Or could he mean Jane Redburne?

"I'm sorry, sir?"

"You don't have to pretend with me anymore, Liberty. Just tell me the truth. You can trust me."

"I'm sorry, I . . . don't understand."

His eyes narrowed. "Never mind. Either I

wouldn't believe your answer or it would enrage me," he muttered.

She shut her eyes against the intensity of his gaze, which was definitely beginning to make her light-headed. "I'm sorry you don't find me more ... trustworthy."

He gave her a strange smile, almost wistful. "I might trust you if I could begin to figure you out."

"Sir?" she said in complete confusion.

"For instance," he continued, "I can't fathom why you wear these damnably ugly gowns."

He traced the line of her collar with one finger, and she felt the air rush out of her lungs.

She took a step back from him. "I strive to maintain a professional demeanor." What she was actually striving for was to breathe properly.

He closed the distance between them. "Yes," he murmured, "your professional demeanor." He placed his hands on her shoulders, pressing the stiff fabric of her wide sleeves into her flesh. "Always so starched and neat and *correct*."

"Y-Yes, sir. I mean, I do my best."

He lifted his hand to her hair. She stood as still as a startled jackrabbit. Slowly he slid the pins from the heavy coil of hair, and she felt it tumble down around her ears.

"Perhaps you try too hard, my dear. There's a time to let your hair down, too." He ran his fingers gently through the mass of curls, arranging them around her shoulders, sending tingles down the length of her spine.

"I ..." she stammered. "I think ..."

"You think too much," he said softly. "Sometimes a woman ought to just feel."

A tiny flag of annoyance waved at the back of her mind. "Just a woman? Never a man?"

His smile reminded her of the wolf's in "Little Red Riding Hood."

"Yes, a man, too. Sometimes the feelings between a man and a woman can be most . . . complex."

"Complex . . ." she repeated, dazed.

He laced his fingers through her hair and pulled her gently toward him, his face inches from hers. "Complex. And very, very pleasurable."

When his lips came down on hers, she thought her knees would give way beneath her. She knew that she should pull away, slap his face, storm off in an insulted huff.

But she couldn't for the life of her seem to manage to do any of those things.

He curled one hand around the small of her back, bringing their bodies close. The other hand he kept laced in her hair, holding her mouth prisoner beneath his.

The touch of his mouth to hers was like nothing she had ever even dreamed of. When his tongue stroked her lips, she felt a hot tendril of pleasure unfurl low in her belly. Her lips parted, and he slid his tongue inside her.

Something primitive and confusing was overtaking her, unholy desire drowning out any lingering voice of caution. She *wanted* his tongue in her, wanted the taste of fine brandy that lingered on his lips. She brought her hands up to cup his head, wanting him closer to her. Yet her desire was not quenched by getting what she wanted, but whetted.

He groaned and slid his hands down to cup her buttocks, hiking her hips against his. The blood sang in her ears as she allowed him to crush his hardness against the softest, most vulnerable part of her.

He took his lips from hers, and she whimpered in protest. He hushed her, trailing a line of kisses from the back of her ear down the length of her neck.

She found herself moaning as she dropped her

head back. His breath was hot on her throat as he nuzzled her, nipping gently at her flesh.

His hands slid from her buttocks and around her thighs to caress their tenderness. He covered her throat in hungry, biting kisses as he stroked her through her skirts, the fabric rough against her skin.

He covered her mouth with his again, and his hands deserted her aching thighs. Her eyes flew open as she felt his hands working the buttons of her bodice.

The shock was like a dunking in an icy pond. She pulled away from his lips. "What are you doing?" she whispered desperately.

His eyes were a green river of longing. "I seem to be unbuttoning your dress."

She pulled sharply away from him, half-disappointed that he let her go. "Mr. Malloy, I don't think we ought—"

He laughed, a low, dangerous rumble. "If you're going to let a man kiss you like that, you might at least call him by his first name."

She gave him what she hoped was a killing look as she hastily rebuttoned her bodice. "I didn't *let* you kiss me. You just did it."

"You kissed me back." He had an infuriatingly insolent grin on his face.

"I couldn't possibly have done that."

"And why is that?"

"Because I don't know how." Liberty lifted her hands to her hair and began nervously to twist it into a chignon.

"You're a quick study." His eyes glowed like fireworks. "Haven't you ever been kissed before?"

"Not like that," she blurted, instantly wishing she could take the words back. She'd made it sound like she was pleased he'd kissed her.

"Why, Liberty," he chided, reaching for her makeshift chignon, "you're trembling."

She drew away from him. "Mr. Malloy, I'm—"

"Zeke," he corrected.

"Mr. Malloy," she insisted.

He took her face in his hands and held his lips an inch above hers. "Zeke."

"Zeke," she whispered, feeling herself melt all over again.

No, she couldn't let that happen. She wriggled free of him and knelt to the ground, gathering her scattered hairpins. "Zeke, then, if you must be pigheaded. Zeke, I won't be . . . well . . . I'm a respectable woman."

He growled, and she straightened quickly. Somehow, kneeling at his feet felt very dangerous.

"You're a respectable woman, but is that all you are?"

She stabbed her hairpins into her chignon, struggling to repair some of the damage he had done. "That's all I am," she said, hoping she sounded certain.

He gave another crooked smile, and her heart skipped a beat. "Bullsh—"

"Mr. Malloy!" She gave him a shocked look.

"It's Zeke, damn you. And you can't stand there and tell me there isn't more to you than this." He gathered a fistful of her sleeve in his hand, mocking her sober costume as he reeled her in like a fish on a line.

"There's more to me than . . . than simple lust," she said, twisting free of him.

His eyes glittered, hungry and hard. "You may find that lust is not so simple as you imagine, my dear."

The flush in her cheeks renewed itself. "I'm afraid I can no longer participate in this scandalous conversation," she said, fighting for her dignity. "If you'll excuse me . . ."

"And if I don't?"

"I beg your pardon?"

"Excuse you. What if I insist you stay here and finish this?"

Liberty took a step back, a little frightened. "I'd refuse, of course."

His laugh was cold. "Of course. The crisp Liberty Brooks, the sensible, efficient Liberty Brooks, would never fritter her evening away tarrying with an oversexed rogue."

Liberty's mouth flew open in shock. "You're not an— You're not a rogue." She simply couldn't use that word.

Zeke's face was serious. "I'm any number of things, my dear. Only a small fraction of which I choose to share with the many hypocrites of Boston society. And I suspect the same is true for you."

"For me?"

He stepped closer. "You're not what you seem either, are you, Liberty Brooks? You have a secret side, too. Tell me. Tell me what you're hiding."

She shook her head. "Nothing. I'm not hiding anything."

He cupped her chin in his palm and brought her face closer to his. He settled a soft kiss on her cheekbone. "Tell me, pretty one," he coaxed.

Her voice faltered. "I . . . I can't."

He brushed feathery kisses across her temple. "Trust me. Tell me."

"But it concerns something that makes you angry."

Zeke froze. After a long moment, he took a step back. "And what might that be?" he asked coolly.

After what had just happened between them, she couldn't keep secrets from him. It seemed immoral to let him kiss her and then to lie.

"Well," she began, taking a deep breath. "I know what you've said about the Underground Railroad, that we must work to change the laws, and not just to save a few individuals. But I just can't believe that you wouldn't help people—if they came your way, that is."

"Is that what this charade is about? You're trying to find out if I'm involved with the Railroad?" Zeke's eyes were as hard and unyielding as New England granite. "Who put you up to this?"

Liberty felt her anger rise like steam from a kettle. She'd known the topic would make him irritable, but she hadn't expected an explosion. "For your information, I do not *scheme*." She bit her lip in frustration, trying to sort out the whole confusing mess. The man was as unpredictable as a rogue stallion. He had clearly jumped to some sort of wild conclusion, but she couldn't tell him the whole truth yet. And she mustn't mention Jane Redburne's name. As angry as Zeke was at this point, he'd call the constabulary in a wink.

"You don't scheme? What would you call this devious little plan you've been cooking up?"

"I haven't been making any plans," she said, hating the lie. "I was merely speaking hypothetically."

"And I'm the king of Mongolia. I asked you a question, Liberty. Who put you up to this?"

She set her jaw. He could storm and shout until he brought the roof down, but she wouldn't betray Jane's trust. "I don't know what you're talking about," she said, and realized it was the truth.

"Butter wouldn't melt in your mouth, would it, Delilah?"

"How can you make such outrageous accusations?" she cried, exasperated.

"I know an evasion when I hear one."

Liberty began to gather her things, scooping papers and shawl and teacup into one precarious heap. "You may stand there ranting like a lunatic if you please," she said, "but I'm retiring for the evening."

"Afraid I'm getting close to the truth?" Anger

now heated the cold expression in his eyes.

"What you are getting close to is a fit of apoplexy," she said, heading for the door.

"I will warn you of one thing, little Delilah," he said dangerously.

She turned to look at him. "And what might that be?"

His eyes were bleak. "I'd strongly advise you to think carefully about whom you choose to trust—and whom you choose to betray."

The hair on the back of her neck prickled, but even with the awkward bundle in her arms, she managed a satisfying slam of the door behind her.

Forty-five minutes later, Zeke had his head sunk in his hands, his elbows propped on Nate Jackson's kitchen table.

"She's beating me at my own game, Nate. Jesus, what the hell have I walked into?"

Nate was clattering around the kitchen, making a pot of tea. Zeke would have preferred something stronger, but Nate's wife, already angry about Nate's risking his life in the rescues, had stormed off to bed, muttering something about masculine stupidity. Jesus, but women were a trying lot.

"Zeke, you're not making any sense. Now you say you had a conversation with Liberty."

Zeke grimaced. "If you could call it a conversation. We weren't actually getting much talking done."

"You don't mean . . . ?"

Zeke nodded.

Nate shot his friend an icy look. "I can't believe you would take advantage of her that way. You can be a heartless bastard sometimes, but I thought that sport at least, you left alone."

"You aren't listening, Nate. I told you, this is serious. I'm not toying with her, I'm . . ." He realized he no longer knew what he was doing.

"I'm listening, all right, and I'm hearing a pack of nonsense." Nate measured the tea with clumsy, unpracticed motions.

"It's just that . . . there's something about her that—" Zeke stopped himself. Nate was right. He *was* talking nonsense.

But Nate was suddenly keenly interested. "That what?"

"That confuses me," Zeke finished lamely. Here in Nate's kitchen, with its comforting, warm glow of lamplight, both his fancies and his suspicions sounded stupid. "It's hard to explain," he said gruffly.

"Not so hard. It occurs to me that you've been in sore need of that kind of confusion for a long time. I just don't understand why you're finally figuring it out now, after all this time."

Zeke felt his heart sink. Nate placed a steaming mug on the table in front of him. "I didn't figure anything out," he growled. "She's nothing but an annoying diversion. Maybe a dangerous one."

Nate sat down across the table from his friend. "She's a good woman, Zeke."

Zeke narrowed his eyes. "She's a viper. Do you know what she asked me?"

Nate lifted a skeptical eyebrow. "What?"

Zeke paused a moment, feeling bitterness fill his mouth. "She asked what I'd do if I were faced with fugitives who needed my help."

Nate nodded. "What did you tell her?"

"What do you think? I told her she was a god-damned Delilah. Did you think I'd tell her the truth?"

Nate looked a little shocked. "Delilah? Why on earth—don't you think that's a little unfair?"

"She tried to weasel her way into my confidence, using her . . . feminine wiles."

"I thought you were the one who sought *her* out. You hired her, remember? And it sounds like you were the one who initiated a conversation that didn't include much talking."

Zeke glared at his friend. "I'm warning you, Nate, don't throw that in my face. She took advantage of the situation, damn it. She thought she could loosen my tongue by trying to seduce me."

"It sounds to me like that's exactly what you were trying to do to her."

Zeke's voice deepened to a growl. "Are you going to listen to me, or am I going to have to take a swing at you?"

Nate sighed. "Zeke, you're blowing this whole thing out of proportion. So she asked you about the Railroad. She's an abolitionist, Zeke, just like we are. She's curious about it, that's all. How could she know you're involved?"

"I could see it in her eyes, Nate. She's keeping something from me."

"You're imagining things."

Zeke took a swallow of his tea, wincing as it scalded his tongue and throat. "I haven't told you the worst part. She's linked with Blodgett."

Nate looked appalled. "Do you know that for certain, or is this another one of your unfounded suspicions?"

"She says he's a friend. Imagine that. Someone calls that murderous sack of dung a friend."

"She's told you this? Used his name?"

"Of course she used his name! I'm certain about this one, Nate." Zeke pounded his fist on the table. "Jesus! How could I have been so stupid?"

Nate sipped his tea thoughtfully. "I don't know, Zeke. This doesn't add up. I've talked with Liberty—she's no traitor to the cause."

Zeke snorted. "Do you have any evidence for that?"

"I can just tell. Call it a gut feeling."

"Well, my gut feeling tells me she's a spy. She's in a perfect position to collect evidence about my

work with the Railroad. By her own admission she
has connections to Blodgett. That bastard would
just love to find a way to bring me down. It'll be
more than a fine and a slap on the wrist for me,
Nate. We both know that."

Nate nodded soberly. If the extent of Zeke's
Underground Railroad activities were revealed
to the authorities, he'd certainly go to prison.
Despite his public protestations, Zeke had personally abetted in the "theft" of hundreds of
thousands of dollars worth of valued "property."

"Maybe she doesn't know why Blodgett wants
the information," Nate offered.

Zeke raked his fingers through his hair. "Whether she knows or not, the result would be the same.
With me in prison, it would be that much harder to
shake up Blodgett's operation. And I'd live to be a
hundred before I ever found Annabelle."

"So what are you going to do about it? Fire the
girl?"

Zeke's mind rebelled at the idea as soon as he
heard the words. "No!" he said before he could
think.

Nate arched one eyebrow. "It seems like the most
logical thing to do."

Zeke's mind worked furiously. "At least I know
her for what she is. If I fired her, I'd never know
who Blodgett had spying on me next. I just need to
make sure that she doesn't find anything out."

"If you're right, she already suspects quite a bit."

"Nothing she can prove. Even Mrs. Biggins
doesn't know about the fugitives."

"You don't trust women much, do you Zeke?"

Zeke looked up at his friend in surprise. "You
mean you do?"

"Some of them."

"Some of them deserve it," Zeke conceded.
"Annabelle, for one. Indigo, maybe."

A frown line appeared between Nate's eyebrows. "Liking people because of their color is as ignorant as hating them for the same reason, Zeke."

Zeke shook his head. "It's not their color. It's their situation. They're freed of all those rules that corrupt polite society. All that . . . *respectability*."

Nate met Zeke's eyes, his gaze steady. "You're thinking about Constance."

Zeke felt the coldness grip his heart. "My father never would have let Anna go if it hadn't been for her."

"It couldn't have been easy for her either, Zeke," Nate reminded him. "Having your father flaunt his . . . affections."

Zeke pressed his fingers into the mug, feeling the stinging heat. "I don't want to talk about that hypocritical—" His voice caught. No more. He would not think about her betrayal anymore.

Nate laid his hand gently on his friend's wrist. "Don't let those memories poison you, Zeke. It's one thing to fight for Annabelle's freedom. It's another to let what happened cloud your judgment."

Zeke scowled and downed the last of the tea. It wasn't brandy, but at least it soothed the tightness in his throat. "Don't lecture me, Nate. I'm not in the mood."

"How unlike you," Nate remarked dryly, dropping the subject for the moment. "So your strategy is to continue as before, then? With Liberty, I mean."

"No, not like before. I was stupid enough to think she might be trusted. And . . . well, I won't go into what else I was stupid enough to think. But now I know her for what she is."

"You know what you *think* she might be," Nate corrected.

"I can't take any risks with this, Nate. It's not just *my* freedom at stake."

Nate reluctantly nodded his agreement. "But, Zeke, please, don't go too hard on her until you're certain."

Zeke stood and pulled on his coat. That conniving little female had caught him off guard somehow, but he was back on track again. The ice-cold mask was back in place. "I'll do what I have to do, Nate. Same as I've always done."

Liberty hugged her knees to her chest, the moonlight pouring into her room. She had cried enough tears, and now all she wanted to do was sleep. But she could not keep the questions from running through her mind. How could he have been so cruel? It wasn't as if she were doing something immoral. She was an abolitionist, as was he. Yet he'd called her a Delilah. Why couldn't he understand that the Railroad was a noble cause, something worth breaking the law for? Plainly she couldn't tell him the truth now. She felt a little dizzy just thinking what he would do if he knew that she planned not merely to help the Railroad, but to shelter a runaway right here in this house.

And the other thing that had happened—the kisses, the words that had pierced her heart with painful sweetness. She shivered. Had he merely been trying to pry the truth out of her so he could thwart her plans? The moment had seemed so real, almost as if he'd really cared for her. Better than a fairy tale—more magical, more wonderful.

She could feel the tears drying stickily on her cheeks, and she rolled onto her side. She was frightened, but she would just have to be strong—not for herself, but for the cause. There would certainly be no help forthcoming from Ezekiel Malloy. But she would hide this fugitive, even if Zeke had her hauled off to prison for it.

Even if he tried to tempt her into giving the game

away with his kisses and his seductive words.

Helping that runaway was the right thing to do. The honorable thing to do. And Liberty Brooks was not a woman to be scared off so easily.

Chapter 10

The busy days slipped like water through Liberty's fingers, and before she quite knew what was happening, it was the afternoon of the Fourth of July. Millie was waiting with feverish anticipation in the front parlor when Liberty arrived. Millie adored a party more than anything, and she was dying to see what Madame Cécie had done with the dress for Liberty. She rushed up the carpeted stairway to her bedroom, Liberty following with a mixture of curiosity and dread.

Millie's taste in furnishings, as in all else, ran to the luxuriant, if not the baroque. Her bed was huge, draped with sugar pink silk hangings and enormous silk cabbage roses. Rich swaths of lace filtered the light through the large windows. Gilt cherubs, pink ribbons, and glass jars of powders and perfumes abounded, and Liberty privately thought Millie's bedroom looked rather the way she imagined a bordello might.

On the bed was a large packet wrapped in paper. Liberty took a deep breath, sat on the edge of the mattress, and slowly, carefully untied the string and unfolded the crisp white paper. She lifted a soft mass of pale batiste from the wrappings and drew her breath sharply. She hadn't realized that Madame Cécie would do so much to change the gown. The fabric was the same—nearly transparent and as soft as a whisper—but Madame had added a

134

sprinkling of meticulously crafted embellishments, including headily perfumed silk roses.

Millicent squealed with pleasure. "It turned out simply *perfect*! You'll be ravishing." Liberty quickly stepped out of her timeworn things, and Millicent rushed about the room, making preparations and assembling her creams and powders. First came a long, hot bath with milk and rosewater. Millicent pulled a fine cambric chemisette and pantaloons from the dressmaker's package, and Liberty reveled in the softness and purity of the sheer fabric against her skin. She pulled the teal silk stockings over her legs and slipped her feet into a pair of soft suede pumps decorated with large blue-red roses. Millie lent her a pair of modest eardrops set with pink pearls and glittering aquamarines.

Millicent held up the tiny corset covered with pale rose satin embroidered with birds and roses.

"Not that implement of torture!" Liberty squeaked. "It nearly killed me during the fittings."

Millicent only laughed as she slipped the impossibly small garment over Liberty's torso, pulling and coaxing her already slender waist into an eminently fashionable seventeen inches. Over the corset came a crinoline and endless sets of petticoats— flannel stiffened with horsehair, calico stiffened with starch and straw, and four skirts of light cotton. Millie curled and ironed Liberty's hair mercilessly into an elegant braided twist held in place by a gold net tucked with fragrant baby roses and tiny black velvet bows.

Finally the dress was pulled over the transformed creature, Millie's maid making a few expert tucks to bring the bodice snugly against the tiny corseted waist. The layers of batiste fluttered with the slightest movement. One sheer flounce lay nearly weightless atop another, building a color that was both delicate and rich, setting off Liberty's smooth golden skin. The dress was cut low, partially exposing a flawless pale back, ripe breasts, and shoulders that seemed to have been sculpted in marble. The fit was very tight through the torso, escaping at the waist into a flurry of flounces like a scattering of pear blossoms. The sleeves were full, gathered into soft bunches just above the elbow with the same small bows, with deep, flowing cuffs framing Liberty's hands. Millicent abandoned the white rice powder she'd intended to use on her cousin, and merely pinched Liberty's cheeks to bring out deep pink roses.

Millie turned Liberty around to see herself in the mirror. Liberty already felt a little faint from the corset, but the view made her positively weak in the knees. Instead of the plain, severe girl she faced in the mirror every morning, she now saw a beautiful, curvaceous woman. A sweep of bare, perfumed bosom and shoulders narrowed to a tiny waist. The many layers of transparent fabric, although perfectly modest, made her look as if she were clothed in nothing but mist and clouds. "Oh, Millie, I can't. I mean, I just, oh, I can't."

Millicent looked at Liberty, slightly jealous but stunned by the luminous beauty she had created. "Jeepers, Lib, you're perfect. You're just perfect!" And she began to prod her cousin toward the wide marble staircase.

The musicians had been playing for nearly an hour when the two came downstairs, their belled skirts seeming to float down the circular stairway. The ballroom was filled with elegantly dressed, laughing guests. Millicent had chosen a patriotic costume—a deep blue tight-fitting jacket of watered silk littered with silver star-shaped spangles, with a sumptuously wide skirt of red-and-white-striped taffeta. A pert tricorn hat waving red, white, and blue ostrich feathers perched on top of her golden curls.

But it was Liberty the room turned to stare at.

Her dress was less flamboyant than Millicent's, and her cousin had been right—the numerous flounces would have made Millie look like nothing so much as a lovely doll. But the gown set off Liberty's taller stature and golden complexion to perfection, the pale batiste fluttering like a shower of butterflies. Not a few men had difficulty taking their eyes from the lush curves of her throat and bosom, so delicately perfumed with rosewater.

Millicent bustled purposefully about, Liberty in tow, making a beeline for Jack Blodgett, who argued forcefully with several other men. Liberty demurely tried to steer Millie away from the captain, but the girl would have none of it, drifting prettily to the sidelines of Blodgett's circle.

"The damned immigrants are ruining the country," Blodgett said gruffly. "The only thing to do with 'em is flush 'em out, like any other kind of vermin—rats, niggers, or otherwise."

Liberty stiffened wordlessly, willing herself not to read the man the riot act right here in the ballroom.

"Jack, darling," Millicent gushed, tired of waiting for the men to notice her. "You do remember my dear cousin Liberty Brooks, don't you? I've convinced her to join our little soirée this evening."

"Captain Blodgett," Liberty said coolly. She had never mentioned her run-in with Blodgett to Millie, wishing to avoid what would only be an uncomfortable situation.

A lime green velvet waistcoat showed from beneath Blodgett's cutaway, and an embroidered peach and sky blue silk cravat was held in place by a sapphire stickpin. He smelled of his usual rum and stale tobacco. Again Liberty was startled by the color of his eyes—the color she imagined a lion's might be.

Those predatory golden eyes met her gaze unflinchingly as he replied in a deep, almost hypnotic voice, "Miss Brooks, I am enchanted." He kissed her hand gallantly, holding her perfumed fingers a trifle too long to be purely respectable. Still, he made no reference to their previous meeting. It seemed that Millie didn't know Jack was wandering the streets of Boston proposing to women he scarcely knew. Liberty was not at all sure she was glad to be in complicity with Jack Blodgett over anything, even so ridiculous a secret.

Millicent gave a high-pitched little laugh. "Sea captains—they're perfectly incorrigible." She gripped Liberty's elbow and steered her to another section of the room, smiling and waving her tiny painted fan.

Millie covered her mouth coyly as she hissed, "Just *what* did you think you were doing?"

Liberty looked dumbfounded. "What did I do? Did you want me to be rude to him? Honestly, Mil, I don't even like the man."

"Well, you must have done *something*. The way he kissed your hand was positively indecent. I didn't lend you that dress so you could throw yourself at every man who looks at you sideways."

Liberty straightened her shoulders. "Millicent Goodall, you take that back this instant or I shall walk out of this room and never speak to you again."

Millicent smiled tightly and blew a kiss across the room to Blodgett, waving adorably. "Oh, all right," she grumbled from behind her fan, "I'm sorry, then. But try not to seem so interested in my young men, will you please?"

"You are more than welcome to your young men, if that vulgarian is any example. Really, Millie, what can you have been thinking to invite him? If he utters a single word to the abolitionist guests, your father's party will be a disaster."

Millie frowned. "The captain is so utterly captivating, he'll simply charm our guests to death."

"Not if you let him go on about the 'vermin and niggers,' he won't," Liberty said. She wondered if Millie even knew what an abolitionist was. "At any rate, managing the captain is your problem. Since you have dragged me to this dreadful party, do you intend to allow me to mix with your guests, or shall we stand in the corner and hiss at one another all evening?"

Millicent looked a little wounded at this, but floated on to drag Liberty to another elegant clutch.

Liberty, recovering her composure, surreptitiously scanned the party, hoping she wasn't too obviously searching someone out. She smiled graciously at Uncle Harry's booming compliments as he introduced her to a group of handsome and bored-looking young men. A red-haired fellow with a dashing mustache immediately asked her to dance. She agreed, a little shyly, and they started off on a rollicking reel. They were both rather breathless when the dance was over, and she was doubly so when he gallantly said, "Miss Brooks, I'll have you know you are the most utterly delightful woman in the room."

Liberty blushed a bit and smiled, not knowing quite what to say, when another equally dashing young man, blond and broad-shouldered, with sweet sky blue eyes, asked for the next dance. She laughed and ran off with him, waving apologetically to her first gentleman.

She was barely able to catch her breath before others, young and silver-haired alike, swept up to glide her out onto the floor again. Aided by just enough champagne to keep her from being tongue-tied, she flirted outrageously, not knowing she had even known how. The champagne and the dancing had brought a delicious warmth to her cheeks, and her curls brushed bewitchingly around her face and neck.

When Captain Blodgett asked her to dance, she

stammered that she was exhausted and that perhaps he might ask her again a little later in the evening. His response was simply to grasp her wrist in one large hand and nearly drag her onto the ballroom floor.

"You're exquisite tonight, I'm sure you know," he said to her as they wheeled around at an almost sickening speed.

His hips were pressed daringly close against hers, and she struggled to maintain a decent distance. "How kind of you to say so, Captain." She recoiled from the sour smell of rum and from his clumsy, overbearing grasp.

"Have you reached a decision?" he asked abruptly, pressing his lips against her ear. "I'm burning for you, Liberty. I can hardly wait to make you my own."

Appalled by his lack of concern for privacy or propriety, she hated being forced to decline him in the middle of a crowd, but she also realized he would be less likely to make a scene in the midst of this elegant group. "I have, Captain. I'm afraid I am far too attached to my work to enter into marriage right now. It wouldn't be fair to you or to my work. I am so terribly sorry." She forced herself to look over his shoulder at the whirling room rather than face those unnatural eyes.

He stepped incautiously on her toe, almost as if in punishment, and the sharp pain sent a hot rush of tears to her eyes, nearly making her curse aloud. His face was a brittle, angry mask. "Don't be foolish, my dear. I never had any intention of asking you to give up your work. I find your projects an indispensable part of your charm."

She forced a smile she did not feel. All this spinning around was beginning to make her quite nauseated. "No, really, I'm terribly sorry, Captain, but I quite prefer the life of a spinster. Of course, I was honored by your offer," she added hastily.

He stopped in the middle of a turn, the music still playing, and stalked away from her, leaving her startled and confused in the melee of dancing couples. She looked around, her face flushed with embarrassment. A grateful young man instantly took advantage of the unexpected opportunity and stepped forward to whirl her around the ballroom at a more seemly pace.

After three more dances she truly was exhausted, and she escaped to a side hall where the music and laughter seemed far away. Parched, and still a trifle shaken from the unpleasant encounter with Blodgett, she wondered if she dared venture out for a lemonade. She decided she was eminently safer in her newfound hiding place.

From a nearby shut-off parlor, she could just make out a pair of voices: Millie's high-pitched chirp, now rather shrill, and Jack Blodgett's throaty rumble. She winced, wondering how she could ever explain Blodgett's awkward behavior away to her cousin. Wait—what was he saying to Millie? Had he decided to tell her the truth, now that he had Liberty's answer?

Overcome with curiosity, Liberty fitted herself into a small nook behind a large fern, bunching her crinolines around her as best she could. If she pressed her ear to the wall, she found she could hear their conversation quite clearly.

"Jack-bunny, if I didn't know better, I'd think you'd been ignoring me," Millie simpered.

"Millie-silly, how can you say that?" he asked reproachfully. "It wounds me that you could even question my undying devotion."

"I'm pleased you and my cousin get along so nicely. My dress is awfully becoming on her, don't you think, darling? The color makes her look a trifle less sallow."

"She's very sweet, of course. But we must feel a bit sorry for her, turtledove, for having to be seen next to you. She's quite presentable, but she can hardly compare with you. She is but a flighty girl; you are a beautiful woman. She has no drama, no finesse! Whereas you, O mistress of my soul, you have the grace and pride of Diana."

Liberty scowled at the familiar words. At least he might have come up with something a bit less hackneyed.

"Jack Blodgett, you're flattering me," Millie said. "No one's looked at me twice all evening; everyone's simply throwing themselves at my cousin. I do hope she doesn't embarrass herself by doing something indiscreet. She's terribly unsophisticated, you know. It's to be expected, of course. What does a half-breed country girl know about life in the big city? Still, ever since she got rid of those freckles, I think she has a certain prettiness."

"Fishwife! She's a common fishwife, my moppet, next to you. Your infinite refinement makes her seem a rough, unmannerly wench."

"Now, darling, we must be charitable," Millie replied, sounding pleased and relieved.

"Of course we must. And, after all, it must be comforting to you to have such a giantess about to protect you. She quite towers over the other ladies. I declare, she's better protection than any man."

Liberty heard the two laugh. She was too accustomed to Millie's sugar-coated barbs to be very wounded, and she understood Blodgett well enough now to know that she had never heard him speak the truth on any occasion, including this one.

There was a silence, and Liberty wondered if they might not be kissing. Ashamed of herself for eavesdropping, she moved to step away from her hiding place, when Millie suddenly asked, "Darling, when do you think you can have those papers together to show my father? I'm simply dying to be your wife, but of course, unless my father's satisfied with your financial stability, well, there's simply no question."

"Oh, plumcake, I *am* a beast to keep us waiting, but my attorney has a number of items to sort out before I can prudently open my books to anyone, even my esteemed future father-in-law. I'm an exceedingly wealthy man, my dove, and I look after that wealth with care and caution."

"I'd hardly have thought caution to be your primary virtue, Captain." Millie's voice was pure honey.

"Ah, with finances only, my sweetmeat. With you, I am a savage beast. How eager am I to be struck down by Cupid's arrow, to be brought to your feet, tamed and gentle, my savagery replaced by the golden yoke of matrimony."

Millie's laugh was no less charming for being carefully practiced. "Oh, darling, if only it weren't for my horrid papa and his dreary insistence on the details of your finances. It's rather like Romeo and Juliet, isn't it? Terribly tragical and romantic."

"How like my sensitive little duckling to discover such an apt comparison. It is precisely like Romeo and Juliet. With one important exception. This play will end in marriage."

Liberty moved away before she thought she would be physically ill. She'd known Blodgett was a buffoon; that much had become clear. But she hadn't realized what a complete charlatan he was. She doubted he had one tenth the money he claimed. And why was he so eager to marry? It obviously wasn't to procure a dowry—Liberty didn't have a penny to her name, which was perfectly obvious to Blodgett. Still, she couldn't believe he had any decent motive. His methods were designed to deceive, and she wanted to know what he was hiding. Millie might have her flighty and self-centered side, but she hardly deserved to be shackled to that deceitful boor.

"My, my, it seems that my secretary is full of surprises," came a deep, soft voice from behind her.

Liberty's heart leapt into her throat, and suddenly she felt unable to move. She willed herself to start breathing again and turned around with what she hoped was a composed expression.

"Mr. Malloy, how delightful. I'm so glad you were able to come."

"So am I, now that I'm here," he drawled, casting his eyes over the expanse of shoulder and bosom revealed by her fashionable gown. Liberty felt a hot blush come to her face. "Taken to creeping around in the shadows, have you?" he continued. "Perhaps your . . . *friend* has not been the paragon of virtue you'd thought?"

"Mr. Malloy, really, you do me an injustice. I was just admiring this lovely fern, and on such a charming pedestal. It quite lights up this corner, don't you agree? And the fronds, they're so . . . well curled."

"When I hear Liberty Brooks spouting such nonsense, I know something's amiss," he replied. "Still, my dear, you quite look the part this evening. I had a notion that behind all that starch was a beautiful, idiotic female waiting to come out."

"Why, Mr. Malloy, what a perfectly horrid thing to say." Liberty managed to extricate herself from behind the fern, glancing around to see if anyone else had caught her eavesdropping.

Zeke took her rather roughly by the hand. "I do hope you can spare your employer a dance? Especially as he taught you how." His eyes gleamed.

Liberty pulled her hand away as roughly as he had taken it. Really, he was the most irritating man she had ever met. "Certainly, Mr. Malloy," she snapped primly. "How could I refuse?"

He led her back to the ballroom, his hand on her waist. Her heart pounded relentlessly, and she felt strangely dizzy. Perhaps she had had a bit too much of the champagne. She gingerly rested one hand on his broad shoulder and placed the other in the warmth of his palm. The musicians were playing a languid waltz, and he gently drew her closer to him as they danced. It was as if his body spoke to hers, forceful, yet drawing a willing reaction from her as the two whirled around the room.

The fairy-tale feelings washed over her again at the touch of his arms around her. The subtle language of his body seemed strangely familiar, this unholy marriage of waists and hips and thighs. His summer green eyes penetrated her as they danced, asking some question she could not fathom. She found her hand curled intimately around his shoulder as their hips pressed more closely together to whisper secret, forbidden murmurings. It seemed they danced for hours that way; perhaps they did. When they stopped, too soon, Liberty did not feel like tossing him a gracefully flippant remark but continued to meet his eyes unwaveringly, a little lost in their depths.

She was a beauty, Zeke realized anew. He would never get used to how beautiful she was when she shed the brittle, hard-nosed shell she so often affected. How could such a golden creature—half-wild even in that utterly civilized gown—transform herself every morning into a model of joyless virtue? And why would she? A woman so lovely, even a penniless one, could have married a man who would give her every luxury her heart might desire.

Unless she had her heart set on Jack Blodgett. Zeke felt the name grate on his consciousness. Was she in love with that unscrupulous bastard?

He was a fool to have danced with her this way. He was too susceptible to the way her eyes flashed up at him, to the soft little chestnut tendrils that were kissing her cheek even now. She was too wild, too willful for this upright city—a natural voluptuary forced to rein in her passions with a false front of perfect, unimpeachable respectability. But a glass or two of wine unleashed the untamed creature within, a creature of passion and darkness. She was all that was magnificent—and lethal—in a woman.

And that magnificence made her vulnerable. Her own passions could become her worst enemy. They'd apparently made her prey to Blodgett's oily flattery. Her passions had no honest place here in Boston, where women turned themselves to their stitching, their children, and their church, leaving only a dutiful submissiveness for their husbands. Did Liberty fancy that by hiding in somber costumes of black and gray, she could escape the fate nature had decreed her?

Zeke was insane to involve himself with her. She was a traitor, Delilah ready with the shears. But he knew her now, knew what kind of woman she was. And that knowledge would give him a new power over her—a power that just might match her disturbing influence over everything he thought and did.

He took her hand in his and led her out to the conservatory, cool and fragrant with trailing honeysuckle. Massive ferns hung from moss baskets, their fronds draping coyly. Potted orchids graced one shelf, pink, white, and purple blooms vying for attention. The air was pleasantly damp and smelled of green, growing things. Huge jungle plants, ten or twelve feet tall, towered over them—concealing a pair of watchful, predatory yellow eyes.

Zeke was silent. Liberty looked at him, puzzled.

"You seem to have gotten over being angry with me," she said, hoping she would not trigger another stormy outburst.

"I'm sorry about that," he said, not sounding sorry at all. "I don't like people meddling in my affairs."

"I wasn't trying to meddle," she insisted. "I was trying to—"

"Hush," he commanded. He laid his fingers on her lips and repeated, more gently, "Hush. Not tonight."

Liberty shivered. The smell of the honeysuckle was filling her with a funny kind of drowsiness, and yet she felt exquisitely aware of every detail around her.

"Cold?" he asked, smiling.

She shook her head. "No, why?"

"You're trembling again. I've told you before, Liberty, you don't need to be frightened of me."

She swallowed hard. "I can't imagine where you get the idea that I'm frightened of you."

"Maybe it's this you're frightened of, then." He took her face in his hands and lowered his lips to hers. His lips brushed hers softly, teasing a low moan from her. He bent to kiss her throat, passing his lips down her neck to her exposed shoulders.

Liberty had never felt so open to another human being, so exposed. He covered her throat with fluttering kisses. She moaned again and dropped her head back when he softly sank his teeth into her. She wanted nothing but to feel this languid heat coursing through her forever. He teased her neck and earlobes with slow, biting kisses before returning to her mouth.

She needed him to kiss her passionately, to be as hungry as she was, but he danced and flirted with her lips, refusing to give himself to her. Each movement of his lips across hers created a secret shuddering within her, a mysterious, dark force she could not control. Almost blind with her passion, she took his head in her hands and pulled him against her.

He pulled back slightly, his eyes shining hungrily in the moonlight. His loins were uncomfortably taut, and he thought with a sudden hot thrill of what it would be like to be buried deep inside her, surrounded by the wet promise of her flesh and the mysterious darkness of her woman's soul. Silently he led her down the narrow wooden back steps behind the conservatory.

Blodgett emerged from his hiding place, his legs sore and stiff from crouching. He muttered an ugly curse under his breath and returned to the party to hunt out another drink. The little whore would pay for his humiliation tonight. He might not be the first to have her, but he would make damned sure Ezekiel Malloy was not the last.

Chapter 11

Zeke led Liberty through the side yard and out to his waiting brougham. She barely noticed the grass wetting her pumps. Jim was nowhere to be seen, probably drinking or playing cards with the other coachmen. "Blast that son of a . . ." Zeke muttered. A smile came to his lips as an alternate plan occurred to him. "Get in," he ordered.

She nodded, mesmerized, wondering why he wanted to go for a drive. The evening coach was spacious, with nearly enough room to stand upright. The seats were covered with dark green thick velvet that was a pleasure to sink into, and she luxuriated in its softness around her exposed nape and shoulders.

He climbed into the coach next to her and again began covering her face, neck, and shoulders with kisses that made her shudder helplessly. She felt a new sense of wickedness. These were not sudden, surprising kisses; they had planned this, had deliberately crept away from the party.

Was this a tryst, then? She worried about what the others were saying, if Uncle Harry had noticed her sneaking off, until Zeke slid his hand over her lisle-robed ankle and let his fingers slowly climb the length of her leg with maddening, circular caresses. She ached with liquid longing, ever hungrier as he inched his way up her calves.

149

A voice deep within her warned that this was a dangerous game. The stakes were high and, once lost, could never be regained. But she couldn't seem to tear herself from this new rush of sensation. The more she tried to resist her feelings, the more strongly she felt the persistent whirlpool tugging at the base of her belly. Eagerly she sought his mouth, hungry to know what he could teach her. He nibbled and teased, their tongues dancing. And in that moment she wished they were a thousand miles from Boston and the need to be respectable.

He slid his hands over her thighs and hips and belly and up to the low bodice of her ballgown, his fingers caressing her through the thin batiste. He nuzzled the swell of her breasts above her stays. A melting heat began to burn in her. "No," she murmured, "don't."

"Don't do this, you mean?" He brushed her breasts with both hands, finding her nipples with his thumbs and bringing them to a humiliating hardness with a single insolent flick.

She gasped. "That isn't fair."

He dipped a hand expertly into her neckline, freeing one breast from the prison of her gown. "Playing fair," he whispered, bending to close his mouth over the now-exposed nipple, "would interfere with winning."

The alarm bells were ringing in Liberty's head again, but she couldn't hear them for the wild charivari taking place in her heart. He suckled her breast, his hands working to free the other. She could think of nothing but that they had been meant for this. His mouth on her and the gentle torment of his hands filled her with something both thrilling and languorous.

He left her breast for a moment to come back to her mouth, kissing her as if she were a sumptuous meal and he a starving man. She strained up to meet him, her hands laced around his head to pull him down against her.

Every sensation seemed magnified. The velvet cushions around her were a sea of voluptuous softness. Her feather light dress weighed on her like iron chains. The air was ice-cold on her wet nipple, puckering it to an even harder tightness.

He took her lower lip and teased it with nibbling bites. She shivered beneath him, caught in wave after wave of shimmering sensation. Her breasts ached tautly, and she arched up to brush them against the smoothness of his jacket.

He groaned and squeezed his eyes shut. "You little witch," he whispered. "Do you have any idea what that does to me?"

"Tell me," she said, shocked by her own brazenness.

He ground his form against her, crushing her beneath him. Everything about him was hard and sinewy. "You make me crazy with wanting you," he said, cupping her breasts in his palms.

Her breathing quickened as he toyed with her nipples again. Pleasure pulsed through her like wet lightning.

He muttered a curse. "You make me so hard, I feel like I could burst." He took one of her hands in his and slid it to the straining stiffness between his legs.

Her heart pounded in her ears as she slid her hands down the length of him, astonished by his size and hardness.

"Oh, God, sweetheart, you're killing me," he said, his voice suddenly choked.

Emboldened by a new sense of power, she slid her cupped hand from the tip of him to the base, feeling his contours clearly through the fine wool of his trousers.

His entire body stiffened. "You'll pay for that," he growled. He bent to take one nipple between his teeth. He closed his mouth over it, sucking as he pushed her skirts up with his hands.

She wrapped her fingers in his hair, wild, hungry. His hands danced over her legs, his thumbs drawing circles on her inner thighs. The sheer fabric of her long pantaloons bunched beneath his fingers.

Slowly he brushed his fingers over the cleft between her legs, and she gasped as a bolt of heat struck her, shooting deep within her womb.

He laughed softly. "I told you you'd pay."

He tormented her with the gentle sweep of his fingers over her. She ached for him to crush her to him, to somehow appease this hunger. But he tantalized instead, building her fever instead of quenching it.

"More," she whimpered, not knowing quite what she hungered for but knowing she was hungry.

He increased the pressure of his fingers by a mere fraction and closed his mouth fiercely over her breast, drawing her nipple between his teeth in a swift, sucking bite.

She cried out softly, and the sound was like a wild rush of wind in her ears.

He gave a low groan as she pressed his head more tightly to her breast, arching her hips to crush them into his tormenting hands.

Suddenly he stopped his maddening movements and cocked his head at the sound of footsteps crunching in the gravel outside.

Footsteps?

Liberty felt her world tilt around her as the carriage began to rock with a sudden, violent motion. Zeke pulled away, sitting bolt upright. Liberty scrambled to arrange her dress as she realized that someone was outside, shaking the carriage. A painful ache, sharp as loneliness, was building in her belly. She trembled with unspent passion as she struggled to tuck herself modestly into her bodice.

"Goddamned bastard!" came an angry shout from outside. "You son of a bitch, Malloy, I'll cut your liver out!" The voice belonged to Jack Blodgett.

Zeke cursed softly. The carriage was dark, but what Liberty could see of Zeke's expression was bitterly angry.

She pulled her skirts back down over her legs, afraid that Blodgett would try to open the carriage door. How long had he been lurking out there? The thought was a little frightening.

"I don't understand—what does he want?"

"Don't you know?" Zeke said coldly.

"What the hell's goin' on in there?" Blodgett screamed. The carriage began to rock sharply back and forth. He was shaking it as if to tumble them out.

"I can't believe he's doing this," Liberty whispered, her heart knocking with fear. She would tell Zeke right now about Blodgett, about his proposal and the way he had lied to Millie. She would tell him that she loathed the pompous scoundrel. But when she opened her mouth to speak, Zeke's eyes were pale and cold, as if he blamed *her* for what was happening.

Zeke scowled. "I'll kill him someday for the times he's made a fool of me."

"Come on out, Malloy, you rich-boy bastard." Jack's voice was wild, insane.

Liberty squeezed her eyes shut. Every single guest at the party was doubtless standing at the top of the steps, peering down at the carriages with intense curiosity, waiting to see who the harlot was who would emerge from Zeke Malloy's brougham.

"Get out," Zeke said roughly.

"I can't," she whispered, panicked. "My hair . . . and my dress . . . Everyone will know."

"You look fine. Just keep your chin up and go on back inside," he said, his voice cold. He twisted the door handle.

"Please, Zeke—I can't. I'm afraid," she said, pleading.

"Of him?"

Liberty nodded.

"He won't hurt you. It's me he's after." His eyes were as sharp as broken glass. "Now, go."

She took a deep breath, gave her hastily straightened bodice one last glance, and stepped out of the carriage. Miraculously, no one was there to witness her shameful emergence. Blodgett alone was slumped over a low wall, his face twisted into an ugly sneer. She ran past him and up the stairs, trembling. He said nothing, and he did not try to follow her.

She jumped, startled, as the sky above her exploded in showers of green, purple, and gold. If she hadn't been so miserable, she would have laughed aloud. Of course—fireworks. Everyone would be on the front lawn watching the display.

The steep climb up the back stairs and the pinch of her dancing pumps barely slowed her down. Her whole being ached, the earlier voluptuous hunger now transformed to a throb of frustration. She made her way to Millie's bedroom to recover, squeezing her wide skirts up the back servant's stairs on the off chance that someone was still in the house to witness her disarray.

She sat in front of Millie's mirror, her reflection wreathed in the lace and ribbons draped over the glass. A stormy cloudiness shadowed her eyes. Her carefully tucked chestnut curls spilled out from the golden net, and she had lost most of the little velvet bows. The dress, which had seemed so fashionable before, now seemed to reveal a shocking amount of bare skin.

She blushed. How could she have let Millie convince her to cavort half-dressed around the ballroom? Just look what it had gotten her—assaulted like a fancy woman in a carriage.

The thought sent a wicked thrill shivering down her spine. Half of her yearned for her studied propriety, longed to climb back into her gray wool and pull her hair tight into its spinsterly bun. But the other half of her—the half that had run as free as the wind back home in Ohio—was almost pleased at this newfound sinfulness.

If only Zeke weren't so savagely angry. It really did seem unfair. He took her by surprise and forced his kisses on her, then seemed to be angry with *her*.

She began to rearrange her hair, settling for something simpler than the elaborate construction Millie had erected, letting the curls fall to frame her face.

Had Zeke really forced his kisses on her? she asked herself honestly. She studied the face in the mirror. It was less the face of a terrorized virgin than one of a shameless, wanton lover.

Blushing at her own immodesty, she threw a thin shawl over her arms. It was an insubstantial trifle, but it covered her throat and shoulders and made her feel more respectable. But even as she covered herself, she knew the respectability was an illusion. The buttery silk caressed her bare skin like a kiss, soft and smooth on the tender flesh where Zeke's lips had been just moments before. She gave a little shiver, cast one more quick look in the mirror, and took a deep breath to calm the butterflies of frustration in her stomach. When she floated back down the stairs to the party, her expression was that of perfect calm.

Most of the younger people were saying their good-byes, off to other parties, other dances. Millie's father had invited only a few to dinner, those people who would impress his partner and the man's antislavery wife. Now that the crinolined gowns had squeezed out the wide front door, Liberty noticed some of the older, more sober guests who had been sipping lemonade on the sidelines.

She was freshly conscious of her décolletage. The exquisite ball gown had pleased Millie's young, fashionable friends, but the group assembling for dinner was considerably more modest. The women still seated in the Goodalls' uncomfortable chairs were swathed tightly to their chins, their hard buckram stays making them look as solid as iron girders.

Liberty took a nervous glance around for Zeke and pulled the shawl up onto her shoulders. He was invited to dinner—was one of the centerpieces of the evening, she knew. She fanned herself nervously, promising herself she would face him coolly. No one would see the desire in her eyes.

There was a clatter from the kitchen, and Millie came sailing out, her color high, a bright smile plastered to her face. "Oh, this room really is so frightfully big!" she gushed, scooping up a stiff-looking balding man as she made her way across the ballroom floor. "Let's move to the parlor for a few moments until dinner is ready, shall we?"

The guests trudged dutifully to the parlor, and Millie flitted about the room, making introductions. The balding man with the prodigious nose was Bronson Alcott, who had brought his sad-faced daughter Louisa with him. Maria Child, a plump woman in russet who looked quite like an attractive little hen, sat talking amiably with an elegant man and his fragile, sharp-eyed wife— Wendell and Ann Phillips. The woman in stiff scarlet taffeta, whose color and disagreeable expression reminded Liberty of a boiled lobster, was Harriet Beecher Stowe, whose serialized story "Uncle Tom's Cabin" had been making such a splash this year. The fat man who wheezed was Harry's partner, Harlon Redburne, with his slim, redheaded wife, Jane, who was dressed in forest green with black silk epaulets. Zeke Malloy had disappeared completely, as had Captain Blodgett.

Liberty nodded in recognition to Jane Redburne, who was fixing her with a purposeful look. Liberty fiddled with the fringes of her shawl. Any other evening would have found her gawking in awe at this gathering of notables. She had always thought of writers as living in some rarified sphere, having nothing to do with average people like herself. Yet here these people were, all eminently mortal, and she was absorbed in her own private drama.

She looked down at her gloved hands and tried to think of something sensible to say.

"Mrs. Stowe," she began, trying for an intelligent tone, "your story in the *National Era* has been positively gripping. Wherever could you have found the inspiration?"

Harriet sat a fraction straighter, her angry expression softening slightly. "It's terribly wrenching, isn't it? I think I must be inspired by God to tell the story of the pathetic, wretched things."

Maria chided her from across the cluttered parlor. "They're not so wretched as all that, Harriet. Let them have their dignity, after all."

"I give my characters the full dignity they deserve," Harriet said, her plump bosom heaving a bit.

"Even you have to admit, you've depicted a rather pitiful bunch," Maria said a trifle acidly.

Wendell Phillips hurried to make peace between the two. "Oh, they have great dignity. Pathos as well, of course, but I think Harriet grants them their dignity."

"A slave's dignity is like a schooner at the docks of discontent," Bronson Alcott said in slow, measured tones.

Liberty wondered if she had heard him properly, but a glance at the annoyed faces around the room revealed that Mr. Alcott made this sort of peculiar statement fairly regularly.

"Well, of course I do," Harriet huffed, arranging the scarlet ruffles of her dress. "The Negroes are so naturally childlike, so much like Jesus. I find them terribly inspiring."

A door slammed, and Zeke Malloy swooped into the room, nearly crashing into poor Mr. Alcott, who seemed to be musing on something with his eyes closed. Zeke's clothes were immaculate, but his right cheek was grazed, as if he had fallen.

Liberty felt herself blush from head to toe. So he had shown up after all. She looked at his strong, elegant hands. The thought of his sinful, feathery touch pushed its way into her mind, no matter how fiercely she tried to banish it. She hoped everyone simply thought her a silly, shy dolt, and didn't guess at the real reason she had gone bright pink.

A moment later Blodgett came in, his lip faintly swollen. Liberty was scandalized as she looked from one man to the other. They had been fighting. The two bristled visibly in each other's presence and removed themselves to opposite corners of the room, yellow eyes and green shooting daggers back and forth.

Though Zeke was plainly familiar to the assembled guests, only Liberty could tell he was agitated; to the rest he seemed the model of easy charm. He murmured his greetings to Wendell, Maria, and Harriet, and kissed young Louisa's hand. Millie rushed to introduce Blodgett around as the bell was rung for dinner.

The Goodalls' beaky, ancient butler served, helped by two of the maids. All of Harry's female servants were remarkably pretty—Patsy had gingery hair and wide-spaced blue eyes, and German Mary was as blond as a butter cookie. Liberty noticed that Blodgett swallowed appreciatively as the diminutive Mary reached past him.

The dishes appeared in a steady stream from the kitchen: tiny golden quails propped up almost as if in flight; thin slices of veal arranged in the shape of roses; puff pastry gondolas filled to the brim with morels, rowing on a sea of creamy pink salmon puree; little brightly colored pagodas made of roast beef and truffles and spring onions. Everything was arranged in some clever shape, and everything was drenched in rich sauces.

Harriet Stowe squealed with delight. "Mrs. Goodall, what a charming table you set!"

"As welcome as a crystal ball to a midshipman," Bronson added.

"Yes, Aunt Lucinda, this is . . . astonishing," Liberty managed. Perhaps she could drown the strange restlessness she felt in the extravagant meal—if she could bring herself to swallow anything.

"Astonishing," Zeke repeated dryly.

Liberty dared a glance at him. He was surveying the table with one of his maddening, dismissive expressions. He caught her eyes, pinning her with a penetrating stare. Flustered, she dropped her gaze.

"Alfonso is a godsend. Our new chef, you know," Lucinda said, smirking slightly. "He's so clever. A perfect terror, of course. The other servants have completely stopped speaking to him. But he's well worth the trouble."

When Patsy and Mary had brought the last dish in, the group began to eat. Even if Liberty had developed an appetite for the peculiar dishes, her tight-laced corset would have kept her from indulging it. She noticed that Louisa, whose stays were unfashionably loose for a nineteen-year-old girl, had piled her plate high. Louisa's father looked disgruntled, taking for himself only a few of the hot dinner rolls and some of the less-elaborately sauced vegetables.

The butler himself poured the wine, as if the task were too exalted to be left to pretty immigrant girls. He began with Harry and Lucinda, then made his way around the table. Wendell turned his glass upside down, declining to drink, and Ann followed his example. Harriet, next to Ann, did the same, as did Maria. Many of the abolitionists also worked for temperance.

The butler, unperturbed, came to Liberty. She looked over at Zeke. He stared at her with something resembling amusement. The scrape on his cheek belied the elegance of his flawless cravat and beautifully cut coat, but he somehow looked the way he always did—carelessly graceful. She thought of the way his voice had broken when she'd touched him. He lifted one eyebrow in surprise as she tilted her chin and let the butler fill her glass with vintage Burgundy.

Jane Redburne refused the wine, although her husband, Harlon, accepted it. Millie, caught up in some private conversation with Jack Blodgett, hadn't noticed the flurry of temperance around the table, and the butler filled her glass unnoticed. Blodgett, touching his napkin to his slightly swollen lip, motioned that the old man should fill his glass to the top. Louisa, after her father shot her a look, turned her glass upside down, as did Bronson. Zeke caught Liberty's gaze as his glass was filled, his eyes a mixture of ice and hungry fire.

She blushed and looked away. He had addled her completely. She glanced down at her shawl, making sure it covered her bosom. Here was a rare opportunity to meet her idols on an equal footing—the great thinkers and writers and reformers of Boston, for whom temperance and abolition went hand in glove—but she hadn't been able to bring herself to look like a prude in front of Zeke.

"So what is it you folks do—play at antislavery, is it?" Jack Blodgett thundered, thumping his wineglass onto the table.

Liberty wished she could sink into the floor. Was the man drunk? Why, why had Millie invited him here tonight? He would embarrass himself and everyone else.

If only he would keep a discreet silence about Liberty's flushed emergence from Zeke's brougham. She remembered with a shudder the humiliating smudge of boot polish across his cheek as Blodgett had clasped her ankles in his office, and fleetingly wondered if he could prove dangerous as well as dishonest. She caught Zeke's thinly veiled expression of contempt at Blodgett's words.

Wendell Phillips pursed his lips and met Blodgett's challenge. "I take it you do not yet support the antislavery cause."

"Bunch of damnable fanatics. Pardon my language, m'dear," he muttered in deference to Millie, whose color had begun to rise.

"We do what we must to serve Jesus our Lord," Harriet puffed, outraged. "There is no shame in being fanatical in the service of Christ."

"The hand of God is like the whispering of the moon," Bronson Alcott said, nodding sagely. His daughter put her hand on his arm to quiet him as Wendell shot him an annoyed look.

"Better to serve the Lord by staying home and taking care of your husbands," Blodgett shot back, his face creased in an oily smile.

Ann Phillips spoke up, her eyes blazing as her pale, thin hands shook. "My husband is very well taken care of, I assure you, sir. And he does the work of a righteous man in fighting the despicable crime of slavery."

"What you do-gooders inevitably fail to understand . . ." Blodgett continued, warming to his subject. Millie shot him a look that could have felled a rabid bear. He ignored her. " . . . is that the nigger is not what you and I would consider a human being. They have their uses, I'll grant you, and they can be fine folks, real good-hearted, but they would never survive a day out of slavery. They need a white man to take care of them."

If Zeke's eyes had been knives, they would have cut Jack Blodgett to pieces.

"I say, Blodgett," Millie's father said, reddening. The table had gone painfully quiet. "That's a little blunt, eh? I think we've heard quite enough on the subject."

"They may be inferior," sputtered Harriet, "but that is a cruel and wicked reason for abusing them."

"Look at your northern niggers," Blodgett said, ignoring the glowers around him. He took a deep swig of wine. "Dirty, shiftless, can't keep a job. Was it really any favor taking them out of slavery?"

Liberty's blood boiled. She took a swallow of wine to try to ease the tightness in her throat, but it only fueled her anger. The man was stupid, hopelessly ineducable. Still, the words were there in her throat and had to be spoken. "And I suppose the failure of Negroes in the North is entirely due to their alleged inadequacies and has nothing whatsoever to do with the way they are treated by larger society?" Her voice was uncompromisingly harsh as she sought to put this barbarian in his place.

Maria, next to Liberty, jumped in. "Hired for the most demeaning work, paid a pittance, kept out of the better schools—is it any wonder they're poor and unhappy?"

"Why don't the rich niggers help 'em, then?" Blodgett said. "I don't see that fancy mulatto boy Douglass building any nigger schools. The only reason he got where he did was the white blood in his veins."

"Frederick Douglass has done a great deal to—" Maria began, outraged.

Zeke interrupted her. "That's your solution, then?" he said to Blodgett, so quietly that Liberty had to strain to hear him. "Masters should rape the prettiest slave girls to mix some of that precious white blood in with the black race?" His eyes flashed with murderous fire, the pupils no larger than the head of a pin.

Liberty blanched. It was hard to imagine a less seemly topic for dinner conversation than miscegenation and rape.

Blodgett met Zeke's stare with a crazy smile. "No, sir. I don't hold with white men fatherin' bastards off of apes."

Zeke's enforced calm exploded as he leapt to his feet, overturning his glass of wine. It stained the white tablecloth and trickled in a blood-colored stream to the floor. Harriet and Louisa gave a little scream as Zeke pulled Blodgett from his chair and hauled him like a rag doll to the center of the room.

Before she knew what she was doing, Liberty found herself between them. "Stop it, both of you!" she hissed. "This is disgraceful. You're behaving like animals."

"You weren't so proper when fancy-britches here had his hand down your dress," Blodgett spat.

Liberty gasped. "Captain Blodgett, I'm quite sure I don't know what you're talking about," she managed, her face scarlet. "You're quite insufferably drunk, and I think you should leave immediately." The blood pounded in her ears.

"I wasn't good enough for you, but Malloy is, is that right?" he slurred, his alcohol-soaked breath stinging her eyes.

"Liberty!" Millie cried, shocked. "What is he talking about?"

Liberty pulled away from the two men, wishing she could disappear like a conjurer's rabbit. "You're not making any sense, Captain. Please leave."

He shrugged off Malloy's grip on his lapels and threw the table one last hostile glare. "I *will* leave. Who wants to have his dinner ruined by a pack of stuffed-shirt fools? You can all go straight to Hell."

"Jack!" Millie shouted, tears filling her eyes as he stormed out of the dining room, his boots clattering in the hallway. Shaking with frustration, she brought her foot down in an angry little stamp and ran after him. Harry immediately took off after his daughter, anxious to protect her from this obviously unsavory, if not outright insane, ruffian. Lucinda threw up her hands, gave a little wail, and escaped to the haven of her room.

Liberty found herself standing on the carpet with Zeke Malloy while a table of nonplussed dinner guests stared at them. Zeke gave her a strange, penetrating look.

She turned away from him. If she kept looking into his eyes, she'd dissolve into tears. She would try to repair the situation with him in the morning, to explain about Blodgett's rantings, but for now, there was a ruined dinner party to patch up. "Please allow me to apologize for the captain," she said, fighting to keep the quaver from her voice. "He was quite obviously drunk, but there can be no excuse for his abysmal rudeness."

Zeke narrowed his eyes. Why was she apologizing for that bastard? It had sounded as if they had parted ways—Blodgett had been jealous and murderously angry—but she still wouldn't let the son of a bitch hang in the breeze. Instead, she made excuses for him, explaining away the ugliness of his words.

The guests at the table fluttered helplessly. "Well, I'm sure I've never met a more disagreeable person," Harriet said, fussing with her taffeta ruffles. "Such language!"

"A garden-variety bigot, I should say," Maria said calmly. "All too common, I'm afraid."

"Agreed, but deuced unpleasant nonetheless," said Wendell.

"The snake of Paradise sheds his skin but once," intoned Bronson to the mystification of all.

"I regret that I must take my leave," Zeke said abruptly. He wouldn't stand here like a moon-struck fool while Liberty Brooks made excuses for Blodgett. "Please accept my profound apologies for losing my temper with the captain. I hope you can forgive me. Good evening." He nodded curtly to the group and disappeared, the ancient butler trotting after him to fetch his hat.

Liberty bit her lower lip distractedly, and turned to the group. "How awful," she said with a nervous smile.

Harry's partner, Harlon Redburne, had begun to wheeze and purple with anger, but Jane was laughing. "An impressive party your uncle has put together," she said to Liberty, wiping her eyes.

Maria laughed with her. "At least the captain didn't have any tomatoes or rotten eggs at his disposal."

"If he had stayed much longer, he might have pitched a quail at one of us," Louisa murmured, blushing when the table erupted with new laughter.

Liberty smiled weakly. Apart from Harriet Beecher Stowe and Mr. Redburne, no one appeared mortally offended. She realized that many of them were probably quite accustomed to meeting rudeness about their beliefs.

"Do you think Uncle Harry will forgive us if we eat some of this food?" Liberty asked, moving back to her chair.

"Lucinda will skin us if we don't," Maria said wryly.

Liberty gave her a grateful smile as the group began to fill their plates and pretend the shocking outburst had never taken place.

Astonishingly enough, the rest of the evening was at least a moderate success. Millie did not rematerialize, and neither did her father. Aunt Lucinda was evidently ensconced in her bedroom upstairs. After tonight's humiliation, she would no doubt stay up there the rest of her days, ringing her little silver bell when it was time to change the cool compresses over her eyes.

Free from Zeke's maddening glower, Liberty shed some of her self-consciousness and entered the conversation around the table. The butler came to her to mumble his discreet questions and announcements, assuming that as nearest kin she would naturally fill in for his employers.

Finally the guests began to make their excuses, and shawls appeared over the taffeta and silk and Louisa's unfashionable calico.

Jane touched Liberty on the elbow, asking, "My dear, shall we give you a lift?"

Liberty gratefully accepted, shuddering at the thought of facing Millie in her cousin's pink and white lair.

Jane lowered her voice, glancing at her husband across the room. "The fugitive arrives tomorrow night," she whispered.

Liberty felt the blood drain from her cheeks. The runaway. How on earth could she have forgotten? "I shan't be able to keep him long," she whispered.

"I know, dear, I know. But we haven't any choice. I shall make other arrangements the very instant it is humanly possible. I am sorry. I know this is terribly awkward for you—" Jane broke off as her husband came to gather her.

"Giving the miss a ride, are we?" he asked jovially. "You've got a good head on your shoulders, girl. Not like that cousin of yours."

Liberty smiled graciously. It was, she had to admit, delightful to be considered the desirable one for a change. "Poor Millie," she said charitably. "Captain Blodgett upset her, that's all. She'll be her old self again in the morning."

"Sounds like that captain's sweeter on you than on her," Redburne wheezed with a wink.

Liberty shivered a bit and pulled the shawl tight around her shoulders. "I'm very much afraid the captain and I don't see eye to eye. He's all Millie's, if she'll still have him."

"The man is an utter boor," Jane said icily. "The child would do best never to speak with him again."

"Hmm, you're probably right," Liberty said, putting any thought of Jack Blodgett from her mind. "Let me collect my things, and we can be off."

She thought of changing her gown, leaving the voluminous pile of batiste with Millie. But she found she wanted to play the part of a wealthy, well-bred young lady for a few more hours. In the morning she would be plain, sturdy Liberty Brooks again, and there would be any number of painful realities to face. Surely there was no harm in extending the charade for the brief drive home.

She took one last look around the dining room. The butler stood stiffly by, ready to show the guests out and begin giving gruff orders to the immigrant girls. Liberty sighed. Her Cinderella evening of glamour and privilege was finished.

And what of the shocking scene in Zeke's carriage? That was a far thornier problem.

Liberty lifted her chin and tucked her shawl protectively around her. She had forgotten herself for a few moments, but she would not make the same mistake again. He'd taken her by surprise, that was all. But she vowed she would never again lose control of herself with Zeke Malloy.

Chapter 12

Jack Blodgett squinted against the bright morning light. He rolled to one side, moaning as a shattering pain exploded against his tightly shut eyelids. Millie sure knew how to throw a party. He ran his tongue across his teeth. They felt furry and tasted sour.

One of these days, he was going to have to stop drinking. Too many mornings like this would put him in the grave. He tentatively tried to pull himself upright, groaned, and sank back into the pillows.

Oh, Christ—he remembered with a sickening shock that Sprigg was coming by this morning. He opened one eye gingerly and squinted at the clock. Nearly ten. Sprigg had been waiting since nine-thirty. Jack almost smiled. The women in this household were beginning to catch on. Six months ago, the maid, Emily, would have tried to wake him up. Now she knew that Sprigg, with his round, gelatinous eyes like hard-boiled eggs, was much easier to deal with than a mean, hung-over Jack Blodgett.

Eggs. He never should have thought of eggs. Fighting the bile rising in his stomach, he fumbled on the bedside table for a cigar. Biting off the end, he lit the tip and relaxed a little as the first puff chased the nausea away. Although it wasn't doing anything for the screaming pain behind his eyes.

Jack swung himself slowly into a sitting position. Not too bad, once his head stopped swimming. He belched, and the vibration sent new spiders of pain scuttling across his skull. He reached for his breeches and pulled them on, not bothering to find a pair of drawers to put underneath. The sickly smell of his own sweat rose in his nostrils, and he quickly put out the cigar, waving away the smoke. When had his stomach gotten so dicey? He must be getting old. You're a disgusting bastard, Jack, he thought, staring at the open buttons of his fly. Can't even convince some brainless woman to marry you.

He gulped down the sickness in his stomach, remembering the night before, that snotty bitch Liberty turning him down with her "of course I was honored by your offer." Then she'd let Zeke Malloy manhandle her.

Christ, he hated that bastard. He hated them both.

What the hell was wrong with her, anyway? Jack was more than good enough for her. He had plenty of money, and he'd made it all himself. His daddy hadn't had a pot to piss in, the miserable old drunk. Too smashed most of the time to do his own job, which was to win at cards. Jack had never met as pitiful a professional gambler as his own father. He could barely remember what his mama looked like. Tired, he thought. She had died when he was still little.

To hell with her for dying. To hell with both of them. They were failures. But Jack was a success.

One thing his daddy had done right was to win that big game against old man Malloy. The stakes were a green-eyed young virgin with skin as smooth and creamy as café au lait. Old Malloy had had the guts to make it big, something his son, Zeke, would never have. Ran a plantation with hundreds of darkies, and he worked 'em plenty hard. He wasn't a softheaded weakling like Zeke. When the old man fathered a kid off of his fancy, he let the brat run around the house for a few years, but he didn't have any qualms about packing her off to another man. Business was business, and anyway, it was probably getting damned embarrassing for the family, having to look after his nigger kid.

Jack shut his eyes, remembering. His own father had wanted Annabelle to cook and clean and to warm his own puke-soaked bed. To hell with that. A night with a beautiful virgin commanded a staggering price in New Orleans. Over the years Jack had made good money peddling Annabelle's charms. Eventually she had financed the business that had, in turn, let him build a big house in Boston and another one in New Orleans, let him buy fancy clothes and the best cigars and all the good rum he could pour down his throat. The good life. In a way, he owed it all to his drunken old man, who had done exactly one thing right in his whole life—won Annabelle off of old man Malloy.

And, he realized, too, he owed it to the cold, beautiful Annabelle, the bitch who had broken his heart.

Jack buttoned his shirt and breathed deeply. He still felt like crap. What he really needed was another drink. Best cure in the world for sour guts.

He gingerly made his way down the stairs, pressing his palms to the sides of his head. His brain felt like it was sloshing around in his skull, and he had a sudden horrible vision of it seeping out through his ears. This meeting with Sprigg was going to have to be quick.

He opened the office door quickly, liking to throw Sprigg off guard whenever possible. The desiccated little man was drumming his fingers against the desk. He looked up, smothering his annoyed expression.

"Stop that goddamned noise," Jack growled.

Sprigg quieted his hands. "I do trust you are well this morning, Captain."

"I feel like the bottom of a piss-pot."

"That's too bad. I won't take up much of your time, then. How is the marriage proposal coming along?"

Jack poured himself a drink. He hated to admit his lack of success to this withered old eunuch. "Not too well. Millie's father insists on looking through the books. And I think I might be in the doghouse with the girl." He winced as he tried to remember the specific details of the night before. What he could remember didn't look good.

"My, that would be rather a problem." Sprigg pushed his spectacles up on his nose. "Perhaps we could create a set of books that would meet with Mr. Goodall's approval. But what of the other young lady, the crusader?"

"I found out she was a half-breed, an Indian," Jack said, taking a swallow of rum. Yes, that helped burn off some of the fog in his head. "I'll be goddamned if I hook up with a woman who ain't white. It's disgusting."

She had turned him down. She didn't want him. She didn't think he was good enough. Christ, his head hurt. He poured another swallow of rum down his burning throat.

"Of course, Captain." Josiah Sprigg bowed his head. He was worried. If this boor couldn't manage to get himself married to someone—anyone— the uncle's fortune would skip to the next in line, and Sprigg would lose a handsome commission. He looked at Blodgett appraisingly. The man was filthy, his clothes were disheveled, and he stank. Sprigg wondered what had gotten into the normally immaculate, if obnoxious, man.

However, the only important thing was that Blodgett pull himself together long enough to convince a woman to marry him. How difficult could that be? He had money, the best bait in the world.

"I shall make the arrangements for a new set of ledgers," Sprigg said, standing. He had wasted a good portion of the morning already, and Blodgett was in no condition to discuss business. "There are some papers for you to sign, and I've brought a new set of blank bills of sale for the next shipment. All you'll need to do is fill in the names and descriptions. You have a shipment going out next week, correct?"

"Week after next," Blodgett muttered, draining the rum. He wished this insect who called himself a man would leave. All he wanted was to crawl upstairs and back into bed. Maybe later that day he'd collar Emily. Nothing too strenuous, just a little release.

He remembered with pleasure the terror in her eyes when he had held a lit candle over her last week, watching the yellow beeswax drip onto her skin. The next day, perfect, shiny round blisters had appeared everywhere the wax had been.

"Week after next," Jack repeated, shaking the distraction from his mind. "Thursday. We've got eight ready, and I got a tip that one of the fugitive ships is leaving next week. I should be able to pick up a few more then. I hate to ship fewer than a dozen at a time. Got to keep the profit margin up."

"Of course, sir, very prudent." Sprigg donned his black silk hat and prepared to leave. "Very well, I shall drop in before you ship off. Good day, sir." He showed himself out, leaving Blodgett alone in his office.

Thursday. Jack hoped Malloy planned to move the runaways before then, to give him a little time to get them settled down before he shipped off. If you shipped them too soon, they got fussy and

wouldn't eat. And a dead slave was worth exactly nothing. But the cargo that was waiting now
wouldn't keep forever either. They could get sick,
or their hides could fester in the damp of the hold.
Sometimes they just up and died, for no reason a
man could see. This business was harder than most
people understood.

Even so, he was glad to be making a run. Boston
was wearing on his nerves. The details of Millie's
party began to seep uncomfortably into the edges
of his memory. It was time to go to New Orleans
for a while, do a little gambling, a little whoring.
He thought of Annabelle, and his throat tightened.
His men had been asking around the city, but there
was still no sign of her. He would have to conduct
his own investigation.

She had to be in the city somewhere—how else
could she live? She only had one marketable skill.
Most whores looked pretty bad by her age, used
up with drink and disease. But Annabelle was as
lovely and fresh as she had been at fifteen. She
should be; he hadn't even sent her out in years,
just kept her at home for himself. He was only at
the New Orleans house for about half the year, and
he paid good money to be sure no one touched her
when he was gone. She had the easiest life of any
slave in the states.

So why had she run away?

Jack knew the reason. She didn't think he was
good enough. She looked at him with those cold
green eyes as if she hated him. He saw those
eyes again every time he saw Zeke damn-it-to-hell
Malloy. Eyes like ice. Eyes that hated to look at a
nothing like Jack Blodgett. Annabelle's voice was
soft, her skin warm, and she knew the moves to
pleasure a man. But her soul was ice-cold.

Annabelle Malloy, a quadroon slave whore,
didn't think Jack Blodgett was good enough for
her. He, who could literally buy a hundred girls

like her. As Jack puffed his cigar and swallowed his rum, one thought throbbed through his head.

Revenge.

Chapter 13

Liberty groaned and pulled the covers tightly under her chin. It was unfair to feel so miserable on such a fine day. The sun streamed through the plants on her windowsill. She propped herself up to watch a squirrel darting along the chestnut tree outside her window.

Her feet ached, her head hurt, and her stomach felt funny. Memories of the night before began to trickle into her consciousness: her daring gown, the smell of honeysuckle, the feeling of Zeke's lips and hands.

She sat upright in bed. How could she possibly face Zeke Malloy today? What on earth could have gotten into her? The dress, the champagne, the flattering gentlemen, all seemed to have released something decidedly wicked inside her. She tried to push the thoughts from her mind—the expression on Zeke's face as he led her down the steps to the waiting brougham, the soft shock of his lips and tongue, the way it had felt when he touched her breasts.

Scandalous.

Uneasiness propelled her to her feet and to the washstand. The water felt cool on her flushed face. At least it was her day off. She would gather her books and go sit in the meadow. Anything to keep from facing him, from looking into those eyes. Anything to keep from thinking about what she had done.

Twenty minutes later, armed with a basket full of books and a few odds and ends for her lunch, Liberty closed the kitchen door behind her. She walked briskly through the orchard and into the cool of the woods. Perhaps the little boy, Tom, would be out today, and she could make friends with him. She would give him some bread and cheese and maybe lend him an alphabet book. She only wished she were feeling better. The champagne, she thought, had made her stomach a bit queasy.

The shack was as empty as it had been before, the wind whistling through the cracks in the walls. Where could the boy and the old man have gone? Why had they been living here on Zeke's property? Perhaps she should ask Zeke about them—he might know where they had gone.

No, she wouldn't ask Zeke Malloy about anything for a little while. She sat at the rickety table and tried to push her thoughts of him into the darkest corner of her mind, to forget that he had kissed her and touched her and made her do those shockingly wanton things.

But had he truly made her? she asked herself again. She thought with a wince of the night she had drunk all that wine and found her hairpins under the table the next morning. After that, she supposed, Zeke had known full well that she was not what she pretended to be. He looked at her the way white men looked at Indian women, the way men had looked at her beautiful mother.

Liberty's half-Indian mother had had little clue to her heritage other than the plaited basket she'd been found in, abandoned on a church doorstep at the edge of town. The minister's wife had taken the baby in, christened her Sarah, and raised her to hold her head high. But when Sarah was grown, even after she'd married John Brooks, men had stared at her and licked their lips and laughed in an ugly way. Despite her delicacy and white-gloved manners, they'd thought of her as an "Injun woman," a cook and a concubine. Such displays had enraged Liberty's father, who would storm and swear all night. But Sarah had lifted her chin, neatly retied her apron, and set about scrubbing the immaculate kitchen or polishing the dustless bookshelves, ignoring John Brook's thundering as if it were entirely beneath her notice.

Liberty lifted her head. She was her mother's daughter, a woman of honor. If Zeke Malloy had unspeakable ideas about her, she would have to shame him into changing his opinion. All she needed was strength and courage—the strength to hold herself as if her spine were made of steel, and the courage to face him down when he turned those lethally green eyes on her.

She sighed and turned herself to the tome in front of her. Last week, after pronouncing himself appalled by her political naïveté, Zeke had insisted she read Rousseau—in the original French, of course—and she was finding the combination of his twisting logic and the resurrection of her rusty French exhausting. "Come on, Liberty," she urged herself aloud. "Keep your mind on what's in front of you."

The door to the cabin flew open, slamming against the wall with a tremendous bang. Liberty leapt from the wobbly little chair, Rousseau sliding to her feet.

Zeke Malloy filled the doorframe, his face stormy. "Just what the hell do you think you're doing here?"

Liberty could feel her heart beating in her throat. She bent down to rescue the book, afraid to meet his eyes. The eyes that had called to her last night, whispering sinful things. "I . . . wanted to get some reading done."

"I spent a tidy sum building Haven House. In the future, you will confine yourself to it when you have reading to do. I must insist you consider this cabin strictly off limits."

Liberty chewed her bottom lip nervously. Really, he was very provoking. After all the chaos of last night, he could think of nothing but issuing unreasonable edicts? "I'm comfortable out here. And I was curious about this place. Do you know who—"

"You will not come here again." He cut her off, his voice low and dangerous.

She found herself lowering her voice to match his. "This text has required all my concentration. I needed some peace and quiet."

He stepped toward her, his long frame and broad shoulders crowding her vision. "Have I been such a distraction?"

She nervously took a step back. "You're not a distraction, Mr. Malloy."

"You cut me to the quick, my dear."

She pressed the book tightly to her chest. "That's not my intention."

"Very solicitous of you. Shall I explain Rousseau to you, then? I can understand that a female might have trouble grasping his arguments."

She set the book on the table with deliberation, then took a deep breath, trying to keep her voice as calm as his. "He writes things that are perfectly contradictory to one another. His ideas are savage and excessively idealistic, and he doesn't understand the first thing about women." She dared to look up at Zeke for a moment, finding one of his dazzling smiles. She thought her heart might stop.

"Your understanding of Rousseau is better than I thought," he congratulated her. "I read him years ago, and I didn't get half so much out of it."

"Why did you give this to me?" she asked, her nerves beginning to fray.

"I thought it would be good for you."

"Well, it isn't good for me. I find it irritating in the extreme," she snapped.

"It's had its desired effect, then," he said.

She glared down at the bound volume. Typical of him to take these jabs at her, trying to throw her off balance, trying to make her abandon her reserve. She shot him a look that she hoped was imperious. "And what effect would that be, Mr. Malloy?"

"To provoke you," he said, the shadow of a smile on his lips.

"Provoke me into what?"

"Showing yourself. Revealing what sort of woman you really are." He took another step toward her, his eyes almost menacing.

Liberty shivered. The room had felt warm just moments before, but now she felt an unsettling draft. "I'm not so very mysterious, Mr. Malloy."

"I thought we'd agreed you'd call me Zeke."

"*I* never agreed." She took another edgy step back, her skirts brushing the table legs.

His eyes lit. "Oh, my dear, but you did. Or at least you didn't protest. It amounts to the same thing."

She swallowed hard. "Is that what you told yourself last night?"

His smile was mocking, almost cruel. "Having a case of morning-after regrets?"

She looked quickly away from him. "Perhaps I am," she whispered.

"I can't imagine why. That dress was entrancing, by the way. It suited you far better than the monstrosity you have on now." He closed the gap between them and took her starched linen collar between his fingers.

Liberty's hand flew to her throat. "I like this dress. I'm very comfortable in it."

"And last night you weren't comfortable?"

She lifted her chin, still not quite daring to look at him. "No, I wasn't."

"Well, you felt damned comfortable to me," he said, stroking her cheek softly with the pad of his thumb.

She shot a look at him then, unable to believe his callousness. "You arrogant son of a—" she blurted before catching herself.

He released her and laughed, but the sound held no mirth. "I thoroughly enjoy you when you're having one of your spells, my dear."

She longed to hurl the heavy-bound Rousseau straight at his smirking face. "I don't have spells."

"Oh, but you do. Spells of, shall we say, frankness. I quite prefer them to your usual stuffiness."

She shot a poisonous look at him. "You find me stuffy?"

He met her look, his eyes bright. "Does your friend Jack have another word for it? Or perhaps you're somewhat . . . freer in his company."

"He's not my friend. I can't stand him, as a matter of fact."

"Please spare me the details of your lovers' quarrel."

"That's the most ridiculous thing I've ever heard! We aren't lovers, or anything like it." Did he really believe that she and the captain were romantically tied?

"You stood there in front of that entirely *respectable* group and defended him." Zeke's mouth was hard, but his eyes looked almost wounded.

"For heaven's sake, it was a dinner party. I couldn't very well just let the two of you thrash one another there in the dining room."

"Stay away from him, Liberty."

"You will not tell me what to do!" she shot. "I am not a child, and I will choose my friends as I will."

"I thought you said you couldn't stand him."

"I can't stand him! I find him perfectly insufferable. But if I decided I wanted to see him, that would be my right."

His eyes glittered like an ice-covered pond. "You're devoting a great deal of energy claiming the right to spend time with a man you find insufferable."

She set her jaw. What gave him the right to make such preposterous insinuations? "Just what are you accusing me of?"

"I wouldn't dream of accusing you of anything. I think your actions speak for themselves. Including last night."

The words sliced her like a razor. She fought to keep her voice steady. "I don't care to discuss last night."

"Strange, I had the impression that's what you were leading up to. Very well, we won't speak of it again."

She looked up at his eyes, and her heart broke. He didn't care. He didn't care at all.

Her face was hot, and her throat tight with tears. He thought she was a harlot, a loose woman who flitted from man to man. Last night had meant nothing to him. Less than nothing. She wished the ground would open up and swallow her forever, so she'd never have to see those green eyes or that cruel white smile again.

"I'm going back to the house to make myself a pot of tea," she said, her throat tight. When she scooped up her books and made for the door, he moved aside to let her pass.

"Oh, Liberty?"

She paused in the doorway, her back to him. "What is it?"

"You won't come here again, will you?"

"Of course not," she muttered through clenched teeth. *"Sir."*

* * *

Zeke watched Liberty stalk off through the meadow and into the trees. Stubborn curls twisted free of her chignon, but her spine was ramrod-straight, anger surrounding her like a cloud.

He felt a twinge of guilt. Normally he didn't think much of men who seduced at night and gave the cold shoulder in the morning. And he had no doubt he would have seduced Liberty last night, if it hadn't been for Blodgett's interruption.

Zeke's cold laugh sounded hollow in the spare little cabin. Well, he finally had something he could thank Blodgett for. Because getting entangled with Liberty Brooks was like skating on paper-thin ice—not just dangerous, but stupid. She was a cunning little spy, he'd give her that. The dress she'd worn last night would have made a dead man hard, yet it had also given her a look of innocence and vulnerability. Just the qualities that would get Zeke to trust her, if he were stupid enough to fall for her act.

He cursed beneath his breath. Like it or not, he *was* falling for her, and hard. When he was away from her, it was easy to see her for the duplicitous creature she was. But when he was with her, things got muddled. He found himself wanting to touch her, and not thinking too clearly after he'd done so, and generally making an ass of himself.

His best defense was to keep *her* off guard. She was only a female, after all. For all her seductive wiles, keeping her confused shouldn't be too difficult.

But as Zeke lowered himself into the hall where the fugitives waited for him, he thought that in keeping her wits addled, he was doing a hell of a job driving himself to distraction as well.

He pushed her from his mind when he saw Indigo's worried eyes. "How is Jake managing?" he asked.

Indigo shifted her baby to her other shoulder

and sighed. "I don't know 'bout them feets. That poultice was doin' real good, but yestiday Jake took a bad turn. This mornin' he could barely stand on 'em. He try to hide it from me, but he an old man, and he ain't so strong now. I'se sorry, but I don't think he can walk on to the next station tonight. We goin' have to cuts them feet off him ef they gets infected."

Zeke shuddered. Please, God, no more maimed bodies. He had seen enough maiming and death to last him a lifetime. "Of course you'll stay until he's perfectly well," he said quickly. "There isn't the slightest hurry. You'll be quite safe here. When you think he's ready, let me know, and I'll make arrangements with the next station."

Indigo bowed her head. "We don't mean to makes trouble for you, mistuh. You done so much for us already, an' we gots no way to repay you. I know we done been here longer than we s'posed to be already."

Zeke narrowed his eyes. "Don't give it another thought," he said brusquely. "You can see for yourself that there's plenty of room. The worst that could happen is that we might get another group of fugitives in, but there's enough space for all. You'll stay until Jake's as fit as a fiddle."

She smiled and pressed the baby close to her. "Thank you."

Indigo breathed a sigh of relief when he left. Maybe that nosy woman wouldn't come around again. Maybe the gentleman would never find out about Tom's encounter with her. When Indigo had heard *two* voices above their heads, her blood had run cold. But their voices had been so low, Indigo couldn't be sure it was the same woman. Maybe it had been a housekeeper, or a lady friend of the gentleman's.

There was no sense driving herself crazy worrying over it. The gentleman obviously didn't suspect a thing . . . yet. One thing was certain, though. If the gentleman knew that Tom had done something so stupid as to get them all caught, he'd pack them off tomorrow without thinking twice about it.

And Jake would die, Indigo thought, if he had to move too soon. She whispered a silent little prayer. Whatever it took, they would be safe, and Indigo James and her little son were going to remain free.

Liberty buried herself in books until well after nightfall. When the clock chimed ten, she blinked wearily, her eyes and back sore, and set aside her books to prepare for the fugitive. Jane had said he would arrive tonight, sometime after midnight.

Jim was in the stables every day, and Mrs. Biggins was always in and out of the gardening shed, so Liberty had been obliged to find a hiding place inside the house. She had decided on an unused bedroom at the end of a shut-off wing, where Mrs. Biggins went only twice a year, spring and autumn, to clean. Liberty had already taken sheets and pillows in, her heart hammering the whole time lest someone hear a noise and come to investigate.

Feeding the runaway was another story. She was not sure how to explain to Mrs. Biggins that she had suddenly developed an insatiable appetite, but she thought the best course was probably to slip into the pantry in the quiet midafternoon and put together a large cold lunch. She hoped the man could get by on one substantial meal a day—she didn't dare sneak food any more often or Mrs. Biggins would certainly ask questions.

Liberty crept downstairs to wait in the kitchen. Mrs. Biggins had long since gone up to bed. Liberty opened the kitchen door and squinted to see if anyone was coming down the path, but the road was empty. Shivering, she shut the door and cut a hunk of cheese and a quarter loaf of bread, wrapping them with a few plums in a large handkerchief.

She sat at the table and turned the pages of *Clarissa Harlowe* listlessly, unable to fall under her usual spell at the tribulations of the persecuted heroine. Liberty's own heart ached like a deep wound, and she had no sympathy to spare for Clarissa. Outside, the wind slapped branches of chestnut and elm sharply against the windows.

She was dozing lightly when a faint knock came at the kitchen door. She woke with a start, ran to the door, and cautiously slid back the bolt.

Two men stood outside, both black, one portly and middle-aged, the other slender and young, with quick movements and large, sad eyes. The older man said in a low voice, "We were sent by a friend in the city."

"Yes, come in," she whispered hoarsely.

The portly man hung at the door. "Well, boy, I wish you the best. You remember what I telled you: Keeps yo' head down an' yo' ears open, an' you goin' do just fine."

The boy bobbed his head and softly mumbled his thanks.

"God be with you, boy," the portly man said as he turned and walked quickly off into the night.

Liberty surveyed her new houseguest. She had imagined that all male slaves were enormous and muscular with very dark skin, but this young man was thin and sensitive-looking, his skin the color of a hen's brown egg. His large, dark eyes fluttered nervously as he looked around the kitchen. "Are you hungry?" she whispered. He nodded quickly. "I have some food for you, but right now we need to get you to your room."

The two walked silently through the house, trying to time their steps so that should anyone hear them, they would sound like only one person. Liberty chose the marble front steps rather than the faintly squeaky wooden servants' stairway. But the upstairs floorboards creaked, and they were at pains to walk lightly enough.

Once safe in his room, the boy fell upon the food, quietly thanking her when he had finished it.

"My name is Liberty Brooks," she whispered after he had wolfed his dinner. "What's yours?"

"Socrates," he said, his voice sad and soft.

She nodded. Slaves were often given classical Greek names, and Liberty had always found it a particularly unkind irony. She took a quick glance around the room. "I think you'll be comfortable here," she said, keeping her voice soft. "There are a few cobwebs and a little dust, but you've got a decent blanket."

"Thank you, ma'am," the boy mumbled, looking down at his hands.

He was so thin. Liberty felt a pang just looking at him. "Listen, Socrates, there are just a few things you need to remember."

"Call me Soko, if you would, please. I don't care for that name the master give me."

"Of course, Soko. Now, you must know that there are several people living in this house. No one will ever come up here, though, unless you give them reason. So don't open the windows and don't make any noise. Do you think you'll be able to do that?"

Soko nodded. "Yes, ma'am."

"For goodness' sake, call me Liberty. I'll come up with some food every afternoon, and I'll bring some water so you can wash. There's a chamber pot under the bed. Do you have any questions?"

He shook his head and blinked his sad eyes.

"All right, then, I've leave you now. As soon as I can, I'll go see the lady responsible for sending you here. She might have some news for you about where you'll go next."

Soko nodded, and Liberty, satisfied that he would not give himself away, left the room, shutting the door carefully behind her. She had to get some sleep. Tomorrow she faced a long workday, after which she would try to meet with Jane.

But a sardonic voice and a pair of mocking green eyes haunted her, and it was hours before she managed to slip into restless dreams.

Chapter 14

In the morning, Mrs. Biggins bustled about the kitchen as Liberty sleepily helped herself to a cup of hot coffee. "Good heavens, dearie, you look a fright," Mrs. Biggins said with real concern.

Liberty poured a comforting stream of sweet cream into her mug. "I'm afraid I slept none too well last night, Mrs. B."

"It's this weather," Mrs. Biggins said confidently. "The wind did rattle things so, it almost sounded like someone was prowling the house."

Liberty gave a violent start. "What a perfectly dreadful idea."

"Hush, child, it was an old woman's foolish notion, that's all," Mrs. Biggins said, concerned at Liberty's ashen face. "I wouldn't have said a word if I'd known you'd take a fright. You know, I could tell you was doin' poorly when I heard you come downstairs last night. You must have a touch of that insomnia that Mr. Malloy is so prone to."

"Yes, certainly, you're quite right, just a touch of insomnia. I'll be quite well again after breakfast, I'm sure."

"Of course you will, child. Now, you go sit down and I'll bring your breakfast directly. Go on, now," she said, shooing Liberty away with a gentle briskness.

Breakfast helped enormously, and after bacon, eggs, and three large mugs of coffee, Liberty was up to tackling a tall stack of letters and leaflets. It was, however, slow going, and she found herself struggling to keep her eyes open.

All too soon, it seemed, her stomach grumbled again, and she looked at the clock on the wall. Twelve-thirty. Nearly time for lunch. Her heart fell as she thought of feeding Soko. The skinny young man could probably eat three five-course meals a day and still look half-starved. She mused that he probably could not read, or she could give him some books to distract him. She thought dreamily that perhaps it would not be such a bad thing to be shut in a quiet room with nothing to do but sleep all day. In fact, the idea sounded perfectly delightful.

She was startled to hear the peal of the meal bell; had she dozed off over her work? She sighed, tucked her book under her arm, and resigned herself to a longer day than she had anticipated.

Later that day, when Mrs. Biggins went into the pantry to gather the makings for dinner, she was surprised to see a thick slice missing from the ham, half the bread and three apples along with it. When she grilled the staff, Bessie, a new kitchen maid, nervously confessed that she had seen Miss Brooks go into the pantry and leave with a plate of food.

The girl was more than entitled to a snack, Mrs. Biggins thought with a frown, but why hadn't she asked her to get it for her? And the miss was one for regular habits—breakfast, lunch, and dinner.

Maybe she had been skimping without knowing it, she thought with horror. She'd starved the poor child. She resolved to double the size of the portions at meals and began to gather the ingredients for dinner, satisfied that she had solved yet another domestic problem in Ezekiel Malloy's household.

Despite her best efforts, it was days before Liberty could find the few hours she needed to see Jane

Redburne. Mr. Malloy had grown more demanding by the day. And on top of everything else, Liberty thought she was coming down with a head cold. But she had ruthlessly pushed the idea from her mind. She would have time to be ill when Soko was gone, not before.

The Redburnes' address was a fashionable one on Beacon Hill, a tall brick house with dark shutters and a gleaming white portico. Liberty sighed as she lifted the heavy brass knocker and thudded it three times. A pert uniformed maid showed her inside to the elegant parlor, where Jane was drinking tea.

Liberty felt out of place in the massive, imposing room. The windows were smothered in heavy plum velvet, and tall cut-glass vases were filled with iris and willow.

"I'm afraid you're not looking quite well, my dear. Please do sit down and share a pot of tea with me." Jane herself looked stunning, dressed in a pale sea green silk day dress, her hair drawn up into a luxuriant mass of auburn waves.

"I really can't spare a moment to take tea," Liberty said, refusing the seat Jane offered. "I have precious little time on my hands lately, and caring for the young man you sent hasn't helped matters."

"Of course, of course." Jane set an eggshell-delicate porcelain cup down on the tea table. "We all have our little concerns. You should be thankful you don't have a household to manage. You really can't imagine the work."

"I think I could better manage a houseful of servants than take in a fugitive slave, on top of working fifty hours a week," Liberty said coolly, beginning to see her virtuous acquaintance in an unflattering new light.

"It's all a question of discipline, dear." Jane smoothed the flounces of her dress. "I'm sure you will find that if you set a schedule and stick to it, you will have plenty of time for all your activities."

"They aren't *activities*, they're *work*." Liberty paced nervously to the tall windows, peering out onto the quiet street.

"Work, then," said Jane indulgently. "I don't see how it matters what we call it."

Liberty sighed, impatient, and rearranged her wrap about her shoulders. "Jane, I don't mean to suggest that every woman have a career, but there are those of us who actually work for a living."

"Oh, of course, my dear," Jane said, a pitying smile on her lips. "You poor little thing. I had quite forgotten your unmarried situation."

"I am certainly not complaining about my *situation*," Liberty replied testily. "I have no desire to marry."

"But we must all marry, dear. It's the only—"

"Jane," Liberty interrupted, working to keep her calm. "Please, what about this young man? When will you find him another place to stay?"

Jane's eyelids fluttered, and she pressed her teacup to her lips. "The Antislavery Society has been looking for a place, but as you know, it's quite delicate."

"It's exceedingly delicate keeping him at Haven House," Liberty reminded her, moving closer to press her point home.

Jane paled. "Yes, of course, we recognize that, my dear. But the Society has decided not to move him until we have a permanent place for him in Canada."

"What?" Liberty pressed her fingers to her temples, closing her eyes against a flood of frustration. "You told me you'd have him out within a few days. What you're talking about could take weeks."

"Or more," Jane mused, then winced. "It's for the boy's good, of course. Every time he's moved, another link is added to the chain. A potentially weak link. The more families he stays with, the greater the chance that someone, perhaps a visitor, will ask a few too many questions or mention something to the wrong people."

Liberty paced the floor, angry. The claustrophobic, overstuffed parlor was beginning to smother her. "So why didn't he stay with the last family he was placed with?"

"Oh, he couldn't," Jane hurried to explain. "You see, Emmaline Brownleigh had planned an enormous party, and—"

"You foisted him off on me because someone else was having a *party*?" Liberty's voice was strained, her disillusionment with Jane Redburne escalating with every word the woman spoke.

"Now, I really can't see that there is any need to shout. It was for security reasons, you understand. He might have been found out."

"And I don't suppose it ever occurred to anyone but me that giving parties is a thing to be avoided when one has a fugitive slave in the house?"

"It's not that simple. There were many factors that—"

Liberty threw her hands up in anger. "Jane, I'm sorry. I'm tired and I'm not feeling well and I'm not getting anything accomplished by arguing this with you. You must find him another place to stay. I can't hide him forever. Call it a matter of security or anything else you please, but he must go."

"Well, since you feel so strongly, dear, I will try, but I must warn you that—"

"No, don't tell me that you may not find someone. Just get him another place to stay. It can't be any harder for another household to hide him from their visitors than it is for me to hide him from Mr. Malloy."

"But—"

"I must get back to work now. Good day, Jane."

* * *

Liberty's boots clicked sharply on the stone steps as she left Jane's house. The damp midmorning air hit her lungs with a sudden, sharp pain. Others in the street walked coatless in the summer heat; women strolled with the most delicate of shawls tossed carelessly over their shoulders. Liberty pulled her own sturdy wrap tightly around her arms, her temples pounding with a nasty headache. But the pain was secondary to her anger, blazing still against Jane Redburne.

The woman had taken advantage of her; she could see that now. To Jane this was all a grand, exciting adventure. An adventure in which other people risked their lives and livelihoods while Jane herself sipped tea in her parlor and fretted over her servants.

She dragged herself to the coach stop, hoping to catch the twelve-o'clock home, wanting nothing more than to go to bed for a solid week and pretend that Soko and Jane did not exist, and wondering if cynical Zeke Malloy was smarter about some things than she'd given him credit for.

That afternoon, Liberty balanced a stack of books gingerly in her arms as she used her foot to nudge the library door open. She was nudging the door closed with her elbow when a heart-sinkingly familiar voice stopped her in her tracks.

"It seems that every time I see you, you're hiding behind a mountain of books, my dear."

She lowered her arms to peer over the stack of volumes. Zeke sat sprawled in a wing chair, his legs stretched in front of him with annoyingly feline grace.

"M-Mr. Malloy," she stammered, feeling her face warm.

"Yes, my dear. I do live here, you know."

She straightened her spine and brought the stack of books back up in front of her face. "I'm sorry to disturb you, sir. I'll leave at once."

He was up and across the room in an instant. He plucked the top two volumes from the stack of books, revealing her face to him. "You'll do no such thing. I'm sure we can work side by side like civilized people."

She swallowed. "No, really, sir, I think I'd prefer to work elsewhere."

"You've been avoiding me." It was a statement, not a question.

"Don't be ridiculous, Mr. Malloy, I've been—"

"*Zeke*," he corrected. "What a thick-skulled little thing you are. Like all women, I suppose."

Liberty pursed her lips. He was only trying to infuriate her. "Any dog can learn to jump through hoops on command, Mr. Malloy. If you're looking for blind obedience, may I suggest a cocker spaniel?"

He laughed, revealing those gleaming white teeth. "Touché. Won't you let me help you with these?" He lifted another book from the stack, revealing her throat.

She pulled the stack a little tighter to her chest. "No, thank you, I'm fine."

"It's the duty of men to assist the weaker sex." He removed another two books. The outline of her breasts showed beneath her dark bombazine dress.

She licked her lips, nervous, and hiked the remaining stack up to shield her bosom again. "I'm more than capable of taking care of myself."

He took the remaining books from her, leaving her arms free. She wrapped them protectively against her torso.

"I've no doubt of your ruthless competence, my dear. But you make a man feel positively unchivalrous, if you don't let him help."

She glanced up to catch a wicked gleam in his eye before he turned away from her to set the books on a table. "I hadn't realized your sense of chivalry was so strong," she said in the frostiest tone she could manage.

Zeke laughed softly and reached out to tuck a wayward curl behind her ear. "Even the most chivalrous of men can forget himself at times. Especially with the right sort of woman."

Liberty edged away from him and reached for one of the books. Her cheek burned where he had touched her. "I fail to see your point, Mr. Malloy."

He was silent a moment, studying her. "That dress is a bit less horrific than the rest," he finally mused.

She stiffened her spine. "I cannot see why you insist on insulting my wardrobe. It's not so different from yours, after all."

"Yes, I suppose that's the problem. Why on earth should a woman want to dress like a man?"

Liberty bent her head over her book, thumbing the pages. "I'm surprised you'd give it any thought. I assumed you didn't have much use for women."

He stepped behind her, peering over her shoulder at the book she was pretending to read. "I'm no fool, Liberty. Even I know that women have their uses."

Her knees felt like damp sponges. "We are every bit as intelligent and useful as men," she said, her voice strained as she flipped blindly through the pages.

"But a woman," Zeke whispered, "ought to look like a woman."

He slid the hairpins from her hair, and she felt her heavy curls tumble to her shoulders.

Her entire body flooded with intense, primitive desire. Her fingers lost their hold on the heavy book, and it hit the floor with a thud. For one awful moment, she thought she might faint.

She sucked in her breath to clear her head and wheeled to face him. "What are you doing?"

"Call it an experiment," he said. He gestured to the tome on the floor. "You're very hard on my books, you know."

She wriggled past him, her skirts rustling. "I don't care for that sort of experiment." She reached up to repair her ruined chignon.

Zeke held her hairpins up for her to see, his eyes mocking. "Miss Brooks, do I not have the right to determine the proper attire for my employees?"

"Please return my hairpins," she said.

"If I determine that I prefer your hair unbound, it shall stay unbound."

"My demeanor is completely professional, including the manner in which I dress my hair. Kindly return my property at once." She held out her hand for the pins.

"I am your employer, and I will decide what constitutes professionalism so long as you are in my employ."

"If my appearance is unsatisfactory, you are free to dismiss me." Damn him and his stupid games! If this had been Ohio, he'd have eaten those wretched hairpins by the time she was through with him. She planted one defiant hand on her hip, the other outstretched for her pins.

He closed the gap between them, clasping her outstretched wrist in one hand. He dropped the pins tightly into her palm. "Your pulse is racing, Liberty," he said, his eyes pinning her.

"I feel . . . I feel a little dizzy," she murmured. To her surprise, it was true. Not the pleasurable confusion she had felt before, but something far less entrancing. Her headache had returned with a terrible vengeance, and her vision was filling with funny white dots.

"Don't tell me you're succumbing to an attack of the vapors." His voice was mocking, but his tone soon changed to one of concern. "Liberty, you really don't look at all well. Sit down a moment until you're feeling yourself again."

She pulled feebly at her wrist, trying to wrench it free of his grasp. It was his fault; he was doing this to her. An odd ringing began in her ears. "I'll be fine," she said in a choked whisper. But her knees chose that moment to buckle beneath her, and it was only Zeke's arms closing around her that kept her from sliding to the floor.

Audrey Biggins hadn't seen Mr. Malloy so angry since the morning he'd returned, with a nasty wound to the shoulder and a worse one to his pride, from a duel with a grizzled riverboat gambler named Five-Spot Blodgett. And, mercy, that had been years ago.

Mr. Malloy had been grilling the staff for over an hour, and poor little Bessie had burst into tears not once but twice. Still, Audrey was almost glad to see the angry spark in Mr. Malloy's eyes. That nice Liberty Brooks had begun to do what Audrey had nearly given up on—bringing Mr. Malloy back to the land of living, feeling folks. But it wouldn't do anybody any good to let him chase the staff off with his scowling and his thundering.

He gripped the table edge and leaned forward, his expression harsh. "We'll go over this one more time."

Audrey cleared her throat. "Beggin' your pardon, sir, but I suspect we've got all the story we're going to get from the staff."

He turned to her, his eyebrows knotted with rage. "Do you understand what happened this afternoon? My amanuensis fainted dead away in the library. Now Bessie here is babbling some kind of nonsense about Miss Brooks and the pantry and some missing apples. We will all remain right here until I get to the bottom of this!"

"Good heavens, the girl had a bit of a spell, that's all. It happens to young ladies at times. And I won't have you bullying my staff."

"We're not talking about some idiotic fainting female, we're talking about Liberty Brooks." His tone was icy, but Audrey refused to be intimidated. She'd taken care of Zeke Malloy since he was no bigger than a hedgehog, and she wasn't going to stand for any more guff.

"I know perfectly well who we're talking about, and the sooner we let the staff go on about their business, the sooner you and I can talk about this foolishness in private."

He shot her a dangerous look. "I see. Very well. You may all go. Mrs. Biggins, I am exceedingly anxious to hear what you might have to say in private about my personal assistant."

"Oh, for heaven's sake," she said, standing and smoothing the folds of her immaculate apron. She patted Bessie's sleeve reassuringly as the frightened girl practically bolted from the room, followed by the rest of the staff.

"What is it, Audrey?" he asked the instant the back door had closed behind the stableboy and the gardener.

Audrey set the kettle on the stove and rolled her eyes to the ceiling. "There isn't anything to ruffle your feathers over, just one or two little quirks the miss has that I don't like to discuss in front of staff. There's no sense letting them hear such things about their betters."

"Mrs. Biggins . . ." Zeke warned.

"I'll get to it, I'll get to it, keep your britches on," she grumbled. "I suspect she's taken a bit of a chill, is all. She's had the Devil of a time getting herself out of bed all week."

Zeke's lips curled into a scowl. "I see."

"I didn't want to mention it in front of the others; it's none of their business, and it gives a bad impression. She's not a lazy girl, Mr. Malloy, I'd stake a month's wages on it. More than likely she's just a bit run-down after those ramblings of hers."

Zeke's eyebrow shot up. "Ramblings? What ramblings?"

"Those walks she takes. And at all hours, too. I've told her it's no good for her health. It's not good for the lungs, being out in the damp."

"What do you mean by 'all hours'? Does she leave this house at night?"

"Well," Audrey said, reluctant to say anything that might get the girl in trouble. "She's been known to. Not that she'd ever do anything that wasn't respectable, sir. She's just one of those souls who needs to get out of doors to think about things."

"What on earth could she possibly have to think about?" Zeke brought his fist down on the table with a loud bang. "Damn it all, I won't stand for this. Doesn't she realize that anything could happen to her, wandering about like that? She could be abducted, or assaulted. . . . God only knows what might happen."

Audrey pursed her lips. She couldn't imagine anyone being assaulted in the quiet countryside that surrounded Haven House. "Well, I suppose it's just possible she might twist her ankle in a ditch," she allowed. "But I'm sure she's learned her lesson, sir. This chill has laid her pretty low."

Zeke narrowed his eyes. "Suppose you tell me just what you mean by a chill."

"Well, she's got no appetite at all in the mornings, but I've seen her bring meals up to her room for lunch that'd choke a man twice your size."

"Go on."

"Well, haven't you noticed, sir? She's so pale, just like a ghost some mornings. And her such a nice, healthy girl."

"Yes, I see now. Thank you so much, Mrs. Biggins. Do you have anything further to tell me?"

Audrey was a little worried at the cold mask that had settled over her employer's features. "No, sir, that's all. I haven't got the girl in trouble, have I? She can't help being sick, Mr. Malloy."

There was something strange in his smile. "No, of course she can't help it. You haven't done anything wrong, Audrey. Thank you very much. I'll take care of things."

Audrey didn't like the tone of his voice, but there was nothing more she could do right now. She'd have to watch and see what happened. She'd step in to protect the girl if he got some bee in his britches about dismissing her. Audrey Biggins wasn't about to let the girl go, not now that she seemed to be thawing the ice that had trapped Mr. Malloy's heart for so long.

"Very well, sir," she murmured. "If you'll excuse me, there are still the parlor flowers to do."

Zeke watched as Mrs. Biggins left the room to busy herself with the big arrangement of lilies, roses, and peonies.

He could scarcely believe it. Liberty was unwell, couldn't eat breakfast, odd fluctuations in appetite, slept late in the mornings.

There was only one possible explanation. She was pregnant.

Damn that unprincipled bastard Blodgett! It all added up—Jack's drunken outrage at the party, her defense of the swine when he'd insulted every guest at the table. And her "long walks" must have been to see him. Perhaps she had even been waiting for Blodgett when Zeke had run into her out at the cabin. The thought made his throat tighten.

He couldn't understand his own feelings. What should have concerned him was the breach of security, but he found himself far more enraged by the thought of Blodgett lying with the girl. He knew that Blodgett was an animal, he had seen plenty of innocent people violated by him. Why was he so agitated over one more?

Zeke thought of Liberty's softness beneath him in the carriage, the way she had arched her back. And he remembered the little waltz she had hummed while they danced in the dining room. A foolish, trivial thing, yet he could recall every detail with perfect clarity.

And she had lied so prettily, insisting that she and Blodgett weren't lovers. Zeke had almost been tempted to believe her.

He'd been right about her all along. She was a dangerous distraction, duplicitous even for a female. He should have been pleased to have her revealed for what she was, but instead he felt depressed and disgusted by his own sentimentality in the matter.

The real question remained; what was to be done? Propriety demanded that Zeke dismiss her instantly and let her fend for herself, but he felt a strange reluctance to do so. What sort of a life would await a sensitive, bright young woman with a baby and no husband? She certainly couldn't teach, and even if she could find work in a mill, who would tend to her baby?

If Blodgett would marry her, the problem was solved, but Zeke did not believe he would. Blodgett was a petty and cruel man, not given to accept damaged goods, even if he had been the one to damage them.

She was sent here as Blodgett's spy. Zeke hated himself for letting her make a fool of him like this. But he couldn't willfully send her into harm's way.

Perhaps he could ship her back to her parents. They could tell people she'd been widowed. Somehow, though, the thought of shipping her back to Ohio and never seeing her again filled Zeke with a deep and profound panic.

He sighed. He would never make a good northerner. He was too inclined to overlook improprieties that would shock a good Bostonian to the tips of his silk socks. Back home, if dark-skinned Sukey were pregnant again, and if the last four babies had borne the master's eyes, well, that was the way of the world. In any case, you could hardly blame Sukey for it.

He swallowed the last of his coffee and grimaced. It was stone-cold. He couldn't change his plans for today, in any event. He needed to arrange the transport of his fugitives. After weeks of resting in the underground room, old Jake's feet were finally well enough to hold him up for a few hours. Zeke was working with a new man, a nervous boat pilot whose commitment to the Underground Railroad was anything but certain. It seemed that everything in Zeke's life had come to a precarious turn.

And Liberty Brooks was starting to lure his mind away from his work with alarming regularity. He couldn't let that happen. This was no time to start getting sentimental.

Socrates was curled up beneath a warm window, clutching a wool blanket around him despite the almost oppressive heat in the unventilated room. He shivered miserably and gave one massive shudder as he sneezed silently. The doorknob to his room turned, and, as he always did, he whispered a silent prayer that it was only Liberty, that he had not been found out, that he would make it on, on to Harlem or on to Canada, anything but back to Georgia.

He sank back into the wool blanket as she appeared in the doorway, framed by the light behind her. "Oh, no," she whispered, crestfallen. "You've caught my cold."

"This ain't no cold, mis'. This gots to be infl'enza, maybe somethin' worse," he said reproachfully, his eyes bright pink. His face was drawn and haggard, and the lovely soft color of his skin had gone a sickly beige.

"I needs to gets somewhere safe. This cough ain't goin' to stay quiet fo'ever. You gots to move me, tonight."

"I've been trying, Jane hasn't been able to find a place yet."

"You gits yo'self over to her an' tells her 'bout how sick I is, I expect she find someplace mighty quick. I kin wait till tomorrow, maybe, but no later."

Liberty was startled by the gentle boy's sudden harshness. He was no innocent child, she realized, but a man who had made a long and bitter trek and would not allow his escape to be jeopardized. Suddenly he was racked by spasms. He wrapped the blankets around him to muffle his nasty cough.

"Tomorrow it is, Soko," she said softly. "I promise."

She retreated to her room and draped her heaviest shawl over her shoulders. It would be dark soon, and after this afternoon she wouldn't be going anywhere at night.

After that embarrassing fainting spell, Mr. Malloy had carried her to her room. She'd regained consciousness in a few moments and tried to get him to put her down, but he'd given her a look that had almost made her faint again. And now she was strictly confined to her room, pending Mr. Malloy's instructions.

She chewed her lower lip distractedly. Well, it *was* a trifle worrisome. After all, she wasn't some helpless female who went around swooning, for Heaven's sake. But she felt perfectly well now, and she resented Mr. Malloy's insistence that she spend the afternoon napping. Getting word to Jane Redburne that Soko must be moved was going to be rather complicated.

She quickly decided that the best course was to send Jane a brief but urgently worded note. True, it would require slipping into the village to post, but that would take less than an hour. If she timed it cleverly, Mr. Malloy would never be the wiser.

Liberty sighed and looked out her window. The sky was oppressively gray, heavy with the threat of rain. Well, there was no sense in thinking of slipping out while Mr. Malloy was in the house, so she might as well get some work done.

She sighed again when she saw the mountain of unintelligible notes that littered her desk and spilled over onto the floor. The lecture she was putting together wasn't going well. She couldn't tell anymore if the lines she wrote made sense or not.

Zeke stormed in, all crash and thunder. She looked up from the pile of work. "Good evening, sir," she greeted him wearily, preparing herself for another tongue-lashing.

"You were supposed to be in your room, in bed," he growled.

"I really feel much better," she insisted, trying for a bright tone of voice.

"You overslept this morning." He fixed her with a sharp gaze, as if waiting for her to crumple at this terrible accusation.

"Yes," she said, swallowing her anger painfully. "I'm awfully sorry, Mr. Malloy. I couldn't sleep a wink last night, and it seems to have caught up with me this morning. It won't happen again, I promise you." She hated herself for groveling, but tonight was not the time to pick a quarrel with him.

"It's not the first time you've overslept," he continued, regarding her expectantly, "is it, Miss Brooks?"

Stay in control, Liberty, she reminded herself. "No, Mr. Malloy, it isn't. I'm afraid I was a few minutes late for work last week as well. I really am terribly sorry." She bit down on her lower lip to fight back the angry words that welled up within her chest. Did he despise her so much, to grill her over a trifle?

"So you admit it." His eyes flashed for a moment with something unreadable, but his voice was calm and even.

"Yes, of course I do, sir. I failed to arrive at work promptly. It was unforgivable. I am sorry." She enunciated the words with slow, careful clarity.

"And your lunch as well," he added mysteriously.

"My lunch, sir?" she asked, bewildered. She felt as if they were having two separate conversations, one for his benefit and one for hers. "I'm afraid I don't follow you."

"You hardly touched it yesterday."

She shook her head to clear away the cobwebs. This conversation would be hard enough to follow, and she was scarcely at her best. "I wasn't hungry," she replied simply.

"Liberty," he said, his voice gentling, "it's all right. I know what's been going on. Of course I understand why you should wish to keep it from me, but there isn't any need any longer."

Liberty felt the air rush from her lungs. She set the notes in her hands carefully down on her desk.

He knew. But how? Had he heard Soko moving about in his room? Had she given something away by sneaking those meals to him? She clenched her fists nervously. Now Zeke would probably feel he had to go to the authorities, and they would send that poor young man back to the plantation. Everything would be ruined, and it was her own fault. Tears of frustration welled in her eyes, and she sank back heavily in her chair, raising her hands to her forehead, suddenly achingly tired.

Zeke felt a pang of guilt for forcing the truth out of her, but it was better this way. Her secret had obviously been weighing heavily on her mind. Now she could make preparations, plan for the baby's arrival.

The sight of her curled up in her chair, more fragile than he had ever seen her, touched him in a way that he would not have expected. He was surprised by the protective pang he felt when he thought of her with child. It might have been his own child she carried, he realized with a shock, if Blodgett had not interrupted them at the party. It would not have been such a terrible thing. He had a fleeting vision of himself driving into the city to fetch pickled eels and imported guava jam.

He shook his head angrily. What the hell had gotten into him? He would not give in to stupid sentimentality. She was an irresponsible girl who had gotten herself into trouble, and that was all. He would help her if he could, but there was no sense making a damned fool of himself about it.

She choked back a sob, her face buried in her hands, and despite himself, his heart ached for her. "Please don't cry," he murmured awkwardly. Kneeling beside her, he gathered her into his arms. "You mustn't get yourself into such a state— it isn't a good idea in your condition," he said softly, caressing her chestnut curls. They were so soft, and she smelled fresh and sweet, like early summer rain.

His words pierced the fog of Liberty's despair. "Condition?" she asked tearily, her cheek resting on his shoulder. He really could be quite nice, she decided, tucked lightly in his arms.

"Well, yes, now that you're . . . unwell. You'll tire yourself if you keep crying this way, and we can't have that," he said, uncomfortable. "After all, being . . . unwell . . . isn't the worst thing in the

world. And I can take care of you," he finished
rashly.

His own words shocked him. Take care of her?
Where the hell had that come from? He looked
down at the girl, curled comfortably in his arms.
Well, maybe taking care of her would be the best
thing. He gathered her closer to him, breathing in
the soft, pure scent of her hair.

Unwillingly, Liberty pulled away from him. It
was too distracting being in his arms that way, and
she was beginning to realize that she might have
gotten things quite mixed up.

"And my illness, that's all you wished to discuss
with me?" she asked carefully.

Zeke felt the familiar sense of a female trying to
take advantage of him. Damn the wench, what the
Devil was she asking for now? He had made his
offer, a damned generous offer. Was she trying to
squeeze him for more? If it had been his child, there
would be the question of marriage, of course.

Marriage? He was shocked by the way the word
blazed in his mind, flashing there like a lighthouse
beacon.

"That is entirely enough, don't you think, my
dear?" he growled, his eyebrows fierce.

Liberty sat back, oddly comforted by his glower.
Thank goodness, he was his old self again, and
he didn't suspect a thing. He'd come up to talk
about how sick she'd been! She nearly fell over
with relief.

"Oh, of course, sir, quite enough. And your concern is really heartwarming. Thank you so much."

Zeke frowned. Of course she was pleased that he
would take care of her, but this frank expression of
relief was a bit . . . well . . . indelicate. And he was
annoyed at the way she had pulled free of him just
as he had declared his intentions, the conniving
minx, as if she had planned all along to secure just
such an offer. He reminded himself that she was

bearing the bastard child of his worst enemy. For one fatal instant he had felt a certain tenderness for it, and for her. But such tenderness could have no place in their arrangements.

"No need to take advantage of my generosity," he said with a scowl. Straightening to his full height, he asked brusquely, "So how are you coming along on that lecture?" There. That should show her that he wasn't a pushover, that he didn't intend to make a fool of himself like some lovesick boy.

"Oh," said Liberty, somewhat startled by his sudden turnaround but too relieved to be very bothered by it. He didn't know about Soko! "I've been making some progress, but I confess I'm a bit behind. I'd like to work on it for the rest of the day, if you don't mind."

"I shall leave for the meeting tomorrow at promptly four o'clock," he said. "I'll need to have the completed lecture no later than two."

"Very well, sir," she said meekly, wondering absently what had turned his temper as he stalked out of the room, his boots heavy on the wooden floor.

She sighed and sank back into her chair. They didn't seem to be able to have the briefest of conversations without one or both of them becoming infuriated. She was always prepared to be reasonable with him, but his stubbornness made it absolutely impossible. "Impossible," she said aloud, the word disappearing into a weak cough.

So why did Zeke Malloy haunt her thoughts night and day?

The worst times were at night, in the moments just before sleep, when, unbidden, her mind would create insanely complicated plots that ultimately led her down the aisle with him, bestowing a passionate wedding kiss in a snow white gown and bright green silk stockings. She violently chased such fantasies away when she was awake and her mind was her own, but as she slipped into dreams, her mind and soul became his, betraying her to his caresses. Many a morning she had slipped painfully from the comfort of his strong arms and broad shoulders into the waking world, the chill dawn replacing that odd warming in her breasts and loins.

She hung her head. Perhaps this wretched cold had addled her faculties. After all, they could scarcely stand to be in the same room together. He didn't care a whit for her; he had more than proven that.

Perhaps she should leave, seek out another position. She thrust the thought to the back of her mind as quickly as it had come to her. She'd think about that tomorrow, or the next day. As for today, there was plenty of work to be done.

Chapter 15

The raps came loud and fast at the bedroom door. "Miss Liberty! Miss Liberty! You've overslept again, dearie."

She blinked in the bright morning sun. Overslept. Again. Zeke would absolutely kill her this time. Liberty croaked, "Thank you again, Mrs. B. I don't know what I'd do without you." The last word died on her lips as she swallowed a painful cough. How was she going to keep this up? She didn't think she'd last another day, much less another week of this.

She pulled herself out of bed, wincing at the pain in her throat as she swallowed. Her mirror revealed skin that was lackluster and too pale despite months of sunny weather. Her eyes were dull and listless, her lips cracked and dry; even her hair was not the glossy chestnut pelt it had been but hung limply, refusing to shine. "Oh, Liberty," she said softly to her reflection. "What are you going to do?"

She appeared in the kitchen in a mud-colored challis that hung on her shapelessly. "Just coffee, Mrs. B.," she said wearily.

"Oh, no, you don't, missy," said Mrs. Biggins severely, her hands planted firmly on her stout hips. "You've been skipping breakfast too often lately, and it's beginning to show. Now, you sit right there and wait for your oatmeal."

"I can't," protested Liberty faintly. "Mr. Malloy'll skin me if I don't have that lecture ready today, and I'm terribly behind. And I have . . . other business to attend to. If I work very hard all day and don't stop for lunch, I think I can do it."

"I've never heard such nonsense in all my life," said Mrs. Biggins with a scowl. "You are in no shape to get past me, young lady, and I simply will not let you start work without a decent breakfast. What Mr. Malloy can be thinking is beyond me, but you can't possibly work like this. Here," she said more gently, pressing a mug of steaming coffee into Liberty's hand. "Go on and sit down, and I'll bring something out in a few minutes. Go on now," she said with a gentle push.

Liberty was sorry to see no newspaper on the breakfast table. Her time would be totally wasted until she could get through whatever Mrs. Biggins cooked up for her. She looked around for at least a paper and pencil to write out a list of her priorities—anything to keep her mind clear and give her a head start. She still had to trudge over to the village to post her note to Jane. And she was hours from finishing Zeke's lecture. She couldn't let him down. He would take it as another sign of her weakness, of the weakness of all women.

Socrates. What to do about Soko? Liberty had failed to take care of him, had underfed him, and now he had gotten ill. She was wracked with guilt at her shortcomings. This disgusting business of oversleeping was only one example. Somehow she had become indolent and selfish. Her workday was two hours shorter than it had ever been, and she had two full, precious days, off, yet she was wasting the extra time in self-indulgence and sloth. It was revolting.

At the rate she was going, she'd be gone from here soon, and they certainly wouldn't put up with this nonsense wherever she ended up next.

When Mrs. Biggins came in with a huge bowl of oatmeal dotted with raisins and slathered with maple sugar and thick cream, she was astonished to find Liberty dozing face down over a pad of paper, on which was written the single word *Sloth*.

After breakfast, Mrs. Biggins was occupied in the parlor and did not see or hear Liberty slip out the back door. Liberty took a deep breath in relief, only to promptly dissolve in a fit of coughing. She trudged down the path to the main road and began to walk, more slowly than she was used to, toward the village.

The sunshine made her miserable. She felt like a prisoner in her own aching head. She had to concentrate on keeping one foot moving in front of the other, and often she was forced to stop to sit for a few minutes by the side of the road until the ringing in her ears subsided.

The trip took twice as long as she'd suspected it would, and she felt as if she'd been pummeled by bandits when she finally returned to her room. Perhaps she really was rather ill, after all. She had felt perfectly fit yesterday, apart from that silly fainting spell, but today something was hitting her with the force of a locomotive.

But ill or no, she couldn't afford to lie about now. Once this lecture was finished and Soko was safely off, she'd take to her bed for a week if she had to.

The leather-bound books felt staggeringly heavy, and after trying fruitlessly to lift a stack of them, Liberty finally decided to move them one at a time from the library to her small desk in the study. The outline Zeke had approved required more research than she had anticipated, so she had devised another, simpler one and hoped that Zeke's thrilling oratorical style would make up the difference. She trudged back and forth between the office and the library, taking special care not to fall off the ladder when she had to reach for a high-placed tome. *I must work harder, I must work faster*, she said to herself as she plodded back and forth, pausing only to look wistfully at the chestnut leaves that brushed against the window of the study. The mass of cool, fresh leaves shaded the room on hot days and made it feel almost like a treehouse nestled in the boughs. She gazed longingly at the massive tree, thinking of her childhood in Ohio. It had been so long since she had climbed the sprawling limbs of an oak, clenching an apple between her teeth so she could munch it happily in her leafy paradise, quietly watching the comings and goings below.

Behind her the clock bonged ten. How had it gotten to be ten? She would never finish this project; she was botching it, and Mr. Malloy would be furious and she would lose this job before she was at all ready to go out and find another. What would happen to Soko then?

Work, she had to get back to work.

Often in adolescence she had been able to make up for lost time in her studies with a last-minute stretch of brilliant concentration, her mind a machine honed to optimum efficiency. That was what she needed now, a good stretch of brilliance.

Zeke found her dozing in the study's window seat. An expensive volume lay sprawled at her feet. "The wench really will be the ruination of my library," he grumbled as he gently shook her awake. His spike of bad temper faded when he saw the unhealthy color of her skin and the bony knuckles protruding from too-thin hands.

She bolted awake with a wide-eyed start. "Oh, Mr. Malloy, I'm not quite finished with the project you gave me. I just need a few more hours," she said, the words tumbling clumsily out of her mouth as she rushed to gather up her spilled materials.

"You need a few more hours, all right. A few more hours of sleep. Liberty, you really don't look at all well. I think you should take the day off," he said.

"No!" she cried. "Your lecture's this evening and I'm—" She broke off, embarrassed. "Well, I'm a little behind."

"Don't be foolish, there's no need to worry about that," he said, pressing his hand to her forehead. She had what felt to be a dangerously high fever. He cursed her silently. How could she jeopardize her health now, when it was so important? "Just show me what you've got, and I'll finish it myself."

"But you shouldn't have to do extra work just because I haven't been able to keep up," she said miserably.

"Miss Brooks, you are being perfectly ridiculous. You must get to bed immediately. You are taking foolish and dangerous risks with your health. Do you feel strong enough to just show me what you already have?"

"Of course," she said, struggling to her feet. "This is silliness, though, really. I'm no weakling who quits whenever she gets a little sniffle, you know."

"I know," he said indulgently. His childhood had exposed him to any number of pregnant women, and he remembered with a certain fondness their peculiar brand of irrationality.

She rummaged through her notes, trying to put them in order as he looked over her shoulder. Finally she nervously handed him a packet and waited for his response with bated breath. She was crestfallen to hear him mumble, "This is terrible."

"Terrible?" she echoed, thinking she might faint.

"The early work is excellent, very thought-provoking, but the later—it's totally incoherent." He gazed at the notes in amazement.

She wrung her hands anxiously. "Well, sir, I realize that it's a bit unpolished, but—"

"It doesn't make any sense, it's totally without focus. This doesn't pertain at all to the outline you showed me." He looked up at her, puzzled.

The kindness of his voice belied the harsh words, but Liberty heard only the reproach, and her chest and throat constricted painfully. She fought to keep the tears from her eyes. "No, sir, it doesn't."

"Well, why not?" he asked gently.

"I ran out of time," she said, losing her battle with her tears. "I read and I read, but I just couldn't put anything together, and I haven't been able to get up at a decent hour all week, and then Mrs. Biggins made me eat breakfast this morning, and I just couldn't—" She broke off completely as she dissolved into tears, her face flushed with fever and embarrassment.

He took her into his arms as she gave way to her sobs, curling his arms around her protectively. Poor thing, of course her work had been incoherent; she was terribly ill. And the baby must be weighing heavily on her mind. It was a small matter to take the early work she'd done and expand the outline for the remainder of the lecture.

Damn the girl, if only she'd told him sooner that she wasn't feeling well, he would have had plenty of time. But she was so obviously crushed, he couldn't bring himself to be angry with her. He felt like a cad to have thoughtlessly chided her like this. What on earth could he have been thinking?

Her crying had subsided to a series of shuddering sniffles when, still curled in his arms, she asked him in a small voice, "Are you going to dismiss me?"

"Dismiss you?" he asked, incredulous. "Do you really think I'm such a heartless bastard?"

"Oh, no, Mr. Malloy, I don't really at all," she said, looking up at him through teary lashes.

He smiled. "Oh, yes, you do," he teased, instantly sorry when she burst into a fresh round of tears.

"No, no, sweetheart, don't cry," he murmured. Too thin and snuffling noisily, she still felt good in his arms.

Maybe he really was a heartless bastard. Why else would she have been so frightened to simply come out and tell him she was too sick to work? "Now, Liberty," he said, holding her at arm's length, "you must promise me something."

She nodded with a hiccup.

"If something like this happens again, and you feel unwell like this, you must tell me. You mustn't overwork yourself in your condition. Your health is of the utmost importance now. Don't kill yourself trying to do something you can't. Just tell me. Can you do that?"

"Yes, sir," she said, her voice still small and quiet. She wondered what had happened to change his demanding attitude.

"Now, I absolutely forbid you to do anything for me until you feel completely better. I want you happy and well. Off you go to bed, and if you get a good day's sleep, you may come down and sit on the porch in the afternoon sun."

She was so exhausted and relieved that for once she couldn't even bring herself to be angry at his patronizing attitude. "Thank you, sir."

He gently pushed her out of the study, shutting the door firmly behind him. She thought for a moment and headed down the stairs.

The door to his study opened again. "Miss Brooks, I thought my instructions were clear. Kindly return to your bed," Zeke said.

Liberty wheeled around. His eyes were kind, but he wasn't about to give a single inch.

"Oh, Mr. Malloy, how considerate of you to watch over me. I wanted a spot of tea and perhaps some broth. I felt too hungry to sleep," she said, her eyes wide in an expression of perfect innocence.

"Very well," he said curtly. "But mind you don't let Mrs. Biggins keep you up all day with her gossiping. I want you back in bed within half an hour."

"Yes, sir," she said meekly.

Zeke returned to the study oddly satisfied. Liberty's pregnancy was turning out to be rather pleasant. If it taught her to heed his word on important matters, rather than challenging everything that came out of his mouth, perhaps it was even a good thing. And she would see, as the time for the baby drew nearer, that he would take good care of her and the child.

By the time Liberty opened her eyes, the sun was lowering in the sky. She sat bolt upright in bed, then sank back a bit, dizzied by the effort. What time was it, anyway? Had Jane sent a return message to her note?

She padded downstairs to the kitchen, finding Mrs. Biggins poring over the household expense logs.

"Oh, heavens, dearie, what can you be thinking to come down here? And without so much as a pair of warm slippers on those feet. It'd be worth my job if Mr. Malloy could see you now." Mrs. Biggins's voice was stern, but her blue eyes were full of concern.

Liberty's toes curled on the cool tile of the kitchen floor. "He's not still here, is he?"

"No, no, he's off to give his lecture. Won't be back till morning, is my guess. Poor thing, you've been sleeping like a baby. Do you feel any better?"

Liberty smiled wanly. "I feel practically myself again," she lied.

Mrs. Biggins pursed her lips skeptically. "Hummph. Well, you still look a fright. Why don't you run on up to bed, and I'll fetch you a nice pot of chocolate. You haven't had two bites to eat all day."

Mrs. Biggins was right, but Liberty was surprised to find herself not at all hungry. "I don't think I could manage even a sip," she said, trying for another smile. "Mrs. B. . . . did I receive a letter this afternoon?"

The older woman narrowed her eyes. "That you did. I've been keeping it for you." She fished an envelope from the pocket of her snowy apron.

Liberty took the letter with studied calm, glad that Mr. Malloy was not here to question her about it.

"It was delivered this afternoon, around four o'clock, by a smart-mouthed little pup in a fancy carriage." Mrs. Biggin's mouth was set in disapproval.

Knowing Jane's tastes, Liberty did not doubt that the carriage was fancy. "Thank you for saving it for me," she murmured, running her fingers over the seal. "Well, I suppose I should be back in bed."

"That letter . . ." Mrs. Biggins began.

Liberty's heart skipped a beat. "Yes, Mrs. B.?"

Mrs. Biggins looked sheepish but determined. "It's not from that Captain Blodgett, is it?"

Liberty's jaw dropped. "Jack Blodgett? Certainly not! Whatever would make you think I was in correspondence with such a . . . such an unprincipled blackguard?"

Mrs. Biggins raised a speculative eyebrow. "I never did think you would, myself. You might do well to tell Mr. Malloy that, though."

Liberty closed her hand tightly around the note. "I've told Mr. Malloy before, I have no connection to the captain."

Mrs. Biggins peered at her. "And he didn't listen, I suppose. Well, all men are foolish and stubborn, and Mr. Malloy more so than most. But I think you'd best tell him again, miss, and in a way he'll listen to."

Liberty felt her cheeks color. "I don't know how I'd ever convince him of anything, Mrs. B. He seems to find me approximately as trustworthy as Benedict Arnold."

Mrs. Biggins nodded. "He gets some fool notion in his head, and it's the Devil to get it out again. I'll talk to him. It's plain enough to me that you've got no business with that nasty Blodgett character."

"Thank you," Liberty said, a genuine smile on her lips. "You're the only real friend I've had here, and I want you to know I'm very grateful for it."

Mrs. Biggins's face crinkled with pleasure. "Oh, hogwash," she said, swiping at her eyes. "You get back on up to bed, you hear?"

"I will. Good night, Mrs. B."

"Good night, dearie."

Liberty somehow managed to refrain from tearing the letter open until she was safely in her room. Jane's stationery was heavy and smelled of violets. Liberty read the short note twice.

Liberty dear,

Rec'd yr message. Of course we shall make arrangements to have the poor creature moved. Tell him to come to Murphy's abandoned slaughterhouse in the North End. He shall be met by men from the U.R. at precisely midnight tonight. Tell him to hide and wait for the signal—one long whistle, two short.

Burn this letter the instant you've read it, won't you, darling? I know we can count on your discretion.

Best regards,
Jane

Liberty's hand trembled as she held the paper to the lamp's flame, then threw it, burning, into her empty washbasin.

Tonight. Soko would be gone tonight, and this charade would be over. An end to the frayed nerves, the skulking around. An end to the web of lies she had been spinning and respinning. She could have wept in relief.

When Liberty opened the door to Soko's room, he was still huddled miserably in the corner, but she thought he looked a little better. "Hello, miss," he said, fairly amiable.

"I have good news for you," she whispered. "You'll be moving tonight. All you need to do is get to Murphy's slaughterhouse by midnight."

"Where's that?" he asked blankly.

"Why, it's . . ." Liberty cursed to herself. Of course he wouldn't know where it was. He had caught only fleeting glimpses of Boston while moving from house to house. He'd never find his way with only her directions, especially as he could not read the street signs, and finding any landmarks at night would be difficult.

She sighed. She would have to go with him. There wasn't any way around it. It would only take one last burst of effort, and she'd be finished with the entire affair. Anyway, she had hours to rest before having to make the long walk again. She would certainly be feeling much better by then.

"Don't worry," she said. "I'll take you there."

"You can't do that," he protested. "You looks poorly yourself, miss. You goin' to give up the ghost if you makes a long walk again. I'se strong enough and smart enough to figger out where's that Murphy's place at by myself."

"You're at least as sick as I am," she countered. "You don't know your way, and I don't want you having to ask anyone if you get lost. I haven't put myself through this so that you can get taken back into slavery, and neither have you."

After some terse whispered wranglings, he reluctantly agreed, and she slipped back into her room just as Mrs. Biggins headed up the stairs with a tray of soup, bread, and a mug of tea.

"Here you are, dearie," Mrs. Biggins clucked, as she watched Liberty change into her nightshirt and climb dutifully into bed. "Just in case you get hungry. That's a good girl. You see if you can't manage a bit of this nice soup."

"Mrs. B., do you think Mr. Malloy is terribly angry with me?" Liberty asked in a tiny voice, feeling suddenly overwhelmed.

"Oh, you know how he is, quick-tempered as the day is long. And if he thinks you were involved with that no-account snake in the grass Blodgett, he'll settle right down when we explain you weren't."

"Thank you, Mrs. B."

"Why, you're welcome, dearie. I'll leave now and let you get your rest. Mind you try and finish that soup now. It'll do you good."

When Mrs. Biggins had left, Liberty summoned the energy to take the soup to Soko. Then she returned to her room, pulled the covers to her chin, and sank into deep, healing sleep.

The room was cool and pitch black when Liberty awoke to hear Mrs. Biggins busying herself with the last few household chores before going off to bed. Liberty pulled herself reluctantly from the soft warmth of the bed, shivering in the night air. She stripped off the nightshirt in one smooth motion and hastily pulled on a cotton chemise, shuddering at the touch of the cold fabric against her warm skin. Her stays were tightened with one quick yank. She buttoned up her warm wool dress, pulled on a pair of thick worsted stockings, and laced her boots. As an afterthought, she wrapped her winter cloak around her before tiptoeing out into the hallway.

Soko was ready when she came into his room, his blankets folded neatly in one corner, his tired brown felt hat perched expectantly above his weary face.

"How are you feeling?" she whispered.

" 'Bout the same. Did you gets some sleep?" he asked, his solemn face concerned.

"Yes, thanks," she said, smiling. "Ready to go?" He nodded.

They slipped downstairs and out the back door, the cool air hitting Liberty painfully in the lungs. She swallowed hard to keep from coughing and focused on the silver stripe of road in front of her, lit only by moonlight. Her knees weakened at the thought of the long walk ahead. She glanced over at Soko, who looked no better than she, and forced herself to rally.

Only one more task ahead of her, one last burst of exertion, and the ordeal would be over. "All right, Soko," she said, her teeth gritted. "It's time."

Chapter 16

In town, the streets were ominous, filled with rowdy men and sinister, twisting shadows. Liberty kept her cloak wrapped tightly around her, the hood obscuring her face, as she walked determinedly on, staring at the road directly in front of her. Every face, every voice, filled her with a sick panic, making the blood rush frighteningly in her ears.

She had decided to make one stop on the way to the rendezvous. Moving Soko like this was dangerous, she knew, likely to get him caught. But she thought she knew a way to make him safe. After one false start, she found Nate Jackson's place.

Soko shot her a questioning look, and she whispered, "Trust me."

Liberty pounded on the door to Nate's small apartment above the presses. A serene, coffee-colored woman answered the door. "Yes?" The woman's voice was throaty, her tone elegant and cultured.

"I'm Liberty Brooks." Liberty threw the hood back from her face. "Is Nate Jackson here?"

Declining to answer, the woman asked, "Will he know what this is about?"

"Not exactly, but he knows me. I work for Ezekiel Malloy," she explained. She touched Soko's elbow. "And this is a friend of mine."

Liberty half expected the woman to turn her nose up at Soko's disheveled, woebegone figure, but she simply showed them into the apartment with a puzzled frown. "I'll get him for you."

Nate's face creased with worry when he saw her. "Liberty, what's wrong? Who's this? Has something happened to Zeke?"

"No, nothing like that."

Nate's wife discreetly closed the doors to the parlor and busied herself noisily in the kitchen. Liberty motioned for Soko to sit, and she tugged Nate to the other corner of the parlor.

A broad grin spread across his face. "Ah, you've finally come to throw yourself at me. I should have guessed. But I have a terrible confession to make— I'm perfectly faithful to my wife."

"Nate, will you please be serious?" Liberty glowered.

"Rather doubtful, I'm afraid," he replied. "At least not while you're lurking so entertainingly."

"I'll try not to lurk, but you must listen to me," she said with a fierce glare. "I need you to prepare some papers for me."

"Work? You came here in the middle of the night to talk about plain old work?"

"I need some papers that look like a pass for a freed slave."

To Liberty's satisfaction, Nate sobered instantly. "Liberty, do you understand what you're asking me to do?"

"To help a fellow soul in need," she replied evenly, glancing over at the miserable figure huddled in one of Nate's chairs.

"To commit forgery and aid and abet a fugitive slave," Nate countered. "Do you have any idea what kinds of penalties are involved?"

"Penalties worse than slavery?" she asked pointedly.

"I think death is worse than slavery," he said,

his voice cold. "If this got around, I could be lynched. There are enough bad feelings about a Negro businessman anyway. I'm hardly eager to fan the flames."

"No one will ever find out. You don't even have to tell your wife. Nate, you have to do this. I've been hiding Soko—Zeke doesn't know about it—and he's a dear, sweet boy. He's caught a wretched cold from me, and I owe this to him. All you have to do is to slip downstairs and print up something that looks nice and official. Please."

"You've been hiding a fugitive without telling Zeke?" Nate was incredulous.

"Well, I could hardly tell Mr. Malloy, now, could I?" Liberty snapped. "If I've heard him once, I've heard him a thousand times—a prominent abolitionist cannot afford to harbor runaways. Rip slavery out by the roots, remember?"

Nate ran a hand over his brow. "This is marvelous. It really is. So that's the secret you've been keeping from Zeke, then?"

Liberty nodded guiltily. "I didn't realize he suspected anything."

Nate gave a strange, choked laugh. "Oh, my dear, you have no idea. So the Railroad sent you here. Why? I've told them a dozen times to get a white man to print their passes. I can't take that kind of risk."

Liberty blanched. "Well, they didn't exactly send me."

He studied her face carefully. "You're not with the Railroad at all. Oh, blast, forget I ever mentioned it. What are you involved in, anyway?"

"It *is* for the Underground Railroad," she confessed, "but I'm not really involved. I'm just doing something for them this one time," she stammered.

"Liberty my dear, you could rot in prison for this one time. The fine for abetting runaways is currently floating at around a thousand dollars!"

he exploded. "My God, this is dangerous business. You have no idea how dangerous."

"And that means I should hide my eyes and cower in my room like a good little girl?"

"How did you get here?" he asked, suspicious.

"I walked," she said quietly.

"You walked?" he roared. "Wonderful! If you wanted to kill yourself, you could have stepped out in front of a train. It would have been much simpler."

"I had no choice!" she shouted back. "What was I supposed to do? Involve Jim in this? Maybe Mrs. Biggins? Mr. Malloy would never have agreed to help me, and I didn't know who else I could trust."

"Something you couldn't do? Something you wouldn't risk?" he mocked. "Amazing!"

"Nate," she pleaded, glancing over at Soko. The young man had slunk down in his chair as if trying to make himself invisible. She lowered her voice. "Bickering won't get us anywhere. But your doing this favor will."

He met her gaze unwaveringly. "Oh, all right," he said disgustedly. "If you can risk your idiot neck for this, I suppose I can, too."

She threw her arms around his neck. "Oh, Nate!" she cried. "I just knew you'd do it! You won't regret this, you'll see."

He untangled himself from her embrace, grumbling, "I probably won't live long enough." He rolled up his sleeves and walked to the door of the study. "I'll do this, but on two conditions," he said.

"Of course, anything."

"This would send my wife through the roof. You mustn't say one word about why you're here. And be careful—she's sharp as an eagle. Make conversation about knitting or something until I get back. I won't be gone long."

Liberty swallowed her resentment at the knitting

remark. "I promise. What's the second condition?"

"That you tell Zeke Malloy the entire story, beginning to end, first thing tomorrow morning."

Liberty gulped, but seeing Nate's unyielding expression, she nodded her head in agreement.

Nate was right about his wife. Mrs. Jackson discreetly avoided direct questions but grilled Liberty nonetheless in a roundabout way that was difficult to evade. Liberty discovered her best strategy was to pretend to be a simpering female with no head for business, herself baffled by this late night errand for the prickly Mr. Malloy.

She was looking nervously at the wall clock behind Mrs. Jackson when Nate returned from the shop. "Here you are Liberty, the, uh . . . rush order for Zeke. Make sure he gets good use of it, after the trouble I've gone to," he said significantly.

"Of course, Nate. Thanks once again for your help on this. Mr. Malloy will be very grateful."

As he showed Liberty and Soko out, he said in a low voice, "Shall I walk you to where you're going? This city can be pretty rough at night."

She shook her head vigorously. "No. If anything went wrong, it would be much worse for you than it would be for me."

He nodded reluctantly, knowing she was right. "But you come right back here when things are settled, and I'll drive you home. All right?"

Liberty nodded gratefully.

"Good night, Liberty, and please be careful."

"I'm always careful," she replied.

Nate, groaning, let her out into the night.

The damp night air chilled Liberty to the bone after the pleasant golden warmth of the Jacksons' rooms. She pulled her cloak tighter around her and motioned for Soko to follow.

Liberty found her way to Murphy's easily; it was no more than two blocks from Jack Blodgett's office. The neighborhood was even worse at night.

Soko slogged along behind her, faintly interested in the machinations of the city but slowed down by his own aching head and pained lungs.

The old slaughterhouse was a large, dark building with a row of small broken windows near the roof. Most of its paint had peeled, leaving only stubborn patches that refused to yield to the elements. The sounds of drinking and gambling and a woman's shrill laughter came from a nearby tavern. Otherwise, the neighborhood was deserted, the moon bright against the water. Liberty resolved to stick to well-traveled, brightly-lit streets when she returned to Nate's, even if the route was twice as long.

Liberty and Soko crouched behind a pair of huge rotted barrels outside the warehouse. There was little chance that anyone would stop them, but their situation was peculiar, and Liberty was anxious to avoid any attention.

A cloud passed over the moon, and a thin, sharp wind passed through Liberty like a blade. Let it be close to time, she prayed. After this, there would be no more crazy projects. She would stick to what she had time and energy for. And she absolutely never, ever would put herself in the position of having to lie to Zeke Malloy again. She had felt a pang every time she looked at him, knowing she was betraying his confidence at every moment. Nate had been right; the only thing to do was to tell Zeke the whole story. He would be furious, but she could no longer live with the lies.

Oh, and there was that matter of Blodgett to clear up. She felt a twinge at that thought, too, knowing it was her fault Zeke had gotten the wrong impression. Well, she had tried to tell him that Blodgett wasn't her lover. But then they had started shouting at each other, and things had gotten so muddled that she hadn't been able to think straight. Would Zeke see her differently when he knew she had no alliance whatsoever with that odious charlatan? She mused that perhaps they would be able to start over, to become friends.

She thought of their tryst in the carriage, and her stomach flip-flopped. Perhaps even . . . more than friends.

The rattle of wheels sounded very close, and Liberty held her breath, keeping herself as small as she could behind the barrels. Several figures emerged from the alley behind the slaughterhouse. The moon came out from behind the cloud, and Liberty could see two men and a woman. The woman gave the signal Jane had told her to wait for. Liberty tapped Soko lightly, and he emerged from his hiding place and walked over to the figures. The men slapped him on the back in welcome.

Suddenly the sharp crack of a pistol sounded, and a crate splintered. Soko's rescuers melted into the darkness, but Soko, slow and sick, was seized by the group of thugs who emerged from the shadows.

"Whaddaya know, a runaway. Sturdy enough boy. Somebody'll be glad to get him back." The accoster was tall, his hair glowing bright in the moonlight. His voice was maddeningly familiar to Liberty, but as she crouched, immobile with fear, in her hiding place, her mind was reeling too fast to place it.

"He looks sickly, boss," complained a small, skinny figure. A third man held the struggling fugitive fast even as Soko protested that he had free papers.

The tall, fair man took Soko's chin in his hand and turned his head appraisingly. "He's not in such bad shape. A little under the weather, maybe, but we can keep him in a separate cabin on the ship. Most likely he'll make it through just fine."

Liberty was feeling appalled that the Underground Railroad rescuers had deserted Soko when the third intruder, who had been holding Soko, suddenly gave a loud groan and sank to his knees. A figure in the darkness—one of the Railroad men—pulled a dark, wet blade from the sunken body before melting back into the darkness.

The tall man cursed. Soko kicked the smaller man squarely in the groin, doubling him over, and ran for the inky side streets.

"Useless little bastard!" the tall man screamed. "Don't just stand there, catch him!" he shouted, flailing his arms in disgust. The small man, limping slightly, ran through the streets, trying to avoid the shadows where, perhaps, the man with the knife might hide.

That voice! An icy sweat broke on her forehead as Liberty recognized it at last. It was Jack Blodgett. *This* was the business he had in town. These were his "exports." Human lives. She was nearly nauseated.

She had to do something. Soko had run off, but would he manage to escape? And where would he go? Liberty's mind was working furiously when a nagging sensation abruptly welled up within her.

No! She had to control it. She couldn't afford to give herself away now. Her eyes stung with the effort.

It was no use. Hidden behind the malodorous barrel, doubled over and pressing her fists against her mouth, she couldn't keep her body from betraying her. The dust, the wet, and her own fear and anger conspired to pierce her lungs as if with knives. She coughed, and found she couldn't stop. The sound echoed loudly through the dark, still night.

"Liberty, no!" Soko shouted from somewhere in the darkness.

"Liberty?" Blodgett shouted, stunned. "Oh, Christ. Goddamn it, Sid, forget the boy! You've got to get her!"

Liberty took a deep breath and bolted for an alley, her heart pounding painfully.

At the end of the alley was a tavern buzzing with music and voices. She had nearly reached the door when two men came out of it, holding each other up. "Well, well, more entertainment for the evening," slurred one in a nasty voice.

"We ain't got no money left," reminded the other with a mournful hiccup.

"Then I guess we'll just have to take what we want," said the first with a chuckle.

She backed away from them, shaking her head, when a pair of large hands gripped her shoulders painfully from behind. "Sorry, fellows, but I saw her first." Blodgett's voice was icy, with no trace of the buffoonery Liberty normally associated with him. The sight of Sid cleaning his dirty fingernails with a long, sharp blade cut short the protests of the two men in the alley.

"Suit yerself," the first man shrugged, and the two lurched off.

"No, don't leave me!" she screamed at the two drunken men. "You've got to help me!" Two massive hands pinioned her, reeking of cigars. She fought to wrench her arms free of Blodgett's bruising grip, but he tightened his hold on her and pulled her sharply back against the powerful, muscular block of his body.

Lightning flashes of memory struck her: the tic in Zeke's cheek when he heard Blodgett's name; the stink of rum and stale cigars; the handsome face smeared with boot polish. Her mind reeled crazily, a hodgepodge of pictures that made no sense, racing, racing.

Then all she saw was Sid bending to pick up a brick. Her head filled with a sudden, searing pain. Hundreds of sparkling dots clouded her vision. The blackness swam up to claim her, and she sank into Jack Blodgett's arms.

BOOK TWO

I am the hounded slave. . . . I wince at the bite of dogs,
Hell and despair are upon me. . . . crack and again crack
the marksmen. . . .
I fall on the weeds and stones,
The riders spur their unwilling horses and haul close.
                    —Walt Whitman, "Leaves of Grass"

Chapter 17

Liberty awoke in a tiny room, the stone floor covered with dirty straw that teemed with fleas. Her skin was covered with bites, but when she tried to scratch at one, her wrists seemed strangely heavy. She looked down and saw that she had been stripped to her shift, revealing her calves and ankles. She wore a set of strange, jeweled metal bracelets, belt, and necklace, heavy and very close-fitting. The metalwork was intricate and subtle, with curving patterns finely wrought in silver and inlaid with gleaming stones of all colors. It had a barbaric look to it, the patterns delicate but some-how savage. Thick iron rings, as large as a Gypsy's hoop earring, were welded to the jewelry. It was uncomfortably heavy, biting into her flesh as she fumbled with the necklace to try to remove the barbarous thing from around her neck.

A man's voice came from above her head. "The collar isn't made to come off so easily, my dear. Neither are the shackles. Made in Persia. Beautiful work, I think. They suit you."

She curled instinctively into a small ball, trying to protect her modesty. The effort of lifting her head to identify the voice made her head swim. Pain, a vicious stabbing pain at the back of her skull. She thought for a moment she would lose consciousness again.

The voice continued. "Of course, they're not purely decorative. If we need to chain you up to the others, they'll prove useful. But I must confess that I use them on you pleasure-slaves simply because I find a woman in shackles incomparably exciting." The man was backlit, and the late morning sun glinted off his blond hair, keeping his face in shadow. The room seemed to tilt at crazy angles, and she felt faintly nauseated. He turned slightly to one side, and she felt an icy shock as she recognized those yellow eyes and that arrogant profile.

She was beginning to remember. Soko ... the Underground Railroad ... Blodgett on the dock. It had been dark. Something had hit her head. And then?

"Come, now, no sense trying to cover yourself up. I've already had a good look at you while you were getting your beauty sleep. Up you go," he said as he pulled her roughly to her feet, gathering both her hands in one large fist.

She turned her head away from him, her face burning with shame at being so exposed. He pawed her breasts carelessly. "These are lovely. They're going to make me a great deal of money."

She felt a cold sweat on her back and forehead. Money? She dimly assumed he had brought her here for his own unthinkable desires. Had he raped her already, while she lay sick and senseless in the dirty straw? But no, the only pain she felt was in her lungs and in the brutal throbbing at the back of her head.

Evidently he had postponed her violation. She would be fully aware when he completed her degradation. The thought momentarily swamped her with a blinding panic.

He had mentioned money. She had to focus on the clues he gave her, so she could figure out how to get out of this mess. Was he a panderer? Very likely, she thought with contempt. Now she knew what had caused her to recoil from him; she had known instinctively that he was a villain, no matter how many times she'd tried to convince herself of his respectability.

She tried to piece together what was happening to her, but her mind veered wildly, a jumble of penny postcards that would not fit together to form a coherent story.

He chuckled coldly. "You're pretty when your eyes fill up with tears," he said softly as he began to fondle her with large, rough hands. "Helpless and vulnerable, the way a woman should be."

"Take your hands off me!" she screamed, wrenching herself away from his pawing. The effort nearly doubled her over as her lungs contracted with icy spasms.

Lightning-fast, he grasped one of her hands in his and bent her fingers back until her mind was perfectly sharp and focused with the pain. "That's right, sweetheart," he said, his voice low and dangerous. "I've spoiled valuable goods before, and snapping the bones of each pretty finger won't bring your price down much. I break fiery fillies like matchsticks, and it would be nothing but pleasure for me to show you how."

The fog that had muddled her mind was no match for this sharp, insistent pain. She realized clearly that defiance would only make escape more difficult. "I'm sorry," she whispered, keeping her voice as subservient as possible.

He sneered, but released his grip on her hand. "Better. Maybe you should call me Master, though. It would do you good to get used to it."

"Master?" Her stomach gave a sickening flip.

"Of course, you won't have the pleasure of calling me that for long. Soon we'll be shipping you out to New Orleans and on to Cuba, to be returned to your lawful master, Don Diego Montoya Veracruz."

"As a . . . slave?" she asked, certain she must have misunderstood him.

He smiled.

"But that's ridiculous. I was born in Ohio. This person Montoya will certainly recognize I'm not his escaped slave. I'm not even a Negro," she said, trying to understand what was happening to her. Blodgett was insane, that much was obvious, but she had to make him see that his bizarre plan could never work.

He released her hand and allowed himself a rough caress of her cheek. "Ah, well, so many of you pretty little niggers have a little master blood in you. It can't really be helped. The immorality of your race and all. And you sure could pass for white, except for your limited intelligence and the fact that you look like a bitch in heat. No respectable white woman has a mouth or a body like that. I can tell," he said, sidling up to grind his pelvis against her nearly nude body, "you're just itching for a ride on a strong, white mount."

She willed herself not to become sick at his hot, sour breath on her face as he murmured the obscenities. "I think you need a little riding lesson right now," he muttered. "You seem to lack the correct attitude." His breath was fast and hot on her neck.

She shuddered, trying to force a calm into her voice that she did not feel. "Captain Blodgett, you know perfectly well who I am. I'm Liberty Brooks. You asked me to marry you, and I declined. Is that what this is about? To punish me? You know this man won't recognize me when we get to Cuba. This charade is pointless."

Blodgett laughed. "He's worn out six *runaways* in the two years I've been working for him. Señor Montoya has some . . . peculiar notions about handling his fancies. It's a rare woman who can tolerate that much pain and survive. I'm fascinated as hell, but it's an expensive luxury. It'll take a few more years on this circuit before I can move to Cuba myself and buy all the niggers I need to do what I please with." The conversation seemed to have stimulated him, as she saw by the huge bulge in his trousers. He shifted uncomfortably and moved to unbutton himself.

Her mind raced as she desperately tried to think of a way to escape. "But don't you think," she said quickly, "that Mr. Montoya would appreciate a virgin? It seems to me that I . . . would command a better price if I were . . . unspoiled."

Her heart hammered as Blodgett considered the notion. Desire glazed his eyes, but the mention of money seemed to have distracted him.

"Señor Montoya has a taste for novelty. He just might appreciate a virgin," he said appraisingly. "When your time comes, you'll just scream all the louder." He gazed at her again, wrapped her hair in his fist, and pulled her head back sharply, forcing her to her knees. "But there is one thing you can do without lowering your market value any."

He fumbled with the trouser buttons and released an enormous, red, distended organ. She turned her face away violently, but he brought her head toward him with a cruel twist of his fist. "Open up, sweetheart. And if I feel your teeth even once, I'll take my pleasure somewhere even less pleasant," he said menacingly. He pried her jaws apart and began to push himself into her mouth, but as soon as she felt the touch of him on her lips, she gagged and bucked back, retching the contents of her stomach over his trousers and impeccably shined shoes.

"You little bitch!" he cried, and struck her hard across the face. Her body, frail and light from illness, flew across the room with sickening ease. Light-headed, she felt a bruise blooming across her cheek.

He crossed the room in lightning strides and pulled her by the hair to her feet. "Don't you ever do that to me again, do you understand me?" he said in disgust. "If you have to puke, you let me know, so you can puke somewhere besides all over my best shoes. Understand?" He gave her body a violent shake that made her aching bones wish they could cry for mercy. "Do you understand?" he screamed.

"Yes," she whispered, wishing he would let go of her so she could sink to the ground and find some peace in unconsciousness.

"Yes, what?" he snarled.

"Yes, Master," she breathed.

"The only reason you're still alive, sweetheart, is that you're worth too goddamned much money to kill right now. But you haven't prevented anything, just put it off. You are going to swallow it until you choke, and you're going to love it. It's only a matter of time." He stalked out of the room, his boots booming in her ears like cannon fire, and she thankfully slipped off into a merciful, inky blackness.

After all these years, Nate thought he'd seen the worst of Zeke Malloy. But he'd been wrong. Nothing he'd ever seen of his friend had prepared him for this. The man who had always been able to pull himself together no matter how ugly the circumstances had been reduced to a raving lunatic, bellowing like a wounded bull. He'd smashed a chair to bits already before Nate had hauled him down to the printshop office, fearing for his wife's china.

Zeke had reached a strange calm now, but that unholy fire still lit his eyes, and Nate was cautious. "Look, Zeke," he tried, "I'm sorry."

It had been the wrong thing to say. The demon-fire in Zeke's eyes raged again, and Nate almost felt afraid of his old friend, the man who was like a brother to him.

"You had her! She was right here, and you let her go!" Zeke's voice cracked with pain.

Nate's stomach twisted guiltily. "I had no idea this would happen, Zeke. No one could have."

For a moment Zeke said nothing. They had been through this a dozen times. "She's gone. He's got her, just like he's taken everything else from me."

"We'll get her back."

"Christ, we don't even have the first idea where he's headed!" Zeke slammed his fist into Nate's desk. "His clippers are all still in port, and they've been as quiet as corpses. There's nothing going out of Boston on them for at least a week. He's found some other way to transport his cargo—he must have."

"But he still has to get them to the same place," Nate insisted. "However he manages it, he'll get himself to New Orleans. It's the only place he can get top price for his load."

Zeke's shoulders sank, his head propped between his hands. "Holy hell, listen to us. We're as bad as he is, talking about 'cargo' and 'loads.' These are human beings, Nate. Indigo and her baby—he snatched them both right off the dock. Jake and Tom were lucky to get away. And now he's got Liberty as well. I never should have trusted that damned new pilot."

"You've got to get hold of yourself, Zeke" Nate said. "We can get Liberty back, but we'll have to act quickly."

Zeke shot him a savage look. "Act? How? Blodgett could have gone in a thousand directions. We'll never find her, Nate."

"There are only two or three viable ways to transport a large group of slaves to New Orleans."

Zeke's jaw twitched. "There are a half dozen good overland routes."

"Blodgett's not a man for wagons and coaches, and it would cost a fortune to ship so many people that way. He'll take them by ship. You can bet on it."

"So why the empty clippers in the harbor?"

"Because we know his routines here in Boston. We know where he docks, where he hires his men— everything about the way he runs his clippers. But there's something we don't know: how he runs his riverboats."

Zeke gave Nate a piercing look. "Steamboat? But that would take him double the time."

"Yes, but half the worry if it throws us off the trail. He has a fleet that runs from Pittsburgh to New Orleans, and Pittsburgh's an easy train ride from Boston. From there we hop a boat down the Ohio, and we're on his tail. I have an old listing of Blodgett's steamboat lines, and it'll be easy to get an update. We can get him, Zeke, I know we can."

The storm in Zeke's eyes subsided a fraction, and Nate almost breathed a sigh of relief.

"I'll get that son of a bitch," Zeke whispered. "First I'll get Liberty out of his clutches, and then I'll crush him like a cockroach. I should have done it years ago."

Nate gave his friend a wary look. "What about Annabelle?"

Zeke straightened his cravat and stood, every trace of wildness gone now. He was master of himself, the icy control back in place. "I can't keep letting Blodgett destroy people on the slim chance that Anna is still alive. She wouldn't have wanted me to. It's time for me to move on and do what I have to do."

Nate shook his head. He'd waited a long time for his friend to come to this. "So it's the real thing this time? No holds barred?"

Zeke nodded. "No holds barred."

"Two weeks ago, this was unthinkable, Zeke. What's changed?"

"I've just realized my own stupidity, that's all. I've been a fool to believe Jack's lies about Annabelle. She's dead. She must be."

What Zeke said was doubtless true, but Nate was pretty sure there was more to his friend's change of heart than that. For years, Annabelle's safety had been the only thing Zeke had to lose. But now there was something new at stake, and Zeke was willing to risk everything for it.

That something new was Liberty Brooks.

Two of Blodgett's henchmen pulled Liberty to her feet before sunrise the next day. The icy early morning air punished her lungs, and a bout of deep, painful coughs overcame her as they yanked her to her feet. Fear overshadowed even her mortification at having these two oafs paw her nearly nude body, covered only by her thin linen chemise and the jeweled shackles. She was seriously ill, and she knew that slave traders were often less than careful with their merchandise. In her weakened state, she might well not survive the passage.

The rat-faced little man spat a stream of tobacco juice and eyed her appraisingly, while the bigger one held her arms behind her. "She oughta make up for the lousy month we been havin'," the little man mused. "Three thousand at least. An' she's got more gumption than most. I'm damned sick of puttin' it to them doe-eyed bitches who lie there not makin' a sound, like they was a thousand miles away. You know this un'll put up a good fight."

The taller man grunted and said eagerly, "Sid, let's do it to her now, huh? She's real pretty. I don't wanna wait fer the captain ta git first grabs."

Liberty held her breath. Panic cut through the mind-numbing pain in her lungs. She had never been so afraid, but she could not even muster the strength to scream, much less fight these men.

"Jesus, Ox, use your thick head for once. If the

captain finds out we took a crack at her before him, he'll take it out of our hides. Besides, we'll have plenty of chance later. The trip takes a couple weeks, with the stops we're makin'. I sure do wish we could, though. Bet she bleeds."

"Whaddaya mean, Sid?" Ox asked.

"I bet she's a virgin, you dope. Ain't you never had you a virgin?"

"Uh, sure, lots of 'em," Ox said, his pride wounded.

"If you had so many, how come you don't know nuthin' about it? A virgin bleeds the first time you stick her, an' they're tighter than you kin imagine. An they usu'lly scream, and cry afterwards. Virgins is the best-quality goods."

"Yeah, yeah, my Susie was a virgin. I remember that bleedin' stuff now. I just forgot, was all."

"You wouldn'ta forgot if she was really a virgin," Sid said wistfully. "Stickin' a virgin is just like drinkin' champagne. After that, you only wanna do it the Greek way, just from rememberin' how tight them virgins is."

"You done a girl that way?" the big man asked, incredulous.

"Sure, lots a times," said Sid breezily. "Just darkies, though. Ain't no white woman would let a man do that."

"How do ya do it?"

"Hell, ya just stick it in, same as the other way. You gotta grease it up first, though, or it don't go in so easy."

"You gonna do that with this one?"

Liberty froze with shock and fear.

"Sure, I might."

"But ain't she white?" Ox whispered.

"Hell, no, she just looks white, you dummy. We're gonna *sell* her in Cuba. How do you think we could do that if she was white?"

"But we done it before, Sid, a couple a—"

Sid's thin lips set grimly. "They was all niggers, you hear?" he said angrily. "Don't you ever let me ketch you sayin' they was white. They was just dirty niggers that could pass for white, you understand? Ox, this is important, so you pay attention, you understand me?"

"Yeah, Sid, I understand. She looks white, but she ain't."

"That's right, Ox. Now, stop jawin', and let's get her moved out of here."

She was too weak to struggle when they wrapped her in a coarse wool blanket. The wool was cheap and scratchy, but she was grateful for the warmth; she knew she would not have survived much longer in the cold. Another spasm of painful coughs wracked her body.

They wound her entire body, including her face, in the blanket, and swung her into the air. Her stomach gave a nauseated lurch when they lifted her, but she fought the urge to retch, afraid she would choke or suffocate. She could hear the sounds of the slums—the rough games of boys in the street, the catcalls of the prostitutes as sailors passed by, the whole tightly wound clock-spring of the city, each person making his way however he could. She never thought she could feel such emotion for the maddening, intimidating place, but now she was filled with a deep pain at the thought of never seeing it again.

They threw her blanket-wrapped body into the back of a wagon. Liberty could feel similarly packaged bodies wriggling beneath her. Had they captured Soko? Who else shared this prison with her? She felt the wagon lurch and roll jumpily down the street. The nausea returned with the wagon's arrhythmic jerk, and she mustered a heroic effort to roll over onto her side, so that if she was sick, it would not lodge in her windpipe.

She was a slave. She couldn't quite make herself

believe it. These men could do absolutely anything they wanted with her, as their earlier conversation amply demonstrated. The only thing they were afraid of was Blodgett; she was fairly certain they would not touch her without his permission. But he, she knew, was more eager than any of them to bed her, probably as sadistically as possible. She prayed his greed would keep him at bay. Sid and Ox's obscene talk nagged at her, feeding her terror.

She began to shudder uncontrollably, although the blanket now felt warm and wet, stifling her with its clamminess. She was cocooned in damp wool, and warm. Too warm. Her head ached mercilessly where she'd been hit, and the pain spread over her like a thick film. What month was this? June? July? Too warm, even for summer.

Escape. Resist. She tried feebly to push her mind to think of a plan. Had to think. But a muggy, irresistible drowsiness flowed into her thoughts, making them as sluggish and sticky as molasses.

Papa, her Papa who had always loved her so much. But that morning he was different. He had started drinking so early, and Mama hadn't said a word all day, she was so angry. And then he'd begun to shout, and no one could make him stop. He told Mama it was her fault all those men looked at her, and then . . . and then he'd exploded. He struck her, and called her terrible things— a mongrel, a half-breed whore. And Liberty had screamed at him then, screamed and pummeled at his broad back, but he'd pushed her away. Through it all, Mama never said a word.

After that day, things had never been the same again. Don't have any more of that whiskey, Papa. See? I'm the smartest girl in my class. I'll keep the house clean while Mama's delivering that baby across town, and I can cook real good, and I don't let my studies fall one little bit. I don't need to sleep or rest. I don't need to take anything for myself at all. It's all for you, Papa. But please don't have another glass. Please, please, Papa.

She was so sleepy, but she couldn't sleep. Unless she was sleeping now. Was she? Too warm to sleep now. Her mind floated far above her body, freed finally from pain and fear. So warm, comfortable. The blanket, it was soaked through. What was that funny noise? The men, the men beneath her, groaning. So many bodies beneath hers, just like Christmas presents wrapped in blankets. Blanket was so itchy before, but now it was just wet, wet all over. Wet and soft and so warm.

His eyes. She dreamed of them for months, waking up, finding herself wet, down there between her legs. Confused. Her nipples hard so they almost hurt, but hurt in a way that felt good. When she saw him, his smile lit up her soul like the rising sun.

He thought she was a slut. A slut. And it was true. She let him do those things, at the party, let him touch her and kiss her breasts, and then he had been so angry. He kissed her, and then she wanted to know more, to go further and further until she was ruined, like a broken milk jug, no good for anything anymore, spoiled and broken and useless.

But she still wanted him, wanted his mouth to do those things again and to make her feel that way. All these nights she had been dreaming about him, dreaming that he would love her in that way that would ruin her, and then she would be all his.

Too warm here, clammy. Hard to breathe. These men were waiting to rape her. The thought aroused in her nothing more than a morbid curiosity. Would they wait until she was well? Or would they assault her when she was this way, locked in other times and places, so far away from her own body? This was not happening to Liberty, but to someone who looked very much like her, maybe a girl in a book. And Liberty herself barely had the strength to turn the pages.

Cold. The damp blankets clung to her, and she could feel the itch of the cheap wool again. Cold, like city streets at dawn, like breaking the ice in the cows' trough at sunup. The kind of cold that pierces bones. She shuddered, her teeth rattling audibly.

The wet cold was drowning her, drowning her like the ocean, salty and deep. So deep, a thousand miles down, she was soulless and mindless as a sea creature, all fins and scales and slippery instinct.

Her body reeled, over and over, spinning out of control. She was a feather on the breeze, weightless, at the mercy of the slightest breath. She was a sack of wet sand, dull and immobile. She was being turned, again and again, losing all sense of up or down.

The sudden bright light blinded her, and she moaned. She shut her eyes against it, but it glowed red through her eyelids. Feebly she pushed her body so that her face was pressed to the cool earth, away from the light's cruelty. A breeze passed over her, starting a new round of uncontrollable shivering as a painful retching began in her throat.

"Aw, hell, she's sick, and we ain't even got on the train yet," said Sid, squirting a stream of tobacco juice.

"Jeez, Sid, she don't look so good," Ox said worriedly.

"I can see that for myself, you dope. What are we gonna do about it, that's what I'm tryin' to figger."

"What seems to be the matter, gentlemen?"

Blodgett's voice made Liberty's flesh crawl, and she began to shake even more.

"Oh, boss," Sid said with unconvincing calm, "glad you're here. It's the bitch we picked up at the last minute in the city. She's pretty sick. I figger if we ship her out now, we'll prob'ly lose her."

"You don't get paid to think, though, do you, Sid?" Blodgett said icily. "We've got to move her, now. This little girl has some friends in very unpleasant circles, not the least of which is the Antislavery Society. Including, my boys, Mr. Ezekiel goddamned Malloy. She'd get away from us in a minute if we delay."

"But, boss, don'tcha think she's pretty sick? She might bring the whole group down," protested Sid.

Blodgett landed a kick at Liberty's midsection. She moaned and retreated into a curled position, another bout of coughing squeezing at her lungs. "She's fakin' it. She gobbled my rod like a whore just this morning. She ain't sick."

Sid and Ox said nothing.

"All right, you morons. If you're so worried, we'll put her in the cabin with the other bitch we trapped yesterday. That way we can keep all the best meat safe in one place, right, boys?"

Sid and Ox laughed nervously and hoisted Liberty up. Her body was cold and slick and completely without resistance. She mumbled as they loaded her into a boxcar, turning her head feebly toward a murmur that sounded like a crowd. But it couldn't be. If there were people nearby, surely they would save her from this. She slipped again into a blackness darker than night.

"Show's over, folks, just a runaway. We're moving on now. Come on, move away." Blodgett shooed the curious crowd away, watching as Sid and Ox loaded the girl onto the train.

You don't act so high and mighty now, do you, Miss goddamned superior Brooks? Blodgett stretched his arms expansively and smiled. The shoe was on the other foot now, and he intended to savor every delectable instant of his revenge.

Chapter 18

❧❧

This light was better, not so bright, but she was too warm again, burning up. Maybe she was in Hell.

I'm burning for what I did with Zeke, for the things I thought about him and the way I let him touch me in the carriage. And for the dreams, sinful dreams.

She fought the shame that threatened to swamp her as she lay semiconscious. Her feelings for Zeke had been deep, deeper than she'd ever admitted to herself. And there was nothing cheap or dirty about them.

It was wrong. He didn't love me. He didn't even like me very much. We weren't married or even engaged. It was a sin, and now I'm being punished. Wickedness, burning. Burning.

Her throat was parched, and she heard only a dry croak when she tried to speak. "Burning . . ."

"Sweet Jesus, she awake," came a gentle voice. Liberty's eyes were weak and the light was dim, but she could see a blurred shape move over her when she tried to speak.

"Thirsty. Please . . ."

"Here you is, just a little bit of water. Mind you don't spill it, now."

Liberty clutched at the tin cup as firmly as her weakened muscles would allow, but it slipped, too heavy, through her fingers, and the warm water spilled over her breasts and shoulders. She began to weep, overcome with frustration, small, shuddering sobs wracking her emaciated frame.

"No, no, ain't no call to cry, now. Look, lookee here, I just wipes you down and you's all clean again. See?" came the gentle voice. Strong, kind hands wiped her chemise with a soft cloth, then dipped the cloth in water and wiped her forehead and cheeks. The cloth felt cool and fresh. The cup was lifted again to her lips, the cool hands keeping hold of it this time. Water flowed past her cracked lips, down her sore throat. Liberty moved greedily for another drink, but the gentle hands took the cup away. "Not just yet. You goin' be sick if you drinks the whole cup now."

"Who . . . ?" Liberty managed, focusing with difficulty on this soft-voiced stranger. "Who are you?"

"I just be a friend. I'se going look after you for a little while. You goin' to be all right. You been mighty sick, but you goin' to live. They ain't no doubt now."

Who? Liberty thought, but before she could repeat the word, she drifted back into fevered sleep.

It doesn't matter what I do. It doesn't matter. I can't keep him from drinking that whiskey, from saying those things to Mama, from getting beat up again. I'm so tired, so tired from everything, and no matter how hard I try, I can't make him stop. Maybe he knows the shameful dreams I've been having about that fancy-talking Boston city man. I'm wicked and lazy, and now I'm being punished. I drove him to this, and now I've got to pay for it.

As Liberty's eyes fluttered open and adjusted to the darkness, she made out the silhouette of a pretty young woman, propped up against the wall, nursing an infant. The woman's close-cropped hair set off the fine shape of her head, and a collar and shackles gleamed on her sculpted collarbone and slender wrists. She wore no more than Liberty, who was shy enough to be glad of the darkness as she weakly brought her knees up to her chest.

"Who are you?" she wondered in a soft whisper.

The young woman's eyes opened. "Don't has to whisper," she said, smiling. "They ain't nobody goin' to hear you, and ain't nobody care if they do. My name's Indigo James. This here be my son, Samuel."

"I'm Liberty Brooks. Where are we?" She still felt physically weak but mentally more lucid than she had in . . . days? weeks? She had no idea how much time had passed, but it seemed like a very long while.

"We on a riverboat, headed I don't know where. They moved us here yestiday. You done slept clean through three days."

"Did Jack Blodgett bring you here?"

"I don't know who he be. Some nasty white man with evil yellow eyes."

Liberty sank back weakly against the rough blanket. "That's Blodgett. You're not really an escaped slave either, are you?"

"You talks a lot for a girl just come through one evil fever. How come you talks so fine? You ain't puttin' on airs with me, is you, girl? Cause they ain't no reason for *that*, now."

Liberty squirmed. "No, I'm sorry, nothing like that. I—I had some city learning, that's all." She found to her distress that the flat, plain Ohio accent that she had worked so hard to squelch would not be put back on like some long-forgotten dress. "Reckon I just spent too much time talking with fancy folks," she stammered, sounding as awkward as she felt.

Indigo squinted in the moonlight. "You's a *white* woman!" she said with a low whistle. "Funny I never seed it when you was sick. On top of all the rest, I gots to share quarters with a buckra woman. What the Divvil you doin' here?"

"Blodgett seemed to think I would pass for a light-skinned Negro. I'm one-quarter Indian," Liberty explained apologetically.

"I seen some yella gals in my time, but y'all be *white*. Crazy white man. Did'n you tell him you be white?"

"He knows very well who I am. I knew him before I was . . . captured. He asked me to marry him once. Do you think that makes any difference to a pig like Blodgett? I could be purple, for all he cares," Liberty said wearily.

"Did he . . . do anythin' to you?"

Liberty's face felt hot. "He tried."

"You didn't let him?"

"I got sick. Then he hit me pretty hard, and I guess I blacked out. I don't remember what happened after that."

"You be smart to let him. I tried to fight it, an' he took me . . . another way."

"He told me he would do that to me, too, if I resisted. I wanted to fight back, but I couldn't."

"I hurt pretty bad for a couple hours, but I feels better now. Least he won't gives me no babies that way. I couldn't stand to bring no baby of his into the world, I surely couldn't. I was four months comin' up North, and I will see my baby in the grave before bringin' him into slavery." Indigo brought little Samuel close to her chest, as if to protect him from her harsh words. "It ain't no human way to live. I been slave, an' I been free, so I reckon I knows."

Liberty's blood ran cold. The thought of giving birth to a baby who could be taken from her and sold at any time filled her with slow, deep panic. She covered her face with her hands and began to cry in tired sobs. She felt the other woman's bare arms encompass her and hold her gently.

"Now, girl, I didn't mean to throw a scare into you. Hush, now. I'se going to teach you how to keeps the babies from comin'. I'se goin' to teach you a mess of things, like you was my own. Thas how it be when you a slave. Your kin be anyone who take care of you. You goin' to need all the help you can gets, ain't you? You still ain't lookin' so good. The fever done broke, but you's weak still."

Indigo retreated to rock her baby, singing a soft, sweet lullabye. Liberty drifted off to sleep, Indigo murmuring words of comfort to chase away the demons lurking in the shadows of her fevered mind.

Liberty's eyes opened when the first dim rays of sunlight brushed her face. She looked around the cramped cabin, wondering why only Indigo and her baby shared her quarters. Had the others been herded into a common cage, left to sweat and sicken until they landed in whatever slave market Blodgett decided on? There had been others, hadn't there? Or had those writhing parcels beneath her on the cart, that unknown, smothered mass of human chattel, been another fevered hallucination?

The cabin was little more than a wood-paneled box, about twelve feet by eight, with a pair of narrow bunks along one wall. Liberty lay on the bottom bunk, and she assumed her protector was asleep above her head. The steady, loud drone of the engines drilled mercilessly into her head, making her teeth hurt. A tiny porthole let in some light, but behind the translucent white glass Liberty could see black bars. A slop bucket sat beside the lower bunk, and there was a hook on the wall to hang a lantern by; these were the cabin's only furnishings. Behind the walls, Liberty could hear the scurryings of vermin, and holes at the baseboards gave evidence of mice or rats.

A pair of brown legs suddenly thrust themselves over the edge of the upper bunk, jeweled shackles gleaming on the slender ankles. Indigo landed on the floor with an agile jump and turned to face Liberty.

"Mornin', girl. You get much sleep?"

"I think so, yes. I still feel tired, though."

"You goin' to feel poorly for months, I 'spect. You was some sick. I thought I was going to have one dead nigger on my hands here. But here you is, alive, and ain't no nigger after all," Indigo said, smiling warmly.

Liberty squirmed at the woman's casual use of a word that made her extremely uncomfortable, but she managed a smile nonetheless. "What was wrong with me?"

"Don't rightly know," answered Indigo. "For one thing, them nasty men done hit your head with somethin' big an' heavy. But you was sick on top of that. It wadn't no yella fever. Infl'enza, mebbe. Ain't no name for most of the nastiness that afflict folks. When somethin' get in your lungs like that, it just squeeze you and squeeze you till you feel like to die. But you's past the worst of it for sure."

"Thank you for nursing me. I think I would have died without your help."

"I don't know's I did so much. I just did what my mama did for us when we was sick—keep us warm and let us sleep and hope the Lord take care of the rest. Better than a white man's way, though, bleedin' the strength from you and givin' poisons for medicine."

Liberty agreed, remembering her mother's horror at the primitive methods of doctors, preferring her own gentle herbs and the power of prayer.

Despite Indigo's friendly company, the days stretched bleakly on, and Liberty longed to be able to take a walk, read a book, even knit. The baby, little Sam, felt the weight of their captivity as surely as if he could understand it, and he cried through the afternoons.

Liberty had chafed against rules and restrictions from the time she could walk and talk, and this imprisonment was the worst kind of torture for her. She stared at the black bars behind the glass in the porthole until she wanted to scream. She memorized every knothole in the planking that lined the cabin. She named the rats, learning to distinguish between their quick gray forms as they emerged in moments of silence. She was no longer afraid of them. They were the least frightening visitors she had.

Indigo smiled ruefully as Liberty concocted one escape scheme after another, bringing her down to earth as she explained the kinds of precautions masters took with "runaways." Liberty felt like a lion in a cage, raging yet powerless, longing to be free. Her legs tingled with the itch to stretch and run, and her whole body felt underused and uncomfortable.

But the women talked and talked, exchanging sad and funny stories and, most important, information. Both were hungry for it, Indigo wanting to know how whites lived, what the abolitionist movement was doing, and what the famous Zeke Malloy was really like.

Liberty in turn had a mountain of lessons to learn: how to prevent a child, how to break things by pretending to be clumsy, how to avoid hateful work by seeming lazy and stupid. And, if the master was truly evil—if he killed too many slaves or raped too many children—how to poison him subtly so it looked like a lingering illness.

As Liberty listened carefully, repeating her lessons to herself over and over because she had no paper or pen, she told herself that she was absorbing the information so conscientiously not because she was headed for slavery, but because it was invaluable research. She imagined herself working with Zeke, sorting through dozens of facts and

anecdotes to illustrate his lectures. He would look
at her with respect, amazed by this woman strong
enough to survive her ordeal and distill it for the
cause. She would write a stirring article for *The
Liberator*, powerful enough to reform the Fugitive
Slave Law at the very least. Perhaps she would lecture on the same platform as Zeke, in halls that had
never before admitted women, the two traveling
together in an atmosphere of mutual admiration.

Thoughts of Zeke filled her eyes with fresh tears.
How could she have been so pigheaded? How could
she have allowed the constant bickering between
them? Most horribly, how could she have let him
think, even for a moment, that she associated with
Blodgett—the man who had beaten and enslaved
her, nearly killing her in the process. Zeke had
been so confusing, one minute seeming to desire
her, the next angrily dismissing her. If only she
could see him again, she knew she would be able
to set everything right.

Yet all her new wisdom was useless. She knew
now that she loved Zeke, but he could never be
hers. Even if she managed to escape—and she
would die before remaining a slave to Montoya—
her virtue would be gone. Zeke would never marry her.

She thought of the night in the carriage, when
Zeke had done those mysterious and wonderful
things to her body. Blodgett had ruined that for
them, too. How she wished she'd given herself
fully to Zeke then, that her first time would not be
rape at a stranger's hands. While thinking of Zeke's
caresses filled her with delicious restlessness, the
thought of Montoya's defilement made her mouth
dry with nauseated panic.

Blodgett often came to their quarters to torment
them, but he was strangely reluctant to defile them
physically. The two men with him, wiry Sid and
hulking Ox, did not dare touch the women until

their boss had taken his fill. They vented their frustrations with low, guttural strings of obscenities and disgusting gestures, concocting explicit, violent threats. Liberty never managed Indigo's trick of divorcing herself from her body. Her obvious, choking disgust, contrasted with Indigo's perfectly neutral passivity, made Liberty a favorite, and the men often seemed to whisper their filth in whatever way made her flinch the most.

"Your body ain't no part of you when a man be hurtin' you that way," Indigo said over and over, exasperated with her friend's apparent stubbornness as Liberty scrubbed her bare skin with water and a rag, trying desperately to wash away the feeling of violation. "You gots to go away to somewheres safe, somewheres in your head. What these boys be doin' ain't nothin' next to what you goin' to find later on. You gots to learn how to fly away now, or you ain't never goin' to survive where they takin' you."

But Liberty could never accept their whisperings, their verbal rape. She shrank with horror every time she heard the bolt slide with a sickening scrape outside the door.

The riverboat trudged downstream, stopping frequently at small and large towns to exchange goods and passengers. As the tedium, the confined space, and the near-daily visits of Blodgett and his two partners conspired to wear the women down, their friendship and long conversations lifted them up again. They spoke as women friends have always spoken to one another.

"You're so beautiful. I wish I were so buxom."

"Girl, you's crazy. Thas just from birthin'. I'd eat a bug to have a teeny little waist like that."

"What use is a small waist when you have no chest or hips? I'm a sack of bones."

"I oughta slap your face. You's the most beautiful girl the Lord ever made, an' here you is complainin' about it. If I had them pretty eyes, I'd never cry again so long as I lived."

They flattered each other outrageously. They were the entire world to each other, the only thing in their lives untouched by evil or disgust. Indigo paid outlandish compliments to Liberty's golden skin and blue-green eyes, and Liberty paid the same to Indigo's creamy coffee-colored complexion and thick-lashed golden-brown eyes. They talked about the webs of their lives before they were captured, their families and their work and the friends they had taken for granted. And they talked about their loves.

"He real tall and strong, I never did see a man so strong. Hands as big as a plate, pract'klly. But a gentle man, he can smile so's to melt a rock. They selled him off someplace in Georgia, I thinks." Indigo was quiet, rocking her baby back and forth as tears slid down her cheeks.

"We're going to make it back, Indigo. We are going to be free."

"I surely hope you right, Libby."

After what seemed an eternity, the air began to carry a wet sorghum sweetness. They could see nothing from the translucent porthole, but the lazy humidity that kinked their hair and made it impossible to think or move told them as surely as any other sign that they were heading into the South. Indigo launched into a whole new collection of lurid stories about alligators and swamp monsters and jealous lovers made murderous by the oppressive summer heat. Stories of Annie Christmas, taller, stronger, blacker, and meaner than any man in the swamp, were Indigo's favorites, especially those that featured Annie tearing off a man's nose or ear in payment for a foolhardy assault.

And sometimes, in the deep part of the night, as the heat lay on them like a damp, smothering sheet, Indigo told of things she'd seen as a slave.

Women rising stiffly before dawn and returning past sunset, rarely catching a glimpse of their own children. A boy whipped, then hung by his hands to "cure" in the smokehouse. Great joyous church gatherings that retained a powerful African magic, as the spirit moved through the congregation like the wind through the trees.

Liberty traded her stories of childhood in Ohio, shooting a bear dead when she was eleven, and having to eat smoked bear meat for six months afterwards, dragging her father out of brawl after brawl over his bad temper and peculiar notions. She even managed to finally work up the courage to stammer out the story of the day her father had gone too far. Blinded by drink and irrational jealousy, he'd raised a hand against her mother, and said terrible things that could not later be unsaid.

But there was no terror in her childhood to compare to Indigo's. The murky, shadowy stories of slave quarters and unfathomable masters chased away many of the phantoms and cobwebs from Liberty's past, and the things that had frightened and shamed her as a child lost their power. It was an odd way to find freedom, but in many ways, locked in a tiny, windowless riverboat cabin, that was exactly what Liberty discovered.

A clear pink dawn lit the gleaming porthole as the steamboat eased crankily down the river. The women could hear the boatmen racing and shouting orders to one another above deck. Blodgett came in shortly afterward, throwing a pair of thin, shapeless dresses at the women, too hurried to stop for his usual verbal torment. "Take off that shit you're wearing and get into these. You have five minutes." His voice snapped like a firecracker.

The women had become accustomed to thin shifts and shackles as their only adornment, and though the jeweled metal chafed their wrists and ankles, their near nudity granted them relative coolness. Liberty felt oddly oppressed as she pulled the tobacco-colored cotton dress over her slim shoulders. Made for a stouter woman, the garment swung low and free over her breasts. The fabric, which must have been coarse when new, was now worn thin and supple with age, and clung to every inch of her body as she moved.

"I've never seen fabric this color before. Do you know what the dye is?" she asked Indigo, working to maintain the fiction of diligent research.

"This cotton grow that color," Indigo replied, pulling a similar garment over her head. "It be slave cotton. They be white cotton for white folks, an' brown cotton for brown folks. Things does tend to go that way down here."

Liberty put her arms around her friend's shoulders. "We'll make it through, Indigo. We have each other, and we'll get through this. I'll get us back home, I promise."

"Don't you see nothin', girl?" Indigo snapped. "Near to two weeks of my good teachin' and you ain't learned a damn thing. They be sellin' us apart, fool! That be the slave's first heartache. You goin' to Cuba, an' they goin' to sell me to some damn ugly white master with wood in his pants. Lord know where I be headed. Why you think they give us these clothes? It be a buyer, girl, it got to be. Ain't nothin' but pain come from tellin' yourself you goin' to gets back home. And even if we does escape, we ain't goin' to be together. When we gets the chance to run, we runs, together or apart. I'm sorry, honey, but that just be the way of it."

"No!" Liberty shook her head forcefully. "No! I have never made a promise I didn't keep, and I'm not about to start now. You are the best friend I ever had, Indigo James, but I swear to you I will slap your face into next week if you don't take that back."

"Hmmph," Indigo muttered, shrugging into her thin dress. "Damn fool girl. Guess I better takes it back then. I'se pretty busy. I'd hate to take up my whole afternoon knocking some sense into your fool head."

Liberty grinned. "All right, then. We understand each other." She started to laugh. "Do you have any idea how stupid you look in that dress?"

Indigo growled. "Suppose you thinks you the belle of the Quadroon Ball with your bony elbows pokin' outa that thing," she said, starting to laugh herself.

Suddenly shouts came from the deck above their heads. The noise of the engines kept them from making any sense of the voices, but an imaginative stream of obscenities made itself clear above the fracas.

"Sounds like nasty old yella-eyes gots hisself a fight on his hands," mused Indigo, her head cocked to listen to the ever-angrier voices.

"But he's the captain! Would one of the passengers really pick a fight with him?" asked Liberty.

"Not a passenger, another boat. They's no end of foolishness along the Mississippi between them boat cap'ns. I expect we's in for a race. It's a wonder we ain't had one yet."

A race? Liberty's heart pounded. These boats, even when well maintained—which this one wasn't, she thought with disgust as one of the rats cleaned its paws in the corner—were dangerous. Newspapers carried reports of steamboat engine explosions every week. And the rivers were full of hidden snags and sawyers, difficult to navigate even at a reasonable speed.

The boat lurched forward, and the engines whined in protest.

Liberty and Indigo looked at each other.

"Just like that nasty man, tryin' to look big any way he can," Indigo said with disgust. "He goin' to end up with a knife in his back and his own mama laughin' over the body."

"No loss," commented Liberty, her own lip curling. Blodgett's employees were not good men, but Blodgett was rotten to the bone. Liberty shuddered as she thought for the millionth time of him throwing himself at her feet, clawing at her ankles, the stripe of boot polish across one cheek. It seemed as if it had happened a million years ago, back when she could not have guessed the depths to which this man would sink.

"I hope he take better care of this boat than he do his slaves," Indigo remarked. Liberty and Indigo were fed a single small bowl of slimy, watered gruel every day, and the thin mattresses they slept on were infested with fleas and bedbugs. The roaches and rats were so plentiful, they had lost all timidity. And the two women knew that they had the best conditions of any of Blodgett's captives; Liberty could hear the moaning of the other slaves from their cabin.

Liberty was not entirely thankful for this preferential treatment, though, because she now knew what it meant. It was the custom to keep "fancies" separate, in order to prevent their being damaged by ruffians in the hold. Their skin must be creamy and unbruised, and most buyers preferred that the girls not be pregnant.

The boat gave another lurch forward, and the engines worked frantically. The din was fantastic; even the rats scurried back into the woodwork to find a safe place to hide. Liberty's head began to hurt as her teeth rattled with the vibration that shook the entire cabin.

Overhead, on the decks, the crowds screamed encouragement to the racing boats. Indigo's baby caught the frenzy and began to cry. Men roared their approval as children shrieked hysterically. Footsteps clattered back and forth, as if the crowd were clamoring for the best view of the spectacle.

Liberty and Indigo jumped as the bolt to their door slid open. Sid stood at the door with his shirtsleeves rolled, sweat beading on his brow and pouring in rivulets down his ashen face. "He'll kill us all this time. I'm not gonna let the bastard take me with him."

The pitch of the engines' whine continued to rise, and an ugly metallic clanking sound began to accompany it.

"It's come with me now or drown like rats," Sid said at the door. "You make up your own minds, but do it quick." He ran down the hallway, leaving the door open.

Liberty and Indigo shot each other a look before following him. They would not put any more trust in Sid than they had to, but for now it looked as though Blodgett really was going to bring the ship down with his madness.

They raced down the narrow corridors and clambered up the stairs to the deck. After their weeks in semidarkness, the light stung their eyes. A rival boat, sickeningly close, careened through the brown water. It was painted a gleaming white, and its passengers waved their hats and hurled insults and refuse.

The clanging in the engine room quickened, as fast now as the ticking of a clock. Liberty and Indigo held back from the throng on the deck, trying to protect their bare feet from the clatter of heavy boots. Indigo clutched the baby to her breast as if no force on earth could shake it away from her. A young woman in a yellow bonnet held tight to the railing as she wept, her shoulders shaking violently. A group of men pushed their way toward the engine room, trying to shut down the boiler before it was too late. The deck roiled in a mass of writhing shirtsleeves and angry red faces as the insistent clanging nearly drowned out the screams and sobs.

The rival boat was close enough that Liberty could make out the mustached faces of its passengers and crew. Eyes rolling and faces contorted, the men screamed out, "Give it up!" and "We won it!" Their faces were split by grins as they mopped their brows. One man gripped the rail, leaned back, and gave a long, low howl, like a wolf.

Liberty jumped as the door to the engine room cracked under the weight of the crowd of young men. The whine of the engines grew more frantic. It seemed as if the boat itself were crying out for pity. The deck lurched beneath her as they pulled a few yards ahead of the rival boat, slicing through the muddy water.

But the clanging dissolved into a hideous grinding, and oily smoke began to pour from the engine room. Some of the men began to throw off their shoes and hurl themselves into the river. Other more gallant souls wrenched the few lifeboats free from their ropes. The woman in the yellow bonnet screamed. Wailing children began to swarm over the deck.

The boat swerved crazily. Acrid smoke filled the air, and the passengers nearest the engine room were bent double with coughing. The grinding gave way to a volcanic roar and a furnace blast of heat.

Liberty's breath was knocked out of her in one sickening whoop. She felt as if a horse had kicked her square in the chest.

The air went quiet and still, and the scene slowed impossibly as she was flung into the air. It seemed to take her body a full minute to fly up over the boat's railing, hit the top of the arc, and make her descent toward the brown river teeming with bodies, moving and still.

Chapter 19

The river felt like brick pavement as Liberty hit it. Water covered her head and filled her nose. Her lungs pounded as she thrashed her way to the surface, flailing against the weight of the water.

She gasped when she broke through the surface, pulling air thankfully into her lungs in gulping breaths. Thank goodness, Indigo was treading water and coughing a few yards away, holding the baby's head up with one arm. Liberty looked around wildly. "The trees!" she called to Indigo, motioning toward the riverbank.

Smooth gray-barked cypress choked the water's edge, buttressed by massive knots of roots covered in bright green slime. They grasped the ropy roots and pulled themselves onto land. Liberty's nose and throat stung as she coughed up river water, and her bare feet sunk into the green-brown muck.

She looked back at the burning riverboat. Flames licked and blistered the white paint. The name of the boat, *Annabelle*, quickly disappeared, the neat red letters swallowed by smoke and fire. People tumbled into lifeboats or jumped into the river, hoping to swim to safety. The woman in the yellow bonnet had found her way into a lifeboat and was bent forward with her face in her hands, her shoulders still shaking. The rival boat had dropped a rope ladder, and the same burly brutes who had jeered during the race now lowered their arms to help sodden passengers out of the water. Someone screamed again and again.

Liberty stood transfixed by the gruesome sight until Indigo pulled at her wet sleeve. "Come on. We gots to put some distance between us and old yella-eyes."

Zeke had hated Jack Blodgett for years, but today he was sure he could murder him. Of the hundreds of insane, destructive moves Blodgett had made, this blasted steamboat race won the prize.

Damn it! Zeke slammed his fist against the riverboat railing. They had been so close to finding her. Zeke had looked up an old friend, David Greystone, in Wheeling, and convinced him to enter into negotiations with Blodgett to buy Liberty. Nate had stayed behind in Boston, conducting his own investigations there. Two weeks of frantic questioning and constant movement down the river had finally led David and Zeke here, to Blodgett's very ship. Blodgett had refused Greystone at first, saying that another buyer had already laid claim to Liberty, but Zeke's friend was a clever and persuasive man. And he had instructions from Zeke to get Liberty back at any cost. He would have closed the deal tonight.

Zeke rubbed the cinders from his eyes. He'd been reluctant to show his face anywhere near the *Annabelle*—a name that had hit Zeke with the force of a hammer's blow—but the boiler explosion had changed everything. Rumor had it that Blodgett had been badly burned. Finally punished by his own brutal arrogance, Zeke thought bitterly. But not before destroying Zeke's life.

And so Zeke found himself here, on the deck of the *Annabelle*, gulping air to ease the harsh sting of smoke in his lungs. The question pushed itself into his mind, as it had been doing for days now. Why was he going through all of this? At first he'd rationalized that he simply felt guilty at having embroiled Liberty in this madness between Blodgett and himself. He'd had some long talks with Nate and Mrs. Biggins, and the pair of them had convinced him that whatever Liberty had been doing, she hadn't been spying for Blodgett.

But there was more to this than guilt, and more also than desire, which would have been Zeke's second guess. Liberty had proven tougher than he'd thought possible. She'd faced him down over and over, even when he had turned on her so coldly after that disastrous night in his carriage.

His mind skittered away from the carriage—and from the way he had treated her afterward. She wasn't merely strong, Zeke was forced to acknowledge. Through all the abuse he'd poured on her, she'd kept her compassion, her humor, even her naïve idealism. Zeke himself had not been able to manage that. He'd battled Blodgett, he'd even battled Boston, but he'd done it by encasing his heart in a stone fortress.

And Liberty Brooks, precisely the sort of prim, overstarched female he least trusted, had come into his life and knocked that fortress down with one blink of those sea-colored eyes.

Zeke squeezed his eyes shut against the smoke, leaning hard against the railing. He'd searched every inch of this grimy rat-heap, but he hadn't found Liberty. The slaves' quarters all seemed to be deserted. Someone had been merciful and let them go, or they had found a way to break free of their prison.

The ship was on fire; it would not stay afloat much longer. But how could he jump ship now, knowing that there was some chance she was still aboard? No, he'd stay and look for her again. Better to burn to death than to live forever with the possibility that he'd abandoned her to die here on the *Annabelle*.

He opened his eyes again, looking down at the river that teemed with lifeboats and bodies. From the corner of his eye he caught a glimpse of two sets of bare female legs as a pair of wet slave women pulled themselves onto the far riverbank.

He narrowed his eyes. Slave women? That was certainly the way they were dressed. One of them comforted a small baby. The other squeezed the water from her hair with unconscious elegance. She was fair, with golden skin and a mop of wet chestnut curls.

It couldn't be.

Of course it could be! Zeke laughed out loud. Once again the indomitable wench had come out on top. He peered after the two women melting back into the cypresses.

Well, hell. He was sure it was her. Once the idea had made its way into his mind, he could see the proud carriage of her neck and the beautiful line of her back and torso. He'd been looking for a figure in dark wool and crinolines, not a slave's shapeless cotton dress. But how would he get to her? Silly chit, running off when she was supposed to wait to be rescued like a good damsel in distress.

He yanked off his waistcoat and threw it to the deck, bending to unlace his boots. He thought a moment and tied their laces together, throwing them around his neck. He'd need shoes if he was going to track them effectively.

He hit the water with a splash and held his breath as he kicked his heels to propel him to the surface. He'd fetch his pack from the other ship and let David know that he'd caught sight of Liberty. There was no time to arrange for dogs or horses; he could only hope she'd leave an easy trail to follow. Just this once, he prayed, couldn't she be a *bit* helpless?

Zeke fixed his eye on the spot where he'd seen her, making a careful mental map of it. He'd find her. His search was nearly over.

The first thing Liberty wished for was shoes. Soft muck oozed between her toes, and snakes darted menacingly among the roots and vines. Twigs and rocks cut at her feet. When they were lucky, they found long patches of dry ground to stumble across. But without warning, the rough grass would give way beneath them, and they found themselves calf-deep in sun-warmed water.

In the water, they were forced to slow down as they tested each step. Pointed cypress stumps poked out of the slime like jagged teeth. Frogs and small fishes shuddered across their legs. Then, as suddenly as before, a dry place would rise up from the muck again, and they could run.

Moving through the swamp was arduous and slow, and they had no idea where they might end up, but they pushed on. No matter how bad the accident had been, Blodgett would want to reclaim his lost property. Maybe he would assume they had drowned, or burned to death in their locked cabin. Had Sid told his boss that he'd let the captives go?

Liberty stopped and stood straight, straining to hear. Was that a dog in the distance? There were so many small noises—frogs, insects, the chittering of birds. With good boots and a shotgun to dispatch snakes, Blodgett could make much better time than they could.

Liberty struggled to keep up with Indigo, who moved more easily through the swamp, adeptly testing her weight and avoiding the worst areas. "The swamp be the runaway's best friend," Indigo said, her breathing only slightly labored. "Slave catchers be skeered to come in here, on account of the snakes and bears. If you moves in deep enough, won't nobody come to bother you. Course, you gots to come out sometime, and that's when they gets you. But mebbe by then we can thinks of sumthin'."

"You've done this before," Liberty said.

"I lived for three weeks in the Great Dismal, and it near to killed me. I swore then that I'd never goes near so much as a mill pond again. But I be more partial to the swamp than the auction block."

Liberty agreed, even as a fat mosquito bit into her cheek. Every step made her head pound where Sid had struck her those weeks before. After so many hours of walking, the monotonous pain made her want to scream, run wildly, break things. She fought another chill of revulsion as something scurried across her bare toes, and followed Indigo farther into the gloom.

Indigo suddenly put her hand out to stop Liberty from moving on. The water rippled as a bony set of green-brown ridges cut across the surface. "Could be a gator," she whispered as they moved to a dry patch. Indigo broke off a heavy tree branch, feeling its heft. She motioned that Liberty do the same. "If you hits them hard on the snout, they gener'lly lets go," she said, her mouth pursed.

Liberty did not feel cheered at the word *generally*.

The ridges moved closer, making a beeline for the dry bank. Liberty and Indigo tightened their grips. The ridges slowed and disappeared beneath the water, and a small, walnut-colored head poked up, two round eyes staring at them indignantly.

Indigo laughed and threw her branch into the water. Liberty looked at her, astonished. "Why'd you do that? Isn't it an alligator?"

"It's a turtle," said Indigo, laughing.

"A turtle?"

"An alligator turtle—a big one. Mind you don't gets your fingers too close. They bites."

"A turtle," Liberty said, disgusted.

"I ain't too disappointed. Myself, I rather be a fool in front of Brother Turtle than a hero for Brother Gator."

Liberty wrinkled her brow and flung her branch into a thicket.

"Mind where you throws that thing," Indigo cautioned. "Swamp bears is mostly peaceable, but they don't care for folks be throwin' stuff on top of them. Only natural. You'd probably come out and eats someone up if they throwed a big ol' branch on top of you."

"Do you really think there could be bears in there?"

"Might be. Might not be. Best not to find out for certain."

They moved on, Liberty newly conscious of how wet she was. The sun was low in the sky, and for the first time that day, a breeze blew through the cypresses, chilling their damp hair and sodden clothes. The hems of their dresses dragged through the water and stuck to their calves, making a slapping sound as they walked.

Indigo stopped. "You smell somethin'?"

Liberty sniffed the air. "Something rotting, and something wet. We've been smelling that all day."

"Keep sniffin'. Somethin' else."

Liberty shut her eyes and focused her attention. "Smoke?"

"Yep."

"A fire."

"You see anything that could catch fire by itself? The way I figger, smoke means folks."

"We've got to head away from it, then."

Indigo tilted her head to one side. "It might just be some trappers. Acadians don't gots much use for black folks, 'cept as fish bait. But I got a notion it be somethin' else."

"Something else?"

"Let's keep goin'. If it what I think it be, we might not be sleepin' with the snakes tonight."

The red sun glittered on the water, and Liberty privately felt that they should simply find a dry patch of ground and curl up into a ball, hoping for the best. The last thing she wanted was to get caught knee-deep in muck after the sun had gone down. Liberty thought that if she felt one more slimy thing scurry across her bare legs, she would go completely mad.

Indigo made her way with certainty now, following her nose. The smell of smoke grew more intense, and after some minutes they could see the white plumes curling through the trees.

Indigo pulled Liberty aside. "Now, you listens to me. You be high, high yella, you understand? You ain't no white girl, you be a New Orleans fancy who ain't never spent much time with black folks. They won't likes you much, but they won't cuts your throat neither. You got that?"

Liberty nodded, wide-eyed. They moved closer to the smoke and heard voices above the nearly deafening twilight chorus of frogs and insects. Slowly, taking excruciating care to be silent, they moved to the thick grove of trees that stood between them and the voices.

Liberty was astonished by what she saw. Seven or eight men and women sat around a campfire, talking quietly, their dark-skinned faces bright in the firelight. Behind them was a large, dry clearing with several crude log buildings plastered with mud and grass. A dog slept in the doorway of one, and a woman nursed a baby in front of another.

Indigo breathed a sigh of relief and whispered, "Maroons."

Chapter 20

The women must have made some small noise, because two men jumped up and were on them in a moment. The dogs began to bark furiously, and the baby wailed. The men held Indigo and Liberty in viselike grips, and one snarled, "Say your prayers, girls, 'cause you ain't never goin' see daylight again."

Indigo stood as straight as she could while the man gripped her neck. She clenched her baby at her side, her knuckles pale as Samuel screamed beneath her grip. "You damned fool, you be blind? You cain't tell runaways when you sees 'em?"

Startled, the man released his hold. "Runaways?"

The other man barked, "You keep good hold of dat girl, you hear me? The catchers could have sent dem on over here as decoys." His accent was musical and lilting, but the tone of his voice was deadly.

The man grasped Indigo again, but he held her more gently.

"Mind the way you holdin' me, Negro," Indigo said insolently. "You think you be a big man, but I'll whip your tail into next week if you don't start showin' some respect, you hear me?"

"I don't think these be decoys, Napoleon. This one too mouthy be workin' for no slave catcher."

"Mouthy?" Indigo cried, indignant. "I hopes I didn't hear you say that. You lets me go and I'll

274

takes a bite out of you that'll make you wish the bears had got you."

"Now, you just calm yourself, wo-man," the man called Napoleon said, enunciating each word carefully in a rhythmic singsong. "You seem to know who we is, but we don't know no-t'ing about who you is."

Indigo shot the man a withering look. "We was headin' for New Oh'lins in a kidnapper's boat. The damned fool be lookin' to race and blowed his own boat up. We been movin' through the swamp lookin' for y'all. Or did I be mistaken—ain't the maroon camps takin' in runaways no more?" Her voice was heavy with sarcasm.

Napoleon's eyes were still narrowed. "How come de other one don't talk?"

"She be a fancy, don't gots much knowledge of the swamp. I 'spect she be a little skeered. She ain't takin' to your friend much, neither."

Liberty was rigid with fear, and her captor loosened his hold a bit.

"That be real gentlemanly," Indigo said, her voice dripping scorn.

"If you know who we is, you know we can't take no chances," Napoleon said gruffly.

"What you thinks we goin' do? Overpowers you?" Indigo asked. "Maybe I goin' to beats you to death with this here chile." She lifted the baby comfortingly to her shoulder, and he quieted a little.

Napoleon scowled ferociously. "Bah. Let dem go, Mingo. Dis wo-man going to be de death of me if we can't get her to shut up."

Indigo and Liberty shook out their arms, as Indigo looked up at Napoleon and spat, "Thank you."

"You wel-come," he spat back. "If you going to ruin us all, best you start now. Come into de camp and get yourselfs warm and dry."

The campfire felt delicious on Liberty's chilled, wet skin.

"Maybe we can find you somet'ing to eat," muttered Napoleon, still disgruntled. Indigo's bravado might have made him trust the two ragged runaways, but it seemed to have done nothing to instill warm feelings in him. Indigo lounged in front of the fire as contented as a cat, stretching her toes and brushing the mud off her feet as they dried.

Napoleon jumped to his feet. "Annabelle!" he called. A green-eyed, kind-faced woman appeared from one of the rude buildings.

"Yes, Napoleon, what can I do for you?" the woman asked, her voice smooth and gentle.

"Dese whores, dey going to sleep in your hut tonight. I hope dey don't give you no diseases."

Annabelle looked pained. "Napoleon, please don't use that word. They were slaves the same as you and I were. They didn't choose to do the work they did, just like you didn't tell the master what crops to grow."

Napoleon looked down at his feet. "Dey sleeping in your hut, if you don't mind," he repeated gruffly.

Annabelle sighed. "That's fine, of course, Napoleon. Will we be building them a hut later on?"

Napoleon shot them a poisonous look. "I don't t'ink dey going to stay long enough for dat."

Indigo tilted her chin. "I don't reckon we will. I doesn't stay where I isn't wanted."

He gave a ferocious scowl and stalked off into the darkness, disappearing into one of the huts. Annabelle walked over to the fire and knelt beside them.

"Don't worry about Napoleon. He's a pussycat once you get to know him. My name is Annabelle." She held out her hand to shake.

Indigo and Liberty warily introduced themselves. After their less-than-hospitable greeting, this cultured, kindly soul seemed oddly out of place.

"You was a slave?" Indigo asked, incredulous. "Truly?"

"My first master was my . . . my father." Annabelle looked down at the ground. "I grew up in the house. My brother—he was white—taught me how to read and write and let me read his books." She laughed, a trifle bitterly. "He even taught me French. He used to say that all I needed to be a true southern lady was piano lessons. And for a long time, I believed him."

"What happened then?" Liberty asked.

"My father's daughter—my *sister*," Annabelle corrected, "began to grow impatient with my presence." She smiled wanly. "As I grew older, the family resemblance grew more acute. She made a great deal of the fact that the situation was not . . . respectable. My father needed to be rid of me, so he gambled me away in a game of cards. I was given to the winner for . . . for what they call a 'fancy.' My brother—he was very young—tried to rescue me. He even challenged my new master to a duel, and got a bullet in the arm for his troubles. The new master and his son took me away to the city. I haven't seen my brother in years. I had news about him from time to time while I was still a slave, but now . . . I don't even know if he's living or dead."

Liberty swallowed painfully. From the sound of it, this woman had had a better education than Liberty had, and had known more wealth and comfort. Yet that had not protected her from slavery. She shivered as a breeze blew through the camp, making the fire flicker.

Annabelle touched Liberty's shoulder gently. "Don't be frightened. Life in a maroon village is rough, and seems a little strange at first, but you will be safe. We are all escaped slaves, just as you are. Napoleon is fine protection for us. He came from conditions that were far worse than anything we've faced—the Caribbean sugar plantations. Our dogs are trained to attack on command. We have plenty of guns and plenty of food. No one will find you here, and if they do, they won't live to tell about it."

Liberty looked up at Annabelle in shock. She had seemed so refined, so cultured. "Doesn't the thought of killing someone bother you?" she blurted.

Annabelle closed her eyes for a moment. "My dear, after what I've seen and the things that have been done to me, I'm afraid I wouldn't have the slightest compunction about carving a slave catcher's heart out." Her voice lost none of its cool, measured tone.

Liberty turned her gaze to the fire. It flickered hypnotically in the breeze. She blinked as the smoke stung her eyes. This wasn't drawing-room politics. It wasn't arguing with Zeke about the fine points of the Constitution, or preparing lectures, or passing out pamphlets. This was the real thing.

The camp stirred with life in the morning. Liberty was surprised to see so many people. More than two dozen men busied themselves around the camp, and perhaps a dozen women and children. In the daylight they could see that although Annabelle's voice was cool and cultured, she wore the same dirty, mud-colored rags as the others. "There's no way to keep anything clean out here, and one simply stops trying," Annabelle sighed as she busied herself making a small fire. "Napoleon and the men will be back soon with something to eat. Most of the men leave in the mornings to hunt, and the women stay behind in the village to make fires and boil the day's drinking water. It's one of the loveliest times of the day."

Certainly Liberty felt relieved not to feel Napoleon's angry gaze burning into her. After Indigo's terse warning and their unfriendly reception, Liberty felt keenly that the maroon colony was the wrong place for her to be. She knew nothing about slave experience; if Napoleon and the others found out she was a quarter-Indian farm girl from Ohio, she was sure it would be the end of her. The colony seemed close-knit, and the runaways seemed to treat one another kindly enough, but their suspicions and hostility—and that casual acceptance of violence—drew Liberty's nerves to the breaking point. She shivered as she remembered Annabelle's lovely, serene face in the firelight as the woman calmly talked about killing slave catchers.

Not that she had not had her own feelings of murderous rage toward Jack Blodgett. Liberty understood completely why these people were so vehement. They had decided to die before they would return to slavery. As it was, they lived in cramped, awkward quarters, with swamp bears and cottonmouths as their closest neighbors. Liberty did not even want to think about what Napoleon would bring home to eat—frogs and spiders, she supposed. Ugh.

She scratched one of the camp dogs behind the ears. He lifted his head, whined, and settled down again, his tail thumping as she rubbed a sensitive spot. Everything here was topsy-turvy. The dogs were as sweet as old Spotty, her childhood beagle, had been. Yet Annabelle said they were trained to kill. Annabelle herself was a mystery. Graceful, beautiful even in rags, educated, and angry enough to slit a man's throat.

And she was beautiful. Her eyes were a bright, clear green. There was something wonderfully familiar about them—they brought back to Liberty the wildflower-dotted meadows around Haven House, and the close-cropped grass of the Boston Common. Her whole manner, the way she carried herself, Liberty was sure she had seen before.

Doubtless in the most aristocratic ladies of the city, she thought.

Napoleon and the men emerged through the trees. It was a strange trick of the swamp that at times even loud noises close by couldn't be heard, yet at others, the peep of a frog a mile away floated across the damp, still air as if it were right next to you. Indigo had said that the swamp was a living place, a creature in its own right, and Liberty was beginning to believe her.

The men had brought home a brace of catfish, and Annabelle's green eyes lit up with pleasure. "Oh, how lovely!" she cried happily. "Fine work, Napoleon."

Napoleon frowned. "It ain't hard to catch catfish dis time of de year. De swamp dries up, and dey get caught in de puddles. The only trick is getting to dem before de bears do."

"You needn't be so modest, Napoleon. You know where every catfish pool in the swamp is and when they'll be full," Annabelle said, her voice full of graceful admiration.

"I *ought* to know after t'ree years in dis dam infernal hole."

"You've been here for three years?" Liberty asked, surprised. How long could one live this way, cut off from decent civilization?

"T'ree years," Napoleon repeated. "Some of de older fellows been here—lessee—Missy had de baby right after dey found dis place, and her boy look to be about five, so I guess de first ones come here 'bout five year ago."

Five years of living in mud buildings and checking the beds for snakes. Five years of listening for the step of the slave catcher. Liberty had been in the swamp for a day and a half, and she would be glad never to see it again.

Annabelle deftly gutted the fish the way some women arrange flowers, her elegant long fingers

incongruous among the blood and entrails. She
threw the offal to the dogs in a fluid, practiced
gesture.

"How long have you been here, Annabelle?" Liberty asked, wondering how long it took to turn a
gentlewoman into a creature of the swamps.

"Six months," Annabelle replied, throwing another catfish on the growing heap of cleaned fish at
her side.

Liberty sighed and picked up one of the cold,
slimy fish, looking around for a knife. Annabelle
lent her one, and Liberty set to work on the
unpleasant task. Whatever she did, she would
not give Napoleon the impression that she was
nothing more than a useless fancy girl. Liberty was
secretly a trifle annoyed with Indigo for having
selected that particular profession for their cover
story. True enough, those were Blodgett's designs,
but the whole world didn't have to know that.

The day passed slowly. Indigo seemed to be
taking great pleasure in her skewering of Napoleon, sniping at the man all through breakfast. By
midmorning, even Liberty was beginning to feel a
little sorry for him.

After a breakfast of grilled catfish, the men took
a nap while the women headed out to look for
firewood and water. It was risky, and Liberty privately thought that the men might give up their
nap to help the women with their search, but
Annabelle explained that the hunting was arduous
and demanding work, especially as the men rarely
used their guns. They saved their bullets for human
intruders.

The search for wood and clean water took the
greater part of the day, and it was late afternoon
before the women finally trudged back to cook the
evening meal. Liberty stumbled beneath the load
of wood on her back. She was hardly a frivolous
female, but compared with the other women of the

camp, she felt pampered and spoiled. She didn't know how to find dry firewood or sweet water in the swamp, and she staggered beneath loads that Indigo and Annabelle carried with ease.

Well, doubtless she would get used to it, she thought, shifting the weight on her back. Whatever she did, she wouldn't appear a weakling in front of these other women. She might be useless at deciphering the swamp's mysteries, but she wouldn't let them think her lazy as well.

The women filed into camp with their loads, and Liberty noticed gratefully that even some of the strongest were rubbing their necks and shoulders. The men had awakened and were sitting cross-legged around the fire, gambling for trifles, while the children played happily in the mud. If it had not been for the mosquitoes, which seemed to have increased a hundredfold since noon, the scene would have been oddly idyllic.

Napoleon's eye lit on them, and he groaned. "Mebbe I stop now, boys," he said in a voice just loud enough for the women to hear. "I don't t'ink too pushy wo-man be so good for my luck."

Indigo's eyes flashed. "Ain't my fault if you dumb enough to lose yo' sorry butt. The good Lord say gamblin' be a sin. Anyways, poker ain't no game for fools."

Liberty grabbed her friend by the elbow. "Indigo, I don't really think you ought—"

Indigo shrugged away from Liberty's grip, her eyes shooting daggers at Napoleon.

He gave her a contemptuous look. "You t'ink you so clever, wo-man, you come over here and play." He and his friends laughed in an infuriatingly masculine manner.

"You thinks I can't? I'd whup your butt like I'd whup an old dog."

Napoleon gave her an appraising look. "You talk big, but I don't see you over here. Just more of your wo-man chatter, like a monkey in de trees."

Indigo managed a dignified tilt of the chin. "I ain't gots nothin' to stake. Ef I did, you be sorry you crossed me."

Napoleon stood up from the fire and walked toward the women. He gave Indigo a searing look. "You got one t'ing to offer. You peddle your ass to white men, why not peddle it to me?"

Liberty would have slapped him, but she'd been a respectable Bostonian for too long. Indigo punched him square in the nose instead.

Napoleon's eyes lit with astonishment. Annabelle raced forward. Napoleon obviously expected her to comfort him, but she wrapped her arms protectively around Indigo instead.

"I'm so sorry, my dear," Annabelle murmured. "Napoleon's often a bit rough around the edges, but he's not normally an uncivilized brute."

Napoleon cradled his nose in his hands. He gave Annabelle a wounded look but wiped it off his face when he saw the rage in her eyes.

"Well, she start dis," he said, his voice like a little boy's. His nose was bleeding profusely. "I don't let no wo-man call me a fool."

"It's about time you stopped behaving like one, then. You've been strutting like a peacock ever since these ladies arrived, and it's time you started behaving like a gentleman."

Napoleon opened his mouth to protest, but snapped it shut again when he saw the unrelenting look on Annabelle's face. He gazed for a long moment at Annabelle, then at Indigo, before turning and retreating into his hut.

Indigo's eyes sparkled with unshed tears. "I don't know why he treat me so wicked."

Annabelle lifted an eyebrow. "Don't you? I think you do. I also think you and he had better settle things between you as quickly as possible. The level of discourse in this camp has grown decidedly uncivilized."

Liberty was mystified. She couldn't imagine why Napoleon had said those dreadful things, but Indigo and Annabelle seemed to understand perfectly.

Indigo wiped her eyes. "You think I should go talks to him?"

Annabelle shook her head. "Not just yet. Give him a little time to mend his pride. That was quite a blow."

Indigo grinned. "I figger he know who boss."

Annabelle gave a quietly radiant smile. "I suppose he probably does."

The women retreated to Annabelle's hut to cook dinner. Annabelle began to skin and gut a pair of fat snakes. Liberty turned her face away. If she was going to eat snake stew for supper, she preferred to know as little about it as possible.

Her heart thumped as the sound of splintering branches came from behind the fencelike thicket surrounding the colony, and angry shouts shattered the early evening calm. Two of the village men had been on patrol, guarding against intruders. From time to time an Acadian trapper would wander into the colony, only to be roughly escorted out again. But this did not sound like a routine scuffle.

Liberty rushed out of the hut to see three men crashing through the thicket. Two muscular guards struggled to keep their grip on a tall figure with jet black hair and eyes as green and hard as glass. The intruder sported a disreputable three-day beard, his clothes were torn and muddy from travel through the swamp, and his hard-edged features wore a look of grim determination.

Liberty thought her heart would stop. The intruder was Zeke Malloy.

Chapter 21

"Let me go, you damned fools! I'm on your side, can't I make you understand that?" Zeke thundered as he thrashed to free himself from the two burly men who held him.

"Napoleon!" one of them called out, struggling to keep his hold on Zeke.

Liberty almost cried out in joy, but quickly realized the potential danger. She lowered her face and looked up at the scene through her hair. What on God's earth could Zeke be doing here? Had he been looking for her? How could she explain her relationship with him to Napoleon and the others? Her heart hammered with a mixture of joy and fear. If they could get out of this, Zeke would take her home, away from snake stew and demon mosquitoes. But it might take some fast talking and a great deal of luck.

Napoleon flew out of his hut, knife in hand, and Liberty prayed the men would not hurt Zeke before they realized he was friendly.

"What your business here, white man?" Napoleon growled.

"I'm looking for a woman. She was kidnapped. I thought she might be here."

Liberty felt an odd thrill beneath her breastbone.

"You a goddamn slave catcher, and we going to cut you apart," Napoleon said menacingly, pressing the edge of his blade against Zeke's throat.

"No!" Liberty cried, springing to her feet.

"Liberty!" Zeke whispered. His eyes warmed, and his shoulders lowered an inch in relief.

Napoleon pressed the blade tightly across Zeke's throat. "So you know de fancy? Were you her master, or just sniffing around another man's property?"

"The fancy? You're a little confused, my friend," Zeke said coolly. "This woman was my secretary. She worked for me in Boston."

Liberty groaned inwardly. This was going to make explaining things very difficult. Maybe even dangerous.

Two of the village men eyed Liberty closely as she rushed to explain. "Well, I did work for him in Boston, but I was kidnapped by a criminal named Jack Blodgett. He was going to sell me in Cuba as a . . . prostitute. Mr. Malloy's a famous abolitionist up North, and—"

One of the men grasped her arm, none too gently, when Napoleon cut her off, muttering, "Go get de other one." Another man pushed his way past Liberty and into the hut.

Zeke looked at Liberty searchingly. "Is this true?"

She nodded. "Blodgett had asked me to marry him, but—"

"Damnation!" Zeke exploded. "When I found out you were going to have a baby, I had no idea—"

"A baby?" Liberty shouted. The blood roared in her ears. "I'm not going to have a baby!"

Indigo emerged from the hut, a dour man beside her. She wiped her hands on her skirts and stared at Zeke long and hard. "Sir, it truly be a pleasure—and a surprise—to see you here," she said.

Zeke was nonplussed. "Indigo?" he said, not trusting his eyes in the falling light.

"Yes, sir. I see you met Napoleon," she said with a saucy smile. "He real friendly, ain't he?"

"Indigo, what are you doing here? I thought you'd been captured."

"Yella-eyes done grabbed me at the dock, along with Liberty. We been travelin' companions ever since."

Zeke groaned and shut his eyes. "I don't know how it is that women manage to get themselves into this kind of trouble."

Napoleon's face had lost none of its suspicion. "I t'ink dey is all up to somet'ing," he muttered, his knife still pressed to Zeke's throat. "We don't know no-t'ing 'bout dese girls. They come in yesterday, de mouthy one talkin' like she own dis place. One of dem has been telling lies—both of dem probably. And now dis buckra sum-bitch come to join dem. It don't make no sense to me."

"You can trust the gentleman, Napoleon," Annabelle said, her voice sounding weary and sad in the twilight. "He's my brother."

Zeke stood very still. Napoleon slowly withdrew the knife menacing Zeke's throat. The camp was flooded with the songs of frogs and mockingbirds as the sun dipped closer to the horizon, painting the sky a fiery red.

"Annabelle," Zeke said quietly.

"Yes, Ezekiel. It's me," Annabelle said, her voice carefully calm.

Liberty wondered that she had not recognized the resemblance before. Annabelle had Zeke's willow green eyes and the same smile, rare and bright as diamonds. Her hands had the same careless elegance, and she held her head as proudly as he.

But Zeke's sister? Liberty had never known he had a sister, much less . . . well . . . someone like Annabelle, the peculiarly beautiful escaped slave.

Liberty remembered Annabelle telling her story in the firelight—the callous father, the slave mother, and the white half brother who had taught her French and fought a duel for her honor, slave though she was. And that proud, angry brother had been Zeke Malloy. Liberty imagined him as a boy, lending books to his sister, fussing protectively over her, teasing her about her lack of piano lessons. He must have been more tender then, less hardened by the world.

To see one's beloved sister gambled away like a diamond ring or a brood mare would turn the gentlest man into a monster. But Zeke was not a monster. He had a relentless anger within him, yes, a savage fire burning in his eyes. But that fire fueled him; it burned beneath all his fierce dedication. He could have become an embittered wastrel. Instead, he had made himself a crusader.

These thoughts came to Liberty in the blink of an eye, as if a curtain had been drawn and she could see a tableau she had never seen before.

But Indigo? How could Zeke possibly know Indigo?

Napoleon looked warily into Annabelle's eyes. He did not yet trust the two new girls and their soft, fancy ways, but Annabelle was another story. Annabelle, the lifeblood of the colony, the highborn lady who worked like a horse and flinched at nothing. His beautiful green-eyed Annabelle, whom he and every other man in the village was secretly in love with, and who had turned them all gently away in that cool voice like bells ringing. Now these intruders—first the women and now this man she called her brother—had pushed their way into the colony and into her affections. Her brother might even take her away. He could not let that happen—couldn't let them steal his Annabelle. She was happy here. She cared for the children and the old folks and for him, Napoleon. They couldn't have her—he wouldn't let them.

He reluctantly sheathed his knife. If he was too

crude now, she would never forgive him. She might even try to leave. Napoleon would deal with the brother in his own good time, but there was no need to hurry the white man's death. The swamp gave time enough for everything.

He held out his hand to shake Zeke's hand. "If you de brother of Annabelle, you wel-come here," he said, his voice hollow.

Zeke drained his face of expression. He knew false hospitality when he heard it; there was plenty to go around in Boston. Yet he had little choice but to trust this angry young man who was his lifeline, and Annabelle's. Zeke had been an angry young man himself, once, and he respected Napoleon's fire and steely temperament. He also knew just how dangerous such fire could be.

And there were more important things to attend to. Zeke stepped forward toward the fire, toward Annabelle. He whispered, "How long have you been free?"

"Six months," she said, looking down at her hands. "They brought me to the city, and I slipped away through the alleys. I hid in a wagon full of chickens until it took me out of the city. I wandered through the swamps for weeks, catching what I could and eating it raw. Then Napoleon found me and brought me here to the maroon village. They've taken wonderful care of me."

"I tried to find you, Annabelle. I tried for years."

The dying light caressed her face and burnished it to a rosy gold. "It would have been impossible. They kept me locked away in the country, away from any talk. There was only an old mute woman to look after me. Her tongue had been cut out. She couldn't gossip, you see—very safe. I used to pray that they hadn't cut her tongue out to look after me." Annabelle gave a little shudder, then quickly shrugged it away.

Zeke stepped closer to her and took her carefully

in his arms, holding her like something fragile and unfamiliar. "Did they hurt you?"

Annabelle took a long, slow breath. "Ezekiel, please don't ask me that question. You don't care to know the answer."

He shut his eyes. "I will exact revenge, *ma soeur*. I failed you once—I won't fail again."

Annabelle looked up at him. "You never failed me, Ezekiel. You fought a duel for me. You gave me an education and a sense of myself. I shall always be grateful to you for those things, for a thousand things."

"I couldn't keep you out of slavery," he said, his voice cold.

"No one could have." Her gentle voice became more insistent, and she took his face in her hands protectively. "Ezekiel, I am a Negro woman. You are a white man. Our father gave me to another man to discharge a debt and to spare your sister's feelings. There was nothing you can do to change that."

"I work every day to change it. I'm quite a troublemaker up North, you know," he said, smiling for the first time.

Annabelle shut her eyes and smiled faintly. "I am quite aware of your reputation in Boston, Ezekiel. That is one of the few things they told me about."

"They didn't hurt you for that, did they?" he asked urgently. "For my work?"

Annabelle smiled as she lied. "No, *mon frère*. They didn't hurt me for that."

Napoleon cleared his throat noisily. "All right, we been staring long enough. Annabelle got plenty to talk about with dis fellow, but de rest of de women can get back to working on dinner. If dey's one t'ing I hate, it's eating after dark, with de ghosts and de alligators putting me off my food."

The women scattered, busying themselves around the cook pots.

"I really must get back to work," Annabelle said, gently loosening herself from Zeke's embrace.

"But it's been a lifetime since I saw you last, Anna. Talk with me awhile," Zeke pleaded.

"I'll talk as I work. There's so much to do. I can't just sit and watch." She gathered a pile of roots and a paring knife, and sat on a mat to peel and slice them. She smiled at him as their identical green eyes met over her deft, swift hands.

Liberty watched from some distance, content to see the brother and sister murmuring and laughing together.

Indigo plucked at Liberty's sleeve. "You knows the gennleman?" she whispered, astonished.

"Yes, he's the man I told you about. Ezekiel Malloy. But how on earth do *you* know Zeke?"

"That be Zeke Malloy?" Indigo asked, a wide grin splitting her face. "That be the fella that hid us in Boston. He gots a little cave underground, underneath a shack in the woods. It be a fine place, I tell you. Whitewashed walls and good things to eat ever' night and time 'nuff for old Jake's feets to heal up proper."

"Old Jake's feet?" Liberty asked, a bizarre realization beginning to dawn on her.

"My uncle Jake. We runs away, Jake and his grandson—that be my cousin's boy, Tom—and me and my baby. Jake and Tom got lucky. They was already in the boat when yella-eyes nabbed me. Anyways, Jake didn't haves no shoes for the whole time we be runnin' from the South. Thinks about how bad your feets hurt now, after one day of runnin', and the ground here be soft. So the gennleman, Mr. Malloy, he be hiding us for near to three weeks until Jake's feets gots better. Tom be the Divvil's own chile, though. He 'most got us all catched when he stole some white woman's purse."

Liberty laughed out loud, startling the dog near

their feet, who shot her a puzzled look as he cocked his ears.

"Indigo, do you know who that white woman was?"

"Some nosy northern lady. She be coming around that cabin at all hours. We could hear her up there callin' and pokin' around. We be skeered to death she find the secret door, but she never did."

Liberty was laughing and holding her stomach. "Indigo, that was me!" Tears rolled down her cheeks, and she nearly tipped over sideways.

Indigo's eyes shot open. "You? That be you makin' all that ruckus? Hell, if I knowed that, I would've come up and gives you a good smack in the rump for throwin' such a fright into us." Indigo started to laugh as well, and the camp dogs gathered around them, panting happily to see such exuberant spirits.

"I had books. I wanted to teach Tom to read," Liberty said, dissolving into giggles.

Indigo hiccuped loudly. "We was skeered to even tells the gennleman about you, for fear he'd makes us leave. We hoped and prayed you don't be pokin' and yellin' while he be there givin' us them first-class vittles. But, hey—you isn't that gal he took a shine to, is you?"

Liberty's laughter subsided. "Gal?" she said, striving to keep her voice nonchalant.

"Sometimes he start talkin' 'bout some gal he know, a real party gal with wild ways, kickin' up her heels and dancin' and the like. Sound like she never did catch him, or he never did catch her. I couldn't rightly tell sometimes who be chasin' who. I could tell he be sweet on her, and I telled him to puts his mind to the job and marrys her, but you knows he be some awful stubborn."

Liberty sobered. Party girl? Kicking up her heels? Was *that* what he had been saying about her? "Isn't that funny?" Liberty said stiffly. "I don't believe I ever heard Mr. Malloy mention such a person. He's awfully dignified, you know. He wouldn't discuss his private life with an employee."

Indigo shot her a skeptical look. She would have bet her good Sunday dress that this was the gal he had mentioned, but Liberty had gotten so quiet. In fact, she had gone all stiff and respectable-looking. If you could look like a schoolmarm in the middle of a swamp with bare, dirty feet, ratty hair, and a muddy dress on, Liberty was doing it.

"Well, anyways," Indigo chattered, "people be tellin' all sort of foolishness to runaways. They figger you ain't never comin' back to tell on 'em, and you wouldn't knows they name if you did. I can't tell you how many whoppers I heared when we be runnin' away."

Liberty smiled at her friend and put an arm around her shoulders. "Thank you," she whispered.

Indigo gave her friend a shy smile. "For what?"

"For helping me to endure Blodgett, and for being strong enough to lead me through the swamp. And for being my friend."

Indigo narrowed her eyes and looked at the ground. "Aw, hell," she said, squirming. "I reckon you would've gots through the swamp all right. Although for a gal who be so full of excape plans, you sure was slow 'bout actually excapin' when we gots the chance." Indigo laughed wickedly.

Liberty gasped in mock shock. "I would have escaped. I was just getting the lay of the land, that's all."

"Gettin' the lay of the land, my butt. You be standin' there gapin' at that boat wreck. You would've catched flies if you would've stood there any longer."

"I would not have!" Liberty said hotly. "I had to

evaluate the situation, didn't I? I was just being careful."

"You be standing there with your mouth hangin' open, gapin' like a trout on a hook. If it wasn't for me, you'd still be there gapin'." Indigo's slim frame was shaking with laughter.

Liberty gave Indigo a sidelong glance and, as quickly as a kitten, pounced on her. "Take it back!" she cried, laughing as she pinned Indigo's shoulders to the mud.

"Agh! Halp! A crazy woman done jumped me!" Indigo shouted, laughing as she twisted and turned to throw Liberty off.

The two rolled around like puppies as the camp dogs wagged their tails, barking excitedly and circling the pair, trying to figure out how to join the game. Finally one black and white hound licked Indigo's face vigorously, while a sleepy gray dog licked at her toes.

"Three against one! It ain't fair! Uncle! Uncle!" Indigo cried, tears of laughter rolling down her cheeks.

Liberty let her go, and Indigo rubbed her rump ruefully. "Damn, girl, you never told me you knew how to wrassle."

"I did two things better than any boy I knew back in Ohio. Wrestle and spit. Bet I can spit farther than you can, too," Liberty challenged.

"All right, all right!" Indigo threw up her hands in defeat. "I said uncle, didn't I?"

As their laughter died, they realized the entire village had drifted into a loose circle around them, including Zeke and Annabelle. Liberty looked down and saw that she was covered with mud, her dress plastered to her bare legs. A trickle of wet mud dripped slowly from her ear, and Indigo had a broad gray-green stripe across her nose.

Liberty, Indigo, and the dogs looked up meekly at the crowd, who broke into peals of laughter. Even Napoleon joined, and for the first time they saw him without a scowl. "Didn't take dese girls too long to get used to de swamp," he said, his face creased jovially.

Zeke gave Liberty a look that curled her toes. He held out his hand, offering to help her to her feet.

She felt her whole body warm as she blushed. "I can't take your hand, I'm covered in mud."

His eyes were warm and questioning and hungry all at once. "So am I. And I told you once before, you'll make a gentleman feel unchivalrous if you don't let him help."

Her mouth felt dry as she extended her hand to him, trembling a little at the touch of his warm palm on hers. He was here. He was truly here.

"Tonight we have a festi-val!" Napoleon announced with a proud, joyous cry. A cheer came up from the village.

Annabelle moved closer to Liberty and Indigo, beaming. She knelt and whispered, "Congratulations, ladies. I think you may finally have earned Napoleon's approval."

Liberty pulled reluctantly away from Zeke and went with Indigo to wash some of the mud from their bare limbs and faces, while the villagers piled more wood on the fire.

Once the fire blazed almost fearfully high, drums appeared from one of the huts. Several of the men began to beat them in a compelling, urgent rhythm, swaying as their hands pounded out the inexorable beat. The others, including the children, began to move around the fire in a circle, their bodies undulating wildly. Napoleon motioned to Liberty and Indigo that they should join in.

Liberty moved tentatively at first, watching a little boy, naked to the waist, swaying and crooning, his eyes half-shut, his shoulders moving forward and back in time to the rhythm. His skin looked shiny and otherworldly in the bright firelight. Liberty experimented with rolling her head from side to side. It made her a little dizzy, but dozens of other bodies moved around her, and she felt their presence supporting her. She moved her torso as the other women did, swaying from side to side as she circled the fire. A crooning wail emerged from the group, rising like a wave on the summer night air. Someone shouted. Another voice responded. The calls resounded back and forth like birdsong, and Liberty was shocked to find her own voice joining the group's. It was as if something had possessed her, taken her over. Arms and hands were thrust out, heads rolled from side to side, and individual bodies moved together like a flock of birds or a school of fish.

Liberty joined in the song, yet she did not know what it was. Words, sounds, music, filled her mouth and floated on the air, but she did not know where they came from. They weren't coming from her as much as through her. A fleeting bolt of fear raced down her spine, but she released it into the air and allowed herself to melt back into the group, circling the spitting, crackling fire.

She found herself face-to-face with Zeke. The three-day beard had changed his face completely, making him seem rougher, less polished. His face was serious, but the tightness around his forehead and mouth was gone. The firelight brightened his eyes to an eerie green-gold.

She pulled away from him as if from a too hot fire, but he stepped closer to her, their eyes locked. She looked deeply into his eyes as the drumming quickened, and she did not take her gaze off him as he began to move his hips in a slow, languid circle. She mirrored him, their torsos separated by a distance of two or three feet but tied together by some invisible magnetic bond. With her eyes locked on his, she could not see his body undulating in the red-gold light as much as feel it. Their bodies did not touch, but the shared rhythm was electrifying.

She felt a fevered thumping deep in her belly, resonating with the inexorable pulse of the drums. Her hair brushed her bare neck, and her shoulders moved freely in the loose cotton dress. He shone with sweat in the firelight, a shining pagan idol. Her lips parted as she felt the spirit of the night, the wet, primitive spirit of the swamp, moving through her to make her thrust her hips in time with his beneath the broad flanks of the cypress.

An elegant hand appeared on Zeke's shoulder as Annabelle, regal and golden as a goddess in the firelight, gently pushed her brother back into the circle. The sacrament demanded an unbroken ring, and Zeke and Liberty's tight dance of two had interrupted the movement of the spirit through the group.

"There is time, my brother, time," Annabelle murmured.

The drumming quickened again, and another shout rose above the circle. The voice of the drum was urgent, beckoning. Liberty writhed with an unknown passion, watching Zeke across the circle from her. The drums, it was the drums that seemed to urge their union, whispering rhythmic encouragement until Liberty longed to strip off her dirty cotton dress and let Zeke take her there, by the fire, the others dancing around them.

She was distracted for a moment by the unlikely sight of Napoleon and Indigo dancing side by side, their eyes locked in a blaze that rivaled the bonfire. Perhaps they were sorting out their differences, Liberty thought vaguely. Their faces didn't look exactly angry, though. She shrugged. The drums were doing odd things to everyone tonight.

A howl rose up, the combined voice of dozens, and the circle widened to make room as a dark-skinned young woman leapt and writhed.

"It is the serpent!" cried Napoleon as he rocked from side to side. "He has come to visit us through Marie. Aieeee! Praise him!"

As the circle rocked quietly, the woman named Marie bent at the waist, her elbows akimbo, and began to shudder. A series of high-pitched yelps came from her mouth, and her head rocked furiously from side to side.

"What is it? What's happening to her?" Liberty whispered, frightened.

"It's the god," Zeke said, having moved quietly around to join her again. "He's mounted her, and she belongs to him until he decides to release her."

Liberty turned to face him, horrified. "A possession?"

"It's the most sacred moment in their religion when a god deigns to enter a human host. The serpent is an especially powerful god. The maroons may take it as a sign of good favor for our arrival."

Zeke showed no trace of the disbelief and terror Liberty felt. She had thought they were merely dancing, not inviting demons to claim their bodies. It was impossible. There was no such thing as demons. Then she remembered the intense, voluptuous desire to fling her dress into the fire and give herself wholly to Zeke as the others looked on. Insanity. Mesmerism, perhaps. Those damned drums seemed to have a message that tried to insinuate itself into her mind, corrupting her. Maybe it was more than insane—it was satanic, obscene.

Without her realizing it, her shoulders had tensed, and she stood rigid by the fire. Zeke touched her gently between the shoulder blades. "Don't be afraid," he whispered, his breath hot in her ear. "The darkness can't hurt you unless you fight it. When you are frightened, it can't pass through you. Relax and let it run through you like wind." His voice was calm, measured, comforting. She dropped her head forward as he began to knead her neck and shoulders.

His touch melted away the tightness and fear she felt, and she became as soft and pliant as a reed. His strong hands moved in languid circles, and it seemed so long since he had touched her, since she had known the feeling of his hands brushing across her flesh.

He stepped closer to her and wrapped his arms around her, enveloping her with his hard, protective body. "I've found you," he murmured in her ear. "Thank God, I've finally found you."

The words made her feel as if she had wings, as if she were flying through an endless summer sky. She settled back into him, trusting him, relying on him to keep her safe in the midst of the odd, frightening ritual unfolding in front of them. They watched as Marie spun and dipped, weird sounds coming from her throat. It was as if her body were being tossed about like a toy by some huge, invisible child. Yet there was no suffering on her face as she writhed; she stared blankly into the night's soft blackness, seeing nothing, fearing nothing. The drums kept up their inexorable beat, keeping a lifeline between Marie and the real world, giving her a signal to follow home when the god had finished with her.

Zeke's hands continued kneading Liberty's neck and shoulders. He brushed the hair from her neck so that it spilled forward onto her breasts. Liberty shut her eyes and let the drumming fill her, feeling the heat of the fire at her front, Zeke's hot, hard body behind her, and the cool night air on her bare arms as she wrapped them protectively around herself.

She felt his lips on the nape of her neck, sending languid shivers down her spine. One hand still kneading her neck, he traced a line behind her ear with the other. Her breathing quickened. She would do anything, anything, to have him keep touching her this way forever, and yet she could hardly bear the pressure building low in her belly.

He slipped an arm around her and stepped back from the fire, bringing her with him. She felt the cooler air on her face, and pressed back into the warmth of his body against her. He cupped her breast in his hand, gently rolling the nipple between his fingers.

She gasped at this new flood of sensation, and at the teeth now nibbling at her earlobe. She felt her heart must be as loud as the drums. The others were still in the circle, watching Marie throw herself to the ground in the throes of the god's embrace.

Zeke tormented her there in the darkness, slipping one hand beneath the loose neck of her dress to brush her bare nipple with long, expert strokes. She moaned softly and wriggled against him, feeling something hard pressed into her buttocks. Her senses flooded with a mixture of shock and pleasure as she realized what that hard, insistent pressure meant. He thrust his hips against the thin cotton of her dress.

She was nearly naked. There were no stays, chemise, or drawers to interfere with his probing hands or that rude, hard push against her buttocks. She was shocked to realize that she was glad, amazed to find herself leaning back into that hardness, as if she wanted him to take her, to stop that unbearable ache. She tilted her hips and rolled back against him.

He gave a surprised, anguished groan that made her smile shyly. This power over him felt delicious. He put his hands around her waist, his fingers nearly meeting before he slid his hands down over her belly to caress her thighs. Liberty shivered as liquid warmth filled her.

His hands on her hipbones, he stepped back farther into the wet darkness, pulling her with him. She melted against him, following willingly. He stopped when they reached the line of cypresses that surrounded the camp.

His hands were bolder now, playing quickly across her breasts, her belly, the tender sweetness inside her thighs. She gasped at the heat building between her legs. Still behind her, he took a fistful of her dress in his right hand and drew it slowly up to her hips. The soft, well-worn cotton slipped like brushed silk across her skin, and she shuddered as she felt the cool night breeze on her thighs.

His fingers stroked her bare thigh, and she swallowed hard. His hand moved, agonizingly slowly, up toward that creamy warmth at the center of her. She shuddered as she felt his teeth on the back of her neck again, kissing her in small, shivery bites. He insinuated one relentless hand farther up her thigh, brushing against the down between her legs. Without thinking, she parted her legs, granting him access to the most private part of her.

He groaned and thrust himself against her, the hardness in his pants rough against her bare skin. She dropped her head forward as he brushed the downy softness between her legs before gently parting her.

She could not be more vulnerable than this. Her hair fell in her face as she panted like a jungle cat.

He caressed her slowly, his hand moving in small, soft strokes against the sensitive bud. She felt the tension build unbearably again, like the last time. She needed desperately to find some release, to know where this unholy twisting path would lead. "Please," she whimpered.

"What do you want?" he demanded. "Tell me."

"I want it to be more..." she whispered, her face hot.

Zeke gave a low, satisfied growl. "Like this?" he asked, his voice husky as he quickened the light movements of his fingers.

"Yes," she cried softly.

"Like this?" he asked again, sliding one finger deep into her wetness, moving inside her with long, deep strokes.

She felt herself clench around him as she closed her eyes. "Yes," she whispered, feeling the tension mount still higher. She would find it with him, the release. She had never wanted anything as much.

He swore softly as she began to twist beneath his probing fingers, thrusting herself against him. "Give it to me," he said, finding her rhythm, feeling her tightening. "Now. I want to feel it."

It was as if she had stepped off a cliff and begun to soar. She arched her back and cried aloud, her mind spinning in the soft black night circling around her.

He slowed but did not stop the movements of his fingers. "Feel good?" he whispered.

"Yes," she said softly, feeling languid and a little faint. The sudden, delicious drowsiness blended with the sound of the drums to drown her in a gulf of warm, liquid pleasure. She succumbed to it, slowly moving her hips against him.

He groaned again. "I want you," he murmured. He seemed to release her for a moment, and she gave a whimper of protest, but he was merely turning her to face him.

She was suddenly shy before him, shy to face this man who had done such shameful and glorious things to her body. He leaned down and touched her lips with his, tasting her with his tongue.

Another wave of longing swept her, and she took his face in her hands and met his kisses urgently. She wanted him as badly as he wanted her, wanted to lose herself in him, to dive again into that slow, deep vortex of pleasure. He slid his hands across her buttocks, moaning softly as he caressed them. Then he grasped her shoulders and knelt, pushing her down onto the warm, damp earth.

He kissed and teased her lips, gently sucking and biting until she hungrily lifted her hips up toward him, pressing herself against his hardness. He traced a line of kisses down her long, proud neck, reveling in the faint saltiness of her skin.

She tensed as he once again pushed her dress above her thighs, but she lifted her hips to free it. He spread the cotton so that her bare buttocks would not touch the ground, and he lowered his head between her legs.

Her eyes fluttered as she felt his lips and tongue on her. She feebly tried to push him away. "No . . . we . . . you can't do that."

"I can and I will," he said, his voice husky.

Despite her protests, she gasped as his lips nuzzled her. She took his head in her hands and arched her back to press against him. His tongue flickered wickedly, darting softly in small, wet circles. He drank from her greedily, as if her wetness were sweet nectar. She whimpered, her need almost animal.

Impossibly, he slowed his movements, denying her. She whimpered again, restless. Her breasts ached, every muscle in her body tensed for release.

As he worked to unbutton his trousers, each flick of his tongue sent her mind careening with pleasure. She was furious with want. "Please," she pleaded softly, not even sure what name to give her own desire.

He lifted himself in one smooth movement and nestled his hardness against her. She felt a shock deep in her belly. Yes, this was what she wanted. She wanted to know what he would feel like inside her. She thought of the way his fingers had felt moving in her, and she moaned.

He pushed his hips so that his hard shaft was nestled between her legs, poised to push inside her.

"Is this what you want?" he asked, his voice quavering.

Her eyes found his in the moonlight, and she mouthed a single word. "Yes."

He shut his eyes and pushed into her. She moaned and tossed her head, taking his bare hips in her hands as if to pull him deeper.

He pushed farther, fighting a tight ring of resistance. Was she a . . . ? He pulled back a fraction and slowly pushed into her again.

Suddenly she cried out, not in pleasure but in pain. Her eyes filled with tears. "It hurts," she said, her voice quivering.

She was a virgin! Zeke felt as if he had inherited the moon. It had all been a pack of lies—Blodgett had never touched her. Zeke felt an insane flush of masculine pride, and he took her face gently in his hands, bending to kiss her. "I'm so sorry, darling," he said. "I didn't mean to hurt you." He kissed her softly again and again. "We'll go slowly. I'll take all the time you need. It won't hurt much longer," he whispered.

Trusting him, she released the tightness in her belly, and he slid in another inch. The pain receded, and she felt a delicious fullness. He felt enormous inside her, but right—completely, wonderfully right. And she wanted more. She moaned and arched against him, pressing her lips to the salty skin at his throat.

Zeke groaned as she moved beneath him. It had been a long time since he'd made love to a woman, and he didn't want to spend too quickly. He wanted to give her a long, slow pleasuring her first time.

He slowly inched into her, marveling at the way she tossed her head and pressed up against him. Her behavior was not practiced, he knew, but natural. A naturally, perfectly passionate woman.

He drew back with a long, slow motion, and she sucked in her breath as he drove into her again. Slowly, slowly, Malloy, he said to himself. He wanted to feel her spend again, to feel her muscles clench tightly around him as she cried out. He didn't care if the drums masked her cries or not. She was his. That was for all the world to know.

He felt her tense, her thighs go rigid. He quickened his pace, testing her, judging her reactions as he moved inside her. She arched her back again and cried out, loudly this time, glorious in her release. Her sudden, fierce tightness coaxed him over the edge, and he found himself crying aloud as he held her close in his arms.

They floated back to earth together, like feathers on a warm breeze. She curled happily into the crook of his arm, reveling in his delicious masculine smell, perfectly contented with the feel of his shirtsleeve on her cheek as she pressed against him. She loved him, and surely he had to love her. He couldn't possibly have made her feel this wonderful if he didn't.

She was his. Zeke kissed the top of her head as he marveled at the wonder of it. This passionate, complicated, confusing woman in his arms had given herself to him completely. The thought stirred him anew, but he looked down at her and sighed. He wouldn't make love to her again tonight, or she wouldn't be able to walk for a week. And he wanted, very much, to love her again tomorrow. And the next day, and the next.

The night stretched above him, huge and fantastic. In the camp, the drums were still beating. Had anyone noticed their absence? Even if they had, what would they say? Loving was no sin here in the swamp. This wasn't Boston.

He smiled grimly. Boston, that thicket of propriety and hypocrisy, suited them both ill.

And there was still the question of Blodgett. Zeke would kill the bastard for what he had done to his sister. For what he had done to Liberty. *Zeke's* Liberty now.

He sighed as he looked down at the woman resting in the crook of his arm. Liberty was fast asleep, her breathing even and calm. *Ah, my little one*, he thought as he watched her sleep. *We still have such a long way to go.*

Chapter 22

Liberty's eyes fluttered open. A mockingbird lit in front of her, burbling cheerfully and cocking a gray head as if to ask, "So what kind of creature are you?"

She smiled and stretched. The morning air was clear and bright, free of the mugginess that had smothered them for days. She sat up and took a deep breath.

She frowned in puzzlement at the soreness between her legs. Then the memories of the night before washed over her: the drums, the fire, the strangely compelling ceremony. In the moonlight, away from the others, she had given herself to Zeke Malloy.

A deep voice came from behind her. "Good morning, sunshine," Zeke said, bending to kiss her chestnut curls. "Did you sleep well?"

She looked up at him. It was uncanny how the stubble on his chin changed him. It set off the summer of his eyes and those perfect white teeth. With his easy smile, his tender eyes, and that rough mountain-man beard, he was like a figure in a dream—her dangerous midnight lover. Except that he was real.

"Good morning," she whispered, hardly sure what to say. She pulled the wool blanket to her chest protectively. Where were they? This wasn't the maroon village, nor its immediate outskirts, but

307

a small, neat camp with a fire and blankets to protect her from the elements.

"We're in my camp," he explained, answering her unasked question. "I didn't want to bring you back to the maroons. You were so fast asleep, you hardly stirred when I brought you here." He knelt beside her and gently stroked the line of her jaw. "How do you feel?"

Confused, was how she felt. This wasn't the Zeke Malloy she knew at all. And she had slept in this strange place, and there was that funny pain between her thighs, and a voice at the back of her mind kept telling her that she had made a terrible, terrible mistake.

She looked up, unable to speak through the tightness in her throat.

Zeke drew her to him, chagrined at having taken her here, in the middle of the swamp. They should have had a week together in the grandest hotel in Paris, sinking into goose down mattresses and swimming in champagne. "I'm sorry, darling," he murmured, his lips pressed against her hair.

"I . . . I'm very confused," she said, fighting the lump in her throat. "I think I need some time to sort things out." The tears squeezed up despite her best efforts, and she hid her face in her hands, swallowing her sobs.

Zeke cursed himself softly and stood. Oh, Christ, he had made her cry. "Please . . . don't," he urged. He had been the happiest man in the world when the sun came up this morning and she had been curled in his arms. And now he felt as if he'd been punched in the stomach.

"I'm sorry," she said, her voice muffled in her hands. She lifted her face, the traces of tears clearly visible on her grimy skin. "I'm sorry," she repeated, her voice steadier this time. She wiped at her cheeks with the back of her hand, like a child.

Zeke motioned to the fire. "I made some coffee.

And there's some porridge." He turned his back to her. "I'll go see what's happening in the maroon camp."

His voice was neutral, almost cold. Liberty watched his back as he disappeared into the brush. Had she done something wrong? Was he angry with her? All she could remember was melting against him like snow into a river.

Crouched in front of the fire, drinking bitter coffee and pushing her spoon around the porridge, she shivered as another wave of longing passed over her. The wicked, knowing way his fingers moved, his lips, his tongue. The hair on the back of her neck stood up, and she shivered again when the breeze blew over her bare arms. God help her, she wanted him again.

She turned to call out to him, but he had disappeared into the weedy thicket. Perhaps it was just as well, she thought with a rueful sigh. She was confused, and Zeke Malloy would only make her more so.

She looked down at her dress. It had been shabby when Blodgett threw it at her through the cabin door; now it was a rag. She felt her face grow hot when she realized what the white spots smeared across the soft cotton were. The dress blatantly advertised what she and Zeke had spent their evening doing. She picked her way out of the camp, looking for a pool of reasonably clean water to bathe in.

Zeke had camped next to a small, clear pool with bright green reeds growing up through it. Liberty pulled off her dress and looked down at her thighs with a gasp. They were smeared with blood. Her monthlies? They weren't due for another two weeks. Then realization came to her in a flood, and she blushed anew. She waded into the pool and splashed cool water over herself.

The water felt wonderful after so many weeks

of filth. Annabelle had given her a small pot of water to rinse off in, but it had been no match for the green-gray swamp mud. After scrubbing her dress, Liberty once again splashed her breasts and face, bending to dip her head into the water. She ran her fingers vigorously through her hair, loosening the caked mud. She had no soap, but she was going to get as clean as she could without it.

The sun was warm, and she stopped her scrubbing to stand straight and let it beat down on her wet, clean face and shoulders. It warmed her breasts, and she felt once again that curious hungry feeling, a heaviness between her legs. She remembered Zeke kneeling between her legs, and she said his name aloud. "Zeke."

"I'm here," came the voice from the brush.

Liberty wheeled around, shocked. "You . . . you were spying on me!" she cried, embarrassed. "What a beastly thing to do!"

"Yes," he said wickedly, "I am a beast." He pulled his shirt off and kicked off his boots.

"What are you doing?" she asked warily, clutching her wet dress against her naked body.

He had removed his trousers and stood before her, defiantly aroused. He stepped into the water, moving inexorably toward her. "I'm going to give you what you want," he said, cupping her chin in his hand as he lowered his face to hers.

The sun warmed her back as he kissed her, and beneath her hands she felt the hard, strong muscles that sheathed his ribs. "I don't know if this is what I want," she whispered.

In reply, Zeke bent to catch her earlobe in his teeth. "You were made for me," he whispered. "Let me please you, my beautiful, perfect darling."

She bent her head back, shutting her eyes against the bright sun as he suckled her breasts, teasing them with gentle nips of his teeth. His hand slid down across her belly and she wriggled against him, her breath ragged.

He took her by the waist and turned her around, grasping her hips tightly in his hands. His hardness pushed against her buttocks, and Liberty gasped. "We can't . . . we shouldn't . . . not this way!"

Zeke chuckled. "I think you'll like it this way, little one." He reached around with his right hand to caress her again, coaxing the moisture from her as he pushed slowly into her from behind.

She gave one long, low moan. She was sore after last night, but once he was inside her, she hardly cared. The touch of his fingers added a tantalizing dimension to his long, slow thrusts.

It was easy to push against him this way, she found, and she ground her hips in slow circles. The water was cool, and the sun warmed their arms and bare torsos. Liberty's toes curled in the soft ooze at the bottom of the pond as she reveled in that rich sense of fullness, gasping as he slid into her slowly at first, then harder and faster, his hand still reaching around to tease her.

She bent her head down between her arms as she felt the now familiar tension build. "Yes!" she cried softly. "Yes, yes!" He quickened inside her to find his release with hers. She threw her head back and gave a long, low moan as he exploded into her.

After a few moments, he gently slid out of her and held her shoulders in his hands, nuzzling her tenderly. They were quiet as the frogs around them sang a riotous chorus, and the water rippled around their thighs in wide, languorous circles.

Liberty leaned back against Zeke, feeling the comforting solidity of his arms wrapped around her. "What are we going to do?" she asked, looking out over the water into the low cane thicket.

"I have a job to do," he said, his voice kind.

"Now that I know Annabelle's safe, I have to stop Blodgett. I've been waiting for years for an opportunity like this."

"Blodgett was the one who had Annabelle?" Liberty gasped.

Zeke nodded. "He threatened to kill her if I put an end to his operation. He always claimed they were treating her decently, but—" He broke off. Zeke knew Blodgett, and he knew Annabelle. She had a new bitterness in her voice and eyes. Her captivity had been painful. "I have to stop him, Liberty. Will you come with me?"

She turned to face him. "Do you really want me to?"

He broke into a broad smile. "Did you think I'd leave you to Napoleon?"

Liberty groaned. "The colony. Zeke, I can't go back there and face those people. They'll . . . they'll know what we've been doing."

"Don't be silly," he said with a teasing smile. "You weren't as loud as all that."

Liberty frowned. "Don't be horrid. Indigo will never let me hear the end of this."

"No, she probably won't." Far from looking concerned, he had an annoyingly pleased grin on his face.

Liberty made one last attempt. "Don't you care about my reputation at all?" she asked, her arms crossed fiercely over her chest.

Zeke delicately removed her arms from across her breasts and ran his fingers from her earlobes to her erect nipples. "Not in the slightest," he said, his eyelids lazily half-shut.

Her face grew hot again. "Zeke," she pleaded.

"Mmm," he murmured, bending down to bury his face in her damp hair. "You smell so fresh and clean."

"Zeke, I—I don't think we should be doing this," Liberty said, her voice cracking. Really, he was making it completely impossible to concentrate, she thought as she arched her back slightly.

He stopped his attentions and stood ramrod-straight. "All right. I'll stop."

She glowered at him and wriggled her shoulders as a small shiver ran down her spine.

He laughed. "You little wench, you want it as much as I do." He cupped her face in his hands and kissed her gently, teasing a little moan of pleasure from her. "Don't you?" he whispered, showering small kisses on her eyelids.

"It doesn't matter what I want," she said. "What would people say if they knew?"

"I couldn't possibly care less," he said, planting a small, sweet kiss on her nose. "Will you come with me?"

She gazed up into his eyes and shivered again. It must be standing naked in the water, she thought. It was giving her goose bumps.

"Yes," she whispered.

It was too late for prudence, and far too late for respectability. The deed had been done. It was time to live as she wanted for a little while, until her sins caught up with her.

And, God forgive her, she couldn't muster an ounce of real remorse.

Chapter 23

The village was quiet when they returned. Even the dogs did not rouse themselves as Liberty and Zeke crept into camp. A black and brown hound lifted his head lazily, twitched his ears, and plopped his snoring head back to the ground with a light thump.

"They were up late," Zeke said. "Even later than we were."

Liberty glared at him. "We don't have to tell the whole world that we . . . we . . ."

"We made love?" he suggested, grinning. God, he felt good. Better than he had in years.

"Yes, that," she said, her face pink.

"You think the folks here in the colony don't make love?" he asked.

"Well, I'm sure it's none of my business," she said tartly.

"Mmm," he said, amused by her shyness. "Well, they do. No one here is going to frown at you or call you names, I can assure you. But I will warn you— chances are they'll consider the whole matter very much *their* business. Be prepared for some rather intimate questions."

Liberty gasped. "Just what do you mean by intimate? You can't mean they'd ask about . . ."

"Just remember, if anyone asks, I'm positively huge," he said with a happy leer.

"Oh, you're awful!" she said, her cheeks flaming to a dark rose. "Honestly, I never met such a primitive!"

"I certainly hope not," he said with mock offense. "I take great pains to cultivate a total lack of manners."

"It shows," she said dryly.

A face peeped out from one of the huts. Liberty groaned. It was Indigo.

She looked at Zeke and beamed broadly. "Sho' be a beautiful mornin', don't it, Mr. Malloy?" she drawled, her eyes twinkling with suggestion.

"Now, Indigo," Liberty cautioned. "It isn't what you think."

"I don't be thinkin' nothin', Libby," Indigo said with exaggerated nonchalance. "I just makes a nice polite remark 'bout this fine weather. It was a touch steamy last night, but I reckon today goin' to be sunny and fine."

Liberty shot Indigo a killing look while Zeke looked on indulgently. "You're both completely impossible," she growled.

Others began to emerge from the huts. Napoleon wore his usual scowl as he stretched and yawned, flexing his powerful arms.

Annabelle parted the grass curtain of her hut, looking peaked and worn. She had dark shadows under her eyes, and her shoulders were slightly stooped.

Zeke crossed the camp to her, stepping around the gray embers that still gave off a few wisps of smoke. "Anna, are you all right?" he asked.

"I'm very well, *mon frère*," she replied, giving him one of her dazzling smiles. The Malloy smile, Liberty realized with a tender pang.

"You look tired," Zeke protested.

"The ceremonies always tire me. The best remedy is to get back to work," she said.

"You work too much, Anna. I know they need

your help here, but you must take care of yourself. I'm worried about you."

Annabelle smiled. "Oh, Ezekiel, it is good to see your face again. But you always did treat me like a china doll. I'm a grown woman now, thoroughly capable of taking care of myself."

Zeke frowned. "Anna, why don't you come home with me, take a vacation from this place? You look as if you could use the rest. It'll still be here if you want to come back."

Zeke belatedly realized the entire village had stopped to listen to them.

"Zeke, I can't leave this place. It's my home now," Annabelle said.

"Let's go into your hut," he said, taking her by the arm. Liberty watched brother and sister disappear into the hut.

Indigo grew closer. "You had best tell him that it be dangerous to try and gets Annabelle out of here," she whispered, her face creased with concern. "They's mighty attached to her here, 'specially Napoleon, and I don't think they'd take kindly to havin' her carted off."

"Zeke wouldn't cart her off," Liberty retorted. "He's just offering her a chance for a better life."

Indigo looked at her skeptically. "They done growed up together in some brick house with a flower garden and a drawin' room. He ain't happy to sees his sister poundin' yams in the swamp."

"Zeke would never coerce Annabelle into doing anything she didn't want," Liberty said. But she was faintly uneasy, wishing she could be as sure as she sounded. Did Zeke want to force his sister to leave the village? Personally, Liberty couldn't imagine that Annabelle would really rather stay here than leave for some more civilized locale. Perhaps that ill-mannered Napoleon was keeping her here against her will.

Annabelle shot out of the hut almost angrily,

saying, "I've told you Zeke, no. I'm staying here."
She took up a stone bowl, refusing to speak with
him any further, and bent to grind a sassafras root
into a mushy paste.

Zeke came and stood behind her. "That's fine,
Anna," he said quietly. "I just wanted you to know
you had a choice. That's all."

Annabelle looked up at him, tears in her eyes.
"What kind of choice is that, Zeke? You want me
to go back into polite society? A society of people
like *her*?"

Zeke tightened his mouth. "Constance has nothing to do with this, Anna."

"People like your sister have everything to do
with it. I can't be anything other than what I am,
and there's no place for someone like me in your
world." Annabelle's voice was almost a whisper.

"I'll *make* a place for you," he said fiercely, "if I
have to thrash every sneering hypocrite in Boston."

Annabelle shook her head. "Can't you see, Zeke?
I can't live that way anymore. I belong here. These
are my people—truly my people. I am grateful for
what you want to do for me, but I've made my
decision."

Zeke was quiet for a long moment. "I've got to
go back to my camp and pack up," he finally said.
"Will I see you when I get back?"

"Of course you will," she said, smiling through
her tears.

The camp was unnaturally silent, and a dog
whined nervously as Zeke left. Napoleon shot a
warning look in Liberty's direction but said nothing.

"Do you think they would try to keep *us* from
leaving?" Liberty whispered to Indigo when the
village had resumed its usual morning noisiness.

"It ain't usual in maroon camps for folks to wander in and out. But we ain't never promised to stay.
Usually they's a swearin'-in. After that, they ain't
no way you gets out, 'cept in a coffin. Napoleon

hate us—that be plain as the dirt under your feet—
so we stands a good chance of leavin' here on our
own feets," Indigo said. Her voice was strangely hollow as she peered into the choked thicket.

"I think we're leaving this afternoon, after Zeke
packs up," Liberty said.

Indigo turned to Liberty, searching her eyes. "Lib,
is you sure Mr. Malloy will want me along?"

"Of course he will, Indigo," Liberty said, shocked.
"He wouldn't leave you here." She looked out at the
rude little village as two naked children played in
the mud. "Honestly, what kind of man do you think
he is?"

"I figger he gots his reasons for bein' in the
swamp, and don't none of 'em take Indigo James
into account. Or my baby neither. He didn't figger to
finds me here, and he didn't figger on takin' me in."

"Don't worry about Zeke. He's awfully resource-
ful," Liberty said.

"What about you?" Indigo asked.

"Me?" Liberty crossed her arms uncomfortably
and looked down at her feet. They were dirty again;
there was no keeping them clean here.

"You," Indigo repeated. "And him. Last night.
You wants me to draws you a picture?"

"Nothing happened last night." Liberty sounded
spectacularly unconvincing even to her own ears.

"Lib, you don't gots to pretend with me. I seen
the way you looks at him, and I knows you loves
him. And I gots a pretty good idea 'bout what
happened last night."

Liberty sighed and twisted her fingers together.
Everything was so complicated. "Things were so
strange, and there were the drums. I don't really
know why I let things go as far as they did."

"But you loves him."

Liberty nodded.

Indigo snorted. "When we be locked in the boat
cabin together, I figgered you for a gal with more

sense. It ain't no sin to lie down with a man you loves."

"We aren't married," Liberty said, staring down at her hands.

"I wasn't married to my baby's father. You think that make a difference in the eyes of God?"

"I don't know."

"The way I figgers, God gots special rules for slaves. You's one of us now, you know. Whatever else you does in life, you knows what it be to be a slave. And slaves ain't expected to follow all the particulars. Even our church don't hold it a sin. They's some they gets married three, four times, 'cause they husbands be sold away. Me, I always figgered I just wouldn't gets married."

"Indigo, who was your baby's father?" Liberty asked.

Indigo turned away, her mouth set grimly. "It don't makes no difference."

"It wasn't the man you loved?"

"Big Sam be sold away mo' than a year before I gots pregnant."

"Who, then?"

"I don't know. Might've been the master. Or one of his sons." Indigo's eyes filled with tears. "They's all pigs, every one of 'em. They ain't no good in that kind of nasty slaveholdin' man."

Liberty reached out and took Indigo's shaking shoulders in her arms. "I'm sorry."

Indigo wiped her tears away with a sniff. "I worked in the kitchen before I gots pregnant. The work was hard—don't let nobody tell you the life of a house slave be easy. I be brung up right, an' I tried to get away from 'em, but they's only so many times they can beats you before you just gives up fightin'. But when I gots pregnant, the missus, she finally figgered out what the menfolk were up to. No way she could pretends she don't see that big ol' belly. She couldn't do nothin' with her husband or her sons, but she could sends the black gal out into the fields."

Indigo's eyes narrowed. "I only wanted 'em to stay away from me, but she looked at me like I'd *asked* 'em to do it. Like it was my idea." Indigo looked down and made an angry face. "Stupid woman. She gots what she deserved in that nasty redheaded husband of hers." Indigo rested her head on Liberty's shoulder as they stood side by side. The two were quiet, looking out into the swamp as the village hummed around them.

Zeke emerged from the brush, a battered black hat on his head and a wicked-looking knife strapped to his hip. His sleeves were rolled up, and his trousers were wet above his boots. He touched his hat to Indigo as he entered the camp, giving Liberty an outrageous wink.

He dropped his pack and made his way to Annabelle's hut. She sat cross-legged in front of a cook-fire, stirring a thick stew. "I've got to be on my way, Anna," he said gently.

She looked at him and rose in a single graceful movement. "Good-bye, *mon frère*. Losing track of you was my only regret when I escaped and came to this place. I'm thankful that we found each other."

Zeke tried once more. "Annabelle, you were never meant for this kind of life."

"I was never meant for slavery," she corrected. "This is freedom, and I cherish it."

"But there's more to freedom than this. You don't have to spend your life bent over a cook pot."

"Zeke . . ." she warned.

"And it's goddamned dangerous, Annabelle. You know it is."

"You know I loathe profanity, Ezekiel," she said icily.

"You can still come with me," Zeke urged. "It's not too late."

Napoleon appeared behind Zeke, his voice ugly. "The lady told you she want to stay. I think you should pack up your fancy whores and get de hell out of my village."

Zeke turned slowly to face Napoleon. "You're an unmannerly bastard, aren't you?"

Napoleon's face was as immobile as a statue as he slowly drew his long knife. "When I leave de sugar plantation, I cut de buckra overseer up into pieces for de dogs to eat. Since den, I make myself a promise dat I don't take no insult from no white man wit'out he pay for it."

Zeke's own shining blade had appeared in his hand. He met Napoleon's gaze without a trace of fear. "For years I took insults from the bastard that raped my sister, hoping that he would spare her life. Annabelle is free now, and I take no more insults from any man, not of me or of the woman I love."

Liberty felt her heart race, gut-wrenching fear mixed with thrilled delight. *Love*. He had said the word, for everyone to hear.

"I let you live when you come here for Annabelle's sake. If I lose my Anna, you lose your life," Napoleon said flatly.

"If you loved Annabelle, you'd let her make her own decisions," Zeke said.

Napoleon's face twisted with rage. "Goddamn your white lying mouth!" He turned to face Annabelle, who was watching from the door of her hut, her grayed complexion the only betrayal of her emotions. "Anna, you tell him now. You want to leave? You can leave. I let him live, and I let you go."

She shut her eyes as if to blot out the glinting knives and angry faces. "I shall never understand the stupidity of men so long as I live," she whispered. She looked Zeke in the eyes. "Ezekiel, listen to me. I am here, and here is where I wish to stay.

This is my home. I'm needed here. I will let no man force me to do anything. Not even you, brother."

Zeke lowered his knife. His jaw tightened for only a fraction of a second. "I'm sorry, *chère*. I was selfish. I wanted you with me. If you've truly found happiness here, then I wish you well."

Napoleon sheathed his blade, his forehead covered with sweat. He extended his hand to Zeke. "You be an honorable man."

Zeke's lips were tight. "Take good care of her. If I find out she's been mistreated, I'll come back here and kill you with my bare hands."

Napoleon smiled. "Dis brother of yours, Anna, he would make a good maroon."

Zeke reluctantly returned the smile. "Liberty, Indigo, are you ready?"

Liberty nodded happily, weak in the knees with relief. But Indigo looked concerned, and she threw a look back at the colony.

"I wants . . ." Indigo began, her voice small. She swallowed hard and started again. "I wants to stay here."

Liberty looked shocked. "Indigo! You can't mean that!"

Indigo looked at Napoleon searchingly. "I wants to stay with him."

Napoleon stepped toward her and took her chin gently in his hand. "You want to stay wit' Napoleon?"

Indigo took a deep breath. "Yes."

He gave a dazzling smile. "Napoleon is a nasty bastard, not a good husband for a beautiful girl who like to live in de house."

"I want to stay with you," she repeated, smiling shyly.

"I don't live like de slaves do," he said contemptuously, throwing a glance at Zeke and Liberty. "A woman come to live in my hut, she marry me."

"I want to marry you," Indigo said.

Napoleon grinned again and gave a whoop of celebration. His face was creased into a smile as broad as his usual scowl was deep. "Wo-man, I hope you know what you getting into. Yes, too pushy woman, I will marry you!"

Indigo beamed and threw herself into Napoleon's arms.

Napoleon laughed. "Dis woman, she t'ink she the man and I the wo-man. You going to learn to be obedient, wife." He took her in his arms and kissed her, crushing her struggling arms at her side.

Zeke laughed and curled his arm around Liberty's waist. "Looks like you've got quite a handful, Napoleon."

"I can manage my wo-man," Napoleon said matter-of-factly.

"Negro, let go of me before I knocks you into next week," Indigo said irritably.

The camp roared at that, and Napoleon smiled sheepishly. "Tonight we have de wedding ceremony, because tonight I bed my woman to show her what a man is!" he crowed.

Indigo blushed, and the village set up a cheer.

Napoleon spared a moment for Zeke and Liberty. "You are friends of my wife. You will stay for de celebration?"

Liberty looked up into Zeke's eyes, and then to Indigo's. "Will it make you sad if we can't stay?" she asked her old friend.

"You two gots work to do," Indigo said. "I be happy to know on my wedding night that you be huntin' down old yella-eyes. Gives him a kick in the pants for me when you catches him."

Liberty and Indigo embraced. "This is what you want?" Liberty whispered.

"Here I has freedom, and I can marry the man I wants," Indigo said.

"Good luck, Indy," Liberty whispered.

"You, too, Libby," Indigo said, hastily wiping a tear from her eye. "Take care of that man. You two goin' to be happy together."

Liberty looked at Zeke. "Yes, perhaps we shall. Good-bye, Indigo." She looked at the little village. "Good-bye, everyone. Annabelle. Napoleon, thank you, and I wish you all well. Good-bye."

She and Zeke began picking their way through the ring of cypresses. "Where are we going?" she asked.

"I'm afraid it's a few days' walk from here. I didn't have time to arrange for horses. But I have a knife and some cooking things—I think you'll be comfortable."

Liberty nodded silently. "I'll be all right."

His smile sent a tendril of warmth up her spine. "You're a tough bird, aren't you, Liberty Brooks?"

"Tough enough to walk for a few days, if it means I'll get out of this wretched swamp." She smiled back at him, nourished by the golden glow in his voice.

"I hope you don't think you'll just be walking, young lady."

She gave him a startled look. "Oh, of course, I've let you carry everything! Here, let me take something from your pack. Do you want to give me the cooking pots?"

He put his hand on her forearm to stop her rummaging about in his pack. "No, you goose. I don't want you to carry. I want you to talk."

"Talk?"

"Talk. The whole story. Beginning to end. Agreed?"

She gulped. "You're sure you couldn't just let me carry the cook pots?"

He gave her one of his stern looks, his eyes flashing like lightning.

She sighed. "Very well, then. Talk, it is."

The trip out of the swamp was arduous, but Zeke seemed to know every stick and puddle, making his way effortlessly with the heavy pack on his back. Liberty had insisted on carrying something, but he took one look at the faint circles beneath her eyes and kissed her lightly, saying that it would hurt his pride to let her carry so much as a handkerchief. She was still not wholly well; she coughed in the morning when it was damp, and after a long day of walking her head ached. He wished he could spoil her silly, bring her someplace where he could pamper her and perfume her and make love to her all afternoon and into the night.

Instead, they walked for days, stopping when the sun was low in the sky. When she asked again where they were going, he softly kissed her forehead and said, "To Paradise." They finally passed from the thick swamp to a flat green landscape of fields, canals, and high roads—the bayou. From time to time they passed an unpainted shack on stilts or a graceful white-columned "big house."

At night he cooked turtle or, if they were less lucky, muskrat. Their only comforts were the fire and the long nights they spent entwined beneath the wool blankets. Liberty had given up any attempt to regain her respectability, and she embraced him eagerly, wrapping her legs around his back to let him deep inside her as they cried out in the still night.

On the morning of the fourth day, Zeke was in fine humor, pressing on so quickly that Liberty stumbled keeping up. They could see the city now—New Orleans, rising above the flat green, about another two days' walk. Was that where they were going?

She thought of returning to civilization. People had a number of unpleasant names for women who made love to men who weren't their husbands. But she thrust the nagging worries from her mind. Zeke had braved so much to rescue her, and she trusted him completely. She would have to do some hard thinking about the confusing changes in her life, but this was hardly the time or place.

They came to a small cottage with wild yellow roses surrounding the door. Unlike the shacks they had seen, this cottage was well kept and white-washed. Above the door was a neat wooden sign with one word painted on it in blue: PARADISE.

"The fellow who used to own this place made the best whiskey in the county," Zeke said. "I bought this place eight years ago when he died. As a young boy I used to come here after I'd gotten into rough scrapes in the city—it makes me feel safe. I hope it will do the same for you."

Liberty looked at him tenderly. Her eyes started to brim with tears. "Thank you."

He gathered her into his arms. "You need somewhere to get well again, to feel spoiled," he said with a smile, lifting her chin with one strong hand and brushing away the tear that glistened on her cheek. "I wrote to the caretaker before I left Boston and told her to get things ready here. I knew I'd find you, and I knew I would want to keep you here with me for a little while."

She explored the house while he checked the stable, where two horses were happily munching hay. The cottage had three bedrooms, plain wooden floors, a pantry full of food, and a fine, sunny kitchen. In the master bedroom, a double-wedding-ring quilt in shades of green, gray, and soft violet covered the massive oak bed. A billowing white lisle canopy kept out mosquitoes. Yellow roses from the front yard filled a blue glass jug on the nightstand, and two wide windows afforded a dazzling view of the emerald bayou.

"This is my room," Zeke said softly from behind her, startling her slightly. "The caretaker set up another room for you, but I'd be happier if you'd share this one with me."

She turned to him and smiled, reaching up to kiss him. How many times now had she pressed her lips to his, felt the same dangerous thump in her stomach that she had when he had kissed her for the first time? If anything, it was more thrilling now that she knew what the kisses would lead to, the delicious, sultry joining of flesh, his heaviness as he lowered himself into her.

The bed felt glorious beneath her, an unimaginable luxury after days of sleeping on rocks and fighting off stinging insects.

"I've been dreaming about making love to you in a real bed, seeing your beautiful hair spilled across a clean pillow," he whispered.

The cascade of lisle floated over them like the roof of Heaven. There was no more walking to be done, no more pounding in her head with each step, no more muskrat half-cooked over a campfire, burnt on one side and mostly raw on the other.

She promptly fell into the deepest, most satisfying sleep of her life.

Chapter 24

L iberty slept for hours, finally awakened by
her own growling stomach and the irresistible
smell of frying bacon. She opened her eyes, and for
one startled instant couldn't recall where she was.
She smiled as she leaned back against the pillows,
remembering. They were back among the clean,
dry comforts of civilization.

A shadow fell across her heart, a darker, stronger
version of the worries that had been nagging her for
days. Soon they would return to the world of polite
society, and they would have to start making some
important decisions.

What did he want from her? She had asked herself
that question once before, when the situation had
been far less complicated. Now they were trusted
friends, and lovers. But would he make her his
wife? She had spilled her entire story to Zeke as
they'd walked, and had tentatively begun to ask
him about their future plans, but all he would say
was that he had to find Blodgett before he could
make any decisions.

She brushed her hair back from her face, wondering if there were any hairpins to be found in Paradise. Her ordeal was over, and in many ways she
was the same Liberty Brooks she had always been.
She had been forced into dishonor, but she could
still choose the honorable path from this point forward.

The late lunch Zeke had prepared was simple but delicious, and she wolfed it gratefully. Later she watched him contentedly as he busied himself pumping water for a bath. Within twenty minutes he had the large tub filled with steaming water strewn with fragrant herbs.

"Get undressed," he said, unbuttoning his shirt.

Liberty blushed. "Zeke Malloy, it's broad daylight."

"It's nearly dark. And anyway, it's only a bath, you scandalous wench. I want you to smell more like you and less like smoked muskrat."

"Only a bath," she mocked, lifting the dress from her body with a single, smooth motion. "I know you for the sinner you are. The second I hit the water you'll be ogling me."

"Who said I'd wait till you got into the water?" he said, his eyes warming. He lifted her into the enormous tub, stepping in after her.

The hot water was delicious on her toes, and she wiggled them happily, holding him gently at the waist. Then she slid her hands farther down to cup the muscular curve of his buttocks.

"And you call me the sinner, you hussy," he whispered as he brought his hands up to her breasts.

She shivered. "You've thoroughly corrupted me," she murmured, pulling his hips close to hers, caressing his buttocks and thighs.

"Amen," he whispered, lowering her into the fragrant, steaming water with him.

His long, strong fingers drew the aches of walking for days from her back and legs. He soaped her thoroughly, running his hands across her shoulders, slipping around to toy with her breasts. He turned her around and took her feet in his lap, massaging her toes and instep, running soapy hands up the length of her calves and around her knees to flirt at her thighs.

She dipped her legs in the bathwater to rinse the lather from them and took the soap from him, a mischievous look in her eyes. She ran her fingers over the hard muscles of his back and upper arms, closing her eyes at the feel of him. She toyed with his flat nipples, then slipped her hands below the water. He groaned and closed his eyes, and she smiled. She caressed him beneath the water, sliding her fingers slowly over the shaft, stopping a moment to cup and caress the soft mounds at the base of his hardness.

He gave an anguished cry. She looked at him and laughed. "Getting impatient?"

"Get out of the tub, woman," he growled, and in a flash he had pulled her, soaking wet, to the wide bed.

He pushed her down with a little growl, but she held one hand to his hip.

He looked at her, puzzled.

"There's something you do for me," she began shyly, "that I want to learn how to do for you."

His eyes widened when she cupped his shaft in one hand and bent to kiss it.

"Liberty, you can't do that," he croaked.

"Why not?" she asked, her eyes wide.

"It's . . . it's not . . ." He lost his voice as she tentatively flicked her tongue down the length of him. He was very silent at her intimate exploration.

The faint smell of him intrigued her. Greedier, she took him into her mouth and sucked wetly, gratified to hear his surprised moan.

She understood now why he did it to her. This way she could know him more intimately than any other—what he looked and smelled and tasted like, where he was most sensitive, what made him writhe uncontrollably. She had absolute power over him.

"Oh, God," he moaned, gripping her shoulders. She slowed her strokes, keeping them steady but slow as molasses.

"That's ... enough ... no more ... I need to be inside you," he whispered. But she gripped his hips in her hands, pinning him with an unrelenting long, slow rhythm.

He gave one last strangled cry, and his hips bucked backward like the recoil of a rifle as he filled her mouth. Liberty filled with languorous pleasure at the taste of him.

"Oh my God," Zeke said, his voice shaking. "How in the hell did you learn how to do that?"

She purred contentedly and slithered up next to him. "You showed me," she whispered.

He looked at her. "You're insufferably pleased with yourself, aren't you?"

She nodded and gave a smug smile.

"Don't think that just because you can turn me into a pile of quivering jelly, you're the boss of this household," he growled, his eyes drifting contentedly closed.

"Aren't I?" she purred, reaching over to bite him softly on the neck.

His eyes opened, and he shot her a ferocious look.

She scooted backward, laughing. "Now, Zeke, it was just a joke. . . ."

He caught her shoulders and pinned her to the bed. "I'll teach you to mind your manners, wench," he said, running one hand insolently over her breasts. He bent to kiss her, hard, pushing his tongue into her as he slid one hand between her legs. She murmured and shifted her weight as his fingers parted her and he lowered his head, grazing her with his wet tongue. He knew her body now, knew the combination of pressure and rhythm to bring her to the brink. He kept her poised at the edge of release a moment, then suddenly withdrew.

She blinked and gave a cry of dismay. He smiled wickedly, shifted his position, and slid into her with one swift motion. She gasped and closed her eyes, bucking her hips as he pounded into her with fast, savage strokes. She twined her legs behind his back to let him deep inside her and was tossing her head wildly when he pulled out of her.

She groaned, guessing his game. "No," she whimpered, "it's not fair."

"Not fair, little boss?" he asked. "I think it's eminently fair."

He kept her there, wild with desire, poised on the edge of fulfillment. Just as she knew the feeling of him inside her would put her over the brink, he pulled away and knelt to taste her. Just when she was ready to melt into blackness at the touch of his tongue, his face was inches from hers and he plunged into her. She pleaded, but he was merciless.

Finally, as he taunted her with his lips and the tip of his tongue, teasing the tight bud of her pleasure with feathery kisses, she exploded, her back arched, her cries ringing in the air. She felt light surround her, her body wet with sweat, hers and his. He did not pull away from her as she clenched her fists and cried out but kept the light, soft pressure of his tongue sliding back and forth. She had not yet begun her descent to earth when the world exploded around her again, then again, every muscle in her body rigid, her voice hoarse from calling out.

"All right," she whispered when it was finally done and she lay shivering atop the quilt, her skin drenched, her eyelids fluttering. The sky had gone dark, and the room was lit only by the rising moon. "You're the boss."

When the sun streamed through the windows in the morning, Zeke wrinkled his nose happily and rolled over. Mmm, something smelled good. He sat up and sniffed again. Biscuits. The woman was an angel.

No, no angel, he corrected himself, remembering the night before. Her passion seemed unbounded. After they had gone to sleep, wrapped up in each other and murmuring secrets in the darkness, she had woken him up in the middle of the night, stroking him to readiness and straddling him. By the time he figured out it wasn't a dream, she had thrown her head back like a wild colt, and he had felt the familiar torrent coming up to claim him. She was no angel, but a devil. A woman who would claim his soul.

He settled back into the soft pillow, smiling. If this was damnation, what kind of fool would choose salvation?

She appeared at the door, dressed in a soft cotton day dress the color of bluebells. "Good morning," she said, smiling.

He grinned. "You look good in that."

"How did you know my size?" she asked.

"I sent the woman one of those ghastly things you had in Boston."

She frowned. "Really, Zeke, I think you might have—"

"Asked you?" he said, amused. "Somehow after you were kidnapped, my letters weren't getting forwarded."

She wrinkled her nose at him. "Well, they're lovely, all of them." She'd found a half dozen cotton dresses in the wardrobe, and dozens of hair ribbons in the top dresser drawer.

"You couldn't have worn all that wool and linen down here," he explained. "You'd roast."

She smiled. "Are you getting out of bed anytime soon? Breakfast is nearly ready."

"What did I ever do to deserve all this?" he asked, standing and stretching.

She looked at him appraisingly. "With a body like that, you have to ask?"

He put on a shocked expression. "Who turned you into such a wanton, eh?" he asked, reaching out to pull her close to him. She wore nothing beneath the cotton dress, a whisper of soft blue-violet cotton the only thing that separated their bodies.

A shadow clouded her eyes, gone almost before he noticed it. "You did," she said with a small smile. "Don't you remember?"

"I suppose I will have to take the blame," he said, bending to kiss her forehead, burying his nose in the rich, clean scent of her hair. "But you've shown no lack of imagination, young lady. I can't imagine a more apt pupil in sin."

She swatted his bare backside, smiling at his yelp. "Get dressed, you heathen. It's nearly time for breakfast."

Liberty watched, amused, as Zeke slathered his biscuits in honey and sweet butter. She lifted an eyebrow as he wolfed them down. "You never ate like that at home."

He eyed her as he swallowed. "I guess the air down here makes me hungry."

"I like to watch you eat my food." She'd spent the morning resurrecting her cooking skills and was pleased to see she hadn't lost her touch. The bacon was crisp, the scrambled eggs tender but not runny, and the biscuits as fluffy as clouds.

Zeke drank deeply from his coffee cup. "I'd eat your food happily for the rest of my days, ma'am," he drawled.

The very air between them seemed to crackle. She forced herself to look into his eyes. "The rest of your days?" she said, trying for a bright tone.

His face creased with concern. "Liberty, I'm sorry."

"Don't be silly, Zeke, what have you got to feel sorry about?"

"It's different here, isn't it?"

Liberty sank into the kitchen chair, looking down at her plate. Suddenly she had no appetite at all. "When we were in the swamp, civilization seemed a million miles away. After being in that wretched maroon camp, everything about my life in Boston seemed so foolish—totally irrelevant."

"And now you don't feel that way anymore." Zeke's voice had chilled, losing the warm, rough timbre she had come to love.

"I . . . I don't know what I feel. It's not that what we have here isn't important to me—it is."

"But not as important as respectability."

She stood again, feeling imprisoned in the small wooden chair. "That's not fair. You make respectability sound like something evil."

Zeke swiped a hand through his hair, shutting his eyes. "I think we have more important concerns than what a lot of society biddies find to cluck over. Why should you care what people think?"

"It isn't what other people think of me, it's what I think of myself," Liberty said, trying to keep her voice calm. She stared at him a long moment, at the rough growth of beard that shadowed his cheek and the high, sculpted planes of his face. He was as hard, as unyielding, as he had ever been. And she wondered how she would ever get past that wall of granite. "Does this have something to do with . . . with your sister? The one who wanted to force Annabelle out of your house?"

The green eyes flew open, pinning her with their ferocity. "I don't want to talk about Constance."

"I think maybe you should," Liberty said, her heart pounding. "Do you really think I'm like her? Do you think I'm so cold? So unfeeling?"

The anger in his eyes wavered, and he turned roughly away from her. "How could you know anything about it?"

"Annabelle told me that your sister—Constance—had been upset by Annabelle's presence in your household. That she had thought it was improper."

"She'd always been bossy, since she was a little girl," Zeke said, his voice flat. "It got worse after my mother died. She's only three years older than I am, but from the time she was eight years old she was mistress of the house."

Liberty stepped toward him, and set her hand lightly on his shoulder.

"I couldn't believe she meant the things she was saying about Anna, not at first," Zeke continued. "I told myself Constance couldn't be that cruel. But she was her father's daughter. All that claptrap about the importance of *family decency*, and then she did the most indecent thing I can imagine. She forced her own sister into degradation."

"I'm so sorry," Liberty murmured, resting her cheek on his head.

He stiffened. "Why should you be? It's not so unusual a story. There must be a hundred southern families *respectable* enough to do the same."

She felt the tears rise in her throat, and she forced them down again. "I would never do anything like that, Zeke. You must believe that."

He twisted free of her light grasp, and turned to meet her eyes coldly. "Must I? I had begun to think you were different, that you were strong enough to ignore all the petty little voices dictating what's proper and what's not. Maybe I was wrong."

Liberty straightened her shoulders. "I am an honorable person," she said, her voice only a little shaky. "I'm not going to apologize for that."

"Honor has nothing to do with what the stuffed shirts tell you, Liberty. It comes from inside. And if you think that loving me is dishonorable . . ." He broke off, swallowing a curse.

"Of course I don't think that!" Liberty said, her throat choking with the sobs she refused to give in to. "But d-damn you, Zeke Malloy, I w-won't be your Injun woman!"

He shook his head. "What the hell are you talking about?"

She moved away from him, away from the anger in his eyes. "I need some time . . . to think things through." She took a deep breath, trying to soothe the painful lump in her throat. "I think we should sleep apart for a few days."

He stood, his chair scraping sickeningly across the floor. "Is this blackmail, Liberty? Are you saying we can't be lovers unless I make a lot of promises to you that I can't keep? I've still got to face that blackhearted bastard, and anything could happen. He could kill me. I could kill him, and be hanged for my troubles."

She shook her head roughly. "You have to do what you have to do. But so do I. If you can't understand that, well then . . . I'm sorry. I don't know what else to say."

She turned and walked into the bedroom, gathering her scattered clothes and a scrap of ribbon that lay on the nightstand.

He appeared behind her, filling the doorframe ominously. "Think about what you're doing, Liberty. Is this Boston all over again? More charades? More pretending we're people we aren't?"

She bit her lip hard to keep it from trembling. Finally she turned to face him, composing herself sufficiently to speak. "I can't continue . . . this way, not until I know where we're headed."

"I told you, I won't make promises I can't keep."

"I know you won't," she said, her voice little more than a whisper. "And I can't turn my back on who I am, Zeke. I'm sorry."

His eyes were hard, shining with unshed tears. "I'm sorry, too, Liberty. I really am."

And minutes later, he was gone.

Chapter 25

Zeke was gone for most of the day. Liberty spent a miserable afternoon trying to drown her thoughts in housework. She wouldn't give Zeke the satisfaction of saying she wasn't earning her keep.

But nothing would go right. The mop bucket tipped over and turned the kitchen into a miniature lake, the bread wouldn't rise, and the milk was sour. Every mosquito in Louisiana seemed to know a secret passageway through the screens on the windows.

Her heart thumped with dread when she heard him return. It seemed to take hours for him to turn the knob of the back door. She stood frozen over the sink, her hand gripping a soapy scrub brush.

"Hello." His voice was cool.

She swallowed and kept scrubbing the sink, sloshing water onto her dress. "You were gone a long time."

"I went into the city."

She pressed her lips together and scrubbed harder, focusing her anger on a faint stain in the white enamel. "That sounds nice."

"It wasn't a pleasure trip, Liberty."

She rinsed the sink and straightened. "No, of course not. I made some supper."

"I brought a few things from town. . . . I didn't know you would cook anything."

She glanced over her shoulder at the packages in his hands. Something wrapped in white paper was sending delicious aromas into the air. "I see. To tell you the truth, I'm not very hungry."

"Liberty, I'm . . . I'm sorry about this morning."

"So am I," she said.

But neither was ready to give an inch. Zeke set his packages on the kitchen table. "I have good news."

She turned to face him. "Your boots!" she cried.

"My boots?" he said, baffled.

"You've just tracked big, muddy footprints across the floor." Damn it, she thought she might burst into tears again. She felt like an idiot. Who cared if he muddied the floors? But her nerves were raw, her eyes and throat sore from crying.

Zeke looked down in dismay. "Oh hell, Liberty, I'm sorry. I'll—I'll clean it up. Why don't you sit down and have something to eat?"

Liberty sniffed hard and blinked the tears away. "Don't be silly. I'll mop the floor again later."

"Don't you want to hear my good news?"

She nodded, but did not meet his eyes.

"Montoya is in New Orleans." He paused. "With Blodgett."

Liberty blanched at Zeke's determined expression. Whatever happened between the two of them, she could not bear to think of him in prison—or worse.

"You're going to fight them, aren't you?"

He nodded.

She saw him afresh then, his sad smile and his beautiful eyes that could take on such a cruel, hard light. And she saw that he could not rest until he had done this thing. She wanted desperately to protect him from the fire storm to come, but she could no more do that than she could turn herself into a fairy princess. He would have to confront Jack Blodgett one last, terrible time.

But maybe there was a way for her to help him—to make this battle a bit less dangerous. After everything he had done for her, she owed him as much.

And after that . . . ? *We'll cross that bridge when we come to it*, she told herself sternly.

"Zeke," she said softly. "I have an idea. . . ."

Liberty's heart throbbed with fear when she awoke at the first light. Maybe this wasn't such a good idea. Maybe something would go wrong. Her pulse hammered in her throat. Maybe. Maybe.

Zeke was already up, angrily rummaging through his wardrobe. He didn't like her plan one bit, but she'd convinced him he had no choice. She wished she could spend the morning curled up with him, pretending the world didn't exist. But it did. Her throat caught painfully as her feet hit the cool floor. She had a job to do. It would have to be done, and it would have to be today.

The choice of the dress was important. It had to be cut low in front, but it shouldn't be too fashionable or seem too expensive. She found a gauzy blue-green wrapper—the sort of dress no respectable woman would be seen out of her dressing room in—with three-quarter-length sleeves, a deeply scooped neckline, and buttons down the front. She slipped the semisheer cotton on without any underthings, and blushed as she studied herself in the mirror. The flimsy garment skimmed her body, molding closely to her breasts and buttocks. Even the faint dimple at the base of her spine could be clearly seen. She felt more exposed than if she had been stark naked. "Scandalous," she whispered to her reflection.

Zeke called to her from the next room. "The horses are hitched. Are you almost ready?"

"Yes," she said, her voice wavering. He appeared in the doorway. She studied her toes, blushing fiercely.

"You're going to have to do better than this, you know."

She looked up to meet his eyes and said in a small voice, "I know." He was resplendent in a deep green brocade frock coat, ruffled white linen shirt, and violet silk waistcoat and trousers. He had trimmed his beard neatly, and his dark silk hat was eminently respectable.

"You look . . . beautiful," she squeaked.

He gave an embarrassed smile. "I feel like a stuffed peacock. I never realized how blasted uncomfortable it is playing the popinjay."

"You look wonderful. Outrageous, but wonderful." Liberty looked down at her hands. "I . . . I don't know if I can do this."

"I understand," he said, sounding greatly relieved. "Let's call this whole insane business off. I'll handle Blodgett on my own." He tugged at his cravat to loosen it.

Liberty swallowed the panic that rose in her throat. "No. We're doing it my way. I just feel so . . . indecent."

"Come here, Liberty." It was a command. She stumbled forward, painfully self-conscious. He lifted her chin and gently stroked her cheek. "You don't have to do this."

She shivered. She *did* have to—didn't she? The scheme she'd concocted seemed to go against everything she'd been so sure of yesterday. And yet, this morning, after a day's consideration and a night's sleep, one phrase stood out in her mind—that honor was a thing that came from inside. What she would do today was not respectable, not by any stretch of the imagination. But it was honorable. And that made all the difference.

She smiled up at him and nodded. "I'm sure, Zeke. Let's go get that snake."

She pulled her cloak around herself, and they walked out to the carriage. The horses shifted impatiently, waiting for the journey to begin.

The landscape was like nothing she had ever seen, a kind of savage Eden. Slaves bent among the dark green of the sugarcane, their voices lifting in a song at once plaintive and hopelessly beautiful.

She shuddered, thinking how close she had come to sharing their fate, or worse.

The passing landscape lulled her back to sleep. She started awake when she realized she was leaning against Zeke's shoulder, soothed by the hard, secure warmth of him. She sat straight on the bench, pulling her cloak more tightly around her.

"We're nearly there," Zeke said, his voice betraying no emotion.

The thought made her panicky and a little sick, but she knew they had no real choice. This was the best way to stop Blodgett, to tear down the barrier that stood between them and the rest of their lives. She only hoped they'd still have something left together when they were done.

They were nearly in the city now, the wide road crowded with people. Zeke's eyes had taken on the coldness she'd seen so often in Boston—the sharp, clear focus of a predator. He snapped the reins as they headed into the glorious wickedness of New Orleans.

The Rowdy Red Slipper was not a gentleman's tavern, although certain gentlemen frequented it. Ladies were not welcome, but a certain type of lady was to be found there in abundance. Rouge smeared stickily on their lips, they eyed one another warily or sat like plump spiders on the balcony, dangling dark-stockinged legs. Men with haunted

eyes tried their luck against well-dressed sharps,
only to slink away more desperate than ever.

Zeke's boots made a satisfying thud on the
wooden floor. He ordered a shot of rye, gulped
it, and ordered another before swaggering to
a round table in an ill-lit corner where four
men played Poque. Liberty followed him the
entire time, her mortification at being in such
a den of iniquity passing nicely for subservient
devotion.

Her heart caught in her throat when she saw
Jack Blodgett among the gamblers. Angry red blisters showed around the edges of the bandages that
swathed his left hand and the left side of his face.
Zeke had told her that Blodgett had been burned
in the boiler explosion, but she was shocked to see
how badly.

Blodgett groped a weary-looking whore and told
her to fetch him another whiskey. "*Je poque de dix,*"
he muttered, sliding a stack of coins to the center of
the table. His yellow eyes widened as he glanced
up and spotted Zeke. He threw his cards face down
on the table. "You? Here? You goddamned son of a
three-legged—"

"So good to see you again, Captain Blodgett,"
Zeke said coolly. "And this is . . . ?"

Seated across from Blodgett was a fine-boned
man with black hair and a pencil-thin mustache.
His hands were long and thin and moved quickly, like insects. Close-set black eyes glittered
beneath his slickly pomaded hair. His cheekbones were high, his nose thin and aquiline.
He could be described as handsome were it not
for the thin, unnaturally red lips that stretched
tightly over his teeth. His beautifully cultured
accent only faintly masked the razor's edge of his
voice.

"I do not believe we have been introduced," he
said.

"This son of a bitch is one of them northern radicals who want to take our slaves away from us," Blodgett spat nastily, loud enough for the entire saloon to hear. He was obviously counting on drumming up support from the murderous-looking thugs at the bar. "I figger we oughta take him out and string him up, to set an example. We don't need no northern boy comin' down here to tell us how to handle our niggers."

"Ezekiel Malloy," Zeke said, interrupting Blodgett's tirade as he offered his hand to the man with the thin mustache. "You might have heard of my father."

"Of course—Jedediah Malloy, no?"

Zeke nodded.

"A great man, well remembered, I assure you. I am Don Diego Montoya Veracruz."

"My pleasure, sir," Zeke said, his voice a silken flow of southern charm. "Actually, I merely came over to thank Captain Blodgett here. I've become one of his most satisfied customers."

"Really?" said Montoya. "I was beginning to wonder if the *capitán* had not lost his old touch. I have been much disappointed recently."

"Have you now? I can't imagine it. Why, I bought this pretty little filly from him not two weeks ago, and she's the best buy I ever made."

Montoya cast his eyes lazily over Liberty and licked his red lips. "She seems delightful."

Blodgett choked to see Liberty there, but he bit his tongue. If Montoya discovered who she was, he would know that Blodgett had lied about her. Montoya had been murderously angry when Blodgett had failed to deliver the frightened young virgin he'd been promised.

"Come on, sweetheart, don't be shy," Zeke said, yanking her closer to the group. "This gentleman wants to get a good look at you." She whimpered and clung to him, nuzzling the ruffles of his white shirt.

"Hell, this little miss is the most affectionate nigger I ever had, not to mention the prettiest," said Zeke as Liberty toyed with the buttons of his shirt. "Come on now, sweetheart, time for that later. Step out and show the gentlemen how pretty you are." Liberty stepped closer, arching her back so that every line of her form was revealed by the thin dress. Her face was burning, but no one looked at her face.

"Course, she didn't come cheap," continued Zeke. "But what nigger of this quality does? I had to pay triple the regular price just to get the captain to sell her to me instead of her original buyer."

"I never sold her to you!" burst Blodgett, unable to restrain himself any longer. "The bitch escaped when we had a little boiler trouble on the boat. Malloy's no slave owner. He's one of them abolitionists from up North. And she knew him from up there. She worked for him. It's a—"

"From up North?" quizzed Zeke loudly. "You don't mean to say that this woman was abducted from the North, do you?"

Blodgett clamped his mouth shut, leaning morosely back in his seat. "Course not. It's . . . she . . . Maybe I'm mistakin' her for someone else."

Montoya's eyes were as hard and bright as jet beads. "I was led to believe this girl had died in transport and was, at any rate, as you so quaintly put it, *Capitán*, a small, plain mouse." His voice had begun to lose its faint veneer of control. "Would you care to explain this, Señor Blodgett?"

Liberty nibbled Zeke's ear, tracing one slim finger across his chest as she crushed her breasts against him.

"She was a little on the shy side when I got her," Zeke said suggestively. "But as you can see, she takes well to discipline."

"Señor Blodgett?" Montoya's voice was insistent.

An audible gasp went through the group as Liberty's hands, roving hungrily across Zeke's body, slid down to the bulge in his tight trousers and she stroked him through the expensive cloth.

"Jesus, girl, wait for it!" Zeke thundered, pushing her irritably aside. She fell to the floor, her hair across her face.

"Señor Blodgett!" The command was sharp as a rifle shot.

On her knees, Liberty thrust her hips against Zeke's calves, moving her pelvis in slow, grinding circles and caressing his thighs with her long, slender fingers. Again he thrust her rudely aside.

"I cannot fathom the reason for this breach, *Capitán*, but I shall have satisfaction," Montoya said icily. "Shall we say tomorrow, at dawn?"

Blodgett purpled beneath his bandages. "Señor Montoya, you can't listen to this rich-boy do-gooder. Old Jed was another kettle of fish altogether," he stammered. "Zeke Malloy is a well-known—"

"My family knew his father well," interrupted Montoya. "He is his father's double, I assure you. Tomorrow, then."

"He's nothing like his father. And the girl wasn't to your taste at all, Señor Montoya. Trust me."

"Trusting you is the furthest thing from my mind, Señor Blodgett. Until tomorrow." Montoya's face was white, his spine rigid, as he walked stiffly from the saloon.

Blodgett looked up from his chair, a feral gleam in his eye. Suddenly he leapt up at Zeke, snarling like a wild animal. Liberty screamed as she saw a blade flash.

As quickly as a panther, Zeke caught Blodgett's hand in his, twisting it brutally until Blodgett released the knife. It hit the floor with a sharp metallic ring. Blodgett swung out with his free arm, which Zeke easily sidestepped before delivering a pair of punishing blows of his own.

Before most in the bar knew what was happening, Blodgett lay sprawling in his chair, and Zeke was cleaning his nails insolently with Blodgett's knife.

"Until we meet again," Zeke said quietly, throwing the knife onto the table. *"Capitán."*

Chapter 26

Champagne bubbled merrily over the tops of the heavy crockery cups as Liberty's laughter mixed with Zeke's.

"Did you see the look on Blodgett's face when he finally recognized you? He looked like he'd swallowed a mouse." Zeke's eyes were bright, and he gestured expansively with his hands.

"When he pulled that knife, I thought I would faint dead away. You were very brave."

He pinned her with his willow green eyes, suffusing her with warmth. "I wasn't the brave one, sweetheart. You were. And one way or another, that duel will break up their little scheme, and you'll have spared a few women from being sold into Montoya's particular brand of degradation." He cupped her chin in his hand. "Thank you."

"You're welcome." She gave a tentative smile.

Their victory over Blodgett made it easier to forget the uneasy truce they had drawn, and supper was a grand affair of fried chicken and biscuits, with a big chocolate cake and elderberry wine for dessert. Laughter filled the cottage by the time they played a game of chess on the hearth rug by the fire well past midnight.

"Checkmate," Liberty crowed, sliding her bishop into position to take his king.

"Checkmate?" He scowled and stroked his rough beard as he studied the board. Well, damned if she hadn't beat him.

He looked up in amazement, but the game was forgotten as he saw her in the firelight. She looked so achingly beautiful, her hair gathered up in soft curls, the dancing flames enhancing the gold of her skin. He felt a familiar tightness in his groin. He'd spent last night alone, and he had no intention of doing the same tonight.

"Liberty," he whispered as he bent over the chessboard to kiss her.

She met his lips shyly, but the touch of their mouths lit a flame that burned as brightly in her as it did in him. She pushed the chessboard impatiently away, scattering pawns across the floor.

God, it felt good to possess her mouth again, to devour her lips and tongue. He loved the soft moan that built in her throat as he cupped his hands around her head and pressed her against him. It made him feel ten feet tall, like a hero who could slay any dragon that might slither across his path. His senses were full of her—her smell and taste and the way she felt beneath his hands. He brushed his thumbs across her breasts, leaving her mouth to sink his teeth lightly into the glorious flesh of her neck.

"Zeke, no," Liberty whispered, her voice ragged.

"Mmm, yes," he insisted as he stroked her hardening nipples. "God, Liberty, you feel so good. I want to be inside you."

"I can't do this," she said, pushing him away from her.

The haze in his mind cleared somewhat, and his gut twisted as he saw tears in her eyes. Instantly he released her. He felt guilty as sin, and irrationally angry. "Damn it, I never meant to hurt you."

She took a deep, shuddering breath. "I know you didn't. I'm sorry Zeke, I j-just can't."

He wanted to do a dozen things at once—comfort her, reassure her, throttle her, and plunge into her until they both cried out in release.

"I w-want you so much," she said.

He gathered her back into his arms, burying his face in the rich scent of her hair. "I want you, too, sweetheart," he said, wincing at the understatement.

"You just want an Injun woman," she murmured into his shirt.

"An Injun woman? I don't even know what that's supposed to mean."

Liberty turned her face up to his, her eyes as big as a frightened child's. "My m-mother, she was part Indian. And people used to give her nasty looks."

"People?"

"Men," Liberty corrected with considerable venom. "Sometimes even . . . my father."

Zeke nodded. "I see. So you don't want to be like your mother."

"Oh, I do! My mother is a very respectable woman. A lot more respectable than I am, actually." Liberty gave a small, shuddering sigh. "I just don't want men to look at me the way men looked at my mother."

Zeke bit back a tart remark about feminine logic. "I wonder how many other secrets you've been keeping from me," he said, one hand caressing the sleeve of her dress. "I didn't even know you were part Indian."

She looked up at him, surprised. "I was sure you would have guessed by now."

He studied the high planes of her cheekbones and the luscious gold of her skin, lightly dusted with small brown freckles. "Never occurred to me," he mused. "And it doesn't matter, you know. I promise I will never think of you as a . . . How did you put it?"

"An Injun woman."

"An Injun woman, then. I don't care if you're a temptress or the most starched, respectable female in Boston. The longer I know you, the more I suspect you're both. I don't care if you're Indian or black or . . . or bright green. You can make me happiest by being what you are. You're Liberty to me, only Liberty."

"Then why . . . ?" She bit back her question, catching her lower lip with her teeth.

Zeke felt the guilt pull at his stomach again. "Why won't I propose?" He sighed deeply. "You know the story of how Annabelle wound up in slavery?"

"She told me about Constance, and about the card game."

Zeke shut his eyes, his mouth dry with the familiar taste of bitterness. "And did she tell you about our growing up together?"

"You taught her French."

"I taught her all sorts of things. After all, I was the one with the tutors and the pocket money. I loved the feeling of being able to make her world wonderful."

"It must have been terrible for you when your father—"

"Gambled her away? Like an object, a trinket?" Zeke felt the old rage well up, threatening to engulf him. He fought it down. "I wanted to kill—anyone and everyone."

"Zeke, I'm so sorry." Liberty's eyes were shining with tears again.

"The thing that used to keep me awake nights was the look in her eyes as they took her away."

"Zeke, you can't torture yourself like this. Your father was the one responsible, not you. It wasn't your fault."

"When we were children, she would ask me if she would be a slave when she grew up, and I would promise her, 'No, never, Anna. If Papa tries to sell you, I shall thrash him.' "

"Oh, Zeke." Liberty's mouth was soft with compassion. .

Zeke cursed himself as he felt the tears sliding down his cheeks. "I was a boy playing at being a man, making promises I couldn't keep. I was the master's son. I thought I could do anything. It made me feel like the prince in a fairy tale to tell her I'd protect her. But I couldn't protect her. That sick bastard Blodgett took her away. He raped her, and he sold her body to other men."

"Zeke, I'm sorry," Liberty whispered.

"I tried to rescue her. I did everything I could think of. I even challenged old man Blodgett to a duel, and got nothing more out of it than a bullet in the arm." Zeke felt the shame claw at him, tear at his throat in horrible, grating noises that he realized were sobs.

Liberty gathered him close to her, and he collapsed in the sheltering circle of her arms. The awful images rushed up one after another, hissing and spitting like goblins. Every word of reproach he'd ever hurled at himself, every nightmare, snaked around his consciousness. But through it all she held him.

Now she knew everything. She knew the story of his shameful weakness, knew precisely how terribly he had failed. But still she held him there in her arms, seemingly unaware of what a useless worm he was behind the trappings of Ezekiel Malloy, respected crusader.

And to his own shock, he no longer felt like curling up and dying when he thought of how he had failed his sister. He wanted to live, and he wanted to make a life with Liberty.

He couldn't quite forget his thirst for vengeance—the wound was too deep, and had been festering for too long. Blodgett would have to die, at Zeke's hands. And maybe Zeke himself would be dead before the next dawn.

Zeke rode into town at midmorning the next day, and when he returned, he had ugly news. "Montoya is dead."

Liberty was silent. It was all very strange. Yesterday he had been alive playing cards, and today he was dead.

"Blodgett's still alive," Zeke continued. "I had hoped Montoya would be a better shot. It's up to me now."

She sighed and turned away. Disappointment squeezed her heart like a vise. When the nightmares of her own childhood had risen to the surface during her captivity with Indigo, she'd found that the light of day stripped them of their power. And she had hoped that last night would do the same for Zeke—would finally light those dark corners of his soul and banish his demons forever. This morning his eyes did seem softer, his face somehow younger and more open. But the demons were still there. Nothing had truly changed. He still needed to face Jack Blodgett, no matter what the cost might be.

"I'm doing this for you, too, don't you see?" Zeke said stubbornly, taking her by the shoulders. "The animal hurt you. He could have killed you."

"If it's for me, then let it go," she said. "I want you alive and safe more than I want Blodgett dead."

Now he was silent.

"It isn't for me, is it?" she continued. "Or even for Annabelle. We're both free now. Killing Blodgett won't change anything."

"I've got to finish this," he said quietly.

Liberty's eyes brimmed with tears. "Zeke, we almost lost each other before because of that man. Now he's between us again."

"I'll take care of myself. You're not getting rid of me that easily." He smiled at her reassuringly.

"After all, one of these days you're going to need me around."

She looked up at him. "I need you right now."

"I mean when you're with child."

Her face drained of color. "What do you mean, when I'm with child?"

"Darling," he said gently, "you must have known what lovemaking is for. You might well be pregnant already."

She turned away from him, stunned.

"I want to make a baby with you, Liberty."

"You might ask me how I feel about it first," she said, her voice tight.

"Did I ever make love to you against your will?" he asked, his eyes narrowing.

"No, but there are things a man can do, things to prevent . . ." she said. Her face was hot.

"Did you ever see me do any of them?"

"I just assumed . . . I don't even know what they are," she said, angry tears chasing away the aching sadness she had felt. God, what had she done? She had bartered her own soul away, and after last night she didn't regret it for a moment. They were tied with a bond that went beyond words or ceremonies, and she would wait for him forever if she needed to.

But she hadn't thought of the fate of a child. She didn't want to bring a baby into the world to saddle him with the horrible name of *bastard*. She would endure almost anything, but her heart broke at the thought of condemning an innocent child to a life of suffering.

"Darling," Zeke murmured, "I'll take care of you. Please don't worry."

"You'll take care of me?" Her voice wavered as she pulled away from him. "Like Blodgett took care of Annabelle? Lock me in a house in the country, guarded by an old woman with her tongue cut out? Isn't that the way it's done down here?"

A vein in Zeke's temple throbbed, visible beneath the tanned skin. "That's what you think of me? That I'm like Jack Blodgett?"

"I don't know what to think of you! Back in Boston you were one way, and now you're another, and I don't know what to think of any of this. I've never been anyone's *mistress* before!" The word sounded ugly in her mouth.

"That much is obvious," he said, his voice dangerous. "A mistress knows how to keep her mouth shut and her belly flat."

Liberty blanched. Then she turned and fled the cabin, slamming the door behind her.

The day was already beginning to heat up. Liberty's throat was tight as she began to run. Through the veil of unshed tears, she couldn't see where she was going, and she didn't care. Damn him, damn him to hell. She might be pregnant. How could she have been so stupid? She was an independent woman, and independent women thought carefully about these things.

The tears began to flow. Zeke's baby. She pictured a dark-haired little boy taking brave baby steps as she held him up by his chubby wrists. She did not want to cry. Crying was not going to help.

She didn't know how long she had run blindly through the woods, but she ended up in a thick grove of trees surrounding a pond. Willows choked the water's edge, and the surface was thick with pale lilies. As she stumbled along the bank, a frog jumped into the water with a splash, and a dragonfly flashed impossibly blue in the reeds.

Zeke wasn't a monster who would hide her away like some shameful secret. He would not leave her alone to raise a bastard child.

But Jack Blodgett was still poisoning Zeke's heart, still infecting him even now that both she and Annabelle were safe. Liberty had not been able to free Zeke from this—he had to exorcise this demon himself. He might even die trying.

Liberty shivered at the thought and stumbled over a root, losing her balance, one foot sliding on the slippery reeds and splashing into the water. Mud oozed over the top of her boot as she tried to extricate herself. The mud was slimy and cold on her clean stockings, and she shuddered as she sank in deeper.

A set of yellow-brown ridges sliced through the water, sending ever-widening vees across the pond's surface. One of those odd turtles, she thought. She hadn't realized a turtle could move that fast.

She felt a yank on her partly submerged leg, something pulling her hard. She shouted, nearly losing her balance completely.

A green-brown elongated head shot up from the water. The head was nearly as long as her arm, and its mouth was open in a horrible toothy grin.

She screamed as a jolt of pure, cold fear hit her. The mouth snatched at her boot, the laces snagging in the jagged teeth. A yellow eye fixed on her, hypnotic and cold.

She screamed again and tried to yank her leg away. The demon had her fast. She could feel its sharp teeth grinding against the boot leather.

Liberty pulled harder at her leg, but the thing gave a sharp tug, and she slipped farther into the cool mud. Indigo's words came back to her: *If you hits them on the snout, they generally lets go.* She grappled for a branch, a root, anything.

The thing pulled at her again with the strength of a dozen men. She grasped a handful of reeds, the rough stems cutting her fingers. Water lapped at her armpits as she slid deeper into the water.

She screamed a third time, a shrill, panicked cry. Could Zeke possibly hear her? And if he did, would he reach her in time?

The beast gave a final swift yank of its horrible grinning head, and she was beneath the water. She could see the entire creature now, the elongated body and squat legs and thick, powerful tail. She began to thrash in earnest, her mind wild with panic, her lungs burning.

Oh, God, she didn't want to die this way, to let this demon thing drag her down where she would never be found. She twisted to try and strike the thing with her bare hands, feeling her muscles burn. No, please, God, no.

A thunderclap sounded overhead, loud as the voice of Jehovah. A dark curving stripe appeared in the murk in front of her. The thunder sounded again—and her ankle was free. The monstrous thing had let her go.

Chapter 27

Liberty's head shot above the water, and she gulped air in grateful mouthfuls. She was alive. She was not going to die. She coughed and sputtered as the wonderful air rushed into her lungs.

"You shore got lucky, lady," a voice said above her head.

She struggled to her feet to face the voice, her boots sinking into the soft mud of the pond bottom.

Two men stood by the water. Their rifles were hanging at their sides, still smoking.

So the sounds hadn't been thunderclaps but gunshots. These strangers had saved her life.

"Thank you . . . thank you so much," she sputtered as she made her way onto the bank, gratefully accepting their hands as they pulled her to shore.

" 'Twarn't nuthin'," one of the men said. The two were very much alike, bearded, grimy, with battered straw hats.

She bent over to cough some of the water out of her lungs and had a nasty jolt when she saw the shocking spread of blood across her dress. Then she realized it was the alligator's and not her own. The dress clung damply to her legs, its hem now black with mud. Her lungs hurt, her nose hurt, and her ankle hurt like hell. But she wiggled her toes, and nothing seemed to be broken. She was alive.

One of the men interrupted her coughing. "Say,

you ain't a lady by the name of Liberty Brooks, is you?"

She straightened up, her eyes watering. "Why, yes, how did you know . . ."

Zeke's heart was ready to explode in his chest. For quite some time now he had been sitting at the oak kitchen table, getting drunk. More misunderstandings. More bickering. And more angry words rising to his lips before he could think things through. Just like it had been in Boston.

Damn her. Everything would have been fine if she hadn't suggested he was anything like Blodgett. Did she really think he would take advantage of her? Her words had been arrows shot straight into his heart.

He should have proposed. But how could he have promised her forever when tomorrow he might be in prison—or dead?

Maybe he shouldn't have mentioned the possibility that she could be pregnant. But how was he supposed to know she hadn't thought of it herself? Just another one of his expectations confounded by that troublemaking little female.

He felt a sharp twinge when he realized how many times his expectations had sorely *needed* a shove in the right direction. And when Liberty Brooks gave a shove, she made it a good one.

Maybe she was right, maybe he couldn't take his revenge on Blodgett. It was an unacceptable risk. But Blodgett was dangerous alive, too. Zeke had won everything back from him now—Annabelle and Liberty. Blodgett would search for a way to destroy them both—unless Zeke made the first move. And that move had to be the right one.

Zeke had been considering just what that move would be when he'd heard the first scream.

He was out the door in a lightning flash, pausing only to grab his pistol. Frantically he scanned the fields, the marshy green plains, the raised levees. No sight of her pale pink dress. She must have headed for the woods. Zeke ran through the trees, clutching his pistol. Where the hell could she be?

She screamed again, and he changed direction. He couldn't be sure where she was—the trees took the sound of her voice and threw it back and forth as if to taunt him. Branches lashed at his face as he ran, his heart pounding not with fatigue but with fear.

A third scream. Liberty was a brave woman—he knew that much by now. This was no mere snake slithering through the reeds that had frightened her. She was in serious trouble. Had her cries come from the big pond, maybe? He crashed into the undergrowth, forgetting the trails, forgetting anything but the sound of her voice. It would take time to get to her. *Please God*, he prayed, *let me be in time*.

He pushed angrily through the brush, waving the pistol dangerously. It was his own fault, his own goddamned fault. He should have gone after her when she left the cabin. He never should have let her leave.

Two rifle shots tore through the air. Zeke's blood ran cold. It wasn't a bear or an alligator that threatened her, then. He was covered in slick, cold sweat. Who had fired the rifle? Was it Blodgett? His heart hammered in his throat. If Blodgett hurt Liberty again, Zeke would cut the bastard's heart out.

Something bit his hand as he thrust undergrowth away. He sucked at the bite while he ran, hoping that whatever it was wasn't too poisonous. He emerged from the undergrowth savage with fear and rage. The pond spread itself before him, the murky water shining dully in the afternoon sun. His shirt was soaked through with sweat.

He scanned the opposite bank, squinting. He spotted two figures there, men with guns, carry-

ing something wet and limp. Something the color
of apple blossoms. Something covered in blood.

"That was easier then I figgered it was gonna
be," Clem said, eyeing the girl. She was slung over
Hank's shoulder like a sack of potatoes. Clem carried both guns.

"Easy for you to say. You ain't gotta carry her,"
Hank said, disgruntled.

"She ain't no more'n a slip of a girl," Clem said.

"Yeah, but she's soakin' wet. She's drippin' all
over me," Hank grumbled. The blood-soaked dress
slapped against him as he walked.

"Closest to a bath you come all year," Clem
offered. "Now, move it, Hank. That was a quick
piece of work, but I ain't happy about firin' the guns.
If her boyfriend's around, we're gonna have him to
deal with, and I ain't lookin' forward to it."

"You wanna go any faster, you can carry her,"
Hank complained.

They crashed through the woods, Hank clumsy
with the added weight. Clem was right; this had
been an easy job. It had only taken those two shots
into the gator, and that green bottle of stuff worked
just like the gentleman had said it would. She went
right out. Dumb kid. What the hell was she doing
out there all alone anyway?

Hank almost felt a pang of guilt. The girl was
pretty, the way your sister could be pretty. She
made him think of pie and chicken dinner and
home. Comforting. Of course, they had saved her
from being eaten by the gator.

Still, Hank didn't believe this girl was the gentleman's sister, the way the gentleman said. His eyes
didn't look like he was lookin' for a sister. Ugly bastard, too, with that blistered face and wrapped-up
hand. And those eyes—goddamned unnatural, like
an animal's, or the Devil's.

He shifted the girl's weight and looked down

with distaste at the blood dripping onto his pants. Gator blood stank something awful. Damn Clem anyway for making him do all the carrying. It was always like that with Clem. But two bucks was two bucks, and the girl had been easy to find. All the same, it wasn't fair.

Liberty had been covered in blood, but Zeke didn't let himself think about that. He thought instead about how to move quickly through the willows, how to become as light and lithe as a lynx in search of prey.

Her kidnappers were clumsy. They left a trail any city slicker could have followed. And Zeke was no city slicker. He wondered briefly if they were arrogant or just plain stupid. He checked his pistol and moved along the trail of broken cane and trampled weeds.

Hank was glad when they reached the gentleman's camp and he could set the unconscious girl down on the ground. Yes, she was sure pretty. Looked like a real sweet kid.

He frowned. He was no pushover, no matter what Clem said. So maybe she was a good kid. So what? They were going to get their two bucks apiece. The kid had been stupid, and now she'd pay for it. That was the way life worked.

Clem cleared his throat meaningfully. The gentleman was staring as if mesmerized into the huge fire he'd built in the heat of the afternoon. The bright light lit his eyes until they almost shone. The burned places on his face were flushed bright red with the heat. Hank wondered how the gentleman could stand it, especially with those blisters. He'd been a handsome fella once, that was easy to see. Poor son of a bitch.

"This the gal?" Clem said. His voice sounded loud in the quiet clearing.

Blodgett looked over at her almost carelessly. "Yes."

"You got our money?" Clem asked. Clem was always the one who asked for the money, who made the deals and stood up for himself. Hank sighed and shifted his feet, waiting.

Blodgett turned the yellow eyes up toward Clem and narrowed them faintly. "Of course. Excuse me a moment."

The back of Hank's neck prickled as the gentleman looked through his saddlebags. He would be glad to be finished with this job. The gentleman gave him the creeps. He wasn't right in the head. Once they got their money, he and Clem would get hold of some whiskey and go off and get drunk and forget all about this crazy bastard.

"Drop your guns," the gentleman said, his voice suddenly all steel. He was holding a pistol leveled at Clem's midsection.

Hank took a sharp breath through his teeth. That dirty doublecrosser.

Clem raised one rifle to his shoulder as fast as lightning, dropping the other one to the ground.

"I won't miss," the gentleman said, his voice strangely calm.

"I'll take you with me," Clem said, his voice ugly.

"I don't give a damn. But I bet you do. Now, get the hell out of here." The gentleman's eyes glowed in the firelight.

Hank felt the fear hit him deep in the gut. "It ain't worth four bucks, Clem. He's gonna kill both of us if we don't clear off."

Clem lowered the rifle.

"Drop it," the gentleman said. The pistol was still leveled at Clem's midsection.

Clem dropped the rifle.

Blodgett smiled amiably and without another word, squeezed the pistol's trigger.

Clem dropped to the ground with a sickening thud, an enraged cry coming to his throat even as his mouth filled with blood. Hank was in the woods like a rabbit, but Blodgett barely seemed to see him go. Clem writhed like a fish caught on a line, gurgling obscenities.

Blodgett turned to Liberty and methodically began to tie her with a rope from in his saddle-bag. Clem flopped and choked a few yards away. Blodgett tied her arms behind her, the elbows meeting neatly. She was covered in blood. Had she been injured? He checked her carefully for marks but found only a small puncture wound near her boot. The shoe had been gnawed by something, but the foot beneath it seemed to be intact.

The ground beneath Clem was wet with gore. The man sputtered one last time. Too tired to protest anymore as the blood rushed out of him to soak the earth, he died.

Blodgett, absorbed in his work, scarcely noticed.

Chapter 28

❧⟳⟳❧

It was hot. Very hot. Liberty could feel a veil of perspiration on her forehead. Her dress clung damply to her. Her arms ached strangely, as if she had been sleeping with them tucked awkwardly beneath her. She opened her eyes tentatively, fighting to return to consciousness.

The heat was horrifying. She was sitting, propped up by a stump. Her head ached fiercely, pain blooming across her forehead and eyelids and down her neck. She noticed she could not move her arms.

Something lay next to her. A man. Dead. One of the men who had rescued her. And who had . . . She fought to remember. Someone had held her arms, and then she'd smelled something medicinal and strong. At the thought of the smell, her head sang with pain.

She spared another glance at the dead man. He was covered with insects. She looked quickly away.

"Did you sleep well, angel?" someone asked her.

She did not have to see him to know who it was. Jack Blodgett's voice had haunted her too long for her ever to forget it.

"My head hurts," she murmured. Her mouth felt as if it were full of raw cotton.

"It's the chloroform. It gives a wicked hangover."

She swallowed and tried to move her arms again. It was no use. They were weirdly weak, and they hurt.

"You're tied up," Blodgett said, his voice almost helpful. She looked up at him. He had removed the bandages from his face, and it looked bad. He would be hideously scarred when it healed. He had lost the look of rage he'd had in the tavern. He seemed beyond anger now, consumed completely by madness.

"So pretty," he whispered, caressing her face with his still-bandaged hand. He dropped his good hand to fumble with the buttons of her dress.

She shut her eyes. This was it. At least she'd had her time with Zeke, had been able to tell him she loved him, had given herself to him. The thought was her only comfort as she realized that Blodgett was going to rape her, then probably kill her. She tried to fill her mind with thoughts of Zeke's arms around her, the sound of his laugh.

When he had unbuttoned her dress to the waist, Blodgett stood and walked toward the fire. How could he bear the heat? Liberty could hardly stand it, but with the burns on Blodgett's face, it must be nearly unendurable. Yet he gave no indication that he was in pain. He wore a neutral, almost pleasant expression as he busied himself around the fire.

He came back to her, holding a long, slim knife in his hand. The blade had been resting in the fire, and he'd wrapped a cloth around the handle to keep from burning his fingers. "I'm going to ruin you," he explained simply. "With this. When it cools, there are more in the fire. First your breasts, and then your face, and then I'm going to cut out the evil place between your legs."

"You—you shouldn't spoil valuable goods that way, Jack," she said, her voice quavering. Stall, she had to stall. "You could still make good money off of me."

"No," he said, his voice almost dreamy. "I have to do this. Then they'll stop screaming."

"Who will stop screaming, Jack?" she asked. She tried to keep her voice cool and soothing, fighting her panic.

"The voices. They told me I have to do this. If I don't, they won't ever go away. I have to mark you and then I have to cut the evil thing out of you, and then you have to die."

"No, Jack," she said, fighting to keep her voice level. "The voices are tricking you. If you do this to me, they won't ever leave you alone again."

"I have to do it," he whimpered. "There are things in my head, like bees, and they sting me and sting me. I have to purify you, and then they'll go away."

"They're tricking you!" she repeated desperately.

"No, they promised me!" he cried, anguished. "I don't want to do it. I love you, the way I loved Annabelle."

"You don't want to hurt me, Jack. I would never hurt you. Untie me now, and I'll show you how much I like you."

"You abandoned me!" he screamed. The ruined face was weeping. "You made fun of me, and then you went away! You're evil, but I'm going to cut the demons out of you."

"I wanted to be with you. I was coming back to you. If you untie me now, we can have a good talk."

"No," he said quietly. "No more talking. You're trying to trick me. It won't work. I'm going to hurt you now."

He moved toward her. Her pulse was pounding crazily in her ears. She held her breath. He pushed her dress open with the knife, and a thin curl of smoke arose from the fabric. She could feel the heat coming off the blade.

He held the knife poised a few inches above her flesh, waiting for the voices to tell him precisely what to do. He could hold the blade flat across her skin to make a long, wedge-shaped burn, or he could use the sharp edge to carve into her. The blade was hot enough to cauterize the wound; he could cut her many, many times before she died. It was important to do it right. If he made a mistake, the voices would never go away.

A pistol cocked from a few feet behind Blodgett's back. "That's enough, Jack. It's time to let her go now."

Blodgett wheeled to face Zeke. The yellow eyes blazed with impotent rage. "I knew you would come! You always come. You ruin everything. I'm going to kill you next."

"I have a pistol, Jack. You can't win this. Put the knife down."

"No!" Jack screamed. He spun and grasped a fistful of Liberty's hair in his hand. "I'll hurt her. I'll kill her. The knife is sharp." As if to prove his point, he sliced through a curl, the blade cutting the large hank effortlessly. The air filled with the sharp stink of burned hair.

He held the fistful of curls triumphantly, waving it like a scalp. "Throw me the gun, or I'll slice right through her windpipe."

The fire between the two men raged like a hot rasp of breath. Blodgett drew a fresh, hot blade from the flames, and Zeke was forced to drop his gun. "Take one," Blodgett said, gesturing toward the remaining knives.

Zeke bent cautiously, never taking his eyes from Blodgett, and picked a squat, heavy knife with a thick handle.

"I can take you," Blodgett crowed. "I can take you fair and square. You think you're better than I am, but you're not. Now I've got everything, and you've got nothing. How does that feel, rich boy? Where's your stinking rich daddy now?"

"You want to fight or talk?" asked Zeke, grasping the knife in his right hand, its thick handle keeping his fingers from getting burned.

"I want to kill you," Blodgett replied, lashing out with a swift, wide arc of the blade. Zeke jumped nimbly to avoid the knife, his heavy boots crashing into the fire. He barely noticed, shifting his position and circling the other man, weighing his options with narrowed eyes.

Liberty was horrified. Everything rested on Zeke's winning this fight. The two men circled each other in the fire's heat. Ash and sparks flew through the air.

Liberty heard something rustling behind her. An animal, perhaps? She froze with fear when she felt the unexpected touch of a human hand on hers.

She clamped her mouth shut on the scream that rose in her throat. Whoever it was, he couldn't be any worse than Blodgett. She gritted her teeth as a knife sawed through the ropes that bound her arms.

Zeke had led Jack away from the fire. It gave Blodgett too much of an advantage. Blodgett didn't seem to feel the heat crisping the hairs on the backs of his arms, but Zeke could.

Blodgett lashed out again, slicing desperately through the air. "I'm going to kill you!" he shouted wildly. His clothes, once bright and neatly cut, hung on him in grimy rags. Swamp mud was ground into the peacock blue linen trousers, and the white shirt was splattered with grease and gore. His hair was plastered to his forehead, sticking to the awful burns on his face.

Zeke was silent. He had been waiting for this his entire adult life. This was the moment when he would take his revenge on Jack Blodgett. Perfect, crystalline revenge. He would cut the bastard's throat and throw him to the voracious ants that swarmed over the corpse in the clearing.

Yet Blodgett was spoiling even this for him. The man was filthy, tattered, and insane. He couldn't even feel the heat of the fire on his burned face.

And he slashed at the air as if he were warding off demons. Christ, for one awful moment, Zeke almost felt a sliver of pity for the son of a bitch.

"You won't ruin this for me," Zeke whispered. The light had begun to die in the sky, yet in the firelight everything glowed with an unholy brightness. The clean patches of Jack's shirt were preternaturally white. Jack's yellow eyes seemed to glow from within his skull. Mosquitoes and gnats sang like violins darting across a satanic arpeggio.

Liberty's hands were free, and she turned to face the man who had released her. He was one of the two who had taken her prisoner. His eyes were kind but filled with horror as he gazed now at his dead friend.

Jack's attention was hindered by the devils swarming around him like a cloud of midges. He tried to wave them away with his knife. Zeke took advantage of the opening and slashed at Jack's unprotected midsection. The knife slit through the filthy shirt with ease, and a thin streak of blood appeared on Jack's stomach. The cut would be painful, but it was not deep. And painful would do Zeke no good.

Jack lurched forward and thrust again at Zeke. He was fighting like a drunk, weaving so that Zeke didn't know where he would turn up next. Zeke moved lightly to one side, but Jack's blade caught him in the left shoulder. The pain was a bright burning. Zeke shifted his grip on the heavy knife.

Liberty bit her lip until tears came to her eyes. She would not scream. She would not cry out. The two men did not see her, nor did they see Hank. She picked up Zeke's discarded pistol.

Zeke and Jack gripped each other, the blood from Zeke's shoulder smearing Jack's shirt. Zeke twisted his wrist and drove the point of his knife deep into Jack's right forearm. Jack's face showed no sign of pain, but his grip on the knife weakened, and he swiftly shifted it to his left hand.

Jack's knife came up at Zeke from this new, unexpected direction. The blade was flat against Zeke's throat before he knew it, the hot metal scorching his flesh. The pain brought his mind into clear, perfect focus. Time moved as slowly as the drip of honey from a spoon. He could have counted the pores in Jack's sweating face.

Liberty crept up behind Jack, gripping Zeke's pistol tightly. She swallowed hard and brought the heavy black metal down hard against Jack's skull, feeling a sickening crunch.

Jack slid gracelessly to the ground, still clenching the knife. The heated blade dragged across Zeke's collarbone, carving a thin red line across his tanned skin. Numb, Zeke barely felt it. He threw his knife aside and looked down at the crumpled man at his feet. Then he looked up, dumb, at Liberty. Someone was behind her, a sad-eyed man in dirty clothes. He looked down again at Blodgett. A red bubble appeared at the corner of Jack's mouth. He was very still.

Liberty flung the pistol away from her with a quick shudder, as if she were clutching a scorpion. Gnats flew blindly against her eyes.

"Oh, Zeke," she whispered, looking down at her hands in horror. Bile rose in her stomach like a fist. "I've killed him."

Chapter 29

Liberty hummed to herself as she cracked two eggs into a big green bowl. "Are you sorry you didn't do it?" she called to Zeke, who was still dressing.

"Do what?"

"Get your revenge on Blodgett."

Zeke didn't answer for a moment. "I got all the revenge I needed."

Liberty frowned at the biscuit batter. Too thin. She sprinkled in more flour.

She shivered as she remembered the horror that had overtaken her when she thought she'd killed Jack Blodgett. He had lain so still, crumpled like a discarded newspaper in the dying light.

Zeke's eyes had glowed with murderous fire, his chest heaving after the exertion of the struggle. Both men's shirts were soaked through with blood and sweat, and blood beaded along the thin cut on Zeke's throat like a necklace.

When Blodgett had stirred, Zeke had held out his hand for his pistol. Liberty hadn't wanted to give it to him. The responsibility for a man's death, even for the death of a monster like Blodgett, weighed against everything she believed in.

But Zeke's eyes had been steady and insistent. Slowly she handed the pistol over, swallowing hard as she mentally braced herself for the moment when Zeke would put a bullet into Blodgett's brain.

Her heart had leapt in her throat in relief when, after a long moment, he'd slid the pistol into his holster and hoisted Blodgett up by the armpits, flinging him over the saddle of Jack's terrified horse.

Zeke's voice from the next room banished the chill that had crept up Liberty's spine. "I guess you got through to me after all. I just couldn't bring myself to do it. Jesus, he looked so bad off, even I felt sorry for him. Anyway, the place he's headed for ought to be punishment enough."

Liberty felt a pang at that. "You don't think the insane asylum will take proper care of him?"

"They won't let him starve, but madhouses are hardly known for their comforts. More than likely they'll keep him fed and that's about all. And he's trapped with his own demons now. That's got to be worse than anything I could have done to him."

Liberty dropped the biscuit batter in fat spoonfuls onto a baking sheet. "It's a terrible thing. Still, I'm glad he's locked up someplace where he won't be able to hurt any more people." Liberty shuddered for a moment, remembering her own captivity at Blodgett's hands. "What do you think will happen to his men?"

"Some of them were killed in the explosion. I guess the others will crawl back beneath whatever rock Jack found them under. Most of them were river men. Maybe they'll go back to that."

Liberty remembered Sid's disgusting treatment of her but also that he had let her and Indigo go when he could simply have let them drown or burn to death in their locked cabin. She slid the pan into the hot oven. "I hope they've reformed," she said softly to herself. "Breakfast'll be ready in a few minutes. What's keeping you this morning, anyway?"

"Come in here and see for yourself."

Liberty wiped her hands on her apron and headed for the bedroom. She stopped short when she reached the door. Zeke had a razor in his hand, and half of his lovely beard was gone.

"What are you doing?" she squeaked in dismay.

Zeke's smile faded to a look of concern when he saw her face. "Sweetheart, what's wrong?"

Liberty smiled weakly. "Nothing. It's just . . . I liked the beard."

"God, Liberty, you can't mean it. It made me look like a dirt farmer."

"It did not," she said hotly. "It made you look like . . . I don't know . . . like the man I fell in love with. It made you look like yourself." She squinted at his half-shaven face. She had to admit, he *was* too handsome to hide behind a beard. But still. "The beard just . . . well, reminded me of the good times we've had."

Zeke set his razor down and turned to her, an incredulous smile on his face. "Good times? Do you mean the alligators, the mosquitoes, or the thugs in the woods skulking around and chloroforming you?"

Liberty frowned. "Well, no, of course I don't mean any of those things."

Zeke was grinning now. "You've got some deep attachment to mud and snakes, maybe? Or to eating burned muskrat?"

Liberty caught his hands in hers, smiling at the face half-covered in shaving cream. "I was thinking more about the nights by the campfire."

Zeke's eyes lit. "And the nights in the bedroom, and the nights in the living room, and on the stairs, and that one afternoon on the kitchen table . . ."

Liberty's face felt hot. "You're making fun of me."

"Of course I am, you hussy. But I've got a good reason for shaving."

"You're not going into town today, are you?" Liberty was disappointed. She hated to be without him, even for a day.

"No, I'm not going into town today. But I'm hardly going to propose to the woman I love with a mangy three-weeks' beard, much less marry her in one."

Liberty blinked dizzily. "Propose?"

Zeke turned back to his shaving mirror. "Yes, propose. And I don't care what you do, wench, you won't spoil it by making me do it with my face half-covered in shaving cream."

Liberty smiled to herself, and she smiled again when he knelt at her feet ten minutes later, his chin smooth, his eyes on hers, asking if she would agree to do the rest of their loving—and fighting—within the bonds of marriage.

"Yes," she whispered, taking him into her arms and heading back to the still warm bed. She thought with a smile that breakfast could wait, after all.

Avon Romances—
the best in exceptional authors
and unforgettable novels!

Avon Romantic Treasures

*Unforgettable, enthralling love stories,
sparkling with passion and adventure
from Romance's bestselling authors*